Praise fo  *ket*

"You can tell that (.... attentive gardener, giving us .... that land and people can heal ....as cultivated characters so memorable that I missed them as soon as I read the last page."

—Robin Wall Kimmerer, author of the New York Times bestseller *Braiding Sweet Grass: Indigenous Wisdom, Scientific Knowledge, and the Teaching of Plants*

"Goodrich masterfully weaves an intricate and deeply satisfying story. It's a beautiful book in its rich language and profoundly honest voice—funny and smart in its observations. *Weave Me a Crooked Basket* is a thrilling read and a much-needed antidote to our time, reminding us we can fully embrace the power of the human spirit."

—Keith Scribner, author of *Old Newgate Road*, winner of the 2020 Connecticut Book Award

"I haven't read a novel in a long time that felt this hopeful, this authentic in feeling, in landscape, in the complexities of the lives of its people—ordinary people who are not only farmers and gardeners but artists and biologists and immigrants, wives and husbands, sisters and brothers. It's a marvelous book, written with immense compassion and honesty, insight and detail. I loved it."

—Molly Gloss, author of *The Jump-Off Creek* and *The Hearts of Horses*

"*Weave Me a Crooked Basket* testifies to a potent vision—small farmers, artists, tattooed hair-stylists, footballers, yoga teachers, schoolkids, and cranky octogenarians rising in community when the engines of Corporate Greed come rumbling their way."

—John Daniel, author of *Gifted* and *Lighted Distances*

"*Weave Me a Crooked Basket* is the good news we've been waiting for: community matters, love heals, care and attention are the greatest of gifts, art is wonderfully re-arranging, the rich soil, well-tended, holds us all, and the work, despite our griefs, goes on. Charles Goodrich has written an exception...... ....utiful, life-giving novel."

—Joe Wilkins, author of *Fall Back Down When I Die* and *The Mountain and the Fathers*

Weave Me a Crooked Basket

A Novel

CHARLES GOODRICH

UNIVERSITY OF NEVADA PRESS | *Reno & Las Vegas*

University of Nevada Press | Reno, Nevada 89557 USA
www.unpress.nevada.edu
Copyright © 2023 by University of Nevada Press
All rights reserved
Manufactured in the United States of America

First Printing

Cover design by Trudi Gershinov/TG Design
Cover images © Shutterstock and Dreamstime

Library of Congress Cataloging-in-Publication Data
Names: Goodrich, Charles, 1951– author.
Title: Weave me a crooked basket : a novel / Charles Goodrich.
Description: Reno : University of Nevada Press, [2023] | Summary: "*Weave Me a Crooked
Basket* is an unconventional love story featuring a makeshift coalition of farmers, artists,
scientists and community members who turn a small organic farm into a work of art
to save it from unscrupulous developers. Facing bankruptcy, Ursula Tunder and her
polar-opposite-brother, Bodie, along with their eco-artist adopted-cousin, Nu, enlist a
ragtag troupe of land-defenders in a festival of resistance."—Provided by publisher.
Identifiers: LCCN 2023003145 | ISBN 9781647791223 (paperback) | ISBN 9781647791230
(ebook)
Subjects: LCSH: Farm life—Fiction. | Organic farming—Fiction. | Community arts
projects—Fiction.
Classification: LCC PS3607.O592254 W43 2023 | DDC 813/.6—dc23/eng/20230208
LC record available at https://lccn.loc.gov/2023003145

For the farmers and gardeners who

care for the soil, the living skin of this

beautiful, improbable little planet

Still there are seeds to be gathered,
and room in the bag of stars.

—URSULA K. LEGUIN

Part I
June 2008

1 · Ursula

Ursula heard the barn swallow's nervous chirping the moment she entered the greenhouse. As she rolled back the sliding door and wedged it open, she saw the bird flapping between pipe-metal rafters, anxious at being separated from her nestlings, Ursula guessed. Sensing the bird's distress, she took a deep breath to slow her own heart rate. Swallows always found their way out, she reminded herself. And with a little luck, so would she.

She crossed the concrete floor and slapped her binder full of invoices onto the army surplus desk. She'd already noticed that the greenhouse's humidity was too high. The overnight temperatures had been warmer than forecasted. Nudging a toggle switch on a control panel behind the desk, she heard the louver vents overhead tip open, and warm, moist air began to stir along her bare arms and face. She drew in a deep breath, savoring the loamy, floral aroma, then sat at the desk and bent to her paperwork.

Ten minutes later, Cat came in. She nodded grimly at Ursula and headed directly to the back of the greenhouse. Ursula knew better than to speak to her. Cat was not a morning person. Though she'd been sober for nine years, Cat had confided to Ursula that she still woke up many a morning feeling like she had a hangover. To spare Cat from having to do any early-morning thinking, they always decided at the end of a work day what her first job would be the following morning. Today, Cat was going to transplant a hundred or so unsold dahlias from four-inch pots into gallons. That would take her an hour or two. Then they could pull the flats for today's deliveries.

Ursula glanced up from her paperwork and saw the barn swallow perched on a pipe rafter near the doorway. The bird seemed calmer now, resting before its next search for an exit. Whenever the swallows started to build a nest in the potting shed, Cat wanted to knock it down, force them to nest somewhere else. The birds could be a real nuisance, crapping on the floor, flapping suddenly in your face. But Ursula couldn't bear to harass them. The birds always reminded her of the child she'd miscarried. After three years, it was probably neurotic to cling to the loss, but she still felt a faint devotion to the almost-child. She was grateful to the swallows for helping her keep her tiny grief alive.

An hour later, Ursula was on her third cup of coffee and her second dose of Tums, and she couldn't find the freaking Safeway invoice. It had to be right here on her desk. She'd taken the phone order herself just yesterday. Jesus, she had to get caught up on this paperwork.

It mortified her how much she neglected her accounting. She didn't mind keeping elaborate seeding charts and production records. She liked graphs and spreadsheets just fine. But filing invoices she couldn't stomach. She had a special antipathy for her Safeway account. Their produce guy, Albert, was in charge of the nursery racks in front of the store, and he couldn't be bothered. He let the plants dry out, or he overwatered them, and he had a lousy eye for display. Last summer she'd made a special effort to help him work up an easy maintenance schedule. He did buy a lot of plants, after all. She and Albert were sitting at his desk by the walk-in coolers in the back of the store, and Albert said he thought he could increase his volume and sell a lot more of her plants if she'd work more closely with him—then, looking soulfully into her eyes, he'd reached over and squeezed her leg. It was all she could do not to punch him. She still needed the account, though, so she'd said, "Excuse me a second," and gone into the employee bathroom and flushed the toilet twice. Now she made Cat do the Safeway deliveries.

"Want me to pinch these petunias?" Cat shouted from the far end of the greenhouse. "They're pretty leggy."

When Ursula stood up, she spotted the Safeway invoice on the seat of her chair. She'd been sitting on it. She swore under her breath. It was a good thing she didn't have to keep her business going much longer, because she seemed to want to sabotage it.

Cat was combing her fingers through the petunias, appraising them like the hair stylist she was on the weekends. There was a whole table full of flats of 'Gypsy,' a new variety that flaunted oversized, overbright purple and gold blossoms. Ursula thought they looked cheap and gaudy—petunias with implants. But Cat liked them. She had predicted that they'd be a big seller, and she'd been right. They'd moved nearly fifty flats already. This was the last of them.

Ursula couldn't help staring at Cat's fingers as they fondled the foliage, grooming out yellowed leaves and plucking the spent blossoms. Cat's shoulder-length hair was dyed chestnut and sprayed stiff. Years of smoking and drinking had left her petite body as tough and lean as jerky. In her tight jeans and plaid shirt with the pearl snaps, she looked like a horse lady, but Ursula knew Cat had never been on a horse. She and her ex-husband had been into motorcycles instead, traveling to rallies around the West, but that was years ago.

Cat was the better grower. Ursula knew her plants, and she ran an efficient business, everyone acknowledged that. But to Cat, the plants were like family. She seemed to divine exactly what each plant needed: food, water, encouragement, discipline. When the farm was sold, the one thing Ursula would truly miss was working with Cat.

"Yeah, they're a little overgrown," Ursula said. "But we have to move them as is. See if Bimart will take a bunch of them on special."

"Okay, but I have a full truck already. It'll have to be a separate delivery. Can Nu make a run this afternoon?"

"No," Ursula said, walking back to the desk with Cat following. She poured herself another cup of burnt-smelling coffee from the grimy pot, pushed her paperwork to the side, and sat on the desk. "He's going to take Daddy to the doctor."

"Nu's a good-looking dude," Cat said. "Wish he'd let his hair grow out though, so his ears don't stick out so bad."

Ursula rolled her eyes. "I'll tell him you said so."

"Do," Cat said. "So, how's it going, having your cousin around?"

Ursula looked down and blew intently on her coffee. How *was* it having Nu here? At first she'd resented him. She didn't like noticing for the first time in months how dirty and frumpy the house was, how boring their meals, how dull their lives. She'd resented having to share the bathroom, didn't like the idea of Nu inspecting her creams, pills, and pads. And she resented not being able to walk naked from the bathroom to her bedroom. But now, after Nu had been here for a few days, she thought it was going to be okay. She'd managed to get the house cleaned. She'd successfully grilled some tuna steaks for dinner last night. And their evenings were a little less dreary with Nu around.

"Daddy really likes having him here," she said. "They like the same movies. John Wayne, Humphrey Bogart. Not my favorites, but watchable."

"Okay," Cat said. She unwrapped a stick of gum and took a few vigorous chews. "But do *you* like having him around? You told me you two were playmates when you were kids."

"Yeah, well, we were kids."

"And now he's a freaking felon. He won't be able to get a job or anything. When is his trial, anyway?"

"He's not a felon, Cat. Daddy's sure they'll reduce the charges. Maybe drop them altogether."

Cat blew a small bubble till it burst with a snap. "So what's he going to do while he's here?"

"Well, Bodie's got more farm work than he can keep up with. And we could train Nu to do some of the deliveries if you want."

"Maybe," Cat said. Ursula knew that Cat liked to handle the deliveries herself. She felt that chatting up customers and bringing back fresh gossip was an important part of her job.

"He probably won't be around long, in any case. He hates rain," Ursula said.

"Pfft. Can't fault him there."

"And he doesn't know an aster from a snapdragon."

"Well, I can teach him plants."

Ursula did a side bend, trying to pop a kink in her back. "Nu took Daddy to the dentist yesterday. He seems to be fine with being his chauffeur."

"Well, if your dad isn't driving, the world will be a little safer."

"And maybe," Ursula said, reaching her arms over her head and lifting herself on tiptoes, "maybe I can even get away for a week or two this summer, if Nu is willing to stick around and look after Daddy."

"You're due," Cat said. Then in her softer, hairdresser's voice, "How's your dad's cancer?"

"Oh, he's doing okay, considering. He had some more melanomas burnt off his face last week, so with all the bandages he looks like a mummy. But the prostate cancer is, you know, stable at the moment. It's not like he'll ever be cured."

"He had that last chemo when, a month ago?"

"Yeah, early May. That was a rough stretch. He talked like he wanted to stop treatments and just die. It was Nu that kept him going, I think."

"How's that? I didn't know Nu was here then."

"He wasn't. Nu was busy assaulting bikers and getting locked up. But that was what pulled Daddy out of his depression—he had to bail Nu out of jail, get him a lawyer, and all that. He drove to Bend right in the middle of his chemo treatments. He didn't see that anybody else was going to help Nu, so he figured he would."

"Helping somebody more miserable than us lifts our spirits."

Ursula made a sour face and dumped her coffee in the floor drain. "You been going to church again?"

"I got that from Julie on my bowling team. I thought it was pretty good."

"If you say so." Ursula went back to the tables and began to pinch a flat of yellow dahlias. She stuck a finger into the soil to test the moisture and reached for the nearest hose.

"Don't," Cat said. "Let 'em dry out. Those tubers don't like being too wet." Cat unwrapped another piece of chewing gum and added it to the mass already bulging in her cheek. "Speaking of miserable, I saw your ex the other day."

Ursula flinched and yanked a dahlia, tuber and all, out of the soil. "Dexter?"

"You have other exes I don't know about?"

"Where?" Ursula asked. She hadn't seen Dexter for more than three years, not since their divorce was finalized. She knew he was back in town, though. Her friend Becca had emailed to tell her that the university had hired Dexter in Ag Econ. Ursula couldn't believe Dexter's gall, moving back to Camas Valley, as if he couldn't sense the cloud of her hatred. Or didn't care. Dexter was a climber. If the next rung of his career ladder was here, Ursula knew, he'd grab ahold and climb over everybody around him.

Ursula figured she'd bump into Dexter sooner or later, and she dreaded it. She couldn't imagine what she'd say to him. "Sorry you're still alive" would be the honest thing, but she'd probably wimp out and just be polite. Fortunately, she hadn't run into him yet.

"Safeway," Cat said. "He was filling a shopping cart with beer and wine. Still likes to party, looked like."

Ursula closed her eyes for a moment, then thumped the side of her head with the heel of her palm as if to clear water from her ears. "Okay. So, what shall we do next? Transplant those celosia or what?"

"I'll transplant. If we're going to have a last crop of veggie starts, they need to be sowed, like, yesterday."

"Last year we hardly sold any starts after Father's Day."

"Yeah, but it was a dry year and everybody had their gardens planted early. This year, it's been so wet..."

"You're right. So, what? Broccoli, cukes, peppers?"

"Too late for peppers. Do some of those Aztec sunflowers."

"Why would anyone transplant sunflowers when they're so easy from seed?"

"Trust me, girl. They'll gobble them up."

Ursula headed for the seed room. Just as she reached the greenhouse door, Cat shouted. "Hey, almost forgot! Bad news. We got whiteflies on the begonias. I pitched the whole lot, but you probably need to spray."

The seed room was a converted u-Haul trailer parked beside the potting shed. Ursula had bought it from a nursery in Canby that went belly up. It was supposed to be temporary, but on the long list of things that needed to be upgraded, the seed room was near the bottom. It didn't have any windows, just a fluorescent fixture that hung low enough to clunk her head on if she wasn't careful. A squeaky exhaust fan whirred nonstop.

She hated the trailer. The moment she ducked into it, her skin began to itch. She raked her fingernails down her forearms and thought about Dexter, whose return to Camas Valley fortified her resolve to leave. She took a breath and exhaled loudly, trying to blow Dexter out of her mind.

Sowing seeds by hand often calmed her. It forced her to stop thinking, to concentrate on the precise task at hand: pinching up seeds, tucking them in the soil. Cat considered seeding by hand a colossal waste of time, and she'd be pissed off if she knew Ursula was lollygagging around in here. So she started to calibrate the pneumatic seeder, a finicky machine that Cat had tamed but that often went feral on Ursula.

Cat had urged her to upgrade to a better seeder. She scolded Ursula all the time about the need to keep up with current technology, and Ursula couldn't really argue with that. She knew that to survive in this business, you needed to keep your labor costs down by adopting every possible efficiency.

But now, mercifully, it felt like her business wouldn't have to survive much longer.

"Hell with it," she said to herself, "I'm doing these by hand." It might take three times as long, but the prospect appealed to her. She could hole up here in the seed room the rest of the morning. She began pulling packets of seeds from several cardboard boxes. She would do the smallest ones, the broccoli, first.

It looked like the sale of the farm was finally going through this time. There had been plenty of false alarms in the past, but now the university had a serious donor lined up. The money was real. And not a moment too soon, because Bodie's debts were mounting fast. She was ready to sell the farm and move on. Their father had signed off on the deal. Everybody involved agreed this was the best solution. Except Bodie, of course. But her brother had had his chance and couldn't make the farm pay. His eight acres of organic vegetables, his eighty-some community-supported agriculture customers, his strawberries, apples, grapes, and hops were not bringing in enough to stave off the banks.

Ever since the city had annexed the farmland to the west, the clock had been ticking for Tunder Farm. A big, new subdivision was creeping their way, a hundred houses a year, with Neville's twenty acres the only land between them. The Tunders owed the city $80,000 in systems development charges for their share of the sewer, water, street, and sidewalk improvements along their road frontage, even though they didn't use, or want, any of them. Their payments had originally been deferred, but the five-year grace period would soon be over. Bodie had poured all his pro football earnings into the farm and maxed out his credit to boot. Ursula could probably extend her loans, maybe nurse her business along for another year or two, but she didn't want to. And she wouldn't have to if the sale went through.

And when the farm was sold, what would she do next? Maybe she'd do some volunteer conservation work. Put her botany degrees to some use again. She'd read a paper last month about a project in Greece that enlisted goat herders to help restore endangered lilies in the Peloponnese. She'd love to work somewhere in the Mediterranean.

She finished sowing the broccoli and remembered Cat's suggestion of sunflowers. Turning to fetch a packet, she clunked her head on the light fixture. She swore, started to punch the fixture, then caught herself and instead patted the light gently. "Bet you'll miss me when I'm gone," she muttered.

She dropped one sunflower seed onto each cell of the planting flat, then prodded the seeds into the soil. Bodie's dream of being a farmer was so far from anything she'd ever expected of her brawny, football-brained younger brother that she'd never been able to give it much credence. But it was a real dream, and he had poured an inhuman amount of energy into it. Well, Bodie was broke now. His schemes had not panned out. He'd had his run. Besides, Bodie had plenty of old boosters and new connections. He could farm anywhere.

Bodie would land on his huge feet. Tunder Farm would change into something else. Ursula let herself contemplate it: a bulldozer rolling over Bodie's cropland, a track hoe taking down the hop barn, then turning to rake the roof off the house she'd been born in. She could taste her father's grief and the bitter tinge of Bodie's anger. But for herself? How did she feel about the prospect? It embarrassed her to admit it, but she felt mostly excitement, possibility, and freedom. If she could pack a bag and leave tomorrow, she would.

2 · Bodie

Bodie's on the tractor, cultivating a field of greens. Spinach, lettuce, radicchio, mizuna. The sun's going to set in half an hour, but that should leave him enough time to finish this section. He squints down at the shadowed rows of succulent young plants.

The way the tines uproot the weeds and cast them onto the ground reminds him of that game against Philadelphia. He was shedding blockers like they were made of spinach. Six unassisted tackles and two sacks, his best game ever. He eases the wheel a tad to the left, keeping the tines a hand's breadth from the crops. At hand-weeding he's a disaster. His huge fingers can't tease out the weeds from the greens. But on the tractor, he is precise, even delicate. He has a steady hand on the wheel and a light touch on the pneumatics lever, keeping the cultivator tines at the perfect soil depth.

He shouldn't be the one doing this chore. Arnold or Juano or even Zebra are all perfectly competent at cultivating. Sure, a lapse of attention can cause a lot of damage quickly, but it's not that difficult to train someone to keep the tractor moving straight down the rows. However, the others are all done for the day, and tomorrow is market, so who knows when one of them will get to this job. And besides, Bodie is in no hurry to go up to the house. He needs some space. He's got too many problems—pest problems, building issues, business glitches. Not to mention his domestic life suddenly going sideways on him. The roar of the tractor is calming. There is a kind of quiet space within the noise, like being on a boat. Zebra likes to call farmers *terranauts*. Goofy, he always thought. But he kind of gets it, too. Farmers are sailors on the earth. And fair sailing it is this evening, the weather sunny and mild, and the soil the perfect moisture for cultivating. The cultivator's shoes are breaking through the ground like the prows of ships, turning bow waves of soil, the weeds rolling over into the surf. Some violet-green tree swallows swoop and dive around him, catching the insects the tractor startles up. Now the birds glide alongside the tractor like porpoises beside a ship. If he loses the farm, maybe he'll get his seaman's papers and join the Merchant Marine.

But wait: he is *not* going to lose the farm. The farm is doing better than ever. They are almost paying their bills. Their customer base is growing exponentially. Their produce, thanks to Juano and Zebra, is as good as any in the valley.

Still, they're hanging by a thread. If Dexter won't defer his loan payments... Well, that's not an option. Dexter will come through. He always has.

Though Dexter called him this afternoon and left an ominous message saying they "needed to talk." Bodie called back an hour later but got voicemail, so now they're playing tag. Bodie's still hoping Dexter will call again. It's late, but Bodie would prefer to hear what's up rather than being left to imagine the worst. Bodie pats the phone in the breast pocket of his bibs. A prayerful gesture, he notices, and snorts mordantly.

It's a wonder he survived that first year on the farm. Emotionally, he'd been a mess, still addicted, three years after he'd washed out of the NFL, to the rush and regimen of football. Coming home to start a farm and grow hops had been either a brilliant career move or a further plunge down his personal toilet. He hadn't known anything about growing vegetables. But he did know a lot of people in town—friends, coaches, boosters, business people, and teachers—and he wasn't afraid to ask for advice. And everyone seemed eager to help out the fallen sports hero, though nobody could quite believe that the former pro football player now wanted to be an actual farmer. A *hobby* farmer, sure. A tax write-off while he looked for a restaurant or a local brewery to invest in. They probably imagined him hosting big parties, entertaining cheerleaders from his former teams. And that first summer his lifestyle would not have disproved their suspicions. Because Bodie did indeed host some big parties, and did in fact sleep with at least one former cheerleader, and several earnest young interns, too. But he really did want to be a farmer, and he worked his butt off at it, with Herculean inefficiency, while the reckless, extravagant habits of his former pro-athlete life ruled his weekends.

He hadn't liked himself for it, but partying and picking up women were things he was good at, and he had needed a win, had needed some cheap confidence-boosting, because he sure wasn't any good at farming. On top of his indifferent crop yields, his poor post-harvest handling practices, and his wayward agronomy, his accounting skills had sucked. His savings had drained away like Gatorade dumped out after a bad road loss.

Now Bodie twists further to watch the cultivator, and a stab of sciatica twitches his thigh. He needs to see the chiropractor, but he knows she's on vacation. He called yesterday. There are two dozen chiropractors in town and he's tried half of them. But Dr. Robinson is the best. All the male doctors look at Bodie's size and brawn and think they've got to out-muscle his spine. Dr. Robinson—Stephanie's her name but he never addresses her as other than Dr.—gentles him with massage and electro-stim, poses him on his right side and, with a whisper and a wrist thrust, pops his fifth lumbar back into line.

Now he feels a buzzing in his chest. Too mild for a heart attack. Fuck, it's the phone. He throws the tractor into neutral and levers down the throttle. He tries to tweeze the phone from the narrow bib pocket with thumb and first finger but it's too tight, so he squeezes the phone up from the bottom like a pimple. By the time he pops it open it's stopped vibrating. He flips the phone open and nearly drops it. The buttons are so small he prefers to use a pencil to punch them. But all he has now are his zucchini-sized fingers. He aims and presses "voice mail."

"Bodie, it's Dexter. Give me a call."

Bodie hits "call back" and gets Dexter's voice mail. "Hey," he says, "it's Bodie. Sorry I missed your call. Try me back. I'll be up till midnight, at least."

He shoves the phone into his hip pocket this time—he's not going to make that mistake again. He sighs and rolls his neck, feeling the gristle pop in his much-abused cervical vertebrae. A turkey vulture wafts up from the river and spirals overhead. Bodie figures there's only enough daylight for one or two more passes. The sun's just dropped behind Marys Peak. A few twists of cloud pinken, and a contrail glows orange like a lit fuse. He throttles up and eases the clutch out.

His first year on the farm had been chaotic, but he did make two important decisions. First, he put in an acre of hops and renovated the hop barn. That had taken a huge chunk out of his savings, but if he hadn't done it then, he'd be even further up a creek now. And then in March, at the start of his second growing season, he'd hired

Fleece. He had put an ad on craigslist for a seasonal farm intern and she had called that evening.

Most of his applicants showed up in blue jeans and sweatshirts, as if ready to go straight to work in the fields. But she came dressed in a brown knee-length skirt, a silky beige blouse and a leather vest with beads and tassels. He felt shabby by comparison, as if he were the one being interviewed. She handed him a neatly printed résumé with a list of references. Felicia Woodson was her name, she told him, "but everyone calls me Fleece."

She had thick black hair. Skin the color of a ripe Bosc pear. High cheekbones, full lips, button nose, though a very large button. And eyes. Oh, my golly, he couldn't look away from those big black-irised globes.

He'd stammered out his stock opening question. "How do you feel about long hours of grinding manual labor for little reward?"

That usually drew a nervous chuckle from the applicant, but she had not flinched. "I like to work hard," she'd answered. "I really want to grow stuff." And then she'd somehow made her eyes telescope toward him and asked, "How little, exactly?"

"How little?"

"The rewards."

"Ah, right," he'd said. "Well, here's the deal." He told her they currently had about eight acres in production, sold produce at the local farmers' markets on Wednesdays and Saturdays, and had eighty-four CSA customers. "That's community-supported agriculture," he explained, though it was obvious she already knew the acronym. He'd offered her the standard package: for thirty hours of labor per week she'd get room and board, free beer, and world-class farming experience.

She'd had, for her part, a couple of conditions: she wanted her own private room, not some dormitory bunk, and, she wanted to bring her flock of six sheep. He said he'd think about it. He had a couple of other people to interview. He'd let her know within a day or two.

That evening he did think about it. He thought about *her*. A lot. There was something forceful about her: her steady gaze, her solid posture. What did she remind him of? A horse? No, a tractor. She was geared low and, he imagined, she could pull all day. He remembered she'd given him her résumé, and he pulled it out of the ratty daypack he used for a briefcase.

She had earned her BS in Soil Science from Camas Valley State the year after Bodie himself had graduated—so she might have seen him around campus, or even watched him play football. He never asked anybody about their ethnic background but she'd included hers anyway. "I am a mix of Kalapuya, Northern Paiute, German, French and Irish," she'd written. "And I'm an enrolled member of the Confederated Tribes." Since graduating, she'd been employed mostly at Lucky Beaver Casino. Bodie could see that she'd worked her way up from greeter to assistant director of community outreach. She was seriously overqualified for an unpaid internship on a shoestring farm. But she seemed to know what she wanted, and she seemed to want to work for him. Or with him, more like it. She wanted to be a farmer.

He had no problem with the sheep. He had several acres in unused pasture. He'd even thought about getting livestock himself, but he hadn't had time. The only glitch: there was no extra private living space on the farm. His other two interns were bunking in an old henhouse he'd roughly converted to a dorm. There was a spare bedroom in the big house, with his dad and Ursula. But he wouldn't risk Ursula's ire by even asking.

He did have a spare room in his own house. It was currently set up as a grow room—windows and walls all covered over with foil-faced insulation—for the half dozen marijuana plants he'd grown last year, an insurance crop. He had appreciated the extra income, but felt paranoid the whole growing season. It was stupid that growing pot was illegal, but even stupider for him to risk getting busted. He could fix the room up for the intern easily enough, hang some blankets over the foil and get the windows opened. There was a bed he could bring over from the big house. But having this intern, this Fleece woman, living in his house would seriously crimp his weekend partying. He liked having his space. He had not had a roommate since he'd shared an apartment with another rookie linebacker his first year in Seattle. That was seven years ago.

Still, there was something about the woman that made him want to stretch, to change. Some better part of himself seemed to be waking up at the prospect of her working on the farm. He called her early next morning.

Her first day on the job, he'd given her to Juano to line out, and Juano had put her to work hoeing beans. That evening, she'd found him in the hop yard, tying up vines. She was a good eight inches shorter than he was. How was it she seemed to look him straight in the eyes?

"I am here to learn how to be a farmer," she'd said. "You're going to teach me that, right?"

"Well, yeah."

"Look," she'd said, "I have no problem hoeing all day. But if you're just looking for cheap labor, that's not me. I'm serious about learning to grow food. Okay?"

She was making a weird challenge, it seemed like, demanding some kind of commitment. He wasn't sure what it was, exactly, but he knew there was only one way to find out.

"Okay," he'd agreed, trying to look as clear and solid as she always did. And from then on they worked side by side. He was a poor and inexperienced teacher, but she was a superb student. She forced him to learn stuff just to be able to teach it to her. In reality, they became students together. And everyone liked Fleece. Juano, Arnold, even the ever-pissy Zebra, all seemed to sense that Fleece was the missing piece. She wasn't taking anyone else's job; she was just filling an enormous gap that no one had even known was there.

She brought her sheep in a borrowed trailer, and she and Bodie strung electric fence around the bottom land pasture. They spent a day tying up hop vines, another day assembling cloches for late-season tomatoes. She could handle tools. She could weed tiny seedlings, working in a full squat like a catcher, which she had been, she told him, for her high school softball team. One evening he showed her his hand-drawn spreadsheets of crop rotations and she popped open her laptop and transferred them to Excel. They started sharing meals, taking turns cooking. They sat together at the table after dinner and pulled out books, and looked at websites, made planting plans, graphed soil chemistry, designed fertilizer regimens. And one night when she'd been there four or five weeks, when they were practically falling asleep at the table, they'd gotten up at the same time and, holding hands like an old married couple, gone to bed together.

She made Bodie feel competent. She made him feel as if he were doing something important. She didn't idealize him, but she did idealize what he was doing, what *they* were doing together. They were a team. Finally, Bodie was once again part of a team. And that made it clear to him how he should treat everyone else: as teammates. He began to take a keener interest in his people—his employees and interns, his vendors and suppliers, and especially all his CSA customers—because they were part of the team. If he could understand what helped them do their best work, everybody's game was improved. Fleece had saved him. Together they would make the farm a winner.

Lately, however, ever since she got pregnant, Fleece was behaving weirdly. She was irritable and weepy. She had started going to visit her mother every week and she'd come home from Yoncalla exhausted. Bodie had not spent much time with Fleece's family, and he kind of hoped we wouldn't have to do so in the future. But Fleece seemed to want to be on a better footing with her messed-up family before the baby arrived. Meanwhile, she wasn't doing all her chores on the farm. The bills weren't getting paid, the website was out of date. Bodie was lucky to find a vet school student to trim the hooves on Fleece's sheep.

Now a tremor in the steering wheel pulls him back to the present. He mashes the clutch and the tractor hunches to a stop. He already knows what's happened, but not how bad. He looks over his shoulder. Yep, he's let the cultivator drift too close to the plants. Twenty feet of row is partially uprooted. He swears and kills the engine. He looks up toward the picnic table on the bluff, hoping that no one is sitting there watching him, then swings down from the tractor to assess the damage. It could have been worse. The spinach plants aren't totally destroyed, most of them just undercut and tipped. If he had a shovel or a hoe, he could tuck them back in just fine. Rather than return to the barn for a tool, he goes back down the rows, toeing the soil back with his boot, firming them up with a light stomp. He hopes no one notices that the tractor has stopped running, hopes no one comes to see if anything's the matter. Where the cultivator has swerved deepest into the rows, several dozen spinach plants are pitched onto their faces. He drops to his knees and tenders the plants upright, swaddles some loose soil around their roots.

He feels a tingling in his thigh. More sciatica. No, it's his phone vibrating again. He pushes himself to his feet and digs into his pocket. His wedding ring snags on the denim. He twists his hand angrily into his pocket and grabs the phone like it's a squirming fish. By the time he tugs the phone from his pocket, it's quit ringing, gone to voice mail. Damn. He's probably missed Dexter again.

He flips open the phone and listens. It's Fleece. The good Fleece. "Hi, Bodie, it's me. I was just thinking of you. I wanted to tell you I think you're going to be a great father. Okay, bye. Love you!"

Bodie closes the phone gently, as if folding a Valentine. He drops back down to his knees and leans both fists onto his thighs. His massive head drops to his chest. If anyone up on the bluff had looked down at him just then, they might have thought he was praying. He takes a pinch of soil and rolls it between his fingers, then places a few grains on his tongue. Gritty, minerally, and rich, it tastes like hope. Now Bodie draws a two-gallon breath, presses the rest of the damaged spinach plants back into the earth, remounts the tractor, and heads for home.

3 · Nu

Nu didn't really want a guided tour of the farm, especially not this early in the day. He'd rather spend the morning sketching and painting. He could explore the farm later, on his own time, in his own meandering manner.

But Bodie had insisted, so here he was, waiting on the front porch. Nu could see him standing in the gravel driveway beyond the hop barn talking to a man on a tractor. Bodie was waving his arms and shouting over the tractor noise. Finally the driver nodded, ground the tractor into gear, and roared off toward the bottomland.

"Sorry for the holdup," Bodie shouted when he finally came trotting down the drive. "Let's rock!" He led Nu toward the overlook, then stopped short of the edge and waved Nu forward. "Okay, cousin. Prepare to be amazed."

Looking out over the bluff, Nu gathered that he was supposed be awed by the prospect, but he didn't really get it. Sure, the acres of orderly fields splayed out below had an interesting geometry and texture, but the palette was too narrow, just green on green. The little oxbow lake curving beneath the bluff added some nice structure, and the darker woods beyond the cultivated fields created an interesting frame, but all in all the scene didn't call out to him as a painter. "Nice," he said.

Bodie led them past the hop barn and past the bungalow where he and Fleece lived, then down the gravel driveway cut into the bluff. They wandered through the bottomland fields clear down to the river, Bodie telling Nu far more than he wanted to hear about his cropping systems, his compost and fertilizer regimens, his innu-merable farm projects.

Bodie introduced him to a small, beautiful, weathered-looking man in a white shirt and bolo tie, smiling under a neat straw hat. Nu guessed the man to be in his fifties. Juano, the farm manager. "A man of the earth," Bodie said, to which Juano made a little bow, acknowledging his due.

"Tus campos se ven hermosos," Nu said.

The dapper man smiled broadly. "Thank you. Tu ves claramente."

Two other Hispanic-looking men did not look up from harvesting cabbages.

"Didn't know you spoke Spanish," Bodie said.

Nu nodded. "Grew up in Fresno."

"My Spanish sucks," Bodie said. "But I'm working on it. Farm workers are mostly Hispanic."

One field over, a raven-haired woman was transplanting seedlings, plucking the little plants from a flat, bending methodically to the ground and troweling them into the soil. Bodie waved at her, but she barely nodded. "That's Zebra. Miss Congeniality. I'll introduce you later."

Beyond the rows and rows of vegetables, they stood at the edge of the field where a man on a tractor was pulling a disc, turning under a cover crop of field peas. The tractor driver had a ball cap pulled down tight to his wraparound sunglasses, and big headphones that bulged insect-like from the sides of his head. Bodie raised an arm to signal him to stop, but the man gave no sign of seeing him. Bodie stepped closer toward the tractor's path and waved his arms, but the driver did not so much as glance at him as the tractor rolled past. Nu heard electric guitar and thumping base above the roar of the engine.

"Wow," Bodie said. "I don't know if Arnold's gonna work out or not." As they walked toward the river, he added, "I hired Arnold on a program the county runs for vets. He was in Iraq, has some serious issues. I can put him on a tractor and he'll drive clear around the planet. But that's about all he can handle."

"Seems pretty focused," Nu said.

Bodie snorted. "Arnold does not have a wide field of vision. Arnold's like a laser."

After they'd toured the bottomland, they walked back up the bluff. Bodie paused in the driveway and nodded toward the hop barn, still thirty yards away. Nu understood that this was the best place to admire the old barn's lines. And he did. It was a beautifully proportioned structure, a good four stories tall, with three cupolas protruding from the ridge, each one maybe six feet square and about the same in height, with louvered vents in the walls. The old barn looked as if it had gotten a tune-up since he'd spent summers here as a kid. Nu remembered the siding had been weathered and warped. And hadn't the whole barn slouched toward the north back then? Now the walls rose plumb and square, and the siding, though still gray and unpainted, looked shipshape.

"You remember playing in there when we were kids?" Bodie asked.

"Yep. Swinging from that rope in the hay mow. Building forts out of hay bales."

"You probably recall," Bodie said, his tone going tour guide, "that the cupolas are for ventilation. Farmers used to harvest hops still on the vine and then hang the whole vines, forty feet long, from the rafters to dry. There were a lot of hops grown in the valley before World War II. Barns like this all over the place. This is one of the last ones standing."

"Can you still climb up to the cupola?" Nu asked.

"Oh, yeah. Check it out sometime. We took the louvers out of the middle cupola so you can see out," Bodie said.

They walked up to the sliding door, where Bodie again paused. "We kept the original exterior, but we've made some changes inside. So here's the new staff room," he said, rolling open the barn-wood door with a flourish. Inside, what had previously been a dark, dirt-floored empty barn now looked more like an elementary school lunch room. The room's walls and ceiling were sheetrocked and painted bright white, the concrete floor brick red. Several long folding tables in the center of the room were strewn with water bottles and lunch buckets, sweatshirts and ball caps. There was a kitchen area in the corner to Nu's right, and next to the kitchen counters sat a big wooden desk with a dusty-looking computer.

"Hey, let me check my email real quick," Bodie said. "I'm trying to get a quote on a ton of diatomaceous earth. Guy's supposed to send it today."

Nu picked up a magazine from one of the tables, *Craft Brewing News*, and browsed the pages while Bodie logged onto the computer.

"Hey," Bodie said. "Got an email here from Dexter, Ursula's ex. He says to tell you hi."

"You're still in touch with Dexter?" Nu said.

"Oh, yeah. He sends me farming articles."

"You two were pretty good friends, weren't you?"

"Kind of. While him and Ursula were married. We went deer hunting a couple of times. Played poker."

"And now?"

"I don't see him much," Bodie said.

The rolling door flew open just then and Zebra barged in. "Bodie," she said. "You cannot put cabbage in field 7!"

Bodie rolled his eyes toward Nu. "Excuse us a sec."

Zebra slapped a spiral notebook onto the desk and explained to Bodie why the next crop of cabbage needed to be planted in field 3, not field 7 as originally planned. Nu heard "club root" and "nematodes."

Peering over the top of his magazine, Nu studied the woman. She was in her late twenties maybe, dressed in carefully ruined cutoff blue jeans and a black tank top. There were half a dozen silver rings in her earlobes, and a silver stud through each eyebrow. Her eyelids were dyed indigo, her lashes long and heavy with gunk. Her chest, arms, shoulders, and legs were covered with tattoos; Nu could see birds, snakes, a turtle, a fox, lots of foliage. The overall theme might have been Noah's ark. Most of the tats were mediocre work, neither sharp nor expressive, as if she had gotten them cheap from student tattooists. But her entire left arm was gorgeously zebra-striped, the pattern rippling as if it were real zebra hide. The sleeve seemed to be quite fresh, and he wondered if the name she was going by, Zebra, might be new as well.

Zebra jammed the notebook back on a shelf above the desk and turned toward Nu. He didn't get his eyes lowered quickly enough and she caught him staring. She stared back, then widened her eyes and stuck her tongue down her chin, a Maori warrior imitation, Nu guessed. She took three long strides till she was an arm's length away, a wave of patchouli fragrance wafting ahead of her. "You are so hot!" she said, then turned and headed for the door, blowing him a little black-lipped kiss as she went out.

"Zebra's a hell of a grower," Bodie said.

"Gay?" Nu asked.

"Who knows? She calls herself 'polymorphously erotic,' whatever that means."

"It's from Krishnamurti, I think."

"Whatever. Under the black ink, she's all green thumbs."

Bodie and Fleece had invited everyone for supper, so around 7:00, Nu, Ursula, and Joe walked down the drive to their bungalow.

"Bodie has *never* invited Daddy and me over for a meal," Ursula said. "So it must be in your honor, Nu."

Bodie was in his backyard, and he waved them over. "We're going to eat out here," he told them, gesturing toward a makeshift picnic table. "The house is a wreck."

Fleece came out from the kitchen and everyone jumped up to give her a hug. After they'd eaten—roast leg of lamb, new potatoes, green salad, all of it grown there on the farm—Bodie revealed the real reason for the gathering.

"We've got some news," Bodie said. "Fleece had her ultrasound today. It's a boy!"

"We're going to name him Joseph, after you, Grandfather," Fleece said.

"Well, you've jinxed the kid for sure," Joe said.

"Joseph Woodson Tunder," Fleece added.

"I love it," Ursula said, leaning over to squeeze Fleece's arm. "Giving him your maiden name for his middle name. That's beautiful."

While the family passed around the ultrasound photo, Nu slipped into the house to refill the water pitcher. The kitchen appliances all looked new, he noticed, but the crowded bundles of grasses and herbs hanging from the ceiling made the narrow space feel like something from another era. Pioneer times, or the 1960s. He went on through the kitchen to peek at the rest of the house. The living room was barren, the walls stripped to the studs. New electrical cable snaked through the exposed framing. A mound of lath ends and old plaster was piled in the corner. Nu shook his head in sad empathy. If remodeling a house while you lived in it was difficult, running a farm at the same time seemed impossible.

Nu returned to the table and refilled everyone's water glass. When he'd sat down again, Bodie thumped his glass on the table. "Sorry to change the subject," he said, "but I've got a bit of an issue I'm going to need some help with."

Nu saw Ursula's jaw tighten and her left hand reach up to clench the braid at her shoulder. Fleece began clearing the dishes.

"The city red-tagged the cottage yesterday. Juano has to move out, like, now."

"Oh, god, Bodie," Ursula said. "Didn't you fix all the stuff they wrote you up for?"

"Everything. Bathroom fixtures, smoke detectors, hand rails. I stopped working on our house to finish the cottage."

"Except...?"

"I haven't had a chance to connect the drain pipes under the house to the new septic system yet."

"Bodie, it's been months! Where does his drain water go?"

"Juano doesn't use the inside fixtures. He uses the Porta Potti by the barn. He doesn't mind."

"Well, just fix it!"

Nu saw Joe close his eyes and lower his chin to his chest.

"I'm trying! All the plumbers are booked up. Underwood's can't get out here for two weeks."

"Two weeks!?" Ursula twisted her braid so tightly it stretched her scalp. Her left eye seemed to bulge. "Jesus, Bodie. So where is Juano going to stay in the meantime?"

"Well, I was hoping..."

"No fucking way! He is *not* moving in with us."

"But Sis..."

"No! We've already got Nu. We're full. No."

"Just two weeks..."

"No! Besides, the city's got your number now. How many other things could they tag you for if they decided to?"

"Why would they do that?"

"Why did they come around now? Somebody is calling in complaints."

"God, Ursula, you're so paranoid."

It was a long-simmering argument, Nu could tell. Ursula sounded convinced that somebody was trying to sabotage Bodie's farm operation by calling in complaints. Bodie didn't think so. Bodie glared at Ursula and guzzled a half glass of beer. Then he sighed. He looked down at the table and said, "It's my fault. I didn't want to spend the money when I could do the plumbing myself. I just never found the time."

"Bodie, you can't do everything yourself," Ursula chided.

"Yeah, but I can't afford to have anybody else do it, either."

"And *your* house? Will it be finished before the baby comes?"

Bodie hissed, blowing out a fine spray of beer-spit. "I've got most of the wiring and plumbing done, but I still have to sheetrock and paint. Then the flooring. Fixtures..." He looked down and shook his head. "Months."

Nu had heard Bodie mention some of the house projects awaiting his attention, but Bodie had made each one sound matter-of-fact and easily accomplished. This was the first time Nu realized *how many* projects Bodie was juggling and how interrelated everything was.

Now that he'd seen the unfinished living room, he understood that the hole Bodie had dug for himself was deep.

"Bodie," Ursula said. "This place is going to kill you."

That touched a nerve. Nu watched as Bodie turned red in the face and growled.

Before Bodie could burst out with anything, Nu heard himself saying, "I can do it."

Ursula had looked his way with interest, but Bodie didn't seem to hear him. Bodie was still grinding his teeth, making a growling sound.

"What can you do, Nu?" Ursula asked.

Nu waited until Bodie shook off his anger and looked his way. "I can finish the plumbing."

Bodie looked interested now, though skeptical. "What do you know about plumbing? It has to pass inspection. The city will be eyeing me close."

It peeved Nu that none of them were aware that he worked as a plumber. None of them, not even Joe, had asked him anything about how he'd been living in Bend. He was used to people shying away from any talk about his art projects. Art talk terrified most folks, made them feel ignorant, and then angry. And he understood that everybody was tiptoeing around his criminal incident. But he had an actual life in Bend. Had a job even. But nobody had asked. "Well, you know, I work for a plumber in Bend."

Bodie did a double take. "Bullshit."

Nu just stared at Bodie.

Finally Bodie chuckled. He laced his meaty fingers and cracked a knuckle. "Well, hey. That's great. That's excellent. You got the job."

It was nearly 10 before they got back to the farmhouse. The family squabble during supper had left Nu feeling grubby and glum. He needed a shower. His duffle bag was in the corner, sprouting T-shirts and socks. Since he wasn't sure how long he'd be staying, he hadn't unpacked. He grabbed a change of underwear and was about to head for the bathroom when he heard Ursula clumping up the stairs, the old fir floorboards and wooden banister squeaking. He wasn't in the mood for any more conversation, so he waited for her to go into her bedroom. Instead she went straight into the bathroom. Nu cracked his door open and listened. After a minute he heard the jangling of the shower curtain and the sound of water.

He flopped down on the bed. Tired as he was, his mind was still buzzing, still trying to make sense of the day's jumbled encounters, conversations and, alas, arguments. No way would he be able to go to sleep yet.

He sat up and reached behind him to switch on the reading lamp and a jolt of pain thwacked across his chest. His cracked rib was healing alright, he guessed, but reaching behind him like that had triggered a nerve. Gingerly, he picked up his pencil and sketchbook from the nightstand. He began filling a page with loops and slashes, working faster and faster, letting the graphite carry his anger onto the paper. Once he'd covered one sheet with a rat's nest of randomness, he felt a bit clearer. He flipped to a new page and drew, more carefully now, a Celtic knot. The pattern calmed him, gave him a place to settle.

He turned to a fresh page, then just sat there, gnawing on his pencil. What, exactly, was he doing here? Sure, the two dirt bikers had threatened to break more of his ribs, but nobody took their threats very seriously. Still, it could be unhealthy to bump into those guys out in the forest, or in an alley in town. That's why Mina and some of his other friends, and his lawyer, too, for that matter, had suggested that getting out of Bend for a while was a good idea.

But why had he come here? He could have gone anywhere. He could have gone to visit Cynthia in San Diego, or his sculptor friend Markus in Fresno. He could have flown to Mazatlán and hung out on a beach for a few weeks.

Well, after he'd been arrested, the first person he'd called, reasonably enough, was his uncle Joe. Joe was the one who had put him in touch with a lawyer, and then, though Nu had insisted he shouldn't, Joe drove all the way to Bend to post his bail. And since then he and Nu had been talking on the phone every few days. He was aware that Joe was dealing with prostate cancer, among other ailments, and he really didn't want to be a burden. But when he'd mentioned a few days ago that he was thinking about getting out of town for a while, Joe had said, "You're always welcome here." So he'd come.

But now he was having second thoughts. Why in god's name had he just volunteered to help Bodie fix his plumbing? Probably he wanted to impress Joe and Bodie, and maybe Ursula too, with his skill, his willingness to jump in and do something no one else wanted to do. Plus, he hated to see Bodie and Ursula quarreling like that. But now he was stuck here for at least a few more days.

He'd brought some art supplies, hoping to do some sketching or painting. Well, that hadn't happened. Instead he'd been pressed into the Tunder Farm labor pool. Yesterday he'd delivered boxfuls of broccoli to the Camas Valley Co-op, driven Joe to a doctor's appointment, and even mowed, at Ursula's behest, the overgrown lawn around the farmhouse. Not that he minded helping out. But if he couldn't find some time to make art, he was going to go crazy.

Nu heard the bathroom door open, then Ursula's bare footsteps slapping down the hall and her bedroom door banging closed. He waited another minute, then grabbed his clean clothes and headed again for his shower. He was nearly at the bathroom when Ursula burst back into the hallway, wrapped in a blue terrycloth bathrobe.

"Wait a sec," she said. "Let me grab my hairbrush."

She disappeared into the bathroom, then came back into the hall and stood blocking Nu's way. "Hey," she said, and paused, tapping her thigh with the hairbrush. "That was really sweet of you to offer to help Bodie out. He doesn't really deserve it."

Before he could respond, she leaned in and given him a damp hug. "And I want to hear the whole story about those biker guys sometime." Then she padded off into her room.

In the shower, Nu tried to puzzle out the sources of tension between Bodie and Ursula. Bodie obviously loved what he was doing, but Ursula, as near as Nu could tell, was not so happy running her greenhouse. And the burden of taking care of their father seemed to fall entirely on Ursula. Joe was still fairly self-sufficient, but Ursula made all their meals, did all the household chores, and it sounded like she spent a lot of time shuttling Joe to doctors' appointments. She had already asked Nu if he would drive Joe to a specialist in Eugene later in the week.

He knew that there was talk of selling the farm, that developers had their eyes on the land. But Bodie, at least, seemed to be settling in for a long run. He was spending some serious bucks on remodeling his house, and the shop he'd built inside the hop barn was not a short-term investment.

Nu stepped out of the shower, toweled off quickly, and returned to his room. He wanted to sketch a map of the land while his memory was fresh. Though he'd spent many weeks here when he was a kid, his memories of the place were just random snapshots—building a fort with Ursula in the hay mow, smoking stolen cigarettes with Bodie in the hidden nook under the grape arbor. He'd never formed an overview of the whole landscape. Plus, the farm was different back then. The bottomland was just plain pasture, rented to a neighbor. There weren't any fields of veggies, no hop yard, no fruit orchard, no chickens or sheep. The hop barn had been a derelict structure, great for playing in, but seemingly on the verge of collapse. And Bodie and Fleece's bungalow had been vacant, boarded up. He remembered slipping inside with Ursula once, their footsteps echoing in the empty rooms.

Taking up his pencil, he drew the hop barn in the center of his paper, then sketched in the farmhouse, Bodie's bungalow, Ursula's greenhouse, Joe's shop. He added Juano's cottage, then sketched in the chicken coop with its fenced-in run, and the county road that marked the northern boundary of the farm. The woodlands, cultivated fields, and rolling pastures he suggested with crosshatches and wavy lines. An hour later, he was still wakeful, but he felt sketched out.

It was after midnight when he finally turned out the lamp. The room was not nearly dark enough. He didn't suppose he would sleep very well. Just a few more days and he could head back to Bend. He wasn't sure whether he was a visitor here, a semi–family member, or simply an interloper. But he sure as hell didn't want to become the farm's designated plumber.

4 · Ursula

It was nearly 8:00 and Ursula was just starting to make supper. Joe was already sitting at the table, reading the local paper.

She'd had to stay late at the greenhouse to spray for whiteflies, and now she was tired and grumpy. Among the many annoying chores that came with running a wholesale bedding plant greenhouse, spraying for insect pests was the worst. She hated the heavy, double-snouted respirator clinched to her face, the clammy neoprene gloves, the acrid smell of the chemicals. She used the least toxic insecticides she could find, but even they weren't exactly benign. Nevertheless, with her slim margins, she couldn't afford to lose a crop to whiteflies.

She poured herself a glass of Chablis and gave Joe a can of beer and a clean glass, then searched the fridge for supper fixings. "Where's Nu?" she asked her father.

"Marys Peak. Said he needed a hike. Said not to wait supper."

She started beating some eggs. "Omelets okay?"

Joe nodded. "They let Kevorkian out."

"Who?"

"Jack Kevorkian. Dr. Death. Served eight years of a twenty-year sentence. They let him out for good behavior."

"Great," Ursula said. She grated some cheddar, cubed and browned some leftover ham. When she tried to fold the omelet, the ham and cheese slid out and the eggs tore apart. Ursula slashed the omelet into shreds. "Sorry," she muttered. "We're having scrambled again. Clear the table, would you?"

Joe tossed the magazine on a chair, then side-armed everything on the table—salt and pepper shakers, four or five bottles of his pills, water glasses left over from lunch, binoculars, bird guide—to the table's edge. Ursula clunked a plate in front of him and sat down with her own.

They ate in glum silence. After a few minutes, Joe looked out the window and said, "Draw the blind, would you?"

Ursula turned and looked out across the yard toward Bliss Fits. The security lamp near the top of the gray wall had come on, its sulfurous eye staring into their yard.

"Fuck," she said, then yanked the cord to draw the window blind. Having the hulking wall of the yoga studio thirty yards from their house was a constant irritation, and they all did their best to avoid mentioning it. For a couple of weeks in May, the light had been out. Ursula suspected that Bodie had shot it with his .22, as he had often threatened, though she knew better than to ask him. But the lamp had been fixed a few days ago, and the nuisance resumed.

Ursula focused on her food. She'd burned the toast a little, so she scraped the black edges off, then slathered on some blackberry jam. She held the jar out to Joe. "Do you think Bodie can get his house done before the baby comes?"

Joe smeared jam onto his eggs and took a bite. After a moment's chewing, he said, "The baby won't care either way."

"Fleece will, though." Ursula took a sip of her wine and grimaced. After the jam the wine tasted sour. "Daddy, did you ever think Bodie would try farming?"

Joe picked up his toast and studied it. "Urse, if you had told me ten years ago that Bodie would someday want to be a farmer, I'd have sold this place then and there."

"You think it's a bad idea?"

"Oh, it's a wonderful *idea*. A noble idea. The problem is, it's a backbreaking reality. Farming is just too hard. From an economic standpoint, it's probably doomed."

Ursula was sadly heartened to hear her father's gloomy prognostication. It jibed with her own sense of Bodie's poor chances of success. But she felt like a bad person for expecting him to fail. "Am I doomed, too, then?"

"Sweetheart, I think both of you kids are nuts. The question is, are you doing something that satisfies you, that you feel proud of? Lord knows I never did anything that made much economic sense."

"Welding was a good career for you, wasn't it?"

"Welding bought our groceries, I suppose. And I had the satisfaction of making so-called art out of some of my failed repair jobs. Not sure that amounts to a career. Your mother's job kept the ship afloat."

Ursula appreciated hearing her father give Alice credit for being the main breadwinner. "Well, Mom loved being a teacher. Even being a principal." Ursula swirled the wine in her glass. "You know, Bodie loves farming. And he seems to be good at it, too."

Joe poured more beer into his glass. It foamed over, and Ursula grabbed a dish rag and sopped up the overflow.

"Do you remember," Joe said, "the summer you and Nu went whole hog into gardening? Your mother set you two up with a couple of beds in her garden. You were probably nine or ten. Nu was with us all that summer because his mother, your aunt Connie, had a string of golf tournaments. You two were together every minute. And Bodie, well, he was the odd kid out."

Ursula didn't recall any of this.

"You had a little patch of sweet corn that was starting to tassel, and the two of you told Bodie it smelled like buttered popcorn. 'Come smell it!' you told him. When Bodie stuck his nose in the corn tassel, one of you shook the stalk and Bodie got a snootful of pollen."

Now it all came back to her. "And he had an allergy attack!"

"Bad one. Face started to swell up. We had to run him into the hospital. He couldn't catch a breath."

"Oh, god, Daddy. I felt so bad."

"Did you? Well, you got over it pretty quick." Joe gave her a sad smile. "Your mother and I thought seriously about selling the farm around then. But the real estate market was down. We wouldn't have gotten much for it at the time." Joe took a thoughtful sip of his beer. "So, whenever I imagined Bodie as a grown man holding down a job, I always pictured him in an air-conditioned office."

"He says that his allergies don't bother him much anymore. Fleece gives him herbs."

"I'm sure she does. That girl has herbs for everything. She wanted me to take some, too. That didn't go anywhere."

Ursula drained her wine and put the tumbler in the sink. "Do you think we should sell the farm, Daddy? Do you want to stay here until..."

"Until I'm dead? Doesn't matter to me. If I was you, I'd sell to the university right now. Much as I mistrust them, it sounds like the donor they've got lined up this time is legitimate. They'd give us a heap of money, and you and Bodie could go off and do whatever you wanted to. This plan that Bodie has—raising vegetables, growing hops, eventually making beer—it all seems pretty dicey. If it worked out, he might be able to hold onto the place. But neither of you would get much freedom out of it."

"I'm afraid that Bodie and I have different ideas about freedom."

Joe nodded. "Yeah, everybody does, Urse. That's the stinker."

Ursula put their dirty dishes in the sink. She glanced at the calendar hanging on the wall beside the stove and gave a start. "Oh, shit. I forgot. You have a doctor's appointment tomorrow afternoon. I'll see if Nu can take you, okay?"

"I can drive myself," Joe replied.

Ursula glared at him. "I'll ask Nu."

When Nu came home just after dark, Ursula offered to make him some supper, but he'd already eaten. He showed her some sketches he'd made of the wildflowers he'd seen on Marys Peak—fawn lilies, trillium, bleeding hearts—then headed up to his bedroom.

Ursula stayed up late, trying to wear herself out enough to fall asleep. She folded a basket of laundry, then watched a cooking show on TV. A half-hour demonstration on how to braise Brussels sprouts might have put some people to sleep, but not Ursula. She was still restless. She neatened up the stacks of bills on the dining room table, and browsed through a couple of seed catalogs. Finally, reading a trade journal article about wholesale nursery trends, she started to nod. Hoping she could sleep at last, she climbed the stairs.

But no. As she lay in bed, her thoughts whirled. She was afraid that at some point Joe was going to refuse more treatments for his cancer. What would she do then? She knew that his surgeries and chemo were horrible, but at this point they were also routine. Their grave, competent doctors told them which to choose among their bad options. There was an odd kind of freedom in not having to make decisions.

And now Fleece was pregnant, and Bodie was teetering on the edge of bankruptcy. She didn't want to think about Fleece and Bodie having to leave the farm right after their baby was born. She didn't want to think about any of it. She wanted to go to sleep.

Sometimes when she couldn't get to sleep, she could quiet her mind by imagining herself walking through the greenhouse and counting the flats of bedding plants—pansies, petunias, lobelia, alyssum—flat after flat, row after row. Tonight, though, after several turns down the aisles, just as she was starting to succumb to the hypnosis, she came upon a begonia covered with whiteflies, and she was wide awake again.

And now her skin itched. She rolled and fidgeted, then flattened herself on her back, hands stiff against the sheets. The chemicals she had sprayed in the greenhouse today might have caused the itching on her arms and wrists. But why was the skin in the back of her knees itching? And now her armpits! It had to be psychological. But wasn't there something familiar about it, this random twitchiness?

Then she remembered: the moon. She got itchy when the moon was full. Not always, but sometimes, if she was upset and sleepless. She flung back the covers, went to the window, and pulled open the heavy curtains. Sure enough, a big white moon drifted overhead. A veil of thin clouds loomed in front of it, so the moon looked anemic, like a pale waif of a girl's face, not the bold, itch-inducing, bully of a moon she expected. But full enough to be the culprit.

More insidious than the moon, however, was the security lamp on the back wall of the Bliss Fits Yoga Studio, its sulfurous light flaring through her window. She still couldn't believe that the city had let them put that ugly building so close to their property line. And it was her fault as much as anyone's.

The letter notifying her parents of the developer's request for a variance had come at the worst possible time. Her mother had been suffering from shooting pains in her abdomen all that winter, but she'd put off going to the doctor for months. Ursula remembered the phone call from her father the day they'd gotten a diagnosis. "It's cancer," Joe said. "Ovarian. Pretty far along."

Ursula had cleared her calendar and driven down from Pullman the next day.

Her mother was all business, lining up doctors' appointments, researching treatments online, talking to any friend or colleague who might have had any first-, second-, or thirdhand experience with ovarian cancer. Alice had assured Ursula that she need not have come, that she and Joe could manage everything just fine.

"Save your vacation time for later," Ursula recalled her mother saying. That "later," Ursula understood, meant after her mother died, when her father would need Ursula most.

But her mother and father hadn't managed things. Alice's cancer had been discovered too late. She'd gone down too fast. And while they were trying, against all hope, to drive the tumors back with radiation, that's when the city's paperwork had arrived, the request for the variance that would allow Bliss Fits to be built so close to their property line. She vaguely remembered seeing a letter from the Camas Valley Development Office, but she hadn't opened it. Nobody had. Only seven months later, after her mother had died, and after construction on Bliss Fits had already begun, did she try to raise a fuss. City staff told her that if Joe—or anyone, for that matter—had made an objection to the variance before it was granted, it would have been denied. But by then it was too late.

If Bodie saw the security light was fixed, he'd probably shoot it out again. He had that farm boy's ease with righteous violence. She envied him that. She felt sufficient hatred to shoot the light herself, but when she imagined doing it, the bullet ricocheted back and hit her. Everything she had tried since her divorce had ricocheted. Even the modest success of her greenhouse business was a total ricochet. She had wanted to show Dexter she didn't need him. She had wanted to prove herself to be a competent grower and businesswoman. Well, she had accomplished those reactive goals. But to what end? She didn't *want* to be running a business. She didn't want to file invoices or spray chemicals or grow stupid hybrid petunias.

She crawled back in bed and clamped her eyes shut. She lay still, trying to picture another life. She imagined herself renting a room in a little Greek village, setting up her research project in the mountains of the Peloponnese. She'd survey all the native vegetation. She'd hire a few of the local men to erect fences around her survey plots to keep the wild goats out. That way she could see which plants grew back if they were protected from heavy browsing.

5 · Bodie

It's a sunny Sunday afternoon, warm for the first week in June, and Bodie is in hog heaven. He's had two beers and three hot dogs. His eyes are full of acres of green grass he doesn't have to mow. Young men in spiffy uniforms—many of them artfully stained with infield dirt this late in the game—throw a ball with remarkable force and grace around the diamond. The game is a pitchers' duel, scoreless after seven. Bodie used to think baseball was boring, but nowadays boring feels pretty good. He won't mind if the game goes extra innings.

He doesn't get to many sports events these days. Fleece is not a fan, and the farm eats up all his time. He does have season tickets for football, but somehow the thrill has gone out of it for him. Maybe once you've been on the field it's not as interesting being in the stands. Also, he gets headaches from the noise, a sad reminder that concussions are forever.

In reality, he has no business taking a Sunday afternoon off. He should be home sheetrocking the living room. But when Dexter emailed to invite him, he eagerly agreed. He needs to ask a favor of Dexter, anyway. A year ago, Bodie borrowed $5,000 from Dexter for the upfront costs to expand his hop yard. Bodie is supposed to start paying back the loan next month, but now, with a baby on the way, he knows he'll need all the cash he can hang onto. And what better place to ask someone to delay payments on a loan than a baseball game?

Dexter climbs the stands with two more beers. "Sorry it took so long," he says. "Ran into the dean." He hands Bodie a plastic cup of Coors Light.

"I'm hoping to have my brewery running in a couple of years," Bodie says, "and get them to sell my beer here."

"That would be a coup," Dexter says.

"Once the fans get used to a local craft brew, this piss," Bodie holds up the offending cup, "can go straight to the toilet without detouring through a human."

There's a man down on the concourse staring up at them, trying to catch Dexter's eye. "Oh, shoot," Dexter says, "the dean wants to introduce me to somebody. Excuse me again."

Bodie watches as Dexter tucks his cup under his seat, then sidesteps back down the row, making "Sorry" faces to the fans whose feet he's trampling on. Bodie takes a sip of beer, grimaces, and looks at the scoreboard. The game's been going less than two hours. Even if it goes extra innings, he'll be home well before Fleece gets back from her mother's. Fleece has never met Dexter, and she doesn't want to meet him, out of loyalty to Ursula. But she knows that Bodie remains friends with him. Still, if he can avoid mentioning who he went to the game with, all the better.

He understands why Ursula divorced Dexter. Dexter had that affair with Susan what's-her-name. It was rude and stupid, and the timing—right after Ursula's miscarriage—couldn't have been more insensitive. But Jesus, you'd think Ursula could let go of it after all this time. It's not like her life has been roses since then. Ursula's chronic unhappiness is like January rain. Day in and day out, cold, wet, and gloomy. Bodie even wonders if part of Ursula's resistance to keeping the farm has to do with his past friendship with Dexter. If she knew they were *still* friends, that he was here at the ball game today with Dexter, who knows what new ways she might find to sabotage his operation.

The fact is, Dexter has come through for Bodie many times. Times, in fact, when his family was *not* there for him. For starters, Dexter was always a lot more interested in football than any of the others. He drove clear to Seattle to see Bodie play for the Seahawks a bunch of times. And then after the injury ended Bodie's career and he moved to Denver, Dexter had kept in touch. If Dexter was flying through Denver, he'd give Bodie a call and they'd go out for a drink.

Denver. Bodie closes his eyes and shivers. Denver was a dark time. He had gone there for his shoulder surgery, and then got some part-time work with a marketing agency. He liked the city okay, liked the fishing and elk hunting in the Rockies. He knew some of the Broncos, of course, and he went to their parties. Mostly he did research. On beer. He sampled every conceivable variety of lager, pilsner, porter, stout. Every ale known to man. Sampled heavily. Researched assiduously. Bodie remembers it all only vaguely. If there were a photo album, all the images would be tilted and blurry. His asthma had come back. He'd gotten soft and fat. But he *was* serious about learning to brew. He'd hung around Stan Weisterman, the famous Denver brewmeister, and actually apprenticed with another guy, Lloyd Emerson, at Golden Lion Brewery.

The winter his mother got sick, Bodie was going to fly home and see her. But he'd gone on another bender, got in a bar fight, and ended in jail. He was too embarrassed to tell his folks, so he called Dexter, and Dexter flew to Denver, bailed him out of jail, got him a lawyer, the whole nine yards. Covered it all and never let Bodie pay him back. Though by the time he got home, Alice had died, a memory that never fails to twist a knot, as it does again now, in his gut.

Dexter clambers up the steps and tramples his way back to his seat. "Potential donors," he says.

"You should have introduced me. I could use some donors."

"When did we score?" Dexter asks, looking out at the scoreboard.

"Asbury walked and stole second. Finney singled him in."

"Sorry I blinked. Looks like it might be all the offense for the whole game."

"I didn't know schmoozing with donors was part of your job."

"It's everybody's job. But I'm doing some admin this year, so..."

"What, like, dean's office?"

"Yeah, I'm the interim associate dean."

"Well, congrats," Bodie says. "And hey, I can't believe I keep forgetting to tell you. Fleece is pregnant!"

Dexter pops out of his seat. "Holy kamoly. That's fantastic!" He holds out his beer and they bump cups, splashing a little on the woman sitting in front of them. She slaps a hand to her neck, turns and scowls.

"Sorry!" Dexter says to her. "But he's gonna have a baby!" The lady shakes her head, apparently unmollified by the happy news. "When's it due?"

"November."

Telling Dexter has made the reality of it sink deeper. Bodie's head reels. He has *so much* to do. Farm, hop yard, house remodel.

"Well, that's just wonderful," Dexter is saying. "Give Felicia a hug for me."

Bodie is lost in his chore list and doesn't really hear Dexter. "I can do it," he finally says. "I can do everything. It might be the hop yard will fall behind schedule, but..." He takes a gulp of beer and comes back to the moment. He remembers his mission. "And in fact, Dex, I need to ask you about something."

A murmur from the crowd. Bodie and Dexter turn back to the action to see the Camas Valley right fielder race to the warning track, leap high, and...nope. The crowd groans. Home run Stanford. Game tied at one.

"Fuck," Dexter says. The splashed lady tosses another scowl over her shoulder. "I can't hang around if this goes extra innings. The wife is making dinner."

Bodie has not met "the wife." He knows the young woman was one of Dexter's grad students in Pullman. "Look," Bodie says, "What with the baby coming and all, it would really help if I could delay a couple of payments on that loan."

Dexter flashes a hard glance at Bodie, then looks down at his beer, waiting, it seems, for Bodie to make his case.

"So, could you, ah, slide the payment schedule back a few months? I can catch up in October after the harvests are all in."

Dexter sets his unfinished beer under his seat. "I'm not sure I can do that, Bodie. Our finances are pretty tight at home," he sighs. "Let me talk to my accountant." Then he turns and looks directly at Bodie. "I am a little worried about this. Maybe you should consider letting the university buy the Tunder Farm after all. You can always find more farmland, right?"

Bodie does not like being stared at like that. He likes to talk business side by side, both parties looking out at something they share an interest in. The farm, the hop yard, the ball game. Bodie looks out onto the ball field. He is surprised to see that Stanford is still at bat, runners on the corners. He glances at the scoreboard. Two outs. Game still tied. As he watches, the Camas Valley pitcher, Gilmore—he's pitched a helluva game, a four-hitter so far, though he's also issued three walks—sets and delivers. The Stanford batter swings late, defensively, and pops a blooper to left. The shortstop scampers out as the left fielder races in, but the ball drops between them. Stanford has a 2-1 lead. CVSU will have to come from behind in the bottom of the ninth.

"Hey, I gotta get home, Bodie," Dexter is saying. "Congratulations again. You're gonna be a great father."

Bodie nods, smiles. He sticks out his hand for a handshake, but Dexter has already turned away.

6 · Nu

Early Monday morning Nu walked over to Juano's house to finish Bodie's aborted plumbing job. The little cottage had been boarded up when they were kids. Ursula had believed that the house held some kind of treasure—jars full of coins, boxes of vintage clothing, or old family photo albums—so one summer when they were nine or ten, the two of them had pried the door open and snuck inside. The three small rooms were completely empty, no chairs, no dishes, no boxes of coins or vintage clothes, just a deep layer of undisturbed dust and a dead mouse in the sink.

Bodie had opened up the cottage for staff housing soon after he moved back to the farm five years ago. The house sat thirty yards or so beyond Fleece and Bodie's big garden, surrounded by a newly planted orchard of filbert trees. As Nu approached, Juano came out the door and waved. In his white shirt and bolo tie with its elegant turquoise clasp, Juano looked like a man heading for an office job or church.

"Señor Nu. Como estas?"

"Muy bien," Nu called. "Es un dia hermosa."

"Hermosa," Juano agreed. "Would you like a coffee?"

Nu sat on the front-porch railing, and Juano brought out two mugs and a couple of pumpkin muffins Fleece had baked.

"Did you grow up on a farm?" Nu asked him. "You're obviously very skilled."

Juano laughed and shook his head. "I'm a city boy. My father was a banker in Ciudad de México."

Nu took a bite of the muffin, waiting to see if Juano would say more. He was curious about the man, but he didn't want to pry.

"He was un pendejo. I left home when I was sixteen."

"Damn," Nu said. "Have you been in the States ever since?"

"Oh, no. I worked in maquiladoras in Juarez. Computer assembly. I was good, so I rose up. I became foreman, made good money. Had a family."

"Ah," Nu said. "And your family is...?"

"My son is in Minnesota. A teacher. My other son and my wife are dead."

"Oh," Nu groaned. "I'm so sorry."

"Long time ago."

The two men fell silent, staring out at Fleece's garden. It was bursting with flowers. Nu recognized dahlias, zinnias, marigolds, but there were many more he couldn't name. A couple of Fleece's black-and-white chickens, Barred Rocks, if he wasn't mistaken, prowled the yard.

"I've traveled in Mexico quite a bit," Nu finally said. "I never came across anyone named Juano."

Juano crumbled the last of his muffin and threw it toward the chickens. The men watched the fastidious birds strut and peck. "When I got to Juarez, you see, I was just a teenager," he said. "My first job was at the big Yanqui chicken farm. For six months I shoveled chicken shit. Guano. And that's why the foreman named me that. They all called me Juano."

"Wow," Nu said. "And now you're just used to it, I guess?"

"That name stuck to me like mierda. Whenever I went someplace new, I would tell people, 'Soy Juan.' But pretty soon somebody would call out, 'Hey, Juano. Que pasa?' I gave up. Soy Juano." Juano looked up at the sky, then turned to Nu. "And you? Your name is not typical, too, eh? Are you maybe Chinese?"

"Vietnamese. My parents came to the States right after the war. They died when I was a baby, and Joe's sister..."

"Bodie's tia?"

"Right. Bodie's aunt Connie and her husband adopted me. They've both passed."

"Ah. An orphan two times," Juano said, shaking his head. "And yet you are family here."

"Yeah, I guess so," Nu said.

Juano pitched the dregs of his coffee into the grass. "Well, I have work to do," he said. "As do you, my friend. You're going to fix my pipes, eh?"

Nu nodded. "You should be able to use your sink tonight."

Nu tugged on the coveralls he'd borrowed from Ursula. They smelled of fertilizer and a peachy skin cream. The morning air was thick with moisture, pollen, and plant odors, so much heavier than in Bend. Nu inhaled deeply, then pinched his nose to stifle a sneeze.

It was kind of a shame to crawl under a house on a pretty day like this, he thought. On the other hand, he always looked forward to seeing what was under a house, and he liked working alone in tight spaces. It quieted his mind. He often got ideas for paintings when he was doing plumbing jobs.

Bodie had already dropped off the black ABS drain pipe and fittings. They were lying on the lawn along with a plastic tote containing primer and cement and the tools he'd need. Looking at the crawl-space opening, he could see why Bodie hadn't finished the plumbing. No way Bodie could fit through that narrow rectangle. It was going to be tight even for him. He wriggled through headfirst and shone his flashlight around the crawl space. Ancient cobwebs dangled from the floor joists like moth-eaten scarves. A pile of old garden hose lay abandoned in the nearest corner. Close beside the opening, there was a sagging cardboard box. Nu lifted the flashlight to peer inside: a pair of rusty muffin tins, a pressure cooker, and a nice-looking hand-crank grain mill, the treasures Ursula had hoped they'd find in the house all those years ago. Against the opposite wall there was a hump of something furry, a dried-up cat or opossum.

Crawling on hands and knees, he took his measurements, writing the list of fittings he'd need on his palm. He scooched back outside, sawed the pipes to length, cut a few short nipples to join the elbow fittings, then crawled under again. He cleaned the first elbow with a rag, swabbed the fitting with primer and cement, then inserted it onto the main drain pipe coming through the floor from the bathroom above. Sprawled on his back, holding the fitting tight while the cement dried, he thought of all the afternoons he'd crawled around the Underground Gardens in Fresno as a kid.

The Underground Gardens, that's where he'd gotten his fondness for caves, and why he didn't mind crawling under houses. The Underground Gardens was a maze of tunnels and rooms excavated from the San Joaquin Valley hardpan by a sun-crazed Sicilian named Baldasare Forestiere. Back in the 1910s, Forestiere had noticed that the best place for an afternoon siesta on a 120-degree summer day was in his employer's root cellar. So he decided to dig himself a cellar—then kept digging for forty years. There were winding underground tunnels with niches for lamps cut in the walls, spacious bedrooms with sleeping nooks carved right out of the rock, and big grottos open to the sky with lemon trees planted twelve feet below grade, their canopies rising up to the surrounding surface. Nu had first visited the gardens with his kindergarten class and fallen in love with the place right then. He'd gone back so often that by the time he was in high school, they'd hired him to help with the never-ending restoration. He even led tours. Lots of people thought the gardens were just an oddity, but Nu believed they were a work of genius. To create something as strange, unique, and beautiful as the Underground Gardens became his goal in life.

In a couple of hours Nu had completed the plumbing. Returning the tools to the shop, he spotted Bodie talking with Arnold. He should have told Bodie that the job was done, that Bodie could call the city for a reinspection, but Nu didn't want to get sucked into any more farm work, so he just left the tools inside the door and snuck away. Back at the farmhouse, he slipped out of Ursula's cobweb-covered coveralls, then quickly washed his hands and face and drove into town.

He needed sketchbooks. He'd been filling them a lot faster than he'd imagined he would. At a crafts store, he found his preferred brand and bought half a dozen. Then he wandered through a couple of little storefront art galleries—a co-op run by some local plein air painters, competent but run of the mill landscapes mostly, then a more unusual kind of gallery for artists who were also developmentally disabled. Bright colors, flat perspectives, but wildly inventive. Monsters, aliens, hybrid creatures. Plenty of smiling faces, but also some scary people. Naïve art, he'd call it. Outsider art. A couple of the paintings suggested a kind of anguish beneath the surface that gave Nu the shivers.

A man came out of the back room. He had on wire-rim glasses and a stiff green beret. Stocky, a little paunchy, in his fifties maybe, he walked quickly up to Nu and stuck out his hand. "Andy Patterson," he said. "Thanks for stopping in."

"Nu Van Nuys. Cool setup you've got here. Are you the curator? Or manager?"

"Nu Van Nuys! Wow, I heard you were in town. Hey, I really, really liked that *Off-Road Vehicle* project of yours. Really good. Really good."

"Uh, thanks," Nu stammered. "How did you...? Did you see my website, or...?" He shuffled backward half a step, trying to get a little space from the man's intensity.

"No, no. In the gallery. Calliope Gallery, right? I read that profile in *Oregon Outback* and drove over a couple of weekends ago. Glad I did, too. Powerful stuff. Powerful. How did you get those wave patterns in the dirt? Did you shape it, or was that the way you found it?"

Nu felt his pulse quicken, as if extra oxygen were being pumped into the room. He hadn't talked art in quite a while. "No," he said, "I didn't want to alter the site. That was the way the dirt bikes eroded it."

"Yeah, yeah. Cool. Brilliant. That is so cool. But look. You got time for coffee? I need to hear more about this. Yeah? Yeah? Okay. Let me just tell Sandra I'll be gone for a bit."

Andy disappeared into the back room, then hurried out and took Nu by the arm. They walked a few blocks through the downtown, Andy talking nonstop all the way. "So, yeah, I'm an artist, too. Paint, pot, fabricate. Whatever. But I've worked with developmentally disabled adults, you know, like *forever*. Group home counselor. Work crew supervisor. About any job you can get without a degree. And the thing is, some of these people, a *lot* of these people are so creative. Art just pours out of them. So I wrote some grants and we got the gallery and studio space going, and you saw the art. God, I just love their stuff! You saw it, right? Don't you love it?"

Nu nodded. He wasn't that big of a fan of naïve art, but he was willing to love it on Andy's say-so. It was something deeper than aesthetics. At the coffee shop, they grabbed an open table, then Nu stood in line to order while Andy circulated among the customers, trading hugs and hellos with several friends.

"Okay," Andy said, once they had their coffee. "I have to hear the whole story. You got arrested, right? And it sounds like the dirt bikers have got, like, a contract out on you."

"Whoa," Nu said. "That's not..."

"Okay, okay. Well, just tell me the whole story. Like, what gave you the idea in the first place? How did you do those paintings? Did you fly over or find some aerials or what?"

Nu felt agitated by the barrage of questions. He put his right hand palm down in the center of the table, staring at it until Andy stared at it, too. After a few seconds, Nu said, "The whole story?" Andy nodded rapidly. "From the beginning?"

So he started with some background, how for the past year the Deschutes National Forest had been developing a new management plan for off-highway vehicles. How the off-road crowd, predictably, wanted more trails, more off-road areas. How a lot of other people—hunters, fishers, some of the ranchers, plus anybody who valued wimpy things like quiet recreation or intact ecosystems—wanted there to be fewer off-road trails. Nu told Andy that his environmentalist friends had worked hard to get people to show up at the Forest Service's information sessions and to submit testimony. But the off-roaders were super well organized, and they had money for propaganda. They were gonna get the plan they favored.

"So, then, one evening, we were looking at some aerial photos. The off-road trails are bare dirt, so they stand out against the darker forest. There are so many of them they make patterns like fish skeletons, or like Nazca lines. It's like aliens made huge geoglyphs on the land."

"I can see it," Andy said.

"Yeah, but they're really just roads. It's like subdivisions were plotted throughout the forest. Fascinating patterns. Beautiful, even. But once you considered the impacts, horrifying."

"Beauty and horror," Andy said. "You were hooked."

Nu chuckled. How cool to talk to someone who understood how an image could just grab you.

"I needed to see it firsthand, not just from old photos," Nu told him. "So I got a friend of a friend to fly me over. Open cockpit, low altitude. God, that was fun!"

Andy grimaced, looking ill. "I can't fly," he groaned. "Phobic. But anyway. Go on. And then you painted from your photographs?"

Nu nodded. He told Andy how the exhibition at the Calliope Gallery had spurred a lot of interest. There'd been some good reviews, a big response. "A lot of people looked at the paintings and say, 'Holy shit! I had no idea. What a huge impact!' And the cool thing was, lots more people got involved with the off-road plan. There were even letters to the editor that made reference to my show."

"And that's what pissed off the bikers."

"Nah, I don't think so. I didn't get any blowback."

"But they tried to beat you up?"

Nu sighed. "No. Here's what happened." He took a slow sip of coffee. "I just wanted to spend a night in the woods. There's this pretty camping spot beside a meadow at the foot of Pine Mountain, less than an hour from my house. It's way out beyond the boundary of the Fort Rock Off-Road Trail System, so there aren't supposed to be any dirt bikers out there. You go past the Pine Mountain Observatory. The gravel ends and the road turns into a bad two-track.

"I heard them first, then spotted them. Two bikes tearing through the woods to my left. I should have just turned around, gone back to town, and filed a report. You don't want to mess with bikers in the woods. But I wanted to document the damage, at least. Maybe get a photo of their vehicle, a license number. So I parked my truck and checked my phone. I had one bar. I didn't really think any deputy would actually drive out there. But I figured it couldn't hurt to call it in. At least there'd be a record. So I called dispatch and told the lady I'd just witnessed illegal off-road vehicles.

"'I've got an on-duty deputy in Millican,' she told me. 'I can't promise you that he'll be able to come out, but I will pass along your information.' Then she said something like, 'And, sir, *do not* engage with the off-highway vehicle users.'"

"You should have gotten the fuck out of there," Andy said. He was visibly agitated. Nu guessed Andy suffered a lot for his imagination and empathy.

"Yeah, no doubt. I figured they were staging from my campsite, so I took my camera and worked my way down the slope. I could see where the bikes had thrashed through the woods, ripped branches, torn through the duff.

"I spotted their pickup, a red Ford F-250, and a blue dirt bike parked beside it. It was broadside to me so I couldn't see the license plates. Figured I'd work my way around farther to the right. I could hear the other motorcycle whining through the woods, and then I saw it, a black bike tearing across the meadow. It roared into camp and parked and the rider dismounted.

"I was hiding in the brush, far enough away I didn't think the guy would be able to hear my camera shutter clicking. But then, above and behind me, I heard some rustling in the brush, and a voice said, 'Well, what do we got here? *National Geographic*?'"

"Oh, man," Andy said, rubbing his knuckles anxiously. "Fuckin' *Deliverance*."

Nu had told the story so many times—to the police, to friends, to his lawyer—that he'd gotten kind of numb to the violence of it. But Andy's visceral response was rekindling Nu's own anxiety. He had to take a deep, steadying breath before he could continue.

"The guy had wavy blond hair, a high forehead. He came out of the brush into the open, and I saw he had a pistol holstered to his belt. He pointed toward the clearing and we scrambled down and joined the other guy. He was smaller than me, had dark hair, his face was all acne scarred. He was leaning against the seat of his dirt bike picking his teeth with a pine needle. I don't remember feeling a lot of hostility coming off either of them. They seemed more amused than dangerous. But, still, I was scared shitless. I managed to suck in a breath and say, 'You know this area is closed to off-road use, right?'"

"'Nope. Didn't know that,' the blond guy said. 'And don't care. The forest don't belong to the government. It's ours to use however we want.'"

"'Okay,' I said. 'I guess we disagree on that. So I'll just head on back to my truck and go home.'"

"'Smart boy,' the dark-haired guy said. 'But leave us the camera.'"

"I lifted the camera strap from around my neck. 'Look,' I said. 'Let me give you the film, and I'll keep the camera.'"

"The little guy snarled and yelled, 'You fucking gook,' and grabbed for my camera.

"I just reacted. I swung my arm up to block him and the camera smacked his forehead. He went down to one knee. Blood was dripping from above his eye."

"And they busted you for assault?" Andy said. "Sounds like self-defense to me."

Nu nodded. "So then the blond guy kicked me in the stomach, and then kicked me again in the ribs, and that's when we heard a siren whoop. Sheriff's suv easing into the clearing, cop over the bullhorn saying, 'Everyone get your hands up where I can see them!'

"The deputy walked over to us and said—" Nu paused a moment. He was a little embarrassed at how practiced he'd become at telling this story. "'What's going on here, Nathan?'"

"Oh, shit. He knew the guy."

"Yep. I could tell I was in trouble then."

Andy's phone rang, startling him. He dug it from his pants pocket, looked at the number, and said, "Damn, I gotta take this."

Nu nodded, and Andy went out to the sidewalk. He was back in a moment. "I gotta go," he said. "My daughter..."

"Right," Nu said.

"But, hey, you should come over to my studio sometime. Soon, right? Okay? Okay? Here's my card."

Nu stood, they shook hands, and Andy hustled out the door. Nu sat back down and stared at his coffee. When he picked up the cup, he noticed his hand was shaking. Revisiting the assault had retriggered his anger, and Andy's agitation had gotten into him, too.

Remembering the new sketchbooks he'd just bought, he pulled one out of the paper bag. He took a pencil stub from his shirt pocket and scribbled angrily for a minute, then threw his pencil down. Closing his eyes, he took a few deep, deliberate breaths. He recalled sitting at the kitchen table last night, watching Ursula as she washed the dishes. There was something ballet-like in her movements as she swayed over the sink, rinsing the plates and arranging them in the drainer, her long braids bouncing lightly against her shoulder blades. He opened his eyes again, turned to a fresh page, picked up his pencil, and began sketching one of those long, intricate braids.

7 · Ursula

Just before dawn, Ursula woke up abruptly. Something was wrong. She reached for her phone to check the time, but it wasn't in its usual place on her nightstand. She lived in fear of losing her phone, and so, of course, she was forever misplacing it. It drove her crazy. She got up and looked on her dresser. Nope. Not in the pocket of yesterday's jeans, either. She pulled on her robe and padded downstairs. Not in the living room. Not in the dining room. Not in the kitchen.

It must be in the greenhouse. Yes. She remembered now. She'd called to cancel that fertilizer order late in the day, and the sales guy had given her some guff. She remembered snapping the phone closed and tossing it down on her desk, but she didn't recall picking it back up again. It could wait, of course, but now she was fully awake. And she really didn't like not having her phone with her. She'd lost it a year ago and the hassle of getting all her contacts reentered had been a minor nightmare. Better just go fetch it. She stepped into her barn boots, pulled a jacket on over her bathrobe, and crunched up the gravel drive.

The sky to the east was paling, the stars beginning to fade. The brightest one—Jupiter, maybe—hovered above the hop barn. A few precocious sparrows were already chittering in the oak grove.

The phone was right there on her desk where she'd left it. She'd just picked it up to check for messages when suddenly the sun rose up above the oak grove and an ocean of light flooded the greenhouse. Ursula looked up from the phone and gasped. Everything around her was throbbing with light. Colors glistened in the air around her as if she were inside a rainbow. The whole long, domed, translucent-walled room with its rows and rows of benches holding hundreds of flats of leafy green plants spangled with flowers of every color and hue was all aglow, supersaturated with light. The air itself seemed alive, atoms drifting like sea plankton gleaming in the radiance of dawn.

"Oh, Mother," Ursula said under her breath. "I wish you could see this."

It didn't last long. Only a few seconds, at most. And once it was gone, it was as if it had never happened, and Ursula couldn't be certain it had. The only evidence was a little pressure inside her, a tingling in her sinuses and thighs, fading fast. It must have been some trick of humidity, Ursula rationalized, each drop of moisture refracting the light like a prism, the water molecules in the air set ablaze by the low-angle sunrays.

She'd started the greenhouse business out of desperation after her divorce, after she'd quit her research position at Washington State to get away from Dexter, after her mother had died and she'd moved back home to look after her father. She didn't have any experience growing annuals on a commercial scale. She hadn't done any market research to determine if the Camas Valley area could support another grower. She'd just needed to do something, anything, to keep from going under. Grieving over her lost pregnancy, angry about Dexter's affair, and depressed by the sudden collapse of her marriage, she'd staggered home and started this stupid business.

The greenhouse had paid her bills, and every once in a while it had dazzled her senses. But she was already thinking about it in the past tense.

After lunch, Ursula drove her father up to Priory Cemetery. Joe wanted to put fresh flowers on Alice's grave.

"I miss Mom," Ursula said, switching a mason jar full of fresh roses for the old jar of withered stems.

Joe nodded. He whispered something under his breath, patted Alice's headstone, and turned back toward the truck.

At home, Ursula got Joe settled into his recliner for an afternoon nap before heading back up to the greenhouse. Cat was pulling the last flats of overgrown petunias. Ursula would take them around to a couple of retailers later and try to unload them.

"Your boyfriend came by looking for you," Cat said.

Ursula scowled. "Who?"

"Nu. He wanted to borrow a pruning saw and some baling twine."

"What for?"

"Said he was going down to the woods to build a hut or something," Cat said. She rolled the loaded cart to the front of the greenhouse and parked it by the door. "Don't give these away too cheap. They still look nice."

Ursula didn't have much luck unloading her overgrown petunias. Bi-mart only took four flats, discounted 50 percent. She still had eight flats left over. Money down the drain.

One last stop—Fleece had asked her to pick up a bag of chicken scratch—and she could call it a day. Ursula was thinking about what to make for supper—a pasta salad with leftover chicken, maybe—when she saw the warning lights begin flashing at the railroad crossing ahead. The car in front of her accelerated to beat the gates, and Ursula thought about racing through, too, then thought better of it and braked hard. The flats of petunias slid forward and thumped the back wall of the truck bed.

The train looked to be a long one, judging by the six—no, seven—engine units. It always slowed down here as it rounded the long curve and turned west toward the pulp mill at Toledo. Ursula thought about doing a u–y, doubling back through town and over the viaduct, but she could see in her mirror that the car behind her was too close for maneuvering. She was trapped. She sighed and shut off the engine. Bronson's Feed Store was right there, just on the other side of the tracks. In brief glimpses between hopper cars, Ursula watched Bobby, the bow-legged co-owner, pack away a display of barn boots from the front sidewalk. She checked the time on her phone: 5:52. He'd probably be closed before she got there.

Ursula reached behind her and adjusted the lumbar cushion. The seats of the pickup had lousy back support. In fact, there was nothing about the truck she liked. A fifteen-year-old Ford F-150, once white, now faded to a blotchy eggshell, it was really her dad's truck, though he'd transferred the title to her. She'd had to sell her much-beloved Honda suv last year, trying to trim expenses. The Ford sucked, but she sure couldn't afford a different vehicle right now.

In her side mirror she saw a man walking up the sidewalk. She recognized the stride from half a block away. Dexter. She felt a mild stirring in her chest. Oh, god, she hated it that she was still attracted to the bastard. Dexter had a loose-jointed way of splaying his feet out to the side. Overpronation. He had heel lifts in all his shoes. It made his gate jaunty, carefree, like a sailor on leave. She leaned forward to follow him in her mirror. He was wearing the drab uniform of academia, a gray suit, the tie loosened, the coat slung over his shoulder. And he wasn't free of care, she could now see. His brow was furrowed and his gaze aimed low to the sidewalk, as if he had a lot on his mind.

Maybe she should have forgiven him, she thought once again. Her father and brother thought so, and some of her friends. "A lot of men have affairs," she remembered Becca saying. "But not many of them confess it and apologize."

She could have postponed the final decision to divorce Dexter. If she had just waited, just suffered through those months of madness, she might have gotten past the grief over her lost pregnancy. If she had waited, time might have delivered its weird soothing, and she might have relented. She might have taken him back. She could still be working as a biologist in the plant pathology lab in Pullman. They could have tried to get pregnant again and she might have a toddler right now.

Or, Cat would be quick to remind her, Dexter might have wasted no time in cheating on her again. Cat had disliked Dexter Blount from day one. "There's something fishy about him," she had answered when Ursula, early on, had asked Cat what she thought him. "I just don't trust him."

As Dexter got closer she could see he looked older, pudgier, his black hair sprouting some gray at the temples, the jowl line more creased. He also had a hitch in his gait, she noticed, as if he might be having hip trouble. Five years older than she, he was still only forty-two. His evident aging made Ursula perversely happy.

He must be heading for the Depot, the restaurant that occupied the decommissioned train station. Her truck was stopped adjacent to the Depot's outdoor seating area, a handful of tables screened from the street by potted shrubs and bamboo. Leaning on the steering wheel, she watched him through the passenger-side window. Dexter turned to pass in under a rose arbor, and Ursula saw a woman stand up at one of the tables and wave. The woman was partly obscured behind a viburnum, but through the foliage Ursula caught a glimpse of a sleek brown bob that curled close around the woman's pretty little ear. Susan Sauer. Dexter gave her a lingering hug. Ursula felt her stomach clench. She reached for her left braid and twisted it.

A waitress approached their table. Dexter cupped his hand behind his ear to signal he couldn't hear her, then pointed toward the train tracks and said something. The waitress nodded and led them toward the restaurant's side door. Through the shrubbery, Ursula glimpsed Susan's expensive, baby-blue sleeveless dress—and Dexter's hand on her shoulder—before they disappeared into the restaurant.

She thought she'd made some peace with it—Dexter's affair, the divorce, having to leave her job in Pullman and move home to the farm. And maybe she had. But her miscarriage still haunted her. Losing the pregnancy had been way more traumatic than losing Dexter. Dexter's problem was that he had asked her to forgive him for the wrong crime. He thought he needed to confess his affair with Susan Sauer, come clean and be absolved. But he didn't have a clue how wounded Ursula had been by her miscarriage. If he couldn't see what that child had meant to her, he wasn't worth her forgiveness.

The crossing bells continued to clang. The interminable train crawled slowly along. Ursula needed to move. She needed to get home and crack open a bottle of wine. With her foot on the brake pedal, she put the truck in reverse and eased backward. The car behind her laid on the horn.

"Oh, stuff it," Ursula muttered, jamming the gear shift back into park. She switched on the radio—NPR's Linda Wertheimer analyzing the burst of the housing bubble—then angrily turned it off. She flipped open her phone. Supper would be late. She should call home, but she snapped the phone shut and dropped it onto the passenger's seat. Around the curve to her left, the end of the train came into sight. In the gaps between the last passing boxcars, just before the crossing gates swung up, she saw Bobby lock up the feed store and drive away.

8 · Bodie

Bodie wakes to a sharp pain in his right hip. He shifts his left knee back and rotates his hip an inch. The pain softens to a dull ache, then suddenly stabs stronger. He rolls onto his left side, knowing it will only aggravate his damaged shoulder. He tries to ignore the twinges in his shoulder for a few minutes before they mushroom into full-on throbbing. He opens one eye and looks at the clock. Just after 4. The alarm won't go off for another hour. Fleece is snoring gently beside him, a funny little sound as if she's sipping at the air. He groans and rolls out of bed. He swallows four ibuprofen, steps into his flip-flops, and goes outside to take a leak.

A few yards along the path into Fleece's flower garden, he chooses a nicotiana plant to fertilize and is rewarded with a whiff of the night-blooming flower's heavy perfume. He inhales deeply, then sighs with the relief of moving his joints and emptying his bladder. He's still half asleep and he hopes to make it back to bed without fully waking. But as he turns to head inside, he sees the nearly full moon rising over the farmhouse, and he remembers: pregnant. Fleece is pregnant and they are going to have a baby. He's instantly, supremely awake. The air reeks of nicotiana. He could eat it with a spoon. The shadows in the moon are the shape of a baby. How had he never noticed that before? He's going to be a freaking father. Unreal.

A breeze from the west raises goose bumps on his bare chest. He pulls a blanket off the clothesline and togas it over one shoulder, then sits on a lawn chair at the edge of the garden. He feels like shouting, like howling, but he doesn't want to wake Fleece. He doesn't know whether he's thrilled or terrified or both. It's as if the moon is working his brain over, releasing knots of mental tension he didn't know he had. Rolfing his mind.

They have so much to do on the farm and all their debts are coming due. And now—holy shit!—a baby on the way. Can he really handle this?

Beyond the garden Bodie hears a door squeak. He sees Juano step onto his cabin porch. Bodie's moon-rush is calming down a bit, and the sibilant hiss of Juano pissing fills him with a deep sense of belonging.

Everything will work out, Bodie thinks. The baby will be fine. The farm will be okay.

He knows it won't help him get back to sleep, but he starts making a mental list of all the tasks he has to do. Put up the new hop trellis. Finish the packing shed wash station. Transplant, fertilize, irrigate. Weed, harvest, market. Fuck, fuck, fuck.

And we have to start getting ready for the Summer Solstice Veggie Fest. We need more help. I need to teach Zebra to manage the CSA accounts, let Juano supervise all the vegetable growing. And maybe I can get some use out of Nu. I never imagined he could do plumbing. Maybe he's good at something else, too.

Oh, yeah—and he grimaces recalling it—and I promised Fleece I'd finish remodeling the house before the baby arrived. A big mistake.

He can get the baby's room painted, no sweat. And maybe finish sheetrocking the living room. Fleece wants him to hire it out, because he really sucks at mudding and taping. But there is zero money for that right now. In any case, he'd damn well better get the washer and dryer hooked back up. The kitchen cabinets will have to wait. As will the new roof and replacing the windows and refinishing the old maple-wood floors.

Bodie shivers in a fresh breeze. At least the baby isn't due until November, he sighs.

How will he be at this father thing? He's never seriously thought about it. What has he learned from football that he can use as a father? Teamwork. Effort. Never give up. Ah, he'll do okay. He catches a vision of himself jogging through the house with the baby tucked under his arm, juking around furniture, and handing off the kid to Fleece in the kitchen. Touchdown.

He pushes up from the chair. The ibuprofen seems to have quieted his sciatica. Maybe he can go back to sleep now. He looks up once more at the moon and notices another, yellower moon, lower down, shining through the limbs of the oak. It's the security light on the back wall of Bliss Fits. "Shit," he mutters. "The bastards fixed it again." He thinks about getting his .22 right then. But the shot would wake up his sister. He needs to wait until she's gone overnight again sometime.

He still can't believe that the city let those buildings go up so close to his parents' backyard. And he can't forgive himself for not being there for his folks when that deal was coming down. He thinks of his mother, sick with cancer. Dying, in fact, though she didn't tell him. And his father, sick himself, trying to take care of her. Joe hadn't been able to spare any energy to monitor the construction going in next door. And the city had let the developers shrink the setback.

And where was he? Bodie asks himself. Drinking himself silly in

Denver after his brief football career went down the tubes, that's where. Doing research, he'd been fond of saying at the time, on beer.

Let it go, he thinks. But the bad light coming from Bliss Fits has reignited his sciatica. He throws the blanket back on the clothesline and tiptoes through the house. He finds yesterday's grubby shirt and overalls on the bedroom floor and quietly, so as not to wake up Fleece, he dresses for work.

9 · Nu

Nu took his coffee out to the back deck. The rising sun had just cleared Bliss Fits, and he placed his chair where he could bask in its warmth. Once the caffeine began to kick in, he picked up his fledgling basket.

Fleece had shown him how to weave slender ribbons of cedar bark into a nice flat bottom, and then how to start rounding up the body. But once Nu took over, he'd immediately botched it, the weave going crooked and gapped. Unabashed, he'd started weaving in bits of junk—a rusty nail, a yellow twist tie, some short lengths of black yarn, one of Ursula's elastic hair ties—and now he had a rat's nest of a basket, vaguely heart shaped. Yesterday he'd woven in two short lengths of surgical tubing, like pulmonary arteries. Aesthetically it was a mess, but it kept his hands busy.

He would never be a fine basket maker, that was for certain. But the basket had given him an idea for a project. He wondered if he could somehow treat the whole farm as a kind of basket. What if he could weave parts of the woods and fields into figures that connected the whole place? Maybe he could sculpture the whole damn farm.

A whiff of some flower fragrance hit his nostrils. He was suddenly aware of the cloying scent of all the backyard shrubs and trees, their overamped photosynthesis. He would never get used to the heaviness, the sponginess of the air here. All the unbridled greenery—the fir trees, the glossy-leaved shrubs, and the ubiquitous blackberries—felt suffocating, while the mawkish pink rhododendron blossoms were just embarrassing. He much preferred dry, austere landscapes. More rocks, fewer plants, and everything in a leaner, subtler palette. Here it was green on green on green, then some gaudy pink, and then more green. An oppressively lush landscape.

But some things about the farm, he had to admit, were growing on him. For instance, he liked sharing meals with Joe and Ursula. He'd even made supper once, a decent lasagna. And he enjoyed watching movies in the evening with Joe. After *Seven Samurai* they'd jumped to *Magnificent Seven,* and Joe had had some pretty astute observations about the techniques that Sturges had borrowed from Kurosawa. Joe, Nu could tell, was happy to have someone to share them with.

And he liked being useful. Whether chauffeuring Joe to his many doctors' appointments or harvesting Bodie's beets or making small plumbing repairs, he could tell that his help was appreciated. Not that the Tunders were much for expressing gratitude. Bodie could be loud and effusive in his thanks, but he was so busy that Nu rarely talked to him. Joe hated being dependent, so Nu did everything he could to downplay his assistance. He didn't expect any overt thank-yous from Joe.

Then there was Ursula, the Braided Norse Warrior. Ursula seemed to be immersed in a great struggle: with Camas Valley Plants, with the farm, with Bodie and Joe, with herself. She could make the simplest tasks seem like combat. Ursula slapping flats of flowers onto the greenhouse benches with root-shuddering force. Ursula in the kitchen, dropping plates and burning toast. Ursula's big bare feet pounding glumly up the stairs. Ursula banging around in the shower—what could she possibly be doing to make such noises in there? Yesterday he had seen her spraying some thistles around the junkyard behind her greenhouse. She had thrust the spray wand at the thistles like a sword, pumping the sprayer handle as if throttling a snake. Ursula the bear. Ursula the angry. Ursula the sad.

He heard the screen door slide open and Ursula stepped out. Nu smelled her lavender soap and turned to greet her. She was just out of the shower, it looked like, wearing her blue terrycloth bathrobe, her loose hair damp and heavy on her shoulders. She looked sleepy and soft in a way he'd never seen her before.

"Good morning," he said.

"Mmmm," she smiled. She pulled a chair into the sunlight and sat beside him. "You made coffee," she said. "Thank you." She sipped the coffee and sighed. She sounded content, though Nu didn't have a lot of confidence in his ability to read Ursula's moods.

He picked up a scrub jay feather that had fallen on the deck and wove it into his basket. Ursula began to brush her hair, the crisp, bristly scritch of her brush sounding like a lone cricket stridulating.

Ursula looked down at his basket. "That's hideous," she said, grimacing.

Nu grimaced back, nodding in agreement. "I'm afraid it might be a window into my soul."

Ursula stared at him, unsure how serious he was.

Nu smirked and chuckled, and she punched him lightly on the shoulder. "You borrowed our pruning saw last week," she said. "Cat said you were building something."

"Oh, just throwing some brushwood together."

"Is it supposed to be art?"

Nu shrugged. "I like making huts." As he poked at his misshapen basket, the collapsed heart with its tattered feather, he asked, "So, what's going to happen with the farm?"

Ursula divided her hair in half and began braiding the side away from Nu. She pulled at it so hard it made Nu wince. After a full minute of silence, she said, "I don't know if Daddy has told you any of this, but the farm is sold. He sold it when Mother died. I was working, married to Dexter, and Bodie was off playing football, and neither of us had any interest in living here."

"What do you mean 'sold'?" Nu asked. "You're still here."

"It's complicated," she said, tugging at the strands of her braid. "Daddy signed a contract with a group of developers, some of the same ones who built Bliss Fits. Those people are out of the picture now, but the university has taken over the contract. They have a big donor who wants to fund an organic farming research center. They've told Bodie that he could stay on and become farm manager, but that's not in writing, and Bodie wouldn't be interested in working for them anyway. Bodie thinks he can buy back the down payment and hold onto the farm. Daddy's lawyer doesn't think the university would let him do that. In any case, Bodie doesn't have the money. He's up to his eyeballs in debt."

"How do you feel about all that?"

"Honestly, I just started the greenhouse for some income to tide me over until I figured out what came next. I'm ready to move on."

"On to where?"

Ursula slipped a hair tie off her wrist and twisted it three times over the finished braid, then started divvying up the hair on the other side. "I want to do science again. Work in the field, preferably. Do you remember my old teacher Marlys? You met her that time you came up to our field camp on Mount St. Helens."

He remembered Marlys. Stocky, loud, direct. Though what he remembered more acutely from that field trip was Dexter. That was where Ursula had met Dexter.

"Marlys wants me do field work in the Cascades for a few weeks this summer. Vegetation surveys. We'd be grubbing around in steep terrain every day, setting up new plots and surveying existing ones. Broiling sunshine. Drenching rain. Mosquitoes. Poison oak. It's paradise."

"Sounds like camping with pay," Nu said.

"Yeah, well, the pay sucks. And I'm not sure I can swing it right now. Not with Daddy needing me around. But maybe once the farm sale closes."

"Why did Marlys ask you? Seems like she could get students to do grunt work like that."

Ursula finished the second braid. She held the ends of the braids in front of her and poked them together as if marrying two ends of rope. "Well, I suspect Marlys wants to get me back to working as a scientist. I think she believes in me. Plus, if you're a professor like Marlys, it's good for your résumé if your students continue working in your field. So there's that."

"Why *did* you quit your research job? That never made sense to me."

Ursula sighed. "It was just too close to Dexter. Like, literally, the lab where I worked was right next door to Dexter's office. I couldn't bear to even see him. And Marlys feels partly responsible for what happened. She never liked Dexter, and she feels like she could have headed him off, but she didn't interfere. And she wishes she had."

"You always liked working as a scientist. Couldn't you have moved across campus or something?"

"Maybe. But at the time, I just had to get out of town."

"Yeah, well, I know about needing to get out of town."

"Right," Ursula said. "Those biker guys. What's going to happen with them?"

"I talked to the lawyer Uncle Joe hooked me up with. She seemed pretty confident that the charges would be reduced to misdemeanors, maybe dropped altogether."

"That sounds promising."

"I should head back to Bend sometime soon, though," Nu said. "Some rich people commissioned a painting, and I need to get cracking on it."

"And see your friends, I suppose," Ursula said. "Do you have a girlfriend or anyone special?"

"Plenty of friends," he told her. "Nobody special." He noticed that one of Ursula's long blond hairs had landed on his pant leg. He plucked it up and used a twig to nudge it into the side of his basket. "So what's Dexter doing these days?"

Ursula glanced sideways at him. "You know," she said, "I need to get to work." She picked up her brush and coffee mug and went inside.

Nu listened to her bare feet slapping across the kitchen floor. He realized he'd never gotten the whole story about Ursula's divorce. Dexter had had an affair, that was about all he knew. And obviously Ursula still carried a lot of anger about it. His own marriage had fizzled in a somewhat similar way. He sometimes wished he'd tried harder to keep it going, but Cynthia had seemed pretty much done with him. Ah, beautiful Cynthia Pyros. Dark-eyed, wavy-haired, fiery little Greek. Painter, sculptor, multimedia, performance, and installation artist. She'd try anything. They'd met in art school, fallen furiously for each other. Then, when his mother died suddenly and Nu inherited some money, he paid off his and Cynthia's school loans, and they got married one weekend in a civil ceremony with just a few friends attending. They'd honeymooned for two months in Mexico, seeking out Diego Rivera murals and chasing down all the artworks of Cynthia's hero, Frida Kahlo. They had remained married to their art as much as to each other, though. Cynthia was addicted to residencies and would go off to Ucross or Djerassi for a month at a time. Nu favored long solo camping trips, followed by art-making binges in his studio in a derelict warehouse out by the San Diego airport.

He came home from a January camping trip at Joshua Tree and found Cynthia sleeping with their friend Jessica. Cynthia had discovered she was a lesbian. Well, what could he say to that? They divorced as casually as they'd married, and Nu moved to Bend. He might have tried harder, but in truth he agreed with Cynthia that they weren't really meant for the long haul. Friends, yes, which they remained. She and Jessica were still in San Diego, married, with a child that Jess had carried. Nu never asked who the father was.

He'd gotten out of his brief marriage a lot easier than Ursula had. Now he prodded the basket in his lap, trying to force it toward round. But the basket was pretty well set now, and it slumped back into its lopsided heart shape.

Early afternoon, Nu decided to hike down to the river. As he walked past the greenhouse, he saw Cat unloading bags of fertilizer from the van. He went over, slung a bag onto his shoulder, and followed her inside.

Cat thumped her bag onto the stack in the potting shed. "How's it going, handsome?"

Nu shrugged. "Can't complain."

Cat came up close and grabbed Nu's hand. "You need a manicure. You know where the salon is, right? I'm there all day Saturday."

Nu looked down at his long ragged nails. Fingernails were handy for flicking open squeeze bottles, tweezing up small items to add to collages, even for using as a stylus to scratch lines in a fresh painting. "I'm good," he said.

As they schlepped more bags of fertilizer, Cat asked him, "How's Joe doing?"

"Seems to be okay. Kind of mopey."

"Mopey's about as good as it gets for those two." Gesturing to a cart loaded with flats of bedding plants parked inside the door of the greenhouse, Cat said, "Help me load these." She wheeled the cart outside and climbed into the van while Nu passed her the flats. He noticed how she crouched like a wrestler, bending from the hips, keeping her back straight. She probably only weighed a hundred pounds, Nu figured. But she was all muscle and no messing around.

"Cat, when was the last time you saw Ursula really happy, would you say?"

Cat stepped onto the bumper and dropped to the gravel drive. "Oh, talking trash on her ex will put her in a jolly state of mind sometimes."

"Dexter," Nu said. "I was never totally straight on what happened between them. He had an affair?"

"With that real estate lady," she said, pushing the empty cart out of the way. "Or yoga teacher, depending on which face you're looking at."

"Susan Sauer, right? Did Ursula ever suspect?" Nu asked.

"Not once. Ursula is not a suspicious person. Or she didn't used to be. She's loyal. She's never been what you'd call cheerful, but if she says she's on your side, you've got yourself a real partner."

Nu pulled a few lengths of string from his pocket and absent-mindedly began to braid them. "Dexter apologized, though, didn't he? Do you think they could have patched it up?"

Cat rubbed her cheeks as if debating something with herself. "Sit down," she said, pointing to a bale of peat moss. She leaned on the bumper of the van, pulled out her pack of chewing gum, offered Nu a stick, and took one herself. "I'm piecing this together from lots of different conversations with Ursula, you understand. This ain't the truth, it's just a partial. Okay?"

Nu nodded.

"Near as I can tell, it started when Joe got the cancer—so we're talking probably five or six years ago—and he decided they needed to sell the farm. Alice didn't like the idea, of course. It was her folks' place, she'd been born right here. But she knew they couldn't keep it up anymore, and Joe promised her a little house in town with a flower garden in the front yard. So she said, 'Okay, if Ursula and Bodie agree.' Well, Bodie was still in Denver, living off his football money, I guess. And Ursula's and Dexter's jobs were just taking off, so they all said, 'Sure, that seems like the best plan. We're not figuring on being farmers, so go ahead and sell the place.'"

Barn swallows were zooming out the open door of the potting shed and swooping down toward the lake, then returning with insects for their nestlings. Nu kept glancing up at them, then returning his focus to Cat.

"So Dexter volunteered to do the legwork on it, and that made sense because he was the one who could stomach banks and paperwork and such. And when it was time to sign up with a real estate agent, why, get this: it was Joe that recommended that yoga lady, that Susan Sauer. He hadn't met her, but she'd handled the sale for Norbert Simpson next door and Norbert had told Joe about her. How would you feel about that? Introducing your son-in-law to the floozy he'd end up cheating on your daughter with? Well, it wasn't Joe's fault, but I know he still feels bad about it.

"Ursula told me she hadn't expected to like Susan. She couldn't imagine liking any real estate person, much less one who taught yoga classes on the side. Two-faced, she'd assumed. But she *had* liked Susan. In fact, they hit it off pretty good. Ursula thought they might become friends. This was—let me think—probably late spring. Yeah, maybe April. Joe had just gone through his cancer surgery. That's why Ursula was visiting. But her mom wasn't sick yet, not for another month or two. So, the way Ursula told it, she went home to Pullman feeling pretty good. Her dad's surgery had gone as well as it could. Her mom seemed to be able to take care of Joe. The plan of selling the farm and moving her parents into town just made sense. It seemed like it would be a big relief all around. And, on top of it all, she liked Susan Sauer."

Cat looked up as a swallow zipped past. Nu waited while Cat took out another stick of gum and worked it in with the first piece.

"Then the shit storm hit. It's a month or two later and Ursula gets a call from her father. Your mother has cancer, he tells her. If you could come home, she'd be grateful. Well, it's a bad time for Ursula to be missing work, what with her field season coming up, but what's she gonna do? She gets people to cover for her and she drives home and spends a week with her folks. Her mother's surgery goes alright, and they get her comfortable at home, and her father seems to be rallying to take care of her. 'We'll be fine,' Alice tells her. 'You go do your field work.'

"So she does. She's up in the mountains in Washington, Wyoming, Montana all summer catching bugs and plants, or whatever it is she does when she's being a scientist. And she calls and checks in, and they're doing fine. Except they're not. The hysterectomy didn't get all of it, and Alice's cancer comes right back, worse. But Alice tells Joe, 'Don't you worry the kids about it. I'll either get better or I won't, and they've got their lives to live.'"

"They didn't say anything to me how bad it was then," Nu said. "I would have come over."

Cat nodded. "Well, you know the rest. Alice has another surgery, another round of chemo, but by Thanksgiving it's plain to see that she isn't going to come back from it. It's just a matter of time."

"And Ursula got pregnant around then, too, didn't she?"

Cat sighed. "Yes, she did. She knew her mom always wanted a grandchild. She thought maybe Alice would rally..."

"And Dexter had the affair while they were pregnant?"

"The son of a bitch." Cat rolled her shoulders and looked Nu in the eye. "About a month before Alice died, Ursula told her she was pregnant. She'd gotten the test the day before in Pullman and driven down. She wanted her mom to be the first to know. She hadn't even told Dexter yet."

A barn swallow coming out of the shed met another bird flying back and the two birds twittered in flight and flapped around each other for a moment right above Cat and Nu.

Cat glanced up and waved her hand as if to shoo them away. "Then her mother died, and she lost the baby. Then she left her husband and her job and her home up there...bang, bang, bang." Cat stood up, turned away from Nu, and slammed the doors closed on the van. "Come to think of it, Nu, I don't believe Ursula's been truly happy ever since."

10 · Ursula

Ursula was working a puzzle with Joe, the two of them side by side on the sofa with the puzzle—a tropical jungle scene, dense with foliage in every shade of green—laid out on the coffee table. Ursula was focused on piecing together a greenish-pink flower while Joe studied a suite of pieces he had sorted out in front of him, trying to assemble a yellow-green snake that twined around a branch.

When she was growing up, there had often been a puzzle in progress on the dining room table. The whole family would work on it together, sitting around in the evening, chatting and puzzling. Except for Bodie, whose hands were too big for puzzles even in elementary school. They hadn't done any puzzles in years, though, and Ursula had forgotten all about the boxes stashed in the upstairs closet until Nu found them soon after he'd arrived. He and Joe had done an easy thousand-piece beach scene last week. Then Ursula and Joe had started this tougher one. Puzzles were supposed to be good for combating her father's cognitive impairment and memory loss, she knew, though saying so might have made him balk at it. Fortunately, he still enjoyed them.

Daylight was fading from the living room window. Ursula got up to turn on a lamp. "More tea?"

Joe scowled at her and shook his head, trying to maintain his concentration. In the kitchen Ursula poured more hot water over her herbal teabag, then rummaged in a cupboard and found some old gingersnaps in a bag. They were hard as rocks but she put them on a plate anyway.

She still hadn't told her father about Marlys's job offer and her desire to go work on plant surveys in the mountains. She knew Joe wouldn't mind. Nor would he think he needed anyone looking after him. But that just wasn't true. He'd forget to take his medications. He wouldn't eat right. And he really shouldn't be driving anymore, not with all the meds he took, and not to mention his glaucoma. She was not going to leave him unattended. That's why the whole thing hinged on Nu. Nu was going to go back to Bend soon, but maybe he'd be willing to return to the farm for a few weeks in late July and look after Joe. It would be a huge thing for her to ask of him, and she didn't know how to broach the subject. But the first thing was to make sure Joe was okay with her being gone.

When she returned to the living room she found Nu standing with his back to her, staring down at the puzzle. He was sweaty and dirty, and he had a couple of messy strands of cobweb trailing down the back of his T-shirt. As she stood behind him he plucked three puzzle pieces from different places around the table and plugged them into the area Joe was working on. Joe's eyes widened. Ursula could see that the pieces Nu had just played opened up the puzzle for Joe to insert his snake.

She set the glasses and cookies on the table. "Have you been crawling under Juano's house again?"

"No. Why?"

She lifted a cobweb off his shoulder.

"Hop barn. I climbed up to the cupola," he said. "The view from up there is awesome."

"Fire trap," Joe said, placing his snake pieces. "I wish Bodie had pulled that thing down."

Nu collected another trio of pieces and added them on where Joe had left off.

"You're a crazy puzzler," Ursula told him.

"I'm good at pattern recognition," he said. "Also, we've done this puzzle before."

Ursula squinted at him in doubt. She had no such recollection.

"Summer of '87," Nu said. He took a gingersnap from the plate and headed for the stairs. "Off to work. Goodnight."

She took a tiny sip of the too-hot tea and tried to remember. She had such a crap memory, at least for family and childhood stuff. Science, geography, things she'd learned in school or read in books—those she could pull up whenever she needed them. But her personal past was pretty hazy. She obviously hadn't been paying very close attention to her own life.

1987? She would have been fourteen, the summer before she started high school. And then it did start to come back to her, parts of it. She had gotten a horse that spring from Norbert, the farmer next door. Rebel was a little Morgan gelding she was supposed to be giddy about, she'd begged and bargained for him hard enough. But she hadn't really bonded with the horse, and it hadn't been Rebel's fault. She had had a fantasy of riding bareback to school, seeing circles of girls interrupt their gossip as she cantered up, all of them gaping at her with envy. But the reality of taking care of a horse—feeding, currying, cleaning the stall, not to mention the hassle of needing a saddle and bridle—hadn't matched her vision of bareback adventures. Her growing indifference to the horse had led to a running quarrel with her parents, who had threatened to return Rebel to Norbert. Ursula kept promising them that she would spend more time with the horse, but she never did much more than feed and water him. One day toward the end of May, she had come home from school to find the horse was gone.

She could not believe her parents had so grossly betrayed her. Her father, in particular, had always extended deadlines for her, helped her find ways to sidestep her mother's mild rules. Now that Rebel was gone, the horse was the only thing she cared about. She skipped meals, brooded in her room, abused her parents with punishing eye rolls.

That was when Nu had come for his usual summer stay. In the past she had looked forward to his visits. Pre-adolescence, they had been buddies, swinging from the rope swing in the hay mow, swimming in the river. But this summer she'd wished he weren't coming. She was unpopular enough already. Having a fourteen-year-old boy cousin on her hands was too embarrassing to contemplate. What would she do with him?

But now she remembered. All that summer they had made art together. She hadn't thought of it that way at the time, but that's what they'd done. Nu had seen a story in *National Geographic* about an ancient giant sculpture in New Mexico or somewhere, made of stones placed on the ground to form the outline of a horse. "It's called an intaglio," he'd told her, bragging, sure, but she'd been impressed. He'd insisted they make one. So they'd used a hoe to gouge the outline of a giant horse in the dusty corral, then filled the furrows with sticks and stones. Other days they'd built elaborate rock cairns along the riverbank, or stacked straw bales into castles in the hay mow. It had turned into a good summer despite losing Rebel.

Ursula still couldn't recall doing the puzzle, though, that summer or any other time. Now she added a piece to the tangled foliage and decided the moment was right to tell Joe of her new plan.

"Daddy, you remember Marlys? My major professor. The botanist." When Joe nodded, she went on. "She wants me to work for her this summer. Vegetation surveys in the Cascades."

"Good," Joe said.

"Yeah, well, I'd like to do it, but I don't want to leave you here without somebody to help you out if you need anything."

"I don't need anything."

Ursula caught herself starting to scowl. She straightened her lips into what she thought of as her neutral scientist's face and said, "Right, but just in case. And to help cook and take you to the doctor."

Joe picked up a gingersnap and tested it with his front teeth. The cookie didn't yield. He looked at it suspiciously and tossed it back onto the plate. "Look, Urse, you should go to the mountains, do your botany. That's what you're made to do. I'll be fine. Or I might fall down and die. I don't really care either way. But you should go."

She tried to maintain the neutral look but she couldn't do anything about the tears. She swabbed her cheeks with the sleeve of her sweatshirt. "God, Daddy, don't talk like that." Joe held an arm out to the side and Ursula leaned in for an awkward hug. "If Nu is willing to stay and help you out, then I'd really like to go work with Marlys for a couple of weeks, okay?"

"Either way," Joe said. "Here, have a cookie."

Just then there was a thump on the floor overhead. They'd been hearing those sounds since Nu went upstairs. He must be lifting weights, Ursula figured.

They worked on the puzzle in silence for a few minutes, then Ursula said, "I've been meaning to ask you about Nu's art. I found a website with photos of his petroglyphs..."

"Pictographs," Joe corrected her. "You're a scientist. You know the difference."

"Sorry. Yes, pictographs. On rocks in the Owyhee Canyon. All those spirally kinds of animal shapes. I liked them. But I still don't understand why he got in trouble over it."

Joe added another piece of snake and squinted up at her. "Are you more interested in the art or the trouble?"

"I just wondered. He keeps getting in trouble for his art. Does he do that on purpose?"

Joe looked up and stared hard at her. Ursula had had to face that rock-steady gaze all her life and it still gave her a chill. She had disappointed him once again. "Ursula," he said, "you haven't been paying attention. I've tried to tell you about Nu's art for years, but you never took an interest."

Ursula scanned the puzzle. "I know. I'm sorry," she said. She tried to shoehorn a piece of blossom into several places it wouldn't fit, poking uselessly. "I've been..." What had she been? Preoccupied with her work? Jealous of Nu's career? Of his friendship with her father? Or just self-absorbed in her loneliness?

"Nu wasn't looking for trouble," Joe said. "Oh, when he exhibited his photos of the pictographs, lots of people were pissed off about them. Some tribal people called it appropriation. Environmental groups called it vandalism. They were on BLM land, and the Feds threatened to bring charges. But, see, nobody could find them. The pigments he used were all plant-based and super-soluble. They faded fast, disappeared. So after a few months, according to Nu, they were gone. People have searched the whole area, but as near as he knows, no one has ever found them. Nothing left but the photographs he made."

Ursula tugged at the elastic band holding one of her braids. "And then, when he got arrested last month, what was that about?"

Her father sighed. He was rubbing his jaw, Ursula noticed, as if in pain. Ah, crap. She'd screwed up on the calendar again. Joe had something bad happening with a molar and she'd finagled him a dentist appointment for tomorrow afternoon, but she was supposed to meet with her accountant at the same time.

Joe pushed up from his chair and headed down the hall toward his bedroom. "Ask Nu. I'm going to bed."

Ursula took their empty cups to the kitchen. She was tired and she had a headache. She didn't really want to talk to Nu, but she needed to find out if he could take Joe to the dentist tomorrow, so she went upstairs and knocked at his door.

"Come in." His voice sounded bright as morning.

Nu was hunched over a drafting table he'd cobbled together out of plywood and sawhorses, working on a drawing of some kind. All he had on was a pair of gym shorts, and Ursula winced when she noticed the big bruises on his right side. Must be where the biker guy kicked him, she figured. But what really drew her attention was the tattoo that covered his entire back, a gnarled, Chinesey-looking conifer, the trunk rising to the left of his spine, and the twisted branches spreading across his shoulders. As Nu sketched, the tree moved, as if leaning in a wind.

She could see that he was working with colored pencils, making a drawing of Tunder Farm. She felt bad about interrupting him, but she was intrigued by the drawing. She went closer so she could look over his shoulder. The perspective seemed weird until she realized that the point of view must be looking down from the cupola of the hop barn. She hadn't been up there since she was a kid.

Nu tossed his pencil down and swung around on his stool. "What's up?"

Ursula backed away a step. She could feel heat coming off him. His face gleamed with a light glaze of perspiration.

She looked past him toward the drawing. "That's cool."

"Thanks. Yeah, I'm pretty excited about it."

Ursula edged up to the drafting table. Something about Nu's drawing made it seem like the farm was moving, spinning around the pole of the hop barn.

"How do you do that?" she asked.

"What?"

"Make it move."

"Oh, nothing fancy. Just bend the radials a little bit and advance the scale."

Ursula gave him a blank look.

"Okay, look." He tapped the drawing with his pencil. "The houses, the shop, everything that's square is bent out of square as if everything is spinning, and the farther away from the zero point we get, I draw things progressively smaller. See, your greenhouse is scaled down a little. Bodie's house smaller yet."

"And twisted more. Like the spiral force gets stronger the farther out you go."

"Yep. That's it."

"And what's this?" She pointed to a little curved-roofed structure in the woods beyond the farm fields.

"Oh, that's nothing. The brushwood hut I've been working on." Nu lifted his arms and bent over sideways, then grimaced.

"How's the cracked rib doing?" she asked.

"It's okay. Kind of catches sometimes."

"I never heard any details," she said. She was feeling a little light-headed, like she might be coming down with a cold. It had been a very long day, and she was worried about Joe, but some little voice told her not to chicken out now. She really wanted to know more about Nu and his art. She also needed to ask him if he'd be Joe's caregiver for a few weeks. "About the assault. What happened with those biker guys?"

She could tell that he wanted to get back to his drawing. She was almost ready to give up and leave him alone when he rubbed his eyes and sighed.

"Okay," he said. "Sit down."

There was no chair in the room, so Ursula sat on the edge of the bed. It was her own bed: this had been her bedroom when she was a child, and the give of the mattress was familiar. Nu leaned past her to grab his T-shirt from the pillow and pulled it over his head. Ursula drew a deep breath and waited. Nu told her about how he'd gone camping, how he'd discovered the illegal dirt bikers, how he'd confronted them and gotten into the fight that led to his arrest. As she listened, Ursula felt afraid and then angry at the two biker guys, then angrier still when the cop arrested him. But Nu sounded fairly calm, sticking to the facts. She could tell he'd repeated the story many times.

"Wow," Ursula said. "And it's not over, right? You've still got your trial?"

"It's over for tonight," Nu said, turning back toward his drafting table. "I really need to work on this while I'm hot, okay?"

"Sure. Of course," she said, and clambered up from the bed. Walking past him, she touched his shoulder and added, "Thanks for telling me about what happened." She was almost through the doorway when she remembered her errand and turned back. "Oh, Nu, any chance you could take Daddy to the dentist tomorrow, at 2?"

"You asked me that yesterday. Yeah, I'm on it."

She nodded, flustered by her absent-mindedness, and went down-stairs to the kitchen, wide awake now. She did *not* remember having asked Nu to take Joe to the dentist. She was really losing it. And she hadn't said a word to him about staying with Joe if she went to work in the mountains. Picking up a crusty frying pan soaking in the sink, she tore into it, scrubbing with all her might.

11 · Bodie

Dusk. Bodie backs the Farmall into the hop barn and shuts down the tractor. He should probably unhitch the brush hog—he finished mowing all the weedy edges around the veggie fields—but he isn't sure which implement they'll be using tomorrow, so he leaves the mower hooked up.

They really need another tractor. The Farmall and the John Deere are in constant use, and some chores get neglected. He only got a chance to mow this evening because everyone else knocked off earlier. He has his eye on a used thirty-horsepower Kubota some guy in Lebanon is selling, but he knows the bank won't give him another loan.

Bodie steps down from the tractor, sits on a sawhorse, and looks up into the shadowy rafters. He loves this old barn. Renovating it and building the staff room inside half of the old structure is one of the things he's proudest of, despite the gaping hole it made in his savings. But he kind of wishes he'd kept the entire hop barn intact, put up a new shop building somewhere else. He remembers how, when he was a kid and the hop barn was dilapidated but whole, the interior space, sixty feet up to the roof, made a soaring, rough-hewn vessel that felt as if it were made for traveling, a vertical boat or a wooden spaceship. Even though his allergies had acted up every time he came in here, he always loved the place, loved the shadowy gloom shot through with pencil-thin beams of light streaming through knotholes in the siding. Loved the acrid aromas of old cow dung, gasoline, and rusty machinery.

In a few weeks he'll be hoisting his hop vines up to those rafters to dry. He can't wait to see them hanging there, to smell that overwhelming tang.

His dream, when he came back home, was to start a craft brewery. That was why he spent half his football savings on the expensive renovation of the hop barn. His better-than-necessary staff room was actually intended to house a startup brewery. Farming was supposed to be just a sideline to generate some cash flow and keep his farm-deferral tax rate. And here he is, more than four years later, mired in debt and vegetables. He barely finds time to make a batch of home brew once in a while.

A sudden sneezing jag nearly topples him off the sawhorse. He pulls out his bandana and blows his nose. It's been another long day, and he's pooped. He trudges toward the house, hoping Fleece has made something good for supper.

Later, after they've eaten—bean burritos, rapidly gasifying in Bodie's belly—Fleece goes out to run the chickens into the coop while Bodie washes the dishes. By 9:30, they're already in bed, sitting with a box of Kleenex between them. Bodie's allergies have gone ballistic, and Fleece has a bad head cold. They make a sad pair, Bodie knows, honking and sneezing, rubbing their eyes.

He's half watching a baseball game on television. The Mariners are getting spanked in Houston. He hates how loud the Astros' crowd is cheering, so he's muted the sound. The latest issue of *Craft Brewing News* is splayed open across his lap. It has an article about new hop varieties he's interested in, but he can't quit sneezing long enough to read more than a paragraph. Hopefully the antihistamines will kick in soon so he can sleep.

Fleece is knitting booties with a skein of her home-spun yarn. At five months pregnant, she is starting to enlarge. Fleece-and-a-half, he thinks of her. They are big people, and the bed was crowded even before she conceived.

"You think Ursula is sweet on Nu?" Fleece asks him.

"Shit!" Bodie hisses. Runners on first and third with one out in the eighth, and Adrián Beltré, the Ms' best hitter, grounds into a double play. He realizes that Fleece has just spoken to him, and says, "Sorry, babe. What was that?"

"She watches him."

"Huh," Bodie says. "I hadn't noticed." He picks up the magazine and tries to read. But come to think of it, maybe he has noticed something. Just yesterday he saw the two of them talking together in their front yard. Tall, fair Ursula with her tight blond braids facing short, swarthy Nu with his buzz-cut black hair and stick-out ears.

Nu had his headed tilted to look up at her, and Ursula's head angled down. It had made him chuckle, actually, how dissimilar they looked. "Stranger things have happened."

Fleece winces and moans.

"You okay?"

She nods unconvincingly. "Heartburn."

Bodie reads about a recently released hop variety, Super Galena, that's supposed to be completely resistant to powdery mildew. His plants are Willamettes and Cascades, and now he wonders if he's already fallen behind the curve.

Fleece glances sidelong at him. "Did the three of you play together, back when you were kids?"

"Nah. They usually ditched me. They were older and liked to do different stuff."

"Like what?"

"Oh, they liked to build forts in the woods, out of tree limbs and old tarps. And they played in the hay mow a lot. But that was killer on my allergies so I never went up there."

"And you were into sports," Fleece says.

"Yeah, yeah. I was always on some team, so they did their thing and I did mine." Bodie grabs the bag of potato chips from the nightstand and offers it to Fleece. She holds up her knitting—no free hands—then leans toward Bodie and opens her mouth like a baby bird. He feeds her a couple of chips and eats a handful himself.

"I'm worried about your father," Fleece says. She puts her knitting aside and blows her nose. "Do you think he'll make it until the baby comes?"

Bodie doesn't like the question. He can't handle the idea of their baby being in a race with his father. He has so much work to do on the house before the baby arrives, but he's had zero time for any of it. Their Summer Solstice Veggie Fest is next Friday, less than a week away, and they're expecting a couple hundred people at the farm. He's been crossing off dozens of chores each day, but his to-do list keeps getting longer. He can't remember if he asked Ursula and Cat if they'd be willing to open up their flower beds for U-cut. He hopes so. Lots of people like to pick a bouquet. Zebra wants him to buy a new canopy for the vegetable stand—the old one is torn in one corner and may go to shreds at any moment—and she wasn't happy when he told her to duct-tape it. And he keeps forgetting to call in the Porta Potti rental! Must order toilets first thing in the morning.

"Daddy's got years left in him," he says, tossing the magazine onto his nightstand.

Fleece sighs. "I sure hope so." Then she says, "Hey, did you pick up the paint for the baby's room today?"

Bodie tenses. This is dangerous ground. Fleece has spent nearly 100 bucks on sample cans of paint. The walls of the little bedroom that will become the nursery are striped with a dozen swatches of green, from a greenish off-white the shade of a cauliflower to the popping yellow-green of a lime. She finally settled on a silvery green the color of the underside of a cottonwood leaf. And after the walls are painted, she wants to add a frieze of leaping lambs. She found some stencils at the craft store. Of all the things on Bodie's to-do list, painting the baby's room does not make the top one hundred. He understands that Fleece is nesting, but the baby is not due until November and the momma bird is just going to have to wait. He will paint and furnish the nursery after the harvest, after the rains begin in October.

"Oh, babe, I'm sorry. I forgot," he says. He lifts the damp handkerchief to his face and gives a massive blow, playing for sympathy. The Mariners get a lead-off double but he can't tell who's coming to bat, so he unmutes the volume.

"Would you turn that thing off! I hate it when you watch sports in bed."

Bodie hastens to switch off the tube. If his watching sports in bed bothers her, it's the first he's heard of it. But many new things have been bugging Fleece lately. Hormones, Bodie can only presume. He blows his nose one more time, turns off the light on his nightstand, and scooches down into a fetal position. His sciatic nerve spasms briefly, and he stifles a groan. "Good night, babe," he sighs. "I'll get your paint tomorrow."

12 · Nu

Nu schlepped his easel out to the overlook and spent most of the morning painting studies of Bodie's fields. At various times, Juano, Zebra, and Arnold passed by in the course of their chores, but no one interrupted him. The pace of work at the farm had ramped up since he'd arrived two weeks ago. There was going to be a big shindig on the summer solstice, with music, food, vendors. "Like the farmers' market downtown," Bodie had told him, "but bigger and funner." That must be why everybody seemed so stressed out lately. The farm had a pulse, and Nu could feel its heart racing.

Around noon he carried his art gear back to the house and found Ursula making ham sandwiches. The three of them ate in silence, alone together, which suited Nu. Joe said he wanted to grab a quick nap before his dentist's appointment. Nu stayed at the kitchen table, sketching. Ursula excused herself, then reappeared in half an hour wearing a sleek tan skirt and a sleeveless blouse the same color as her Nordic blue eyes. Her braids were coiled formally on top of her head.

"Wow. You look like you're going to a wedding," Nu told her.

"More like a funeral," she sighed. "Meeting with my accountant. I don't know why I get dressed up. Helps me cope with bad news, I guess."

"Well, you look good," Nu said. "You'd brighten any funeral."

She punched his shoulder, then leaned down and gave him a peck on the cheek. "Thanks for taking Daddy," she said. "It's nice having you around."

Joe wasn't one to grouse about pain, but the toothache seemed to have broken through his stoicism. He'd been snarling the past two days at anyone who came close.

But when Joe strolled back out of the dentist's office, Nu could see he was a different man. Not that he was smiling, exactly. The left side of his mouth was slack and droopy. Drugged numb, Nu supposed. Joe's hooded gaze and pinched scowl were gone. There was a light in his eyes Nu hadn't seen for days.

"Nowacain," Joe slurred. "Miwacle dwug."

On the way home they stopped by the paint store. Bodie had asked Nu to pick up a gallon of custom-mixed interior latex. Nu expected Joe to wait in the pickup, but Joe climbed out and followed him inside.

"Well, look what the skunk drug in!" one of store clerks called out. He was a small, colorless man nearly Joe's age. "Joe Tunder. How the hell you been?"

While a younger clerk put the can of paint on the shaker, Nu listened to Joe and the older clerk trade barbs and catch up on a few mutual friends, one of whom, a man named Lenny, had died just yesterday.

"Heart attack," the old clerk said. "Sally found him dead in the recliner when she got home from playing bridge."

Joe sighed but didn't say anything, just waved goodbye to the clerk and followed Nu out the door.

"Sounds like you used to be a regular customer," Nu said once they were back in the truck.

Joe nodded, the look on his numbed face unreadable.

Driving past Asbury Park, Joe jerked his thumb at the parking lot and said, "Pull in."

The moment the truck was parked, Joe clambered out and walked unsteadily toward the city's big rose garden. He didn't pause until he'd come to the very center of the extensive plantings. When Nu caught up with him, Joe was inspecting an ornamental welded-steel pergola the size of a living room. Climbing roses were trellised up all six legs of the pergola, and the canes were tangled above like a green roof. In the warmth of the afternoon, the fragrance was as thick as at a perfume counter.

"I made this," Joe said, glancing overhead. Then he poked his stick at the steel leg where it was bolted to the concrete footing. Nu could see the metal was flaked with rust. Joe shook his head wearily, then headed back toward the truck. "Needs paint."

Nu dropped Joe off at the farm and drove back into town, wondering what he was getting himself into. From last week's brief encounter, he couldn't tell whether Andy Patterson was an insightful potential collaborator or a busy-body con man to be avoided at all cost. This much he'd learned from some online research: Andy was connected. If the local art community was a web of interwoven relationships, Andy was the spider sitting hungrily in the center.

Andy's place was in a neighborhood adjacent to the university, a mix of small hard-used houses and cheap apartment buildings. Most of the front yards were abandoned to weedy bark dust, but here and there a yard sported nice plantings of shrubs and perennials, or raised beds rampant with vegetables and flowers. He found the address Andy had given him, a generic '60s ranch-style house painted turquoise with apricot trim, and parked at the curb. A big pile of mill ends filled most of the driveway. One of the overhead doors of the two-car garage was tipped open; this was Andy's studio space, Nu supposed. He stepped quietly inside, hoping to get some idea of Andy Patterson's art—and hence his personality—before he announced himself. Meandering guitar riffs, the Grateful Dead, maybe, poured from speakers hung in the corners. Nu saw Andy at an easel across the room, painting with rapid slashes.

Andy looked up and saw Nu and his face brightened as if Nu were a long-lost friend. Nu took a deep breath, bracing himself for Andy's intensity. He waited by the door while Andy tossed his brush in a jar, wiped his hands haphazardly on a rag dangling from his belt, and charged across the room. "Wow," Andy said, sticking out his hand. "Nguyen Van Nuys. Mr. Nu. Oh, man, thanks for coming!" Nu shook Andy's hand and felt a dab of wet paint sliding between their palms.

Andy's eyes never settled, never stopped moving. Even when they were face-to-face, he seemed to be looking at Nu sidelong, this way and that. Nu noticed that Andy's lips shifted constantly through micro-expressions—smiles, frowns, grimaces—as if his mind was experiencing surprise, concern, sadness in rapid succession. It was exhausting just watching him. What must it be like for Andy, enduring that restless inner experience? The shadowed and slouching skin beneath his eyes suggested he didn't sleep much, at the very least.

Andy put his arm around Nu's shoulder and led him on a tour of the studio. There was a big layout table cluttered with paper, mat board, big shards of stained glass, a box full of frame molding. Then came a long workbench dominated by handmade wire mannequins. In the far corner, Nu saw a potting wheel beside a slop sink. There were paintings everywhere. Oils and acrylics, mostly, hanging from wires, leaning on easels, resting in stacks against all the benches. Andy was promiscuous in his choices of media, obviously, though painting seemed to be his main thing.

They completed the circuit around the studio and arrived back at the working easel. Nu leaned close to inspect the painting in progress, and Andy fell uncharacteristically quiet. The focal point of the painting was a riot of bright flowers spilling over a concrete wall. Beyond the flowers, a street stood eerily empty, canyoned by windowless, tall buildings, gray and indistinct, buildings that reminded Nu of Bliss Fits. They weren't bombed-out; it wasn't post-apocalyptic. They looked more like they'd been sucked dry. The flowers shouted for attention, but the eye kept shifting uneasily back toward the buildings.

"I like it," Nu said. "Impressive, how the buildings feel insubstantial but menacing."

"I call it *Flowers in the Aftermath*," Andy said. "For a show next month in Portland. Needs something, right here. Don't you think? What? A tree? A persimmon tree!" Andy plucked the paint brush from the jar and waved it at the canvas, then tossed the brush back. "I don't know. What about you? What are you doing out there on the farm?"

Nu shrugged. "I'm the resident plumber."

"Good. Plumbing is good. But you're doing art too, right?"

"Some drawing. Fleece is teaching me to weave baskets."

"Good. Good. But you should make art. Maybe land art. That's one of your things, right? Can't we do something with that farm? We should art it up, don't you think? Come on, man. You gotta make that place sing."

"Yeah, well, it's not my place," Nu said. "I'll be heading back to Bend pretty soon."

"Rats. I was hoping you'd be around a while." Andy maneuvered them back out the garage door, and now he gestured to the pile of scrap wood in the driveway. "Mind helping me stack this? Got to get my wife's parking space open before she gets home from work."

There was a ramshackle woodshed made of pallets and old metal roofing right beside the driveway, and the mill ends were easy to stack. Each time Andy bent to pick up some wood, he grunted and sighed. He was older than Nu had realized. His manic energy was youthful, but the man was getting on.

"Have you got a studio over there in Bend?" Andy asked.

"I've got a garage, like yours. Bigger, though. Log-truck garage."

"Damn," Andy said. "I could sure use more space. What are you working on?"

"Well, I had started putting together an installation, a follow-up to those paintings in my show. Trying to do something out in the forest. I was going to string some nearly invisible weavings, like spider webs, across the off-road trails, then video the motorcycles tearing through them."

"I can see it," Andy said, grunting as he picked up some lumber. "And this would be out there where you got your ribs kicked in?"

"Same general area."

"I admire your chutzpah, Van Nuys. But are you sure you want to tangle further with those biker guys?"

Nu chucked some lumber onto the pile and changed the subject. "So, how long have you lived here?"

Andy, already holding a couple of pieces of lumber in one hand, bent to pick up another but fumbled it—all the pieces went clunking to the pavement. "Crud," he said. "Almost forty years. We own the house and plan to stay till the bitter end, even though we're surrounded by dumpy student housing, as you noticed."

"What brought you to Camas Valley?"

"Did a stint in the army, then came here for school on the GI bill."

"You served in Vietnam?"

"I did," he said. "Pencil pusher. No shots fired."

It sounded to Nu as if that was all Andy wanted to say about his military career. "What's your wife do?" Nu asked.

"Suzie's a nurse at the clinic. A phlebotomist, to be precise."

"She draws blood all day?"

Andy nodded. "She likes her job. Perfect complement for a shiftless artist."

"But you work too, right? At the gallery."

Andy clacked a block of lumber onto the pile, pulled a handkerchief from his back pocket, and mopped his sweaty face. "I figured out a long time ago that the kinds of art I make aren't going to bring in much money. Luckily, I fell into working with the DD people."

"I hope I don't have to work as a plumber much longer. I just got a commission to do a painting for a couple in Bend..."

"Congratulations!" Andy interjected.

"Thanks," Nu said. "They're uber-rich techies building a huge bomb-proof vacation home where they can wait out the apocalypse. And they want one of my paintings on the wall of their bunker."

"I hope they're paying you a shit ton of money."

"Five grand," Nu said, and immediately felt embarrassed to be bragging.

Andy whistled, impressed. "Sounds like you are on the very precipice of success, Van Nuys. Now your troubles really begin. Will you totally sell out, or stay true to your art?" Andy returned to stacking, and the two of them worked quietly for a few minutes.

"You know," Nu said, "selling art is just dirty. I'm not even sure how I feel about shows and galleries. Or grants. All that art bureaucracy shit." Nu clunked a length of lumber onto the stack. "Have any advice on how to cope with capitalism?"

"Yeah. Marry a nurse."

"I'll keep an eye out."

"Any interest in teaching?"

"Not really," Nu said. "I always figured teaching would pull from the same pool of energy as the art. And I don't think my pool is that deep."

"Oh, everybody's little pool is tapped into the Big Aquifer, don't you think? There's always more creativity you can pump up, Van Nuys. But I hear you about teaching. It can be a drain. And the pay sucks. I wouldn't go that route if I were you."

As they finished stacking the wood, Nu asked, "But you teach, don't you?"

"Sometimes, at the community college," Andy said. "Adjunct. Shit pay." He got a push broom from the garage and swept the sawdust and splinters under the shrubs. "Better to do something else for money, keep the art free," he said. "Your uncle tried teaching, then went the second-job route."

"Joe? Joe taught? What did he teach, welding?"

"Art, man! He taught sculpture in the art department. I had him for a class my first term here."

"No way," Nu said.

"Oh, come on, man. You know this."

Nu did not know this. He wasn't even sure he believed it. Andy Patterson was throwing too much stuff at him all at once.

"You know about Joe's art, right? And how he got fired by the university?"

Nu had some vague memories of Joe having worked for a time at the university. But that was before he was even born.

"I've got photographs. Hell if I know where, but..." Andy chucked the broom into the woodshed and disappeared into the garage. Nu followed him into a partitioned-off room in the corner. Andy's office, it looked like. There was a desk with an old computer on it, bookshelves lining two walls, and teetering stacks of big art books rising from the floor, pillars of books taller than Nu, leaning precariously together. Andy was digging through a file cabinet. "Shit. It's an album I put together. Shit, shit, shit. Ah, wait, here it is."

Andy placed the album on the desk and flipped through the pages. "So, we had this rally, you know. Vets Against the War. I started the local chapter myself."

Nu looked down at the wide-angle photos—professional-looking, black-and-white eight-by-tens. A steely, overcast sky, shiny-wet sidewalks, people milling around with unopened umbrellas. One photo showed a knot of men in sports jackets, white shirts, and skinny black ties. Faculty members, Nu guessed. Another focused on a trio of co-eds in miniskirts, their knees, even in black-and-white, looking cold. Then a couple of photos of guys in military uniforms, eyes up, shoulders back. Most of the people in the photos were smiling, with here and there a smattering of angry-looking faces, a few fists raised.

Nu turned the page and there he was: a very young Joe Tunder with a full, neatly trimmed beard, wearing a corduroy sport coat over crisp-looking overalls, standing next to a tall sculpture, looking bemused and aloof.

Andy tapped the sculpture. "Your uncle Joe made her, *The Sorrowful Mother*. Here's a close-up." Andy flipped to the page he had in mind and inspected the hand-lettered text under the photograph. "*Grieving Mother*. That's it."

Nu leaned down close to study the photo of the sculpture. The woman's tall body was entirely concealed in a shapeless gray cloak, as unrevealing as a nun's habit. But her bent neck and the slope of her back spoke heartbreak. Her face was a ceramic mask, Nu guessed. Her broad cheeks and full mouth seemed bloated with grief.

"Joe was thinking Liv Ullman," Andy said. "He had a blown-up photo of her, a still from *Cries and Whispers*, hanging on the studio wall. And look at her hands."

Nu bent closer. The woman's hands appeared to be carved from a single block of dark, glossy wood. Her right fist tugged at the three middle fingers of her left hand as if she wanted to rip her fingers right off.

"Oh, my god," Nu said, shaking his head. "What agony."

The two men stared down at *The Grieving Mother* for a moment. Then Nu broke the spell and looked up at Andy. "Where did you get these photos?"

"I took them. I shot for the local paper sometimes." Andy paged further into the album. "Here's the story," he said, pointing to some tear sheets from the *Camas Valley Gazette*.

"May 3, 1970," Nu said.

"Day before Kent State."

"Three years before I was born. And you say Joe got fired?"

Andy bobbed his head up and down, side to side, up and down again. "To tell the truth, Joe wasn't a great teacher. His style was like, 'Okay, here's the studio. Here's the supply cabinets. Y'all make some art, okay?' It worked for me and a few others, but some of the kids needed more structure. But everyone liked Joe, and we were all pissed when his contract was terminated. Everybody knew it was retaliation. Political activism was bad enough from the students. But the administration was sure as hell not going to let its faculty get away with that shit."

"Huh," Nu said. "I did *not* know about this. Joe as an art teacher. Wow." He bent down to study one of the photos more closely. "Do you have any idea what happened to this sculpture, the *Mother* thing?"

"Nope."

"Joe's never mentioned it to me. I know he did a lot of sculpture in the past, but there isn't much evidence of it around the farm."

"Well, you need to ask him, don't you?"

13 · Ursula

Tuesday evening, Ursula rummaged through the refrigerator. She found a bag of shredded cheddar, a pint of sour cream, and a tub of salsa, and plopped them all on the table. She asked Nu to harvest a head of lettuce from the backyard garden while she heated a can of refried beans and warmed tortillas in the toaster oven.

"Ah. Burritos again," Joe said.

"You have a problem with burritos?"

Joe said nothing, just cleared the table and set out silverware. Nu came back into the kitchen and started making a salad.

They'd barely eaten when a car honked in the driveway. Joe grabbed his jacket and hobbled out the front door. He had told her that Lenny Green had died yesterday, and some of the man's buddies were gathering for an impromptu memorial. Beer, poker, and bullshit, Ursula figured. She remembered Lenny, a carpenter who'd remodeled their kitchen back when she was in middle school. He and Joe had been part of a group that played cards once in a while, so that must be who was getting together tonight. Her father almost never did anything social anymore, and Ursula had been surprised when Joe told her he'd be going out. But she knew it would be good for him, too, however sad the occasion.

Nu cleared the table. "I'll do the dishes when I get home," he said.

"Where are *you* going?" Ursula asked.

"Gallery opening with Andy, that artist guy I told you about."

After Nu left, Ursula wandered from the kitchen through the dining room and on to the living room, where she stood gazing numbly out the front windows. The gravel drive was empty. None of Bodie's farm workers were in sight. She couldn't even hear any machinery. Strange. It was only a quarter to 7, but it felt like the farm was abandoned.

She couldn't remember the last time she'd been home alone in the evening. Must have been last fall, when Joe had spent a couple of nights in the hospital. She loved solitude, she always told herself, but now that she had a little she felt antsy, adrift. She wandered back to the dining room, where manila folders full of invoices were splayed out on the table, her account ledgers waiting to be reconciled. She shivered with revulsion, turned quickly into the kitchen, and reached into the cupboard for a wineglass. A postcard pinned to the crowded message board on the wall beside the doorway caught her eye— "Yoga Classes with Becca Bayer," featuring a photo of her friend in lavender tights and gray leotard doing the Standing Warrior pose. There was a class on campus at 7:30, the card said. Ursula put the wineglass back on the shelf and trotted upstairs to change.

She got to campus a few minutes early, parked in the lot behind the Women's Building, then sat behind the wheel of the truck. She wanted to walk into class just as it was beginning, so she wouldn't have to speak to Becca until the end. She really didn't know what she would say to Becca beyond "I'm sorry," but she hoped an hour of yoga might bring her, if not clarity, at least a smidgeon of courage.

She and Becca had been best friends twice in their lives. The first time had been their senior year in high school. They had grown up in Camas Valley and gone to the same public schools, but they'd mostly run with different crowds. Becca was prettier—her body slender but ample in all the right places, her round cheeks and big brown eyes framed with a mop of brown curls—and more popular. She was good at volleyball and modern dance and got lead parts in school theater productions. Her yearbook entry listed an obscene number of clubs, activities, and honors. Ursula was a mere biology nerd. With her frizzy hair, flat face, and flatter chest, she affected a disinterest in boys, and she tried to obscure her height in a slump-shouldered slouch. Fortunately, there were ample social outlets for her type: she spent most of her weekends on Sierra Club hikes or Audubon birding trips.

But in the spring of 1991, their last semester of high school, Ursula started making facial salves from beeswax, herbs, and floral fragrances, and suddenly she became popular. Lots of girls wanted Ursula's salves, including Becca, but Becca also wanted to learn how to *create* them. So Ursula invited her over. Her mom gave them some space in the laundry room where they could make a mess, and the two them spent hours together, cooing and laughing over their concoctions.

Their instant sisterhood began to dim as high school wound down toward its frantic culmination, and after graduating the two of them left Oregon in opposite directions. Becca enrolled at UW in Seattle, Ursula at UC Santa Cruz. Ursula remembered them talking on the phone a lot the first few months, but they never followed through on their promises to visit one another. Pretty soon they were immersed in their new college lives and they barely kept in touch.

Their second stint of best friendship occurred ten years later, after they had each married, Ursula to Dexter, Becca to Randy, and they all wound up living in Pullman. Dexter and Randy had research jobs in Ag Econ at Washington State. Becca worked as a garden designer for the biggest landscape contractor in town and she also taught yoga classes at night. Ursula ran the university's plant pathology lab, identifying pests and diseases—fungi, nematodes, viruses—on sick plants that farmers brought in, a challenging job she enjoyed. "I'm a plant detective," Ursula had liked to say when someone asked about her work.

For a couple of reasonably happy years, the four of them spent a lot of time together. They went on a spectacular ten-day backpacking trip in the Canadian Rockies one summer, and during the school year they had dinner dates at least once a month. The women got together on weekends whenever they could, and sometimes Ursula signed up for one of Becca's yoga classes.

Then it all fell apart. Ursula had picked over the details too many times, dissecting that year of unfolding disaster, from her mother's sudden illness to her own miscarriage, from Dexter's affair to their ugly divorce. Time and distance, work and wine had gradually weaned her from her near-constant worrying over the story. But one part of the disaster still mortified her. While Ursula was in the final throes of her marital breakdown, Becca had been diagnosed with stage three breast cancer. Within days, it seemed, Becca had gone in for a radical mastectomy, and Ursula, ostensibly her best friend, had been practically a no-show. She'd visited Becca once in the hospital, then staggered out of town the next day. She didn't regret leaving Dexter, but she should have found a way to support Becca more.

Becca and Randy had moved back to Camas Valley last fall, when Randy started his new job at CVSU. Ursula had seen Becca only once, briefly and awkwardly, in the dairy aisle at Fred Meyer. Ursula had been relieved to see that Becca's beautiful brown hair had grown back, and Becca assured her that she was cancer-free. Since then, Becca had called Ursula several times to suggest they get together, and each time Ursula responded, "Definitely. Super busy right now, but let me get back to you." And then she hadn't followed through. And the longer she'd put it off, the more ashamed of herself she'd become.

Now Ursula slipped into the big basement room and unrolled her mat in the very back. There were twenty-five or thirty people in the class, mostly women in their fifties or older, plus a few men, and she didn't know any of them. She peeked through the crowd, trying to see Becca without being seen. When she spotted her, she noticed that Becca's hair was shorn close to her scalp. Ursula felt a gut-stab of fear, anger, and grief. Becca's cancer must have come back, she imagined. As Becca guided them into the Mountain Pose and then into the Triangle, Ursula tried to concentrate on the movements. She had no doubt that yoga was a beneficial practice, good for body and soul, but she'd never enjoyed it much. Her mind was just too busy. She wobbled a lot. But she hadn't come for health and composure, she reminded herself. She'd come to try to reconnect with Becca.

A miserable hour later, Ursula lay in the Corpse Pose, her mind still churning.

"Relax your toes," Becca intoned from the front of the room. "Relax your calves."

Ursula issued her muscles a stern command—"Relax, damn it!"—then continued her nervous train of thought. She shouldn't have left town without telling Becca, for sure. But she'd been crazy at the time, insane with grief and anger. Still, none of her anguish had been Becca's fault. The only thing Becca had done wrong was to suggest—one night, drinking wine in Becca's kitchen, right after Dexter confessed his affair with Susan Sauer and asked Ursula to forgive him—that Ursula might want to think about giving Dexter a second chance. Becca had just been a close friend offering some caring advice, but it hadn't been what Ursula wanted to hear at the time.

"Relax your buttocks, your belly, your chest. Picture a clear sky. You're floating, held up effortlessly by the generous air."

Ursula lay on her back, rigid with tension, her thoughts in a tangle.

"Ahhhh," Becca intoned. "Beautiful. See you all on Thursday."

Ursula let out a ragged breath, struggled to her feet, and began rolling her mat.

"I've been hoping to see you!" Becca said, walking swiftly across the room and folding Ursula into a big hug.

"Yeah, I get so caught up in running my business. It's nuts."

"Doesn't your season wind down pretty soon?"

"A couple more weeks. Our fire sale is always the first weekend in July. But things are slowing down. That's why I'm here this evening." Other women wandered past, exchanging hugs and goodbyes with Becca.

Ursula had planned to suggest that she and Becca get together sometime and catch up. Now she stood back, watching Becca talk to an older woman. They both laughed and blushed and the woman reached out and touched Becca's stomach, and Ursula realized that Becca was pregnant. How incredibly dull of her not to have noticed during class. Becca was just barely starting to show, but still. Ursula felt a little surge of disgust at her own self-absorption. Now she was too embarrassed to even look at Becca. She slipped into her clogs and headed for the exit.

"Ursula," Becca called from behind her. "We should get together soon!"

Ursula wanted to duck out as if she hadn't heard, but some better part of her stopped and turned. "Let's do," she said. "How about coffee? Tomorrow maybe?"

"Wonderful. Say 10:00 at the Jumping Bean?"

Ursula arrived a little early and found a table where she could see the door. Becca came in right on time, wearing a filmy gray hiking skirt and a sleeveless blue top, looking as if she'd just stepped out of a yoga magazine.

Ursula felt grubby in her blue jeans and T-shirt, but she'd just delivered an order of plants on the way here, and she had to get back to the greenhouse right after. Cat was already pissed at her for being away from work so much lately. Ursula stood to hug Becca. "I didn't even know you were pregnant. How's it going?"

"Oh, I love being pregnant! Morning sickness. Fatigue. Sudden cravings. It's all good."

"When I saw you a few months ago—at Fred Meyer, remember?—your hair was long." Ursula raised her eyes to Becca's short-cropped hair. "I was afraid..."

"Nope. Cancer's gone. I cut my hair again for a friend who just found out she has a brain tumor." Becca shook her head and frowned. "So many women..."

"Oh, god, isn't it true." Ursula reached across and took Becca's hand. "I'm just glad you're okay. Will you be able to nurse?"

Becca smiled. "Left boob's as good as new. And how about you? How's your business doing?"

"Too well. I work all the time. That's why I haven't made it to class."

"You know I teach the same yoga class right next door to you, at Bliss Fits. You can come to that one if it's easier for you." Ursula felt her face redden. Becca noticed and said, "Oh, sorry. I forgot. Susan owns Bliss Fits. You probably avoid the place, huh?"

"I've never set foot in the whole complex. I don't even know what businesses are in there."

"You drive by it every day!"

"I look the other way. At the llamas and alpacas across the road." Ursula made a sheepish face at Becca and shook her head. They both laughed. Ursula said, "It's so petty!"

"No! I understand. She totally screwed you."

"Well, technically, she screwed Dexter, and then Dexter screwed me." They laughed again, though it was seriously not funny. This was good, Ursula was thinking, getting some resentments off her chest, laughing at herself. "Do you see Susan much?"

"No. Every couple of months maybe we run into each other. She's not teaching anymore."

"Really? Not teaching?" All this time Ursula had imagined her nemesis right next door, teaching yoga to students clueless about her duplicity. So much animosity she had aimed through that concrete wall, and now it appeared to have fallen on innocents. Or even on friends, like Becca, teaching yoga in that space Ursula had so demonized.

"No. She's back to real estate full time. I guess the financial crunch hit her pretty hard. Last time I saw her she looked really stressed out. The business center is half empty. Susan was certain that, if she built it, they would come. But it hasn't happened like she was hoping." Becca looked around the café as if to be sure no one was eavesdropping. "Did you know that Dexter is back in town? He got hired in Ag Econ."

Ursula sat up straighter and felt her jaw clench. "Yeah, I saw him the other day at the Depot. With his arm around Susan."

"Oh, god, Ursula. That must have hurt." Becca reached across the table and covered Ursula's hand with her own.

Becca's sympathy touched some still-vulnerable place. Ursula felt as if she might start crying. She took a sip of her tea to steady herself.

"You know," Becca said, "I don't think I was a very good friend to you when you were going through all that. The divorce and everything."

"Becca, no. I'm the one who was a lousy friend. You had your mastectomy, you were going through chemo. And I just left town."

"That was a rough time for both of us. I wish I'd reached out more."

Ursula shook her head. "You tried. I just couldn't respond. I was in shock, depressed."

"Dexter's affair was unforgiveable. I know Randy thought you and Dex should have given it another try, but it's never that easy, is it?"

Ursula fingered a braid, and rubbed the bristly, loose end on her cheek. "The thing nobody understands is that I might have gotten past the affair. I'm not that big a prude. It was losing the baby that did it. When I miscarried, Dexter was like, 'Oh, shoot. Well, let's try again. Up and at 'em.'" Ursula sighed. "But I was wrecked."

"You were grieving."

Ursula nodded. "I was. I wanted a baby so bad. I already knew that Dex and I weren't all that well suited for each other. We didn't talk. We didn't really enjoy each other's company that much. But we'd made a child together! That was worth everything. Worth trying to make the relationship work."

"I didn't know this. I thought the affair was the big shock."

Ursula shook her head. "Losing the baby," she said. She closed her eyes and let her head loll, then looked back up at Becca. "He never gave that child another thought. I hated him for that. I sure as hell wasn't going to 'up and at 'em.'"

"And that was before the affair even."

"Yeah, well, I guess what with my grief, my withdrawal, Dexter figured he had permission to go fuck Susan. Anyway, I *still* had my doubts about leaving him, even then. I mean, everybody told me I should give it another try. He did apologize, after all."

"For the affair. But he never did understand about the miscarriage?"

"No. And I have to tell you, when I saw him with Susan yesterday I felt...," Ursula squeezed her eyes shut, searching for the word.

"Affirmed?" Becca suggested.

"I was going to say triumphant. Like I'd won the lottery."

"Wow. I never knew Dexter was that big a dick."

"People don't. He's very charming."

"So, you said you saw him with Susan. Do you think he's cheating on his new wife?"

"It didn't look like a business meeting."

14 · Bodie

Bodie's lying on his back, his head and shoulders weaseled in under the double sink in the packing shed. Nu is kneeling on the concrete floor, reaching under the sink with a big crescent wrench, trying to get a firm grasp on the P-trap drain fitting. Bodie tightens his grip on his pipe wrench. He's lying on a length of angle iron, part of the sink's base frame. He has thrown his sweatshirt over it for padding, but the metal is still trying to separate his fourth and fifth lumbar vertebrae. His bad hip is howling.

Above him, Nu repositions his grip on the wrench. "Ready?" Nu asks.

Bodie grunts affirmative. He can see Nu's face contort as he leans back on the wrench and growls.

Nothing.

The chrome-plated drain pipe they're trying to loosen is stuck tight. Bodie knows how hard it's screwed down because he installed it himself a week ago. He even used a cheater—a two-foot length of galvanized pipe slid onto the wrench handle—to get extra leverage. He couldn't understand why it was so hard to turn down, but he reefed it until it wouldn't budge another millimeter. Cross-threaded, it has leaked badly ever since.

He should have waited to fix it until after the Veggie Fest. He has a thousand other chores to do before Friday, and he's nuts for trying to squeeze in this plumbing job now. But Nu offered to help, and he figured what the hell. He is grateful to Nu for connecting Juano's plumbing to the septic system, but he's still not sure exactly what to make of Nu. In the struggle over whether to sell the farm or keep it, Bodie suspects that Nu sides with Ursula. Anyway, Bodie just wants to get this job done as quickly as possible so he can get down to the fields and check on his crew.

They try again. Nu grunts and mutters something Bodie can't understand, maybe swearing in Vietnamese. Still no movement.

"Where's that cheater?" Nu asks.

"Fuck, I don't know. Look over by the tool chest." Bodie lays his head on the floor and flexes his neck. His back is on the verge of spasming. He should wiggle out and stretch himself, but it took long enough to scooch under here in the first place. He hears Nu clanging through tools. The clatter reminds him of how Fleece rifled through the kitchen drawers last night looking for a spatula. Angrily. Unhelpfully. You can hear a person's mood in the how they handle things, and Bodie hears anger and frustration in Nu's banging around now. It's stupid. A two-foot-long cheater isn't hiding under the socket wrenches. It's either there or it isn't.

And now he remembers. "Wait!" he calls. "It's in the corner, with the scrap."

Fleece has been cross-threaded lately, too. Tight, touchy, leaking bad vibes. The pregnancy has hit a rough patch. It's confusing to Bodie, and scary. They have this unspoken system, this division of labor that works so well for them. And it isn't even a guy and gal thing. Like, he cooks sometimes, he does laundry. And she slaughters the chickens, no problem. And they don't keep track or even bother to tell each other. Everything just gets done.

Until now. These days, the past week or so, Bodie has no idea whether Fleece is taking care of her sheep, doing the grocery shopping, putting gas in the truck.

Like those shattered beer bottles. Who'd have thought?

In the past, Fleece always kept the refrigerator stocked with beer. He had never really thought about it—it was just one of the things she did. There was always cold beer in the fridge. Until last night. Last night he came in, late, tired, crusted with sweat and dirt, and there was no beer in the fridge. Jesus, that hurt. But he didn't say anything. It wasn't her job, after all. It was just that she had always done it, and now his world was tilted out of joint. Oh, well. He put three bottles in the freezer. They'd be cold by the time he got out of the shower.

But then Neville called. The sheep were out. They were grazing in his backyard. Fleece was already in bed. She'd been sleeping fifteen hours a day lately, it seemed like. So he threw some tools in the bucket of the tractor and drove down to the bottom. Found the place where the oak limb had flattened the electric fence. Sawed up the limb. Fixed the fence. Walked through Neville's little wood lot into his yard, where he found the sheep. Neville's grass was thin and dry, and sheep aren't *that* dumb. So they were easy to get started back home to their lush, green pasture. It was well after dark by the time he got back to the house, ready for a cold one. But when he looked in the freezer, the beers were whacked. Frozen and shattered. He almost wept. Six warm beers later, in fact, he did.

That's about how he feels now. Stressed to the max. Not just his spasming back and his screaming hip, but his mind. Frozen up and about to explode. He can't hold everything inside much longer.

But now Nu is back, slipping the wrench onto the fitting, the cheater over the wrench handle. The growl in Nu's throat as he bears down gets loud, then the cross-threaded metal begins to screech. The metal moves, painfully. Bodie hurts all over, but the fitting moves. Nu sets the cheater aside, levers the wrench. It's free. One job done, a hundred thousand to go.

The rest of the morning Bodie hustles from chore to chore. He drives the Farmall down to the bottom and helps Juano stretch shade cloth over three of the big crop tunnels. Just as they finish, Arnold jogs up and says they're short on irrigation pipe.

Bodie pounds a fist to his forehead. "Crap. I lent a couple of hundred feet to Neville two weeks ago. He hasn't returned it?" He sends Arnold off to Neville's with the Farmall and the pipe hauler. Then he walks back up to the packing shed just as Zebra returns from the Wednesday market.

"Could have sold twice as many tomatoes if we'd had them," Zebra tells him. "People wanted to know when we'll have peppers. I told them Friday at the Veggie Fest, right?"

Friday is their usual CSA pickup day, and all their regular customers will be coming to the farm. That's always a busy day already. But Fleece had the idea of doing something special on the solstice, so they dreamed up the Tunder Farm Summer Solstice Veggie Fest. They've invited a couple of other vendors—Helen Cortland with her willow baskets, Bobbie Elbow's Brat Master BBQ cart, he can't remember who all. A friend of Zebra's will do face painting and temporary tattoos, and they have a local bluegrass band, Camas Valley Grass, lined up to play. They put an ad in the co-op newspaper and posted flyers all over town.

And Bodie has a new batch of ale ready, too. It's home brew so he can't sell it, and only a dozen gallons, but he plans to sneak a pint into each CSA box. It's a terrific batch, one of his best yet, a smooth IPA with a sweet strawberry finish. Everybody says that Bodie has a nose for beer, and it's true. No flattery there. It's just a god-given talent. He even feels it's his calling, to become a brew master. That's what keeps him going through all his setbacks and all his formidable debts.

He had hoped that the farm's website would be updated with news about the Veggie Fest, but that was one of Fleece's jobs, and he's pretty sure she hasn't gotten to it yet. She might be coming out of her funk, though. When he dashed home to grab some lunch, she was up and dressed. She even had a couple of sandwiches made for him.

"I feel great," she said, as if her week of bad temper had never happened. She was all lovey-dovey, rubbing up against him like a scent-marking cat. "Let's take a picnic to the river tonight."

An hour later, he stops by the packing shed to check in with Nu again. Nu has managed to remove the U trap, and he thinks he can recut the cross-threaded ends of the stainless steel pipe. Bodie watches as Nu eases Joe's pipe threader onto the end of the pipe, carefully torqueing the cutting head into the buggered threads. Bodie doesn't say anything. He can tell Nu needs to concentrate.

He daydreams ahead to this evening's picnic with Fleece. Their sex life has never been particularly inventive, just steady and nourishing. Slow cooking, Fleece likes to call it. *Pot roast* is their code. The meat just falls off the bone. They'll be kissing and petting on the sofa, and one or the other will ask, "Wanna make a pot roast?" Bodie likes it that way. Slow and easy. He had actually grown tired of the high jinks with the cheerleaders he used to pick up, and since he and Fleece got together they've kept it pretty straightforward. Lately, though: nada. Even though the midwife has told them that having sex during pregnancy is just fine, Fleece has not been interested.

In their three years together, they've only done it outdoors a couple of times, but the spot that Fleece has suggested for their picnic, a pretty knoll overlooking the river, is a place where they made love once before. So Bodie is hopeful.

"It's gonna work," Nu says. "I'll need to go buy a new P trap, but I think the threads on the pipe will be fine."

Bodie gives him a thumbs-up and heads back out to the fields. Things are looking up. Bodie has always been sensitive to momentum, the way a game can suddenly shift, the holes start opening up for your running backs, the fumbles start bouncing your way. And he feels it now. Positive momentum.

It's 7:30 by the time they start for the river. The field truck, a '54 Chevy pickup faded to overcast gray, with no license plates—no doors, for that matter—is only used on the farm. One of Bodie's early interns, a Deadhead named Fox, christened the truck and painted its name on the front of the hood in rainbow lettering: "No Further." Now the old truck bounces over the rutted road down the bluff, bumps around the edge of the veg fields, rolls over the knoll where the pastures begin, and coasts down to the river's edge. Bodie sets the parking brake and grabs the cooler. Fleece brings two chairs and a blanket.

They settle into their oversized sling chairs. A breeze spangles the flat green river. On the opposite bank, cottonwoods flash the pale undersides of their leaves. Fleece unpacks the basket and the cooler. She's brought pork chop sandwiches, a bag of their favorite gourmet potato chips, a jar of pickles, and a half dozen of her special pumpkin-ginger muffins, which she calls Bodie cakes.

Bodie opens a root beer for Fleece and a beer for himself. "To you, my pretty bride," he says.

Fleece smiles and adds, "And to the baby."

"Yes! To the baby!" He reaches out with his bottle to twine arms with Fleece, but they get tangled and Bodie spills some beer down her tank top. Fleece giggles, and Bodie leans over and licks the beer from her chest. He's ready to lick her everywhere, but Fleece is hungry for the actual food. She kisses him firmly then turns away and starts unwrapping the sandwiches.

Bodie leans back into his chair. It's a beautiful evening. Mallards are chortling somewhere downriver. Sheep bleat from the pasture. There are a few pesky flies and mosquitoes, but no yellow jackets. Three fluffy cumulus clouds sail overhead.

"Mama Cloud, Papa Cloud, and Baby Cloud," Fleece says.

Oh, her cheeks are as red as raspberries. She looks delicious. Bodie wolfs down his sandwich and guzzles a second beer. Now he hauls himself out of the sling chair and flops down on the blanket. He might have tweaked his back a little there, but no matter. He opens his arms for Fleece to come to him, and she kneels and turns, leaning back against him. Bodie wishes they'd put the blanket closer to the stump so he could prop himself up on something. His glutes are clenched, his erectors cramping. He shifts a hip so he can nibble Fleece's neck.

"Mmm," she murmurs, her tone mushy, and he is instantly flooded with lust.

Lip-locked, faces mashed, they're engaged in some big-time tongue wrestling when Fleece abruptly stops. Bodie opens his eyes to see her staring at him. Suddenly she wallops him on the forehead. "Mosquito," she says, still in that mushy, sex-drunk voice. "I got her."

Their kissing resumes. Bodie introduces breast fondling, thigh rubbing. Zippers are unzipped, T-shirts tugged stickily over heads. Fleece is cooing and moaning. Bodie hears a great pounding of hooves in his blood and tries to calm himself. He's been known to jump the scrimmage line ahead of the snap. He has tugged off Fleece's beachcombers and is poised over her like a diver ready to plunge off a cliff when the hoof-pounding reaches a crescendo and three impossible horses gallop into the clearing, followed closely by a mewling centaur.

Christ. It's fucking Neville, chasing his escaped herd on his four-wheel motorcycle. The horses whinny and wheel. They stare down at Bodie and Fleece, nostrils flaring. Neville skids to a halt. He tries not to stare at them, tries to say something—an apology, Bodie imagines, or a solemn promise to drown himself in the river—then revs his engine, which launches the horses back into flight, and the whole horrible mirage hurtles away.

Bodie is mortified, homicidal, and suddenly very, very tired. He collapses into Fleece's arms. His limp thing will not rise again. He could sleep for days. He could break down and weep. But, after just a moment of profound, death-like rest, he rolls over, picks up kissing her where they left off, reaches down into her warm, slippery place, and, with his massive sensitive linebacker's fingers, he finishes her off.

15 · Nu

Nu could hear Bodie, at the head of the packing line, holding forth on beer-making arcana. "The secret's in the terpenes," Bodie was saying. "Your hop variety is going to determine most of that, but soil acidity can influence it, too." Bodie was in high spirits today. Nu guessed that the prospect of a lot of people showing up at the farm fueled Bodie's mood.

There were four of them in the shed, packing vegetables into the CSA boxes, while the rest of the farm crew was out in the yard setting up the produce stand and canopy tents, or posting the signs directing visitors to the bicycle parking, the hay ride, the Porta Pottis. It looked as if there might be a decent turnout for the festival. Summer solstice fell on a Friday this year, so Fleece had suggested creating something special, the Tunder Farm Summer Solstice Veggie Fest, to get more people out to see the farm. Zebra had designed the posters and Nu had helped her tack them up around town. They'd sent an email to all eighty-four of their CSA customers, promising live music, games for the kids, and the season's first bell peppers. "5–9 p.m. at Tunder Farm."

Bodie's primary audience was Ursula's friend Becca, second in the packing line, who'd volunteered to help today. Her job was to artfully arrange a head of broccoli and two bunches of Swiss chard around the head of cabbage and pint of home brew Bodie started each box with. Nu was third in the line. His task was to pull tangles of just-harvested carrots from the field bin and make up bunches of eight carrots each, twisting a yellow wire-tie around the green tops. He was slow at it, fussing too much to get the tops neatly arranged, and both Zebra and Becca on either side of him occasionally reached in and bundled some carrots to keep the line moving.

The other reason he was slow at his job was because he kept glancing sidelong at Becca.

"You probably don't remember me," she'd said when she'd first arrived. "But I used to hang out with Ursula when we were all teenagers."

Oh, Nu remembered her. Vividly. Back then, those summer vacations when he was staying at the farm, he'd found Becca gorgeous, alluring, and totally out of his reach. What he remembered most was how he ached with longing and loneliness whenever she was around. Now, with her round, green eyes, her high Slavic cheekbones, her rosy coloring—she'd mentioned her pregnancy right away so that Nu wouldn't have to do the awkward male thing of finding a way to ask—and especially her close-cropped hair that accentuated the subtle landscape of her skull, she was even more beautiful. As an artist, Nu was having a hard time keeping his eyes off her.

Becca seemed to be fascinated by Bodie's brewing insights, drawing him out with intelligent technical questions, while Bodie yammered about fining agents and mash pH. Nu was not much interested. Bodie was so big and loud that even his most reasonable and detailed expressions came out sounding like sales pitches. It was unfortunate, Nu thought, because Bodie was smart, a lot smarter than he sounded.

It had taken Nu a while to recognize it, but Bodie had made himself into a very competent farmer and businessman, and Nu had no reason to doubt that Bodie was going to become an expert brewer someday as well. Craft breweries were popping up everywhere. Bodie might be able to catch the wave.

The band Bodie had hired, Camas Valley Grass—three middle-aged white guys, banjo, guitar, and fiddle—had set up on the lawn across the drive. They'd been warming up for a while, and now they started off with a hornpipe.

Becca was saying something, but it took Nu a moment to realize she was speaking to him.

"Excuse me," he stammered.

"Your home is in Bend?" she asked.

"Bend? Oh, right. Never thought of it as home, exactly. I live in a garage."

"I hope it's a nice garage."

"It's huge. Studio space, mostly."

"You're an artist?"

Nu turned to face her, wondering how to answer the question. Becca's green eyes regarded him steadily, and he had to look back down at his carrots. "I try," he finally said.

Zebra shouldered in just then with a fresh bin of produce. Nu caught a whiff of patchouli and armpit, and nearly got an elbow in the face as Zebra upended a bushel of carrots into his crate.

He turned back to Becca. "Ursula tells me you're a landscape designer."

"Yes, but I'm finding there isn't much demand for my services here. I'm thinking of trying something else. I might like to work with my hands more."

"You could take up plumbing. High demand for plumbers."

Becca laughed. "Well, maybe not that hands-on. But growing plants like Ursula does, that appeals to me."

Nu had fallen behind on his carrot-bunching again, so Becca pulled a handful from the bin and quickly twist-tied a bunch. The band played a banjo-heavy version of "Blackberry Blossom," then slid straight into "I Saw the Light."

"Ursula said you would be returning to Bend soon. For a hearing? About that scrape with the law you had?"

Nu nodded. "Not sure when, exactly."

A steady stream of people had begun pouring into the Veggie Fest. CSA customers were lining up at the end of the packing shed to claim their boxes. The band jumped from one upbeat number to the next, picking up the tempo as they went.

Nu wanted to talk further with Becca, or better yet just gaze at her glorious skull, but she suddenly stuck out her hand. "I have to go," she said. "I teach a yoga class this evening. I just wanted to come by to say hello and see the farm again."

Before Nu could think of anything cordial to say, she shook his hand, gave Bodie a passing hug, then strode down the driveway against the flow of the arriving crowd.

As Nu stepped out of the packing shed to watch her depart, he spotted Ursula and Cat cutting bouquets from their flower beds out front. When he'd first arrived at the farm, he'd thought the flowers growing out along the road were just for show, but he now knew that they were another cash crop. Ursula and Cat sold bunches to several local stores.

Ursula had been grumpy at breakfast this morning. Nu supposed that she wasn't a big fan of the festival. Bodie's little successes, however modest or temporary, could threaten her preferred outcome: selling the farm and everybody moving on. But now, wheeling a cart load of cut flowers up the hill, she looked happy. She smiled over at Nu and began arranging her buckets full of flowers in the produce stand. She'd been working hard, judging by the sheen of sweat on her arms and face. Sprays of loose hair that had sprung from her braids gleamed in the early evening sun.

More people were arriving for the Veggie Fest. Lots of people, Nu realized. A tall man in clown garb began juggling fruits and vegetables beside the produce stand, and a dozen or so children instantly surrounded him. Nu realized the juggler was Arnold, the hyper-focused Iraq vet. It was the first time Nu had seen Arnold without his headphones on.

Bodie came up behind him. "Can you help Fleece?" he asked, pointing.

Nu saw that the produce stand was already mobbed, and Fleece was alone at the checkout counter. He crossed the driveway, cut through the line of kids waiting at the face-painting booth, and ducked inside the canopy that covered the produce stand. "What can I do to help?" he asked Fleece.

There were probably forty varieties of vegetables for sale, neatly arrayed in crates, bowls, and baskets on the display tables. Already a dozen or more people were picking over the produce—tomatoes and strawberries looked to be the hot items—and Fleece was totting up sales on the ancient cash register.

"Bag," she said.

Soon it was chaos. People were swarming in and around the booth. Nu was hustling back and forth to the walk-in cooler to bring over more produce. There was still a bevy of people in the packing shed getting their CSA boxes. Whole families had parked their bikes beside the driveway, leaving their kids to pick grapes from the arbor. Kids were racing around spitting grape seeds at each other.

Nu spent the rest of the evening in the booth, busy the whole time. Lots of people came by to hug and congratulate Fleece, asking her when the baby was due. Her little cedar-bark baskets were selling fast, mostly to women in their twenties and thirties, Nu noticed. They were probably hoping that some of Fleece's fertility was woven in. Kids dashed up to show off faces painted with cat whiskers or zebra stripes, and the band's spritely folk music made the air feel lightly carbonated. Fleece kept up a running conversation with customers while she checked them out, the cash register adding its silvery *ka-ching* every time she cranked the arm to open the cash drawer.

Restocking the tomatoes—people were taking them right out of his hand before he could set them on the table—Nu glanced up and saw that the gravel parking area out front was full, and more cars were starting to park on the shoulder of the county road. He noticed Ursula and Cat out in the flower beds, helping people u-cut flowers. Four or five kids were chasing one of Fleece's chickens. The skittery bird looked like it might regret being free-range this evening, alone so far away from its coop.

At one point Nu looked up to see a police car with lights flashing stop beside the string of vehicles parked along the road. Cops. He felt a rush of tense memory, recalling the deputy sheriff who'd rescued him from the dirt bikers but then charged him with assault. Nu saw Bodie trot out and talk with the cop standing beside his cruiser. Bodie was waving his arms and pointing toward the front pasture, and it looked to Nu as if Bodie and the cop were both laughing. Bodie trotted over to the fence and opened a gate, then circulated among the customers, and people began going out to move their vehicles off the road shoulder. The cop stood at the head of the driveway for a few minutes, directing traffic, then he climbed into his cruiser, whooped his siren in a farewell salute, and drove off.

By the time the last of the CSA customers had picked up their boxes and the final visitors were heading for their cars, the produce stand was pretty well pillaged. The last tomato had been sold an hour ago; the last basket of strawberries was gone before that. Zebra and Juano were schlepping a few boxes of unsold collards, turnips, and summer squash back to the cooler. Fleece was counting the money in the till.

Nu saw Joe sitting in a lawn chair in the shade of the maple tree near the house. He walked up and stood beside him, looking back at the aftermath of the Veggie Fest. "It's cooler up here," he said.

Joe nodded and chewed on an unlit pipe.

"How long have you been watching the show?"

"I saw the police car flashers, so I came out for backup. But it looks like Bodie has the cops bought off."

Ursula and Cat sauntered up, swinging a basket full of zinnias between them. Cat handed a red flower to Joe and a yellow one to Nu. Ursula had zinnias tucked in her braids and a little yellow daisy painted on each cheek. Then Zebra trotted over from the packing shed, wearing a necklace of daisies and a crown of little pink roses.

"Love the crown," Nu told Zebra. She lifted the circlet and placed it on his head.

Fleece arrived with a basket of perfectly ripe strawberries she'd somehow saved. Even to a food dunce like Nu, they tasted ambrosial. Bodie was still supervising the cleanup. Nu saw him hand some money to the three band members, then Bodie danced a jig and twirled around once, and the musicians all laughed.

Bodie looked up their way, and Fleece waved to him. He jogged over to the packing shed, and grabbed a six-pack of beer from an ice chest, and came trotting up. "That was a blast," he said as he handed around the beers.

"You done good, bro," Ursula told him. She took her beer and saluted her brother, then reached around Nu's waist and gave him a quick squeeze.

"Thank you, guys!" Bodie said. "You're a hell of a team." Bodie held up his hand toward his father for a high five.

Joe slapped Bodie's palm and said, "You have a lot of fans, son. That was fun to watch."

Nu looked around their little circle at the smiling, tired faces, and heard Bodie, who'd been carrying the farm on his back for four solid years, let out a very long sigh.

16 · Ursula

Xerophyllum tenax. The name was on Ursula's tongue when she woke the next morning. She sat on the edge of the bed for a moment, feeling uncommonly grounded and refreshed.

She was aware that calling plants by their Latin names seemed snooty to some people. But ever since she'd taken her first botany class in high school she'd fallen in love with scientific nomenclature, and once in a while she would wake up with a Latin binomial on her tongue. It always felt like a good sign.

Xerophyllum tenax. Beargrass. Also called basket grass or turkey's beard. That was the species Marlys wanted Ursula to survey. Marlys had a huge complicated multiyear grant, funded by the National Science Foundation, the Bureau of Land Management, and several tribes, to assess the condition of a variety of food and fiber plants traditionally used by the tribes in the Cascades. Marlys's specialty was huckleberries. She was one of the country's foremost authorities on *Vaccinum sp.*, having published fifty some papers and contributed chapters to many textbooks. When Marlys had called last week she'd told Ursula that the beargrass was already beginning its extended bloom season, and it looked like it would be a big year. Ursula imagined the creamy inflorescences rising from their baskets of leaves like huge, slow candles. She couldn't wait to get into the mountains.

She pulled on yesterday's blue jeans and T-shirt and went downstairs. Coffee was already made, a little stronger than she preferred, but it was nice that Nu had brewed a full pot. She poured a bowl of cornflakes and sat at the table recalling yesterday's shindig. It was the most fun she'd had in a long time. Plus she'd sold a ton of flowers. She was happy for Bodie, and happy that they were on good terms at last. She could leave for the summer with a clear conscience. Slightly clearer, anyway.

But she wasn't going to leave unless Nu was willing to stick around and look after Joe, and she still hadn't gotten up the nerve to talk to him. She'd had a couple of opportunities but just couldn't make the ask. She wasn't sure why. It was kind of a big deal, sure. But Nu had already learned to handle most of the caretaking tasks: meds, doctors' visits. And he and Joe really got along well. They'd watched every Kurosawa movie they could borrow from the library. She'd heard them debating whether to do John Ford or Ingmar Bergman next. Two dreary choices as far as she was concerned, but then she wasn't being consulted.

Meanwhile, she should just plan on going into the field. She should help Cat put the greenhouse to bed. Start organizing her gear: sleeping bag, foam pad, camp stove. Where was her tent stored, anyway? She wasn't sure, but it would turn up.

She'd just finished her cereal and set the empty bowl in the sink when she remembered that, in a moment of rash enthusiasm out under the maple tree at the end of the festival yesterday, she'd invited everyone over for dinner tonight to celebrate. Ugh. Why the hell had she done that? Oh, well. Bodie said he'd grill brats and burgers, so that was easy. And Fleece offered to bring a dessert. Ursula considered making something special—Thai salad rolls, maybe—but then decided to go with the standard offerings: potato salad, steamed green beans. She could raid Fleece's garden for salad greens. Hors d'oeuvres? Checking the fridge, she discovered a rind end of Swiss and some mold-speckled cheddar. She'd need to make a run to the co-op.

She refilled her coffee mug and stepped outside. A breezy morning. It felt like the weather might be changing.

She strolled around the house and saw Nu gathering up yesterday's beer bottles under the maple tree. The yard looked like a traveling carnival had just broken camp. Bodie's crew had put away all the perishables, but otherwise it was pretty much as they had left it. Rectangular outlines of smashed grass indicated where booths had been dismantled. Fleece's chickens picked over the Veggie Fest trash.

Nu looked up and waved. She walked out across the lawn.

"Morning after," she said, letting her eyes drift over the debris.

"It must have been fun. I was working too fast to notice."

"And now you've got cleanup detail. Did Bodie ask you to?"

Nu shook his head. "I offered. His crew had to go do Saturday market."

"Want a hand?" Ursula said. They began folding up tables and taking down the canopies, working in tandem as if they'd done it before. Within an hour they had most of the trash picked up, the tables and tents stacked in the packing shed. Bodie's crew could take it from there.

"How's your drawing of the farm going?" Ursula asked.

"Oh, fine. You know, it's just meant to be a blueprint. A bird's-eye view," Nu said, looking up at the hop barn.

Ursula followed his glance. "Is it hard to get up to the cupola?"

"Not at all," Nu said. "Want to see it? It's a pretty sweet view from up there."

Ursula trailed Nu into the hop barn. He started climbing the ladder nailed to the east wall and, taking a deep breath, Ursula followed. The rungs were just two-by-fours, the top edges worn smooth from eighty-some years of hands and feet. Three stories straight up. Next came a narrow catwalk—a pair of two-by-six planks screwed onto sleepers attached to a massive beam, with a two-by-four handrail at waist height—leading out to the very center of the barn. Ursula surprised herself by strolling nonchalantly onto the catwalk, her hand sliding lightly along the handrail.

At the base of the final ladder she paused to look down at the interior of the barn. The flat roof of Bodie's staff room occupied half the space below her. She shook her head at the audacity of Bodie contriving to build his new room *inside* the old hop barn. She recalled how the carpentry crew had taken down the siding from the west wall of the barn, removed some of the massive support posts, and erected temporary beams to support the absent framing, all to give them access to the interior of the barn. It had cost more—like, *a lot more*—to do it that way. But Bodie was nostalgic about the hop barn. And it seemed as if Bodie had had plenty of money back at the beginning. Even rookie football players got paid way more than scientists, Ursula supposed.

The other half of the barn was more or less as it always had been, with its massive, rough-cut posts and beams, the tall, windowless walls clad on the exterior with straight-grained Douglas fir clapboards.

"Need a hand?" Nu was looking down through the opening in the floor of the cupola.

"No. I'm coming."

She went more slowly up the final ladder. Pausing to look down had triggered a slight queasiness, a sense of exposure. But when she stepped up onto the cupola platform and turned from opening to opening, she was back again in her body, giddy with the height but entirely present.

"Wow!" she said, sidling around all four sides before stopping to look east toward the Cascades. "What a glorious view."

"Yeah. And look at that storybook farm. The people who live down there must be very happy."

She glanced down toward the front door of her house just as Joe shuffled onto the stoop in his bathrobe and slippers. "I heard they were grumpy old bears."

"Only before breakfast," Nu said.

Ursula growled and clawed the air with her long fingers. "So, your map thing," she said, leaning back on the west wall. "It's looking down from up here, right?" She thought she could feel the cupola sway ever so slightly in the breeze. A barn swallow shot past the east window, its cobalt feathers catching the sun.

"Yeah. The map is just to help me see the whole place and think about what I might want to make out on the land."

"And?"

"Well, what I think I want to do is to create stuff all around the farm out of found materials."

"Stuff?" Ursula said.

"Yeah, like brush shelters, woven mat fences, sculptures made from dead wood maybe. All over the farm. All connected."

"Connected how?"

"Sorry. I know I'm being vague. I won't really know until I do some work on the ground." Nu screwed up his face in concentration, then held his hands out as if cupping a bowl. "Fleece has been trying to teach me to weave baskets, which I totally suck at. You've seen the results. Those cedar withes have to be woven just right, and I don't have the patience. I'm more into making big, gross, messy things." Nu waved his hands as if tossing hay in the air. "So, I might try using branches and bark and stones and whatever to make sculptures all around the farm. They could be messy and goofy, or neat and pretty, or I don't know what. Put them out where people would maybe just happen to find them. And I'm trying to weave the whole thing together somehow: the farm fields, woods, buildings, pastures…"

"Cool," Ursula said, hoping her puzzlement would come out as enthusiasm. "Have you talked to Bodie about this?"

"I made a deal with Bodie. He'll ignore my art if I'll do his plumbing."

"Sounds more than fair."

Ursula looked down and noticed Joe sniffing a rose beside the front door. She squelched an urge to call out to him. Instead she took a deep breath and looked directly at Nu. She wished there was a little more space up here; he was only an arm's length away. "It sounds like you're maybe planning to be around for a while?"

Nu turned away from her and leaned out the south opening as if trying to see something down by the river. "It's still kind of one day at a time," he said. Then, turning back toward her, "Why do you ask?"

"Well, I mentioned to you that Marlys wants me to work for her this summer."

"Yeah."

"And I was wondering, if I were to go work in the mountains for a few weeks, would you be willing to look after Dad?"

Nu turned away again and looked out to the west. Did she hear him sigh? Ursula realized with a jolt what a huge thing she was asking. She'd been imagining it was no big deal, that Nu had come here to help take care of Joe anyway. But it *was* a big deal. It was a serious commitment.

"I need to go back to Bend sometime. Got a call from the attorney yesterday. They dropped the charges."

"Nu, that's wonderful! So you're totally free?"

Nu nodded. "Yeah. I'm free from that little nightmare, at least. I still have a painting to complete, and I'm way behind on that."

He bounced on his toes, letting off some tension, Ursula figured. She waited for him to continue.

"So. Looking after Joe," he said. "What's that entail? Doctor visits? Monitor his meds?"

"Yeah. Make sure he eats, gets outside some. Doesn't drive."

Nu winced at that one. She understood. She didn't like taking away her father's mobility either. But he was a real danger behind the wheel.

"For how long?"

"Just a few weeks. And I could come home on weekends."

"Let me think about it."

Ursula couldn't tell which way he was leaning.

Nu looked toward the square opening in the cupola floor. "You want a hand starting down?"

Ursula shook her head. "You first," she said. "I need to go real slow."

17 · Bodie

Some hangovers are special. Bodie's, Saturday morning after the Veggie Fest, is like having a toothache *and* the flu. Head, joints, limbs, everything aches. After his surgery for the shoulder injury that ended his football career, he'd stayed on hydrocodone too long and got himself a nasty little addiction. That horrible week he finally went cold turkey—that's how shitty he feels this morning.

Fleece takes pity on him and makes Bodie cakes. Along with bacon and eggs and hash browns, the carbs begin to dampen the throbbing behind his eyes. Bodie is pathetically grateful. "I couldn't survive without you," he says, finishing his second pumpkin muffin.

"Duh," Fleece says, and blows him a kiss.

Bodie would like to go back to sleep, but he has chores to do. Some of the crew are already off doing the farmers' market downtown. Zebra usually comes in on Saturdays to irrigate, but not today. She asked for the day off to take a visiting friend to the coast. He steps into his boots and goes down to the fields. First stop is the seedling cloche. He'd be hard-pressed to remember what to do, which seedlings need to be hand-watered, what beds have drip lines that have to be manually turned on, what overhead sprinklers to run and for how long, but Zebra has left him detailed written instructions. He follows them to the letter, too groggy to trust himself to cut corners. It's difficult enough even with her directions. Which of these seedlings is cauliflower and which is cabbage? He can't tell them apart at this stage. Jesus, why must farming be so complicated?

In the three hours he spends getting through Zebra's list, the brittle pain in his head turns gradually to dull fog. His body has used every available calorie to muffle the pain, and now he's hungry again. He needs more carbs and then, hopefully, a nap. As he trudges numbly toward the back door, he concentrates on just keeping moving. Left foot is food, he tells himself, right foot is sleep.

Bodie clumps into the kitchen.

"Boots!" Fleece barks at him.

Bodie looks down at his muddy barn boots. "Sorry," he mutters, and retreats to the mud room. He has to sit down to tug his boots off, teetering on a mound of coats and raingear piled on the bench. Then he shuffles back inside in his socks. Fleece is waiting by the refrigerator, proffering another Bodie cake. He accepts it, along with the bear hug she wraps him up in. Leaning heavily on her, he sighs, then reaches his right arm all the way around her neck to take a big bite from the muffin.

It's late afternoon, and Bodie and Fleece are painting the baby's room. Bodie is grumpy and ashamed. After lunch, Fleece allowed him to take a nap, on the condition that he promise, *promise*, to help her paint the baby's room when he woke up. He had promised her four or five times in the past and always weaseled out of it. He knew he would not have the strength for further weaseling today.

Now here he is, brush in hand, the smell of the latex paint reminding him of hospitals, of all his shoulder and knee surgeries.

Fleece is humming along with Bonnie Raitt's "Angel from Montgomery" from a CD her sister mixed for her—Dixie Chicks, Enya, Bruce Springsteen—the music loud and echoey in the bare room.

She is plying the roller, slathering on the silvery green paint in time to the music. Bodie's job is to cut in the ceiling edges. Under the best of circumstances, which these are not, he is the wrong man for the job. Up on the step ladder, he holds the cutting brush with both hands and drags the paint-sopped bristles left to right. The green line wavers onto the ceiling's off-white. Dabs of green appear in odd places. He wipes at them with a rag.

"Leave it," Fleece says. "We can touch it up later."

The CD ends and Fleece wipes her hands to change it.

"Can we have some quiet, please?" Bodie pleads.

Fleece *tssks* him, but shuts the music off.

Grateful for the silence, Bodie remembers something. "You got up in the middle of the night, didn't you?"

"Yeah. I had a dream and I wanted to write it down."

"Must have been special. Want to tell me?"

Fleece loads her roller with paint, then closes her eyes for a moment. "Okay, yeah. It was here on the farm, maybe. There was a huge plank house with the sides all opened up, like a big picnic shelter, where we all lived. I was outside tending to a camas oven buried in the earth. The baby was in a sling on my chest." Fleece takes a long, deep breath as if smelling the memory. "And then over a ways there was a fire pit with racks of salmon drying. Ursula was there, and some other women, my mom, my sister. They were making jerky at a big table on the other side of the fire. And out beyond them there were all these raised garden beds in a fancy pattern, like Versailles or something, except they were overflowing with all kinds of vegetables. A geometric jungle of fruits and vegetables. And beyond that, surrounding us, there was this gigantic curtain of foliage, so it felt like we were in a hidden grotto."

"Hops, maybe?" Bodie says.

"Oh, my god, they *were* hops. Except a hundred feet high."

"Any men in that picture?" Bodie asks.

Fleece picks up the roller and lays down a couple lines of paint. "Oh, yeah. They were all over in a corner drinking and gambling."

Bodie waits for her to give him a smile or a wink, but Fleece just keeps on painting.

"Okay. Anything else?"

Fleece stops painting and closes her eyes again. "And then," she continues, "and then there was this fountain that appeared in the middle of the yard. It just popped up. A beautiful fountain with elaborate tiles, cobalt blue and sunflower yellow. It was shooting water up higher and higher till it looked like it might crash over the plank house, and that's when I realized—I *really* had to pee. That's when I got up."

"Wow," Bodie says. "Sounds like Shangri-la. Or like you're trying to go native on me."

"I am Native."

"Yeah, but, still…"

Fleece takes a few more swipes with the roller. "If I go native, will you be my bison?"

"Sweetheart, I will be your shaggy old buffalo and your rolling hills and your tall-grass prairie."

"And I will graze in your grass. There will be flowers dangling from my lips."

"And we'll roll together in the mud wallow…"

"And stampede over the cliff!"

18 · Nu

Nu fetched himself another beer, sat back down at the table, and picked up the little mat he was weaving. Fleece had given him a bagful of dried cattail leaves—rejects, she'd told him, only good for practicing with—and he was trying to teach his fingers to plait the flat blades without looking. Nu had watched Fleece once, weaving a mat while talking with other women, barely attending to her work, and he wanted to learn to weave like that, too.

Dusk was coming on, the evening still warm. The mosquitoes were getting annoying, but Nu could tell that everyone was glad to be outdoors anyway. He looked down at his mat. He'd missed a tuck in the previous row. He growled under his breath and tugged it apart, then glanced across the table at Ursula. She and Fleece were talking about maternity clothes.

"I can let out a couple of your skirts if you want," he heard Ursula say.

Fleece turned her head in a pretty way. "I didn't know you sewed," she said.

"I don't. But how hard can it be?" And the two women leaned together and laughed.

Nu looked past them into the over-green backyard. This domestic harmony shit was not really his cup of tea. He should pack up and move along.

Ursula looked across the table toward him. "I love that screen, Nu," she said.

That afternoon Nu had tacked an old beige bed sheet onto a frame of two-by-twos, painted an oak branch on it, then hoisted the big rectangular canvas from a limb of the tree near the back fence. It was a lousy painting, the leaves a fake bright green, but it served its purpose. He'd strung it up to screen out the security light on Bliss Fits, and he'd lucked out on the placement. It was close enough to the light to shade the entire deck.

"Thanks for doing that," Ursula said, and pooched her lips into a semi-kiss.

Now everyone turned to gaze up into the oak tree.

"Yeah, thanks for the shade, dude," Bodie said. He flipped a burger and grease flames leaped up again from the grill. "Makes it a little harder for me to shoot out the light, but I'll manage."

Nu saw Ursula frown at the reference, even though she hated the security lamp as much as Bodie did. She'd shoot it herself, Nu was pretty sure, if she thought she could get away with it.

Nu was already on his fourth beer of the evening. He was celebrating. They all were. Bodie had pulled off his big Veggie Fest. Ursula was just about done with her greenhouse season, and she'd made her peace, it seemed, with her brother. Fleece was smiling beatifically, her pregnancy giving her cheeks a rich glow, though for some reason she had a big streak of green paint in her hair. Even Joe seemed to be in a frisky mood. Adorned with fresh white bandages on the melanoma burns on both cheeks, he stood next to Bodie at the grill, telling him, judging by the fragments Nu could overhear, about a long-ago welding job gone embarrassingly wrong.

Nu figured he had the most to celebrate, though. Like not being a felon. Not going to jail. Not being fined thousands of dollars. It wasn't quite a done deal yet, but his lawyer had told him on the phone that the DA would *not* be taking the case to trial. The charges would be dropped. He lifted his glass in a solo toast to his own soon-to-be-expunged criminal record and took a deep drink.

Closing his eyes, he basked in the murmur of the voices around him. He tried to listen without distinguishing actual words, relishing the music of the voices, the cadences and tones. How comforting, to hover at the edge of a conversation he didn't have to take part in.

He suddenly recalled eavesdropping on the family one evening when he was a little kid. It might have been the first time his mother dropped him off for a long summer visit, while she went off to play golf on her LPGA tour. So he would have been four. They were having supper, and he'd already eaten most of his meat loaf when he suddenly decided to slide off his chair and hide under the dining room table, hoping no one would notice. Everyone above went on talking as before. Aunt Alice always did most of the talking at the dinner table, while his Uncle Joe was quiet and stern. But when Alice paused, maybe to take a bite to eat, it was Joe who broke the brief silence. "Where's Nu?" he asked.

Nu had expected Ursula to immediately snitch on him. Surely she'd seen him slip from his chair. But to his surprise, Ursula had said, "Yeah. Where *is* Nu?"

Then Alice and even Bodie echoed the question. "Where is Nu?"

"Well, he'll show up," Alice said. "At least for dessert."

Now, as Nu eavesdropped on Fleece and Ursula's conversation, he felt again the same stew of emotions as that little boy. Pride at his stealth. Guilt over his deceit. Happiness at the sense of belonging.

A strange sensation, belonging. Where did one feel a sense of belonging? He searched his body. Maybe his skin was slightly more alert. And maybe he felt a vague sensation of spaciousness in his belly.

Across the table, next to Ursula, Fleece was massaging one of her breasts. "I wish the baby would get here already. Pressure."

There was a sudden sizzling sound, and Bodie shouted, "Whoa!"

Hamburger fat flamed up from the grill. Nu's stomach rumbled.

Something blue caught his eye. He looked up to see a scrub jay land in the vine maple behind Bodie. Now the jay hopped down onto the deck railing, close beside Bodie at the grill. Nu admired the bird's insouciance, testing its proximity to danger.

He still hadn't decided whether or not he was willing to stay at the farm when Ursula went to work in the mountains. He didn't want to disappoint her, of course, but he was a lot less motivated to stick around if she wasn't going to be here. On the other hand, he had to admit that the farm was beginning to interest him more. Not the farm as a labor-intensive vegetable-producing business, exactly, but the farm as a place that might inspire some art. Question was, would he actually have time to work on art if he were caretaking for Joe?

Then there was Ursula. Twice today—after they'd climbed down from the cupola, and again when he'd come into the kitchen an hour ago to help her prep for dinner—she'd opened her arms wide for a hug, then held onto him a little longer than a cousinly embrace might have called for. He'd been surprised at how truly trim her long waist was, and he liked how her cheek smelled of her musky olive soap. She'd even reached up and rubbed the back of his neck with her long, calloused fingers. So, what was that all about?

"Burgers are done," Bodie said.

Nu helped the women fetch salads, a watermelon, and a plate of fudge brownies from the kitchen. Bodie plopped a burger onto each person's plate. Pickles and tomato slices were passed around, ketchup and mustard slathered onto buns, glasses refilled with iced tea or beer. Bodie appeased the scrub jays by tossing a handful of chips onto the lawn, although it only emboldened them. They hopped around the edges of the deck, haranguing the picnickers.

During a quiet spot in the commotion, Ursula leaned forward and lifted her glass. "We have a lot to celebrate," she said. She looked at Bodie, then Fleece. "Your Veggie Fest thing was a huge success. Even I had fun." Glasses clinked. Their huzzahs scattered the jays. "Here's to you and your baby," she added.

"You look gorgeous, Fleece, honey," Joe said. "I'm so happy for you both."

Bodie leaned over and squeezed Joe's shoulder affectionately. It was hard for Nu to believe that for a couple of years Bodie and Joe had barely been on speaking terms. Just the other night Joe had told Nu that he still kept expecting Bodie to revert to full-time partying. He couldn't quite believe that this new Bodie was here to stay. Nu studied Joe and wondered what was going on in the old man's mind. Would the arrival of his first grandchild make Joe want to stay alive longer?

A few quiet moments went by as they all tucked into their food. Nu, hiding behind sips of beer, snuck glances at Ursula. He was watching her when Ursula firmed up her jaw and came to some inner decision. She clanked her glass against the table to get their attention. "I have a bit of news myself," she announced.

"Bodie!" Fleece shouted, pointing toward the grill. One of the scrub jays had landed on the side board and was eying something. As they watched, it flapped up over the grill and grabbed a bun and flew off toward the shrubbery, a tongue of grease-flame licking after it. Whether the bird's wings got singed, Nu couldn't tell. The jay had disappeared into the cover of the rhododendrons.

"Signs and portents," Bodie intoned. "When a jay steals your bun, cover your assets."

Everyone chuckled nervously. Bodie's joke was a little dark for the occasion.

As if to restore the bright mood, Bodie said, "Hey, we have some more good news, if you can believe it. And this is almost as big"— here Bodie looked down at Fleece's belly—"as the baby. I made a deal to supply hops for the Tapster. Bob Brundidge is fronting us money to put in five more acres of hops."

Bodie paused, inviting congratulations, which were duly offered.

"Who is this guy?" Ursula asked.

"Bob Brundidge. He owns Camas Valley Tapster, the biggest craft brewery in town."

"And how big a deal are we talking about?" Nu asked.

"Big. He wants to source all his hops locally. We'll be in some kind of partnership. I might even try growing some barley for him."

Joe asked something about hop culture, and Bodie launched into one of his "future of brewing" monologues that Nu was not interested in. He looked across at Ursula. She was twisting her braid, her face shrouded, her eyes focused somewhere over Bodie's head.

"Hey," Bodie said loudly. "I hate to change the mood again, but here's some bad news. Got a call from Zebra this afternoon. She fell off a rock at the coast and sprained her ankle pretty badly. Might have torn a ligament. She's in a walking boot for at least a week, maybe more. So, we're seriously shorthanded heading down the stretch." Bodie took a deep breath. "The thing is," he said, holding his half-empty glass up and gazing into it as if trying to divine the future, "well, Ursula, we were wondering, Fleece and me, if you'd be willing to help get us over the hump this summer?"

Ursula had wound her braid tight, tugging her left eyebrow upward. Nu realized that Ursula had not yet told Bodie about her offer from Marlys, her plan to be gone for part of the summer.

"Like how?" she said.

"Well, since your nursery season is almost over, if you just could, like, help manage the farm, just till Zebra's back..."

"No. I can't do that."

"With Juano and Arnold knowing everything, it shouldn't be that big a deal..."

"No, Bodie. I'm not going to be here."

Bodie blinked and flexed his jaw back and forth. He looked as if he'd just been sucker punched. "Say what?"

"Remember Marlys? My old professor? She wants me to do field work around Mount Adams for a couple of weeks. I told her I'd do it."

Bodie choked his glass with both hands. His jaw had quit moving and Nu saw a mean stitch at the corner of his lips. "Wow. That *is* news. You're going to go count marigolds with Marlys. Hey, thanks for telling me about that."

"She just called me a week ago. I've been thinking it over. Marlys says there might be a job for me in the fall, too, but I'm not making any plans."

"No plans! No plans! Doesn't that sound nice? Sis, we can't run a farm without plans. Planting plans, irrigation plans, time sheets. And now I've got building plans, permits! Fleece and I are going to have a baby, for chrissake. And we've got this once-in-a-lifetime opportunity to make a decent income from this sorry-assed farm, and do something important for the planet at the same time..."

"For the planet?! Jesus, Bodie. I will grant you that your little scheme for growing hops is pretty cool. Good for you. But local beer to save the planet? You're over the edge there, little brother."

"Yeah, maybe I am kind of naïve, thinking my family might stand behind me. But at least I'm not sending my customers home with pretty flowers full of poison."

"Look, asshole, I used a small amount of an entirely legal insecticide *once* to save a crop to make my loan payments on time. Which is something you haven't been doing lately."

Joe got up and stood behind Bodie and Fleece for a moment, putting a hand on each one's shoulder. Then he sidled around to stand behind Ursula. "Can't Juano pick up Zebra's work while she's off?" he asked.

"Juano is maxed out. We need more help here."

"Can't you hire someone else? How about Neville?"

Bodie snorted. "Neville sells car insurance, Dad. He hasn't farmed since high school."

Fleece reached around the table for the dirty plates, and Nu helped pass them to her. She got up and disappeared into the kitchen.

"Look, Pop, are you okay with Ursula just walking out on you like that? You need somebody..."

"Not that you could be bothered," Ursula hissed.

"You are so tight-assed. No wonder Dexter dumped you."

Joe raised the palm of his hand toward Bodie. "That's enough. You'll have to find some other help. Maybe Nu can lend me a hand while Ursula's in the mountains. Would you stick around for a few weeks, Nu?"

Nu felt anger swarming inside him. Everyone was taking his role in this family drama for granted. This was the bad side of belonging. But what could he say? He looked toward Joe and nodded.

Bodie glared at Ursula. "Were you going to even ask me about it?"

"Bodie, did you ask me when you went off to play football? You left home, you left the farm, you left this family, and you never came back once for six fucking years. You nearly missed your own mother's funeral. And now suddenly you're running the place. Well, you can have it." Ursula grabbed a couple of brownies, angrily wrapped them in a paper napkin, and pushed herself out of her chair. As she marched past Bodie toward the kitchen, she added, "*If* you can pay off all your loans."

Part II

July 2008

19 · Ursula

Ursula was down on elbows and knees, surveying a plot. A hot breeze raked across the south-facing slope, and shards of basalt bit into her skin. Ursula paid them no mind. She was completely focused on the flora. Some of the plants growing on this exposed, thin-soiled, high-elevation site were stunted and sun-burnt, but many of them were perfectly at home here. And there was a wondrous variety of species. It fascinated her, how harsh conditions sometimes increased the diversity among plants, where tiny variations in soil composition, shade, or moisture created very different microbiomes in close proximity.

She was only supposed to be counting the food species here— huckleberries and elderberries primarily—but she couldn't help admiring all the outliers. Here was an old half-dead manzanita bonsai'd by the wind. And here a seedling juniper as tiny and delicate as a fern. Lanceleaf and spreading stonecrop. Payson's Whitlow-grass. A yellow lomatium, probably *martinandalei*. Not to mention all the immaculate lichens clinging to the rocks, and even a few burnt-looking mosses, a gorgeous array of plants no home gardener could ever hope to emulate.

From behind her and just downslope, Valerie asked, "Got any numbers for me?"

Ursula stood and grinned down at her field partner. "I think we got all the targets. I was just ogling the extras."

"I noticed."

Valerie's all-business attitude seemed to bring out a wayward streak in Ursula, a willingness to steal a few moments from science for beauty. She stood up and looked off to the south at Mount Hood, its snowy heights sporting a pale-pink ring of cloud that perfectly encircled the summit. "Oh, my god," Ursula said. "Look at Wy'east!"

Valerie glanced over her shoulder "Yep, still there."

Ah, another jaded grad student, Ursula thought. She doesn't know how lucky she is to be here.

Ursula consulted their map and cross-referenced their location with the GPS device. The next sample plot was a couple hundred yards across the slope, around the curve of the mountain in a more gently sloping, east-facing drainage. The two women picked their way around a dense copse of alpine fir and waded through tangled thickets of manzanita. As they rounded the slope, they passed out of direct sunlight, and the temperature dropped ten degrees. Ursula realized that even with her sunglasses on, she'd been squinting all day. She pushed her bush hat off and let it hang on her back, then removed her sunglasses and rubbed her eyes. She heard a small stream burbling deep in the draw below them.

This was the final plot they'd survey today. It was mostly waist-high bushes of *Holodiscus discolor*, ocean spray, with huckleberry and elderberry interspersed. It wouldn't take long. "Last plot is yours," Ursula said, reaching out to take the data logger from Valerie.

Valerie sighed and pushed her way into the dense vegetation. "One *V. membranaceum*," she called out. "One *Sambucus racemosa*."

Half an hour later, they had climbed back up to the old log landing where they'd parked the car. Marlys and D'lanta were already there. D'lanta had dropped her jungle fatigues to her ankles and was slathering poison oak lotion on the inside of her thighs. "Fuckin' shit is driving me crazy," she said, then looked up and grinned. "But did you see that doughnut cloud on the top of Mount Hood? God, that was so cool."

"Wasn't it gorgeous?" Ursula said. "Almost the same color as your calamine."

"Did you make it to all your plots?" Marlys asked.

"Yep. Fifteen today, half a million to go," Ursula answered. "Valerie drove me like a mule."

"Or a graduate student," Valerie said, smirking at her.

"Same difference," Marlys said, as she chucked her daypack into the back end of her dust-plastered SUV. "Let's load 'em up. Who's cooking tonight?"

"You are," Valerie said. "What are we having?"

Marlys lifted her eyes in fake surprise. "Is it really my turn? Well, okay, I guess we're having pb and j's."

D'lanta groaned and threw the plastic bottle of calamine at her.

Marlys, cat-quick, caught it and tossed it in the car. "Salmon," she said. "Wild caught. With capers and olive tapanade. If you're good."

She threw her ball cap into the car, shook out her seriously tangled curls, and blew a kiss toward each of them. "Which you are. Verily."

Ursula pulled off her heavy boots and sweaty socks and slipped into her sandals. "You guys should go ahead," she told them. "I need to call home."

The three women got into Marlys's rig and headed for their camp, a couple of drainages to the west and a thousand feet lower. Ursula guzzled from her water bottle, and found a granola bar in the cargo pocket of her field pants. Now that the day's work was done, she realized how tired she was. Muscle-tingling, bone-buzzing tired. Many of the plots they'd sampled today had been on brutally steep slopes. Her glutes and thighs were beyond sore. And she had some poison oak on her right forearm. Not in her crotch, luckily, like D'lanta had it, and not between her fingers, the absolute worst.

She wouldn't mention her weariness on the phone. She'd tell her dad she was fine. Which was true. She was just fine. Happy to be in the mountains. (And *away* from home, another thing she would not mention to Joe.) She scooched up onto the hood of her pickup and punched Joe's number.

After five rings, she got the answering machine. "Tunder residence. Leave us a message."

It must be ten years since her father had recorded that, Ursula realized. His voice had been so much clearer and stronger then.

"Hi, Dad. It's me. I'll try back in a few. Love you! Bye."

It was nearly 7 already, later than she'd said she'd call. But there were plenty of innocent reasons why Joe might not answer the phone. He was in the bathroom. Or out on the deck. Whatever. She'd hang loose here for ten or fifteen minutes and try again. The setting sun blazed above the Coast Range in the west, a blaring orange ball. Tilting her bush hat to screen the low rays, she studied Wy'east looming before her to the south. The bangle cloud had come undone and now streamed off to the east like a wind-blown scarf.

Ursula shucked off her long-sleeved shirt and rolled up her pant legs. She scooted farther up the hood of the truck. The sun-warmed metal felt good on her aching butt. She leaned back against the windshield, closed her eyes, and let the sunlight massage her tired body. It had been another good day. She liked working with this all-woman crew. They were all so different. D'Ianta was tireless and ebullient, always chattering about friends and family, while Valerie was just the opposite. Valerie could sit in her camp chair reading by flashlight, and Ursula would be lucky if she saw Valerie so much as turn a page. It was a little creepy how inert she could seem. Last evening in camp she'd walked up to the folding kitchen table as Valerie meticulously chopped veggies for a stir fry. Nothing but her hands moved. Valerie had one ear bud in and the other one dangling, and Ursula heard the propulsive rhymes of an angry-voiced rapper. But Valerie's face was neutral, her lips firm and straight, no particular tension showing in her eyes. Ursula paused beside her, planning to ask if she wanted help with dinner. But Valerie did not look up, so Ursula let her be.

Now she roused herself and dialed home again.

"Hallo," Joe answered.

"Hi, Daddy, how're you doing?"

"Still breathing."

"Any doctor news? Are you feeling okay?"

"No complaints."

"Good. How is Bodie doing?"

"Haven't seen him. Must be fine."

"And Nu? What's he up to?"

"Oh, he's out and about. Cutting willows for a wickiup he's building."

"A what?"

"He can show you when you get home. When's that gonna be?"

Ursula had told her father before she left for the mountains that she would come home in a week. It had already been ten days. She really didn't want to get sucked back into any family dramas, and she'd been thinking about asking if he'd be okay with her putting it off for another week. But now she was curious about Nu's project, and she probably should go down for a quick visit while things were on an even keel. She needed to restock her food supply, anyway.

"Friday. I'll be home for the weekend."

"Alright. Well, we can catch up then."

"I'll be late, so don't wait dinner for me. Love you, Dad. See you day after tomorrow," Ursula said, and folded her phone.

The sunlight was waning, but she still wanted to take a dip on the way back to camp. She was smelly and crusty with sweat and dust. There was a little lake just off the road a couple miles back. The mosquitoes would be bad, but she really needed a quick rinse.

Ursula drove downhill and parked in a pullout along the road. She grabbed her towel with her change of underwear rolled up in it, and followed a well-trodden path fifty yards or so to the lake. She wouldn't use any soap in this pretty alpine lake, she'd just rub off the grime with her calloused hands. She unlaced her boots and tugged off her clothes as fast as she could, knowing the mosquitoes would soon be on her. And here they came, instantly and in numbers, harrying her about the legs, arms, face. She didn't bother to slap at them—it was hopeless. She walked quickly but deliberately, so as not to stub a toe, into the lake.

The water was glorious. Chilly, not cold. The bottom was mucky, but the muck was just a few inches deep, with only a few sticks in it. Clean muck. She stepped carefully, trying not to stir it up too much. The bottom sloped evenly. In a dozen slow strides the water came up to her breasts. She crouched until her chin was level with the surface. No mosquitoes had followed her. She couldn't help thinking how fine it would be if the planet was rid of mosquitoes. The ecologist in her knew better, but there it was.

The loud branch-cracking sound from the woods to her left startled her. Her toes clenched in the squishy lake bottom and her calves tightened. She kept her head low to the water, scanning the shadows along the shoreline. The sound was made by a deer, most likely, or possibly a cougar or bear. There was only one kind of animal she was truly afraid of, especially with her clothing piled on the shore: men.

But it was a bear. Ursula let out a quiet sigh. Her left calf had been on the verge of cramping. She shifted her weight to her right leg and gently flexed. The bear ambled along the lakeshore, chuffing and grunting as if talking to herself, loudly sniffing the evening air. When she found Ursula's clothes, she nosed them around. In the dim light Ursula could see the bear pick up something light-colored, her sports bra probably, and mouth it.

Since Ursula was mostly underwater, she figured the scent of her dirty clothes was far stronger than her own smell. The bear was not likely to notice her. If she rose up and shouted, the bear would almost certainly take off running. But that would be rude and possibly dangerous—a startled bear could do something stupid. And besides, now that she was past her fright, Ursula wanted to watch the bear, even if she was eating her underwear.

When Ursula heard more rustling from the woods, she was glad she hadn't shouted. She knew what made those sounds and now she was frightened again. Not panicked and adrenalin-flooded as a few moments ago, just soberly, alertly scared, as two cubs trundled out of the woods. A sow with cubs was another animal altogether. One of the cubs scampered up to its mother and tried to take Ursula's bra from her mouth. The other one dug his snout into the mother's belly, as if wanting to nurse. They were surprisingly small for this far into summer, Ursula thought, not much bigger than cocker spaniels.

The mother bear peered out into the lake. She lifted her head to snuffle the air. Oddly, Ursula's fear had vanished. She felt as if she were just part of the lake now, kin to the bears and the cedar and firs and the mountains surrounding them. Whether minutes elapsed, or just a few seconds, Ursula had no idea. The bears ambled along the shore and gradually disappeared back into the forest, but Ursula didn't move. In fact, she *couldn't* move. She couldn't find her feet or her hands. She was too large and dispersed, just a body of water. Finally she felt a spark glowing deep inside her, an embryo of grief-and-joy that gradually grew back into her renewed body. She waded ashore, retrieved her bear-chewed sports bra, found her towel and her clean clothes undisturbed where she'd set them on a log, and dressed slowly, as if in a dream. She was crying quietly, though she wasn't sure why.

That evening, Ursula and Marlys outlasted the grad students for once, talking quietly by the campfire till past 11. Finally, they doused the fire and headed for bed. They would have to get up at dawn to begin another long day in the field.

Their camp was at fifty-three hundred feet, so even though the daytime temps were in the upper seventies, there could be frost overnight. The temperature was already dropping fast and Ursula shivered as she undressed and shimmied into her sleeping bag. She was bone tired, but her mind was still awake. It had to be the tea. Valerie had shared a pot of green tea after supper, swearing it would help Ursula's body recover from the day's punishing labor. The tea had been delicious and soothing, and had in fact seemed to ease her weariness, but now she was keyed up. She'd probably have to crawl out in the night to pee, too, a real nuisance when you were zipped up tight in a mummy bag. She was glad she'd decided to pull her sleeping pad outside and bed down under the stars, though. If she couldn't go to sleep at least she could watch for shooting stars. She gazed up through the small oval opening in the surrounding conifers, where the sky was clotted with stars. That lacy mantilla of light across the center of her view would be the Milky Way.

Along with Valerie's caffeine, there were other things lighting up Ursula's mind, not the least of which was Marlys's epic good news. Marlys had taken a phone call out on the slopes this afternoon and learned that her grant would be renewed for two more years. She'd be able to synthesize all her data, keep her grad students employed, and extend the research to include not just food plants but fiber plants too. And she wanted to hire Ursula to head up the fiber plant research. Though Ursula couldn't imagine a better job, she'd told Marlys she'd have to think about it.

Ursula had not thought about the future in a long time. She hadn't been able to imagine any good futures, so she hadn't tried. Now the future was beckoning. She would let herself imagine it tomorrow, but not tonight. Tonight she needed to sleep.

She did not want to think about the bears now, either. She had surprised herself by not saying a word to the other women about the intimate visitation. She wasn't sure why she was feeling so protective of her experience, but she somehow knew that it was better to keep it to herself. She could see the bears even now, the sow and her two small cubs, at the periphery of her thoughts, but she was afraid that if she looked at them directly, if she tried to affix some meaning to the encounter, they'd disappear for good. So she stared into the night sky instead.

The late-risen gibbous moon backlit the branches of the old mountain hemlocks that stretched overhead, their ink-dark limbs etched onto the sky like dendritic calligraphy. She felt herself drifting off. She was back at home, leaning behind Nu again as he drew his map of the farm, gazing at his smooth-skinned shoulders, at the pine tree tattooed on his back. The tree began to move, its limbs reaching out from Nu's back, slowly encircling her until she was totally wrapped up in its branches.

20 · Bodie

Sweat pours off Bodie's forehead, pooling and stinging at the corners of his eyes, while his ears, inside the bulbous noise protectors, feel like they're being boiled. He'd like to ditch the muffs, but the roar of the tractor is deafening. Arnold keeps the John Deere's engine revved high, the augur turning fast. They sheared a bolt while drilling their second hole this morning, when Arnold tried to push the augur too hard into the ground. Bodie had a spare bolt in the shop, fortunately, and now he's told Arnold to keep the rpms under 2,200.

Bodie glances up at the sun, a prickly, yellow thistle overhead, then looks down at his watch: 12:22. It must be ninety degrees already, way hotter than normal for this early in July.

This additional acre of trellis will double the size of Bodie's hop yard. He and Arnold have already dug more than half of the eighty-one holes. He'd figured it would take them two full days to drill all the holes, but at this rate, if Arnold is willing to work late, they may be able to complete the job by early evening. The soil moisture is ideal for digging. Bodie watches the dirt, his beautiful class 1 Chehalis silt loam, spool up light and friable from the augur. He shakes his head for the hundredth time at the thought of the stupendous ice age Missoula floods that roared down the Columbia, eddying seventy miles up the Willamette Valley and depositing six feet of this luscious soil on the valley floor. Lucky the farmer who gets to grow food in the spoils of that colossal disaster.

His hop plants, rooted cuttings he started himself, are growing nicely in a big cloche behind his house, ready to be transplanted in the fall. The twenty-foot-long pressure-treated poles for the trellis are stacked in several big piles out beside the driveway. He can already imagine the poles in place, the cable strung between them and the hop vines twining up the guide strings, the foliage spreading into a resinous and fragrant canopy overhead.

Building hop trellis one acre at a time is not cost effective, but it's all he can afford for now. *More* than he can afford at the moment. He has not made any payment on his past-due account with Cascade Farm Supply for months, and they won't ship his trellising cable until he pays up. He told his family that Bob Brundidge was fronting him money to put in more hops, but that was a stretcher. He's been pressing Brundidge to partner up with him, and he *is* hopeful, but no deal has been finalized.

Bodie mops his brow with a filthy bandana. He could be running the tractor himself, make Arnold do the hand work. He *is* the boss, after all, the owner of the show, the supposedly big kahuna. But Arnold is so happy on the tractor, and Bodie feels some satisfaction in how well the sketchy vet has succeeded at working on the farm. Plus, Bodie doesn't really mind digging. Hard manual labor keeps him from thinking. From worrying. Anyway, he's not sure he'd trust Arnold to measure the depth of each hole properly. Bodie has wrapped a ring of electrical tape on the shaft of the augur at the four-foot depth. When the augur has drilled down so the tape is level with the ground—a judgment call, since loose soil mounds up around the hole—Bodie gives Arnold a throat-slit signal. Then, while Arnold lifts the augur and moves the tractor twenty feet down the line and gets in position to bore the next hole, Bodie scoops out the remaining loose soil with the clamshell digger and confirms to his satisfaction the hole's final depth.

Bodie suddenly feels woozy with the heat. Digging may keep him from thinking, but it's torturing his back. The posthole digger should have longer handles so he could keep his lower back straight. As it is, he can't really get his legs under the lift. He has to lean over and hoist the soil with arms, shoulders, and lower back. His erector muscles are screaming. He straightens up, rolls his shoulders, and stretches his neck up and back, but his head starts to spin and he nearly falls over backwards. He steadies himself with the posthole digger until his head stops spinning.

Arnold is staring his way, the tractor already positioned to begin the next hole. Bodie staggers over and eyeballs the augur for vertical.

He pushes the shaft toward the tractor a few degrees, then nods okay, and Arnold engages the power takeoff.

Bodie stares groggily as the augur bores into the earth, the spiral of steel twisting deeper and deeper into the ground. He tries to ward off thinking about his debts, but he feels himself being augured in. For the past two years, Fleece has kept the books for the farm, and she's the one who deals with Gary, their accountant. But last month she'd insisted that Bodie come along for her meeting with Gary and get up to speed on their finances. He wasn't sure whether this was Fleece clearing some bandwidth to deal with pregnancy and motherhood, or Fleece getting him to face up to just how bad their fiscal situation was. Either way, it had been a sobering experience, depressing even, as Gary walked them through the numbers. With their present income, they could probably cover expenses for four, maybe five more months.

In the past he and Fleece had played some minor shell games with their money, moving chunks here and there to cover short-term debts, or to pick up a few points in interest. But the shells are all empty now. Worse than that: under every shell is another debt. By autumn, he'll be unable to pay anything toward his bills with several building supply outfits. Unable to make his payments on the tractor. Unable to cover the payments on his Farm Credit Union operating loan. Unable even to make payroll. The thought of not paying his employees makes his stomach churn.

Arnold draws the augur out of the latest hole and waits for Bodie to check it for depth. Bodie isn't sure he can lift another ounce of dirt. He chucks the clamshell digger into the hole and saws a finger at his throat, signaling Arnold to shut the tractor down. It's time for lunch. Bodie watches as Arnold ambles over to the pickup, switches his ear protectors for his headset radio, grabs his box of leftover pizza from the cab and, juking to the music, disappears around the front of the hop barn.

In the sudden quiet, Bodie shucks his own ear muffs and mops his face with the damp bandana. He's afraid he may be getting sick. He has a headache coming on and his throat feels swollen. He plods over to the pickup, retrieves a water bottle from the cab, and guzzles down most of a quart. From the passenger's seat, he grabs a plastic bag containing his lunch. He leans wearily on the tailgate, draws out a stale bagel, a slab of cheddar cheese, a slender English cucumber, and half a dozen Early Girl tomatoes. Alternating bites, he chews through the food without tasting any of it. Ten minutes and he's finished. At the spigot beside the back door to the hop barn, he splashes his face, then returns to lean on the tailgate.

He knows it could be a mistake to even sit down. Weariness is always just one step behind him these days, and threatening to catch up. If it gets to him now, it could swallow him whole. Weariness, like a human-sized leech, sucking him dry.

In the past, he has only felt such muscle fatigue after football games. But back then, within hours or a day at the most, that leaden feeling would pass and his body would begin to lighten again. This is different. This hasn't let up for weeks. He wakes up tired and aching in the morning and two cups of coffee only puts a thin buzz on top of his fatigue. His twitching calf muscles wake him up at night. Even drinking doesn't lighten his mood or his step. He had two beers last night, hoping a little alcohol would give him the energy to pay some bills, but he fell asleep in his recliner. If his sciatica hadn't stabbed him awake after an hour, he might have slept there all night.

On top of being weary, Bodie has to admit that he's lonely. Lonelier than he can ever recall being. Fleece has been away all week, gone to take care of her mother, who's suffering a flare-up of shingles.

He'd practically pleaded with her not to leave him. "This is a really bad time for you to be gone," he had whined.

"Uh-huh," Fleece had replied, giving him her sternest look. "It wasn't very thoughtful of my mother to end up in the hospital right now, was it?"

If he has ever doubted how much Fleece is responsible for keeping the farm together, the past four days have refreshed his memory. On top of his own impossible load of chores, he has had to assume all the tasks that Fleece routinely and uncomplainingly takes care of. Fleece tends the chickens and sheep. Fleece cooks, cleans, and does most of the laundry. And especially, Fleece takes care of all of the farm's marketing, ordering, billing, and bill paying. These are all tasks that he has promised her he will take care of in her absence but, aside from feeding the animals, he hasn't kept up with any of them.

And with Ursula gone to play scientist in the mountains, he's had to help out his father more, too. Bodie took Joe to the doctor on Monday and sat for most of an hour in the waiting room. He had tried to do some business on his cell phone, then gave up and dozed with a *Sports Illustrated* splayed out on his chest.

But worse than all of the extra chores he's had to pick up, Bodie just misses Fleece. He misses hugging her, smelling her skin, feeling her boobs squashed against his chest. He misses her every tone of voice, from her melodious low and absent-minded humming when she's happy to her raw and booming profanity when she's pissed. He misses her brown eyes. He's never really thought about it before, but Fleece has a way of taking things in with her eyes, like she's visually inhaling her surroundings. Fleece doesn't so much look out from her eyes, he realizes, as she welcomes the world in. Oh, she can turn her eyes into probes, needles, even truncheons if she needs to, if she comes up against someone being mean or stupid or hostile. But at home with Bodie, she is usually gentle toward him and toward everything. She fondles her gathered bundles of lavender and grasses hanging from her ceiling racks. She pets her skeins of yarn. She nuzzles tomatoes, melons, figs as if they were old friends, dear friends she is going to properly adore before she eats them. She practices adoration, Bodie realizes with a jolt. She loves the world bodily, with her hands and her nose and her tongue and, especially, with her eyes. She drinks the world in through her eyes. And Bodie misses being drunk by her.

He forgets to love the world sometimes. In fact, the world has always seemed like an adversary. The world is the opposing team, right? And with a roster that deep, the world is not going to be beaten. The challenge is in how brilliantly you play in defeat, how smart and skillful and athletic you can be as the world beats the crap out of you.

After half an hour, Arnold comes back and climbs onto the tractor, and Bodie picks up the postholer, and on they go. He staggers through the afternoon in a near delirium, saved by his old athlete's habit of drinking tons of water. After every few holes, he refills his bottle from the standpipe by the hop barn. He remembers one of his coaches saying there are always deeper levels of energy that one can tap. Quiet the mind and the body will find them. He knows that to be true. But he wonders what the cost might be if the body draws too deeply on those reserves. Is the reservoir finite? Can it be sucked dry?

Finally, hours later, Arnold throttles the tractor down to idle and looks inquiringly at Bodie. Bodie doesn't know what the problem might be, then looks around and realizes: they're done. The last hole has been drilled. He signals Arnold with a vigorous thumbs-up and mouths "Thank you!" Arnold returns a crisp, military salute, pauses to trade his ear muffs for his headset radio, then throttles up and puts the tractor into gear. As Bodie starts to gather the tools, tossing posthole digger and shovels into the pickup, he sees Arnold backing up, wheeling faster than he should toward hop barn. Without slowing much, Arnold hits the right wheel break and cranks the steering wheel, pivoting the tractor ninety degrees.

Bodie has a premonition of what's about to happen. Before he can shout, he watches the augur, daggling from its three-point hitch, swing out from the vertical and clip the water spigot beside the barn. Water gushes up waist high from the shattered standpipe.

"Stop!" Bodie shouts. But Arnold is oblivious. Bopping to the beats from his headset, Arnold grinds the tractor into a forward gear and hurtles off toward the equipment shed.

21 · Nu

Kneeling beside the trench, Nu glued a PVC coupling onto the arm's-length section of new pipe. He was covered in mud, his lower back ached, and his thumb throbbed where he'd raked the hacksaw blade over the meat of it. Digging up the broken pipe to repair the break had taken twice as long as it should have. Nu had hoped to be finished before lunch and have a few hours in the afternoon to work on his wickiup. But nothing had gone as planned. Now it was late afternoon, and the sun, reflecting off the side of the hop barn, was cooking him. Sweat was streaming into his eyes, but the sleeves of his T-shirt were so muddy he knew better than to mop his face. Even for a Fresno boy, a desert rat who loved the heat, the glaring sun was brutal.

Last night he had been on the back deck sketching the wickiup he was planning to weave out of willow branches. He had a place in mind for the brush shelter, on a grassy bank just above the river. After failing for weeks to get going on an art project, he was excited by the idea of a wickiup and eager to get started.

That was when Bodie showed up, trudging around the side of the house, mud on his boots and overalls, mud smeared on his haggard face. Arnold had busted a standpipe, Bodie told him. He had to shut off the water to the whole barn. Would Nu help him fix it early tomorrow morning? Please.

What could he say? Okay. He would help.

Then, when he'd met up with Bodie at the barn at 6 this morning, Bodie was looking more worn down and defeated than he'd ever seen him. Bodie told Nu he was really, really sorry, but he needed to go to Yoncalla and pick up Fleece from her mother's. Fleece was not doing well. Depressed, maybe. Some pregnancy thing. Nothing serious but she wanted him to come and get her. So, could Nu...?

It took Nu all morning to expose the broken pipe. Enough water had gushed out to quagmire the whole area. Hand-digging the sticky, shovel-sucking mud was grueling. The clay stuck to the shovel to such an extent that Nu had to fetch a piece of old plywood to bang his spade on, to make each heavy glob let go. It would have been a lot easier if he could have waited two days for the mud to set up, but Bodie couldn't be without water in the barn that long. His crew already had to run hoses from the big house to the packing shed in order to wash this morning's veggie harvest for market. Nu had heard them complaining as he loaded his shovels and plumbing tools into a wheelbarrow.

He had to get out of this situation. He had not come here to be everybody's grunt. The farm was a sinking ship, and Bodie was just delusional if he thought he could make it sail. Clearly Ursula wanted out. And Joe, Joe had pretty much given up. He was just waiting to die. Every once in a while Nu saw glimmers of life, like last night when Joe got interested in his willow sculptures. But mostly Joe just napped in his recliner or moped around the house.

Nu didn't mind taking Joe to appointments. He didn't mind cooking and housekeeping. He didn't even mind helping Bodie around the farm, or Cat in the greenhouse. But altogether, it was eating him up. He didn't have any friends here except Andy. And he didn't have any time to make art. Or, if he had a few hours here and there, he didn't have any clarity. Any vision. All he had was an awful itch inside, some serious, nerve-twitching friction between where he was and where he wanted to be.

Which was, where? Bend? Fresno? An unnamed canyon in the Black Rock desert?

Now that his criminal charges had been dropped, he could certainly go back to Bend. He'd never given much credence to the threats against him, but with the bike-and-gun crowd, you never could be sure. Still, the ruckus over his *Off-Road Vehicle* exhibit would have died down by now.

Nu applied solvent, then cement, to the final fitting, the slip-joint that would marry his new pipe section to the old main line. Soon he could backfill. Lying on his belly with his head over the open trench, he slid the fitting into place. A perfect fit. He held the joint together for a minute while it dried. Then he wiped his hands as best he could with a muddy rag and, sitting on the ground beside the trench, ate an apple left over from lunch. He needed to give the cement a few more minutes to set up firmly before he started backfilling.

Just then Joe came stalking around the side of the hop barn, his scarred face scowling. "We were due at the doctor's twenty minutes ago."

Nu banged his fist on his forehead and threw his apple core in the hole. "Oh, fuck, Joe, I'm so sorry. I..."

Joe turned and lurched away. "I'll be in the truck."

They'd gotten to the doctor's office forty minutes late. Joe was still apologizing to the receptionist when a woman in pink scrubs opened the door to the inner offices and called his name. Joe followed her, not even looking back at Nu.

Nu took a chair near the entry. He knew he was pretty dirty, but now he took stock. He had streaks of dirt all down his bare arms. His hands were still muddy, and the bandage he'd wrapped around the cut on his left thumb was completely brown. His jeans were filthy, his boots looked like they'd been dipped in a mud fondue. An older woman sitting across from him looked at him as if he smelled bad, which was entirely possible, then cast her eyes toward the entry door. No denying who'd left those muddy footprints.

Joe had a right to be angry at him, Nu supposed. He'd completely forgotten about Joe's appointment. In truth, Nu was kind of glad to see Joe get riled up. Joe had been so listless and depressed lately. He had hardly been out of the house since Ursula left. He hadn't even filled the bird feeders. He had tried to interest Joe in watching some baseball games together, but the Mariners were on a long losing streak and playing miserably. Joe said he couldn't bear to watch them.

Nu took off his boots and set them out in the foyer, then asked the receptionist if there was a restroom he could use. He washed his arms and hands and removed the bandage from his thumb. The hacksaw wound was ragged and dirty and began bleeding again as he scrubbed some of the mud out. He couldn't see any first-aid supplies, and he sure wasn't going to ask. But he did find an antiseptic towelette to drape over the cut, and there was a box of disposable vinyl examination gloves on the counter. He stuck his fingers into a glove and rolled the cuff carefully onto his hand. It held the towelette in place and made a decent temporary dressing.

He returned in his sock feet to the waiting room, grateful that the glowering old lady was no longer there. He picked up a copy of *Time* magazine, then closed his eyes and sighed. He imagined packing his clothes up and driving to Bend, settling back into his studio space, facing once again the blank canvas he was supposed to fill for the Furmans.

The nurse opened the inner door just then and summoned him. Shaking his head to clear his thoughts, Nu followed the nurse into one of the examination rooms. Joe, in a chair against the wall, didn't look up at Nu. The oncologist, Dr. Sable, if Nu remembered correctly, sat at a desk with a computer monitor turned to face them. Nu could see what looked like a chest X-ray on the screen.

"Nu, thanks for joining us," Dr. Sable said. "Joe agreed it would be good to have another family member here for this. Okay?"

Nu was still shaky from his day-long ordeal trying to repair Bodie's pipe, and still embarrassed about forgetting Joe's appointment. He had no idea what was coming, but he nodded okay.

"So, you want to hear it straight and simple, right, Joe?" Dr. Sable asked. "Well, here are the facts. Your cancer has spread. It's metastasized into your lymph system and lungs. See these little white spots, here, and here?" He pointed with a pen to the features on the X-ray. They could have been fly specks on the monitor glass for all Nu could tell.

Joe looked sideways toward Nu. He took a breath as if he were going to ask for Nu's opinion. Then he turned back to Sable. "Sounds untreatable."

"No, no. There are things we can do. We can step up the chemotherapy or try some more radiation..."

Joe raised his hand to stop him. "I meant to say 'uncurable,'" he said. "You can treat me to death, I understand that. But I'm not going to beat this, right?"

"It's a question of time, Joe. How much time you may have, and how you want to spend it."

Nu missed some of the details that came next. He must have zoned out, in denial or panic or something. But the upshot, he gathered, was that with aggressive treatments, Joe could probably live six to nine months, a year at the outside. If he stopped treatments, they could keep him comfortable and reasonably pain-free, but he'd only have months.

"How many months?" Joe asked.

"Three, tops. Probably less." Dr. Sable said. "Why don't you go home, talk to your kids, and think about how you want to proceed."

"Been thinking about it for a couple of years now, Doc. I'm done. I'm interested in your pain meds, but no more chemo, thanks."

22 · Ursula

Ever since Ursula had come home from the mountains, Joe had been in surprisingly good spirits. "I like having a project," he'd told her.

Only Joe. Only her scarred-up, burnt-out welder, widower, and sometime artist father would think of dying as a "project." It had brought her to the edge of tears, where she'd teetered all day.

After lunch Joe insisted on going over the plan for his funeral and the provisions of his will. He said he was leaving some money and a few artworks to Nu, and the rest would be divided evenly between her and Bodie. Ursula knew that Bodie was reeling over Joe's imminent death, barely keeping up with the unrelenting farm work. He had

finally admitted defeat, though, accepted that he wouldn't be able
to service his debts, so they'd all be able to move on now. The farm
would be sold to the university. Divvying up their father's assets
would be fairly straightforward.

Bart, the hospice nurse, arrived late in the afternoon. The three of
them sat at the kitchen table while Bart described the pros and cons
of the various pain meds available to Joe—Roxanol, Oxycontin,
Dilaudid—as casually as if they were looking over a menu at a nice
restaurant.

"I might try them all," Joe said.

Bart smiled kindly and answered, "You probably will."

It kind of bugged her, actually, how chummy those two were acting.
She didn't feel as if *she* could be in good spirits. She was supposed to
be serious and businesslike, with a sad, grave demeanor, wasn't she?
And she didn't like their gallows humor, either. Bart was a good guy,
she could tell, and an excellent nurse. She just wished somebody else
would help her carry some of the grief around here.

Just two weeks ago, up in the mountains, she'd felt at the top of
her game. Doing field work. Sleeping under the stars. Encountering
those beautiful bears. Like camping with pay, Nu had called it. But it
was even better than that. It was camping with high purpose. Trying
to describe the impacts of logging and road building, decipher the
signals of climate change, puzzle out complex plant-animal interac-
tions. She'd loved sharing that rugged, purposeful life with her tiny
band of competent, independent women.

Well, that was over, at least for this summer. And in truth, Ursula
knew she'd never have quite that experience again. She'd already
had it twice in her life, her first time as a grad student and then
again, ever so briefly, two weeks ago. Now her days were going to
be seriously constrained. More so than ever. Joe kept telling her to
go back to the mountains, but she wasn't going anywhere. She was
staying home with her father. She wanted this time to be with him,
to just look at him, to touch him, and maybe even talk with him.
Talk about all the stuff they'd hidden or skipped over all their lives.
About how they both missed Alice. About how much it had hurt
Ursula when she'd lost her pregnancy.

On the other hand, she had to admit that her father's good humor was pretty inspiring. She couldn't imagine it would last. Gruff old Joe was sure to resurface. The ogre would return to rule his moods in the coming days, weeks, months. To help her cope with those trials, she was grateful that hospice would be on hand. She'd appreciated how matter-of-factly Bart had outlined the administration of Joe's many medications, his options for massage, counseling, dietary advice. Hospice would send a volunteer musician to sing songs for Joe if he wanted. (He didn't, of course.) It was really impressive what an array of services they provided. Healthy people should be offered such decency.

If she concentrated on the process and avoided looking too hard toward the end result, she knew she'd be okay. It would be like climbing the ladder to the cupola. You focused on the ladder rungs, and you tried not to look down.

When Joe decided to take a late-afternoon nap, Ursula used the free time to fold the laundry. It appeared that none of Joe's clothes had been washed while she was in the mountains, much less any towels or bed linens. So this morning she had changed Joe's sheets, sorted through the overflowing hamper of clothes, and washed three loads. She felt guilty putting them in the clothes dryer on this hot summer day, but she just didn't have the energy or the time to hang things on the line.

Now, as she folded Joe's old khakis, she noticed how neatly patched at the knees they were. Her mother's long-ago handiwork. His blue chambray work shirt was threadbare and soft. She held it up and rubbed it to her cheek and had to squeeze back tears.

There were a few of Nu's clothes in the mix—two pairs of shorts, one of blue jeans, a couple of T-shirts—which she folded and set aside. But most of the clothes were her own, from the duffel bag of dirties she'd brought back from her time in the field. She folded tank tops. Tossed bras and panties in a heap. She smoothed the wrinkles from her favorite sage-green cotton blouse, then folded her cotton-poly field pants. She loved those pants. All the nifty pockets were just a fashion affectation for most of the kids who wore them on campus, but in the field she used them all, for carrying nut mix and granola bars, for stashing plant samples or unfamiliar mushrooms she'd take back to key out in camp.

She folded a tan T-shirt and tossed it on the pile with her other shirts, then picked it back up and inspected it. It wasn't hers; it was one of Nu's. It had a line drawing of animals, woolly mammoths, maybe, from one of those Paleolithic caves in France. Incredibly lifelike. She checked the label. Men's medium. They wore the same size. She refolded it, thought for a moment, then placed it on her own pile.

She carried the clothes upstairs and put hers away, then paused before the door to the guest room, her childhood bedroom. Nu's room. She hadn't been in it since he'd left, and she really didn't know whether he had taken everything back to Bend with him, or if he'd left some of his things behind. She paused at the door, wondering if she were trespassing. How would she have felt if Nu had gone into her room when she was gone? Honestly? The thought of it gave her a little thrill. What would he be looking for? Oh, he'd just be snooping around, trying to get a glimpse into her private life, a whiff of her secret self. Was there anything in her room she would not want him to discover? Not really. It embarrassed her to have to say so, but if she had a secret inner life that she wouldn't want discovered, she couldn't think of any evidence of it. She had never kept a diary, for instance. Whatever photos she'd saved were in albums downstairs, available to anyone bored enough to peruse them.

No, there was one thing. A small box of baby clothes. When she got pregnant, her friends had given her tons of baby things, boxes and boxes of clothes and toys suitable for newborn, infant, toddler. She'd gotten rid of almost all of them soon after the miscarriage, one of the few tasks she'd managed to complete in those weeks of house-bound depression. But she had saved a few special pieces. A pair of tiny booties that Becca had knitted, one pink and one blue. A set of three onesies her mother had gotten her on the last shopping trip they'd done together before Alice died. Ursula's pregnancy had been a great joy to Alice, the only happy distraction in her rapid decline.

Nu would never find the box. It was on the highest shelf in her clothes closet. She hadn't taken it down since she stuck it up there. But if he did happen to find it, what would he think? He would know. He would understand.

She pushed open the door and went in. He hadn't taken everything.

She'd been holding her breath, she noticed, and now she almost laughed with relief. His weights were on the floor, along with a black yoga mat. Leaning in the corner, a walking stick with animal faces freshly carved into it. She was especially glad to see that the bird's-eye drawing of the farm was still on the drafting table.

His bed was made, casually. She picked up a pillow and sniffed it, smelling the faint earthy fragrance of his scalp. On the nightstand beside the bed was a novel, *Grapes of Wrath*. She knew the story from seeing the movie, but she was pretty sure she'd never read it. And under the novel was one of Nu's sketchbooks. She picked it up and sat on the bed with the sketchbook in her lap, considering. Why had he left it here? Was it okay to look inside? She turned it over and opened it from the back. There was a drawing on the last page, so the book was full. That's why he'd left it behind.

She turned to the beginning. The first couple of pages looked like a child's scribblings, like the kind of aimless loops one makes when trying to get the ink to flow again from a dried-up pen. The third page had a Celtic knot design, and further along there were many pages of woven baskets in every stage of completion. All the drawings of baskets seemed to be exercises, drawn quickly, unrevised. But even so, she could pretty well guess what materials Nu was depicting: the flat ribbons were cedar bark, the round, twiggy stems were maybe willow, and the fine, thin lengths would be grasses or reeds. Except for those strangely expressive chicken scratches on the first pages, there wasn't really anything personal revealed in the sketchbook. Except then, toward the very back of the book, she discovered a dozen or more sketches of long braids. Her braids.

After supper, Joe went into the living room to watch the Mariners game. Ursula rinsed the dishes and put them in the dishwasher. It was time to leave for yoga class, but she was too sad and rattled to go tonight. She poured another glass of wine and headed for the deck. On second thought, she went back to the fridge and grabbed the whole bottle. Whenever Bodie was over, she would pull out the cheap stuff because she knew it offended him. This Chablis was in a half-gallon bottle with the finger-hold on the neck, a sure marker of poor taste. But it wasn't half bad if it was really cold. She smiled to herself and flopped into a sling chair.

It was still hot out, but a hesitant breeze was nudging the oak leaves. Nu's makeshift screen still shaded the Bliss Fits' lamp, though a pall of artificial light fogged the upper canopy. They should move the deck to the front of the house, it occurred to her, to get away from that damned light. Not that it mattered now. She noticed the alyssum in one of her planters was wilting, so she dragged a hose over and watered everything.

There was something weird under the rhododendron. Bright blue. She stepped off the deck, went across the lawn, and bent down. Ah, it was that scrub jay from the picnic—no mistaking the scorched tail feathers—lying in the leaf litter, desiccated, its eyes eaten away by ants. It *was* a sign, just as Bodie had said. She couldn't say why, but the dead bird filled her with a weird sense of peace, or maybe resignation. It was probably just the wine, but in any case she was beginning to feel somewhat in tune with her fate. All would be well, one way or another. She heard a mallard quacking from the lake, mocking her, no doubt, and then a huge bird flew overhead, a blue heron, trailing impossibly long legs. She'd always imagined she'd do more bird watching on the farm, but somehow she'd forgotten. She drained her glass of wine, stuck her finger in the bottle handle, and wandered around the side of the house. She ambled along the drive and paused beside the hop barn. The evening air was still heavy, the sky braided with red contrails. Swallows—no, they were bats—stitched between the barn and the darkening trees in the yard. She thought about climbing back up to the cupola, but realized she was too tipsy. In any case, it wasn't a place she wanted to go alone.

Wandering farther along the drive, she heard Fleece's chickens palavering on their roosts, and a dog barking from the new subdivision to the west. As she approached Bodie's house, she stepped more deliberately, trying not to crunch the gravel. She had spoken to Bodie only briefly a couple of times since she'd gotten home, always focusing solely on Joe's medical care, and she sure didn't want to see him tonight. Whenever she recalled Bodie insinuating that Dexter had had reason to "dump her," her anger flared up afresh. With her free hand, she gave the house the finger.

She followed the drive down the bluff. The road was rutted, and her sandals didn't have the best grip. A cobble rolled under her foot, and her ankle tweaked. She staggered, but caught herself. She hadn't been in the bottom for a while. Not for months, now that she thought of it, not since she'd helped harvest pumpkins last fall. The rows of Bodie's vegetables stretched away like a labyrinth. Sprinklers hissed over the middle fields, the arcs of spray trailing ghostly rainbows. When they were kids, the bottom land had all been boring pasture. Her parents had rented the land to Norbert, then to Norbert's son, Neville, who ran a few steers on it, or some years just cut it for hay. She thought suddenly of her little horse, Rebel, remembered riding him here in the pasture twenty years ago. Rebel would be long dead. Ursula hoisted the bottle on her elbow, tipped it up, and took another gulp. "Here's to you, Rebel," she said aloud.

She thought she heard music, or maybe it was just road noise from the highway across the river. The Farmall was parked ahead. As she approached, she could tell the music was in fact coming from the tractor. There was a headset radio on the vinyl seat spilling out heavy rock music. She'd seen the army vet, Arnold, wearing it. His batteries would be dead by morning. She set her wine bottle on the gear box and switched the radio off, then climbed onto the tractor.

The breeze was picking up, and the wine was kicking in. Sitting in the high seat, watching the sprinklers pulse and turn, she felt oddly serene.

She'd driven this tractor before, she suddenly realized. Just once that she could remember. Summer. She must have been fifteen. The hay had been cut and baled but not picked up yet. There was rain in the forecast and Neville hired Bodie to help. Ursula, wanting to be useful—or important or strong or something—had offered to help, too. She was tall and, she thought, strong, but she could just barely lift a bale of hay. Bodie was two years younger but he could lift a bale one-handed. Neville had let her drive the tractor and wagon from the barn, along the drive, and down the bluff. Then Neville took over the driving. Bodie picked up the bales and tossed them onto the wagon. Ursula, standing on the wagon bed, thwacked a hay hook into the bale the way Neville had showed her, dragged the bale to the back, and stacked it. She could only manage to get the bales stacked two high. Periodically, Bodie would leap onto the wagon, brush her aside, and stack the bales higher.

At one point Bodie had picked up a bale from the ground and flung it in a high arc toward Ursula. "Snake!" he yelled. And she had seen it—a long tan snake flying out from the bale that was headed toward her. She had shrieked, staggered backward, and fallen against the stack. The bale landed snake up and slid toward her. It was a gopher snake, lolling halfway out of the bale, and she could see that it was dead. But her heart was roaring. She launched herself off the wagon and knocked Bodie on the forehead with the handle of the hay hook. He fell onto his back and her momentum carried her on top of him.

"Get off me!" he shouted and shoved her away.

The gash above his eye was oozing blood. Ursula remembers now how she felt: exultant. Should she have felt some remorse? Did she feel remorse now? She couldn't find any. There had been so few times in her life when she had felt on top of Bodie, but that was one of them.

Bodie had never bullied her so much as simply been the bull that he was. He had seldom gone out of his way to torment her, but his ordinary, everyday acts had accomplished as much even without intending it. He didn't purposely block a doorway, just positioned himself, leaning nonchalantly, so no one else could pass. Pretending not to notice *you*, waiting there patiently to get through. Or maybe he wasn't even pretending. Maybe his seeming obliviousness toward others was *genuine* obliviousness. That would come in handy for a football player, she imagined. Charging over opposing players as if they weren't even there. Or starting a farm when you had no experience whatsoever, oblivious of the many wise voices counseling you not to.

Well, she was on top of him now. All she had to do to see that the sale of the farm became final was...nothing. Her silence would accomplish the knockout blow.

23 · Bodie

When Bodie returns home after driving Fleece back to Yoncalla, he calls the livestock buyer and arranges to have the sheep taken for slaughter. He had been afraid Fleece would argue, or worse, get depressed. But she seemed to be the old Fleece again. Unsentimental, pragmatic. "Wherever we wind up, we can get more lambs in the spring," she'd said, steady as the seasons.

Fleece's mother is out of the hospital but needs round-the-clock care. Fleece will be staying with her for a week or more. Meanwhile, Bodie has a shitload of things to do to lighten the ship, to see if he can keep this wreck of a farm afloat a little longer. He calls the Farm Supply and cancels his order for hop trellis cable, then the feed store and cancels Fleece's order for chicken scratch. He talks to Gary, the accountant, to find out how much money he has left. Not much. In fact, he owes a lot more than he has in hand. Gary tells him they can juggle it forward for another few months.

Then he calls Dexter to make a date to meet him at his university office. He doesn't know what he'll tell Dexter other than that he doesn't have the money, that he won't be able to repay his loan until the sale of the farm is finalized in January. He gets Dexter's answering machine and leaves a message.

He walks out to the bluff top and watches his crew finish up the day's chores down in the bottom. He sees Arnold on the Farmall cultivating beans. No one drives a tractor straighter than Arnold. A true terranaut, hand firm on the tiller. Zebra is harvesting lettuce, cutting heads of romaine with a long knife and tossing the heads in a blue plastic bin. Gabriel, Pedro, and Jesus are schlepping irrigation pipe from the pumpkins to the Brussels sprouts, each of them balancing a twenty-foot length of aluminum pipe on one shoulder as they step gracefully over the rows of plants like a trio of high-wire artists.

He shakes his head sadly and plods back to the house. At 7 p.m., he eats a sandwich. He has waited until now, but now it begins. He takes a six-pack and settles into his recliner in the bare-studded living room. He opens a beer and drinks half of it in one draft. He smiles at the bottle and tips it up, belches, and says to the unfinished walls, "Bodie, old boy, time to liquidate your assets."

Just before sunset, Bodie staggers out the front door and pisses in the yard. Someone is walking past the hop barn. Ursula. The braids. Swinging something in her hand that looks like a head. She's decapitated somebody, Bodie chortles. Good for her, the bitch.

Bodie drinks more beer. Takes a leak out the back door. He wanders the house, eating chips and guacamole. Half a pan of chocolate brownies. He pisses out a window. Smokes a joint, his head spinning. I could grow dope again! he thinks. But even this drunk he knows his enthusiasm is fake. He doesn't like what pot does to him. Makes his appetite boil and his mind go dizzy.

Hours later he wanders toward Ursula's greenhouse. Has an idea. He'll trash her plants. A barn cat yowls and leaps from the shadows. Bodie yowls back at it, then barks. As he staggers past the farmhouse a yellow light stabs him. The security lamp on Bliss Fits! That's right. They fixed it again. The sons of bitches.

Feeling clearer now, a little clearer, he returns to his house. Slaps himself. Remembers. The .22 is in the kitchen. Between the fridge and the counter. Behind the mop and broom. Shells in the drawer with the silverware. He loads. Steady. With a purpose.

He returns to the farmhouse. Walks into the backyard. Not creeping. Walking tall. It's his house, too. The first shot misses, but not the second. That chuffing explosion of a blown-up lamp. So satisfying.

Late next morning, Bodie is splitting firewood. The maul arcs up and hurtles downward with terrible force. Bodie puts his muscles into it just as the steel strikes the wood and he feels the shock travel up his arms all the way to his shoulders. A smart man lets gravity do the work, he knows. Lets the maul head fall down of its own weight, the wedge of steel shouldering the wood apart with momentum's finesse.

But I ain't smart, he's thinking. I'm a chump. I'm a busted, out of luck chump.

The fir round blasts apart. The halves go flying.

The morning's getting warm. The sweat that stains his T-shirt is mostly last night's beer. He's been at it for probably half an hour, chopping as hard as he can. He doesn't need the firewood. There are cords and cords already split and stacked in the barn. What he needs is the punishment. His head is pounding from his hangover, concussion-quality hammer blows, but he got used to that kind of punishment long ago. Football headaches, hangover headaches—the price you pay. You can't let them slow you down.

Failure, though. That's another matter. That'll stop you cold. He sets the maul aside and hefts a big hunk of wood onto the block. He stares at the Douglas fir round, inspecting the growth rings. Must be a hundred rings. Some are wide and some are narrow, but each one goes all the way around.

All the parts of Tunder Farm fit together. The row crops. The CSA. The hop yard and Fleece's sheep. Even Ursula's fucking flowers. They are all connected. He can see it. He can taste it. Why won't they hang together? What's the tissue, or the rope, or the sinew that seems to be fraying? What is it that should be holding them together, but isn't?

Money. Right.

He rubs his hands on the legs of his jeans, and picks up the maul. He's looking for a natural crack in the wood to aim at, but he can't find any. It's such a beautiful round. Where did this come from? Who would have cut down a tree with grain like that?

Oh, yeah. He traded Brian Simpson a CSA subscription for three cords of this firewood. It's all connected. Even when it's broken. Even when it's wrong.

The police car rolls up to the house nice and easy. When Bodie woke up in the recliner this morning, his rifle was leaning against the side of the chair, and he remembered. He regrets many, many things in his past, but shooting out the Bliss Fits security lamp is not one of them.

Any coach will tell you, *Never admit defeat.* And any lawyer will tell you, *Never confess to a crime.* But Bodie is tired of denying the facts, and when the cop asks, he does both.

24 · Nu

Driving north on 97 from La Pine, Nu got stuck behind a glut of semis. With his windows down—the AC still wasn't working—he ate diesel fumes and road dust all the way into Bend. At least he had the mountains—Three Sisters, Three-Fingered Jack, and Mount Jefferson—to gaze at along the way. Last winter's snowpack had been poor, and the shoulder-cloaks of the mountains looked dirty and threadbare, but the mountains were beautiful nonetheless.

He was tired and filthy, his fingers encrusted with dried blue

PVC cement. He figured it would take him one more day to finish replumbing Hector Perez's cousin's double-wide.

Hector owned the converted truck garage where he lived, and Nu did plumbing jobs for Hector in exchange for rent. There were days he'd rather be a plumber than an artist, anyway. He'd had a string of them lately. When he came back to Bend two weeks ago, he was hoping to make some quick progress on the Furman commission. But he was still stymied. Having to fulfill somebody else's idea for a painting wasn't motivating him.

Mina said working as a plumber was a terrible waste of his talents. She even suggested he had some kind of self-destructive impulse. Mina had sold more of his paintings than anyone else, by far. She was the closest thing he had to an agent, and he valued her opinions. But he disagreed with her about his day job. Working as a plumber grounded him and kept him out of debt. Plus, plumbing was something useful he could do when the art wasn't coming. The muse would return at some point—she always had so far—and then he'd be free to hole up and paint.

He stopped at a Chinese takeout for some moo goo gai pan, then drove through his light-industrial neighborhood and parked the truck at his back door. He sat behind the wheel for another minute, trying to quell the dread in his stomach. Home was the place his unfinished painting waited.

He'd lived and worked in the converted truck garage—the Loft, he'd named it—for nearly three years now. Hector Perez had built the apartment—a big, all-purpose kitchen/living room, a ten-by-twelve bedroom, and a bathroom with a decent fiberglass bath/shower—in one bay of the three-bay log-truck garage not long after he'd gotten his green card and brought his wife and two kids up from Mexico City. The floor was just oil-stained concrete, and the whole apartment was cold and dreary, but Nu had hung the walls with posters and paintings, and there were sculptures, woven baskets, and ceramic bowls and vases arranged on his secondhand end tables and bookcases.

After a shower, he nuked the takeout in the microwave and ate straight from the carton with the disposable chopsticks. He really should call the farm and see how Joe was doing. He'd been putting it off for days, afraid Ursula would answer the landline. He didn't want to talk to Ursula again yet.

The thought of the blank canvas waiting for him in his studio on the other side of the wall made the Chinese food rumble in his stomach. He didn't believe in artist's block. He had plenty of artist friends who complained bitterly when their work stalled, but Nu considered that weak, bourgeois bullshit. He never got blocked, never completely stuck, because he always had a dozen art projects going in any number of media. Only lazy fools waited for inspiration. You had to jump-start your own insights. Draw, paint, or sculpt your way into it. He could always find something to work on.

Until now. Now—ever since he'd returned from the farm—the blank canvas standing on the main easel out in the studio, the canvas that was supposed to become the Furmans' painting and pay his bills for a few months, that big empty canvas was sucking every hint of inspiration out of his world. He'd never experienced anything like it, and now, in addition to being scared and angry, he was also kind of ashamed that he'd never felt the least bit of sympathy for any of his friends when they'd whimpered about being blocked.

He chucked the takeout carton in the trash and went through the door into the studio. Log trucks once parked here; now it was the space where Nu committed art. He toggled a pair of light switches. In the far corner two rows of hanging fixtures fired up. The walls in that corner were sheetrocked and painted white. Half a dozen folding work tables corralled his painting area. They were all paint splattered, a couple of them empty and ready for projects, the rest piled with draft paintings, tools, and supplies. Standing among them were several easels holding studies and sketches in various media. The biggest easel, displaying a blank canvas nearly the size of a sheet of plywood, stood portentously front and center. Nu stared at it for a moment, then switched the light off and turned back to the kitchen.

The next day, Friday, he finished plumbing the double-wide and drove home late in the afternoon. He shucked his grubby clothes and showered, then peeled the blue cement from his fingers with a pair of tweezers. After a quick ham and cheese sandwich, he drove downtown. It was the final day for his *Off-Road Vehicle* exhibit. Once the gallery closed at 6 p.m., he had to dismantle the show. He had tried to coax a couple of friends into helping him, but he hadn't gotten any takers. Mina would probably hang around, but she would be dressed in her work clothes—high heels, expensive dress, and lots of turquoise and silver jewelry—and she wouldn't offer to help. No big deal. He could manage.

He lucked out with a parking spot right in front of the gallery. He'd lied to Mina on the phone last week when she'd asked how the Furman commission was going. "Making progress," he'd told her. Now, as he gathered up his packing supplies to take inside, he debated whether to come clean, tell Mina he was totally blocked and might need more time to complete the Furman painting, or continue to smile and lie.

The gallery door swung open as he approached. "Van Nuys! Entrez!"

"Andy! What the fuck?" Nu was startled, though maybe not totally surprised, to see Andy Patterson holding the door open. Andy was becoming a pop-up personality in Nu's little universe.

"I saw that the show was closing, so I came for a final gander. Can I help you take these babies down?"

Mina came out from her office in the back, high heels clicking smartly on the parquet floor.

"You two have met?" Nu asked.

"Mr. Patterson has been telling me about his gallery in Camas Valley," Mina said.

"Pretty cool, huh?" Nu said.

"Admirable," Mina replied.

"Did we sell anything else?" he asked. Mina had told Nu yesterday that only one of his nine paintings, the smallest one with the cheapest price tag, $800, had been purchased.

"No. But we got a lot of good press," she said. She reached under a counter and came up with a bottle of cheap champagne and three plastic flutes. Popping the cork and filling the glasses, she said, "Here's to art, however unremunerative." They bumped glasses, and Nu noticed how lame the non-clink of flimsy plastic sounded.

"We also got a lot of inquiries," Mina added. "I'd like to hang your show again in San Diego, in January. I assume that's alright with you. I think we'll sell more of your aerial paintings yet."

"Of course," he said. "Thanks, Mina. I can't begin to tell you …"

"No, you cannot," she said, tipping up her glass. "But you may give me a hug."

Nu set down his glass and wrapped his arms around his benefactor. Mina was not a hugger. He understood that this invitation to embrace her was a mark of his special status. After a moment she pushed him away. Andy was waiting with his arms open.

"Not you," she said, and turned to leave. "My husband is fixing a late supper. You'll lock up, Nu? And let's talk soon."

Way back in art school, Nu had developed a system for packing up his artwork. He'd sewed poplin slipcases for individual paintings, and built a crate with Plexiglas dividers. Now he climbed the stepladder and removed a painting from its hanger. As Andy held open a slipcase, Nu lowered the painting into it. Nu carried it to the curb and slid the painting carefully into a slot in the crate.

As they worked, Nu said, "You didn't really drive over the mountains just to see my show again?"

"Call it an added perk," Andy said. "I think I told you that my daughter lives here. Right? I came over to see her."

"Ah," Nu said. "And what's her gig?"

"She's a river guide. Terrific outdoors woman. A force of nature. Just back from a week on the Middle Salmon. She couldn't believe I'd met you."

Nu gave Andy a puzzled look.

"I told her about your pictograph project out there, and she was all agog. You know how river guides make up stories to entertain their clients? You know, by the campfire at night? Well, they've got one for the Owyhee River about *you*. Your disappearing pictographs. The way she likes to tell it, they were made by the ghost of an old Paiute shaman. Medicine symbols that disappear in a day. If anybody ever finds one, it connects them to a spirit helper."

"Oh, god. I wish I'd never done those," Nu said. "Pretty embarrassing."

"Heard you caught some flak about it. Cultural appropriation, eh? Ah, well. You'll have to make more art to atone for it."

Nu couldn't tell if he was being ribbed or consoled. The Owyhee canyon was such glorious country. He was glad his pictographs had safely disappeared, but it seemed now that stories about them persisted. And stories were even harder to erase than marks on rocks.

They worked silently for a few minutes. Nu could tell Andy had something on his mind.

"I heard about Joe," Andy said finally, his tone somber. He let another quiet moment pass. "A buddy of mine works at hospice."

Nu didn't know what to say. The one time he'd spoken to Joe on the phone, he'd asked him how he was holding up. "I'm right on schedule," Joe had said.

Nu stared at a blank stretch of wall. "When I hear myself say, 'Joe's dying,' I get an image of a white space with a gray man-shaped hole in it. But I don't really believe it's happening." He closed his eyes and sighed. After a moment he went back to the task at hand, climbing the ladder, removing the last painting from the wall.

"I've tracked down a couple of Joe's sculptures," Andy said. "I thought we might try to mount a small retrospective before he's gone."

Nu leaned the painting against the wall, and faced Andy. "What? Some of Joe's sculptures are still out there?"

"Local people have them. I called around. They're willing to loan them to us."

"I didn't know any of his work still existed."

"Well, there isn't a lot. A couple of bronzes, a couple of wire sculptures." Andy was getting animated again. "But it would be so rad to bring them together, wouldn't it? Don't you think?"

"Joe worked in bronze? Like, lost wax?"

Andy nodded. "I've seen two pieces. A frog and a raven. Stunning."

"Wow. Well, yeah, sure. How can I help?"

"Yeah. Right. Let me do some legwork. Okay? Find out exactly what we can pull together. Okay? When you come back to Camas Valley, we'll talk to Joe and make a plan. Alright? Alright."

They finished packing the last of the paintings, and Andy headed off to meet up with his daughter. Nu thought about going home, but realized he wasn't ready to face the Loft just yet. He always felt depressed after taking a show down, regardless of whether it was a success or a bust. Either way, it was a kind of death. A beer might help resurrect him.

He wasn't much for drinking in public places, but he did have a favorite hidey-hole, a taproom with decent, inexpensive pints and a row of two-person booths along the wall in back, away from the main hubbub. Sulking alone in close proximity to others sometimes lightened his funk. He could stretch a couple of beers into an hour of self-pity.

As he pulled into the parking lot, he thought briefly of his paintings in the back of the pickup. Their retail value might be as much as 20K, and his flimsy pickup shell would not withstand even the smallest crowbar. But no local thief would have a clue how to unload the paintings. Even Mina wasn't having much luck moving them. He decided to risk it. He was about to swing into a well-lit parking spot when he saw the red F-250 pickup again. He was sure it was the dirt biker Nathan's. He could tell by the dualies and the blue motorcycle lashed in the bed.

He had returned to his old campsite just this past weekend. Craving some forest time, needing to get away from the art-shaming blank canvas in his studio, he'd almost headed west into the Cascades. But he decided he should go back to the meadow, to the scene, as the saying went, of the crime. The thought of encountering Nathan or Smitty there scared him, but he couldn't bear the thought of abandoning that beautiful meadow to the bad guys. In the end, his love for the place carried him past his fear. And he was glad he'd gone. He'd been anxious and angry when he arrived, but he took a long hike up to the base of Pine Mountain, then, toward sunset, he built a juniper-wood campfire in the stone-lined pit under the big ponderosas. He tossed in some twigs of sagebrush, and the acrid smoke was pure medicine. He hadn't realized how wound up he'd been all week until he noticed the tension begin to drain out of his face and arms. Later, he heard gunshots somewhere to the south. Target practice was common, even "normal," for the National Forest lands out there. Gunshots in the dark, however, would be alcohol-and-testosterone-fueled revels, and the sound made his skin crawl. But eventually the gunfire ceased and the stars came out. He doused his fire and unrolled his foam pad and sleeping bag, and the only shootings from then on were meteors.

Nu was glad he'd swallowed his fear and gone back there, but tonight he wouldn't risk running into Nathan and Smitty in the tavern. He rolled on through the parking lot and back onto the highway. There was beer at home.

He drove back to the Loft and unloaded his paintings, feeling like a failure and a coward. He didn't want to be alone, but he didn't want to talk to anybody either. He did a quick inventory of his available diversions. Plenty of junk food. Half a rack of beer in the fridge. And the DVDs he'd checked out from the library, *Battlestar Galactica,* ten episodes, good for many hours of mind-numbing violence.

Beside the TV on the coffee table, he noticed the cardboard box full of cedar bark he'd brought from the farm, a batch of rejects Fleece had given him to practice weaving with. He pawed down to the bottom of the box. Yes, there was his badly started, asymmetrical basket with the surgical-tube arteries poking out from the cedar withes. "You'll never be a weaver," he said aloud, then picked out a slender ribbon of bark and began threading it through the unfinished ribs.

25 · Ursula

Ursula gathered her hair and coiled it heavily on her head. She backed under the shower and let the hot water pummel her shoulders and neck. It was her second shower of the day, a rare indulgence. She'd gone more than a week without a shower when she was in the mountains, so she figured she'd built up some credit. She nudged the mixer valve a few degrees hotter, till the steaming water stung.

Even in this midsummer heat, her hair would take hours to dry. But Becca wasn't coming until 6. She'd have time to braid it before then. Or maybe she'd leave it down. Ursula was hoping to rekindle her friendship with Becca, though she had an additional purpose in mind as well. After yoga class on Wednesday, Becca had mentioned that her mother had died this spring. Ursula wanted to hear more about Becca's experience with hospice.

Becca had sounded pleased when Ursula had invited her to come for supper on Sunday. "Oh, I'd love to," she'd said. "When I came to your festival thing last month, it brought back so many memories."

Ursula had deep-cleaned the kitchen after lunch. She'd planned to vacuum the whole house, too, but she'd run out of steam. Now she did a minimal tidy-up of the living room, neatening Joe's piles of magazines on the coffee table, folding the ugly gold afghan her mother had crocheted and draping it over the back of the sofa. She picked up a framed photo from the table beside Joe's recliner. A wedding photo. Joe in a gray tweed suit and blue tie, Alice in a long blue satin gown. It wasn't the formal shot. That, she noticed, was still propped up on the mantle. This candid photo must have been taken just after. If she'd seen it before, she'd never looked closely. Young Alice and young Joe—they were in their late twenties when they married, she remembered—smiling into one another's eyes with wide-open delight. Though her parents had seemed reasonably compatible and mildly happy when she was a child, she'd rarely seen them caught up in anything like this wild joy.

She was surprised to see a tear fall onto the photo. Weird. She didn't feel sad. But those were definitely tears streaming down her cheeks. She didn't have any of the physiological reflexes that usually accompanied weeping. No tightness in the chest, no catching of the breath. Just clear, copious tears. If anything she would have said she was fairly content. Happy to have been able to spend those few glorious weeks in the mountains, to have resumed, however briefly, her work as a scientist. Now happy to have the house to herself for a few hours. Happy to have reconnected with Becca.

She set the photo back on Joe's table and straightened another stack of magazines. A pamphlet slid off and coasted to the floor and she bent to retrieve it. *What to Expect with Hospice*. Now her chest clenched. Now the sobs came and the tears fell in earnest. God. How could she even think of being happy? With her father on death's doorstep?

But she was. Even sobbing now, even grieving his imminent death, she was happy. Moreover, Joe was happy, too, as near as she could tell. He'd even told her so.

"It's all good," he'd said just this morning, and smiled like he really meant it.

How strange was that?

Ursula heard Becca's car crunching up the gravel drive. She stepped outside and waited on the front porch. Becca parked, then clambered out of her car. Leaning on the car door for a moment, she took a deep, deliberate breath, then straightened herself with effort. Ursula saw she was wearing baggy gray sweatpants and a lightweight orange hoody that clung to the curve of her pregnant belly. Becca was not as tall as Ursula, but with her elegant, yoga-teacher posture she usually seemed taller. Taller and lighter, floating an inch from the floor. Last Wednesday when they'd talked after class, Becca had radiated vitality. But now Ursula could see she looked pale and stooped.

Ursula hurried out to welcome her with a hug. "Becca! How are you? You look a little..."

"I got a damned bladder infection."

"Ick. I hate those." Ursula looked back toward the house. "Come on inside. Nobody else is home. Bodie took Joe to the coast for the day."

"A father-son outing. Nice."

"Yeah, I'm sorry Daddy's not here, but it's pretty neat that he and Bodie are spending the day together," Ursula said. "Are you hungry?"

"Always. But I need to pee first. I just drank a pint of cranberry juice."

Ursula led her inside. "You know where the bathroom is, right? I'll be out back."

Ursula had their supper all ready. She took the tray of food out to the deck, filled two glasses with water from a pitcher, and fussed with the place settings. She poured herself a glass of Chardonnay and took a couple of sips.

"What the fuck is that!?" Becca said.

Ursula startled and sloshed her wine. She hadn't heard Becca come onto the deck. "What's what?"

"That. That wall."

"Oh. Right. You've never seen it from here. That's Bliss Fits."

"Holy crap, really? It's huge. And right on your fence line. How did they...?"

Ursula let out a big sigh. "Here, sit down. There's chicken breasts. And a tempeh salad if you'd rather." She pulled out a chair at the table for Becca and set a plate in front of it. Becca eased herself into the chair, still glancing sidelong at the hulking gray building as if it might pose an active threat.

"I'm having wine. What can I get you?"

"I'd love to get nice and drunk. But I have to be healthy, right? For the baby?" Becca made a pouty face. "Just water." She stabbed a chicken breast with her fork, hoisted it straight to her mouth, and tore into it. After a couple of bites she plopped the meat back onto her plate, the fork sticking straight up like a handle. "Seriously. How did they ever let that hideous wall get built so close to your house?"

Ursula felt the old grudge boiling up from wherever she'd stuffed it. "Susan. And Dexter. They did that."

Becca made a growling sound. "But how? Aren't there laws? Like set-backs or something?"

"Oh, man, Becca. It was awful." Ursula peeled the skin from her chicken, then picked off the little tatters of skin still stuck to the meat. "It was right after Mom died and Dexter and I split up. Daddy had his first bout of cancer and he just couldn't deal with it. Mom's death seemed like the end of the world to him. He hated that wall, but he just couldn't fight them."

"And Bodie was...?"

"In Denver. It was right after his shoulder injury. And I was still in Pullman."

Becca stabbed the chicken breast again, then pulled the fork back out and dropped it on her plate. "Can we just go for a walk?"

"Absolutely. Let me put this away." Ursula said, and when Becca started to gather dishes, added, "No, you just sit. Only take a minute." She gulped half her glass of wine, piled the food and dishes on a tray, and took it all back to the kitchen.

They followed the side yard around the house and Ursula led them along the lane through the farm buildings.

"When I was here for your festival," Becca said, looping her arm lightly around Ursula's waist, "I was remembering our mad chemist phase in high school, when we made those facial salves. I was here a lot then. But it's been fifteen years, at least."

"Whew. A couple of lifetimes ago, right?" Ursula said.

They strolled past Joe's shop and then past the hop barn. Becca halted suddenly and spun them around. "Is that the barn we played in?"

Ursula nodded.

"It was practically falling down."

"It leaned some. Bodie put a lot of money into restoring it. There aren't many old hop barns still standing."

"It's pretty. So tall and straight. Good posture!" She grinned at Ursula and they both laughed. Becca seemed to be recovering her energy and humor. She tugged them around and walked them straight to edge of the bluff. "Oh, my god! That's Bodie's farm!"

Ursula felt her eyes suddenly dilate, as if she'd walked up to the edge of the Grand Canyon. There it was. Bodie's farm. Lush fields, intricate tapestries of color and texture and geometry, all of it radiating some kind of glow. Bodie's fields oozed fecundity. There was an aura, a vaporous exudation of health, verdure, vitality. And it wasn't just her imagination. Though the sky was cloudless and the evening air still brittle with heat, she could see a gauzy, gossamer cloud hovering over the crops. It must be moisture rising out of the soil? Or transpiration of gases from all those leaves? Her scientist mind wanted an explanation for the mysterious quickening of the air below. Whatever made it, the insects liked it, too, judging by all of the swallows swooping and veering through the haze.

"It's just gorgeous," Becca said, pulling Ursula closer. The two of them stood gaping at the fields, swaying a little as if to keep their balance as the Earth rolled beneath them. Ursula quit trying to analyze the field-cloud and just gazed at the scene below them. It *was* beautiful. It seemed riotously alive. She was afraid to breathe. Or else maybe she didn't need to breathe. Maybe the whole world was breathing for her. She was acutely aware of Becca's fingers on her waist, and her own hand touching Becca's taut belly.

Becca spoke first. "I've missed you, Urse," she said, giving her another squeeze. "My friend Sally told me how beautiful it is here. She has a CSA subscription and comes as often as she can. I didn't understand it until now. Next year I want to come help you in the greenhouse, learn how you do it."

"If there is a next year," Ursula said.

Becca pulled her arm away and frowned at Ursula. She started to say something in reply, but then gestured ahead and said, "Let's go down there."

They walked in silence past Bodie and Fleece's house, then descended the bluff via the steep gravel lane. Becca skidded once on a loose pebble, and Ursula took her hand. They walked past a plot of beets, their red-veined, deep-green leaves aglow in the slanting evening light. Then rows of white cauliflower, then a tangled patch of unstaked tomatoes, then a sprawl of squash vines. Under the big leaves they could see lumpy beige fruits already larger than Becca's pregnant belly. "Hubbard squash," Ursula said. "They'll get bigger than a wheelbarrow."

The sun was lowering, but the air was still very warm. Ursula noticed sweat beading on Becca's brow and she steered them into the shade at the edge of the oak woods.

They sat on a makeshift bench—a two-by-ten spanning two rounds of firewood—and Ursula pulled a bar of good chocolate from her skirt pocket. She tore the wrapper and set it on the bench between them.

"Ooh," Becca said, and took half the bar. "So, you're working with Marlys again?"

"Was. Until Dad…" Ursula's voice caught. Becca put her hand on Ursula's shoulder, and they sat quietly for a minute until Ursula could go on. "Yeah, I was out in the mountains doing plant surveys last month. Which I love. I didn't want to come down, but, well…"

"Will your job be there, after…?"

Ursula shook her head no, but said, "Maybe. Not this summer. But Marlys has work for me in the lab in the fall."

"In Pullman?"

Ursula nodded. "If I can. Depending on Dad. And selling the farm."

She tried to take a bite of chocolate but it made her gag. She turned toward Becca. "What I wanted to talk to you about was hospice. We've started it, and it's fine, but can you tell me about your mom…didn't she have hospice?"

Becca scooted closer and put her arm around Ursula. That was all it took to set Ursula off; she began sobbing and didn't hold back this time. She wasn't sure how long she cried—it seemed like several

minutes, though it may have lasted just moments. Finally she lifted
her face from Becca's shoulder, sniffled a few times, and was finally
still. Becca gave her a handkerchief and she daubed at the tears,
then blew her nose.

"I'll tell you all about hospice," Becca said. "But first, sorry, but
I have to pee again." She got up and followed a faint path into the
woods.

Ursula looked out over the fields. On the far side someone—Arnold,
probably, judging by the bulbous headphones—was moving irrigation
pipe. Even at this hour on a Sunday, people were out working the
farm. And it was Bodie who had to assign the tasks and keep track
of it all. A row of sprinklers spouted mare's tails of water over a plot
of waist-high corn, rainbows glimmering within the spray.

Becca returned from the woods scratching her backside. "Gah!
A mosquito got me on the butt. They never used to bother me, but
since I got pregnant they *love* me. Did you know about that sculpture
thing in there?"

Ursula shook her head. "What is it?"

"Come on." Becca led her into the woods.

Twenty yards in, under a gnarly old oak tree, there was a small hut
made from downed limbs. It had to be Nu's work. It was a rough
A-framed kind of structure, pairs of oak limbs lashed together and
joined by a ridge pole. The sides were loosely woven willow branches.
It looked like a big, messy pup tent.

"It wouldn't keep out the rain," Ursula said.

"It's kind of pretty, though," Becca said. "It's like the total opposite
of the hop barn. All slouchy and porous."

Ursula looked at Becca, then back at the hut.

"Where is Nu anyway?" Becca asked.

Ursula slapped a mosquito on her knee. "Back in Bend. He was
looking after Dad while I was in the mountains. He really stepped
up. But it was hard on him, I guess. And he's got his own stuff he's
dealing with. He left as soon as I got home." She really didn't want
to talk about Nu.

"I had such a crush on him," Becca said. "Did you know that?"

Ursula perked up and shook her head. "When?"

"Summer before sophomore year, I think. Yeah. We were at a

party at Sally's house—you were there; remember it?—and Nu told me he'd just gotten a tattoo. He asked if I wanted to see it, and I followed him into Sally's parents' bedroom. He closed the door and pulled off his T-shirt. It was a little spider web on his left shoulder. Nothing special, really. But oh, my god, what a body!" Becca closed her eyes and sighed. "I asked him if I could touch it and then I ran my fingers over the tattoo. I could have fallen into that web."

"Did you...?"

"I might have, if Nu had made a move right then. But he didn't. He just smiled that little smile of his and pulled his shirt back on."

Ursula pictured the intricate tree branches now tattooed across Nu's shoulders and back. She blew out the breath she'd been holding. "Close call, huh?" she said.

"Oh, I'm glad nothing happened. We wouldn't have been a good fit. And besides, he was sweet on you."

"Bullshit." Ursula shook her head vehemently. "We're cousins."

Becca got up and stretched her back. "Whatever," she said. "Anyway, let's not go there, because I have something else important to talk to you about."

Ursula stood up, too, and stretched her calves. She didn't much want to hear another "important thing" right now. Becca was rolling her shoulders, flexing her neck, as if getting ready for a wrestling match. Ursula nervously rubbed the backs of her hands.

"Okay, look," Becca said. "I didn't know whether I should tell you this or not, but I can't sit on it anymore." Becca turned to face Ursula, then glanced up into the trees.

"Jesus," Ursula said. "You're scaring the shit out of me."

Becca turned back to her. "Yeah, I'm sorry. Here it is. It's about your farm. Has the university told you who the big donor is?"

"Yeah. Rondoni or something."

"Edward Modini is the guy. He's the founder and CEO of Earth-wide Farms. Ever heard of him? No, but you've eaten his lettuce. It's the brand they sell at Safeway, Fred Meyer, everywhere. In those plastic tubs."

"That's organic? CVSU said the plan is to build an organic farm research center."

"Listen, you *did not* hear this from me." Becca shook her head nervously. "If Randy finds out I told you..."

"Okay. I promise."

"You know, Ursula, Randy told me your whole family was ready to be done with the farm, and you were all pretty excited about CVSU's proposal. But now I've seen firsthand that Bodie wants to keep the farm. And I can see why. It's so beautiful here."

"Yeah, but Bodie's broke. We have no choice," Ursula said. "And besides, if it becomes a research farm, I can live with that."

"Yeah, maybe so. But I think you should know the whole truth. When CVSU has been talking to you about the research center, they've been leaving out one word."

"Okay..."

"What Edward Modini wants to fund is an organic farm *marketing* research center. He wants to fund research into how organic can develop more consumer products and capture bigger markets. He wants to fund *industrial* organic agriculture. CVSU doesn't care about the land here. They have no intention of farming. They just want a place for their buildings."

Ursula squinched up her face. "Does Randy support that?"

"Ursula, the chance to land a multimillion-dollar donation, to build a state-of-the-art building, a named center, and add faculty lines... This is the university's wet dream. Randy would get some great new projects, a lab, grad students." Becca rubbed her belly and grimaced. A cramp, Ursula guessed. "Ursula, it's such a mess. And it was Dexter who closed the deal."

"Dexter? He wasn't even here. He was still in Pullman." Ursula's head was spinning. She sat back down on the bench and gripped the seat.

"Randy figures Dexter will get promoted to assistant dean."

"The fuck!" Ursula blurted out. "How did this happen?"

"Through Susan. Susan worked with Modini when she was doing real estate in California. Selling farmland was her specialty, I guess."

Ursula's thoughts were reeling. She did not want to hear this, did not want to learn there was anything dubious about CVSU's offer to buy the farm. Her tenuous peace of mind about returning to work as a scientist, about letting Bodie sink or swim, about taking the money from CVSU and everybody just moving on—it was all predicated on the university's offer being legit. But she couldn't square the notion of Susan Sauer's involvement with any kind of legitimacy.

"So they've been lying to us all this time?"

"Technically not. Their contract with your dad says, basically, that the land will be used for a research facility and your family will be commemorated in the naming. But none of that is binding. Once the deal is closed and some time is allowed to pass, then Dexter will come back to his dean and say, 'Oh, by the way, Modini has some new stipulations. He wants to focus on *marketing* research. And in order to recover some of the costs for the building we have a buyer lined up for five acres of the property to develop compatible retail space.' That's Susan's perk. Everybody wins."

"The hop barn? Bodie's fields?"

"The hop barn will be a parking lot. I don't know about the farmland. I've heard Randy talking to Dexter on the phone about trying to sell the bottomland to the city for soccer fields."

Ursula looked out toward the fields, at the tapestry of plants with rainbow-laced irrigation spray flying over it all. At the far end, she saw Arnold mount the old Farmall tractor and putter up the drive. "Why are you telling me this? If Randy finds out..."

"I don't want him to know. Okay? Can you keep me out of this, please?"

"Yeah, but..."

"Look, it's just not right. What they're doing to you. To Bodie. I'm sick of how the university bullies the whole community. And to tell you the truth, Randy is not that happy about it either. It's gone farther than he expected. Part of him would like to get out of the deal, but he feels like he's in too deep at this point. He'd be relieved if the whole thing fell through."

Ursula picked up a stone and tossed it in her hand, then hurled it into the woods. She really didn't want to care that much about what Becca was telling her. So what if it was marketing research? So what if the house and the hop barn got torn down? There was nothing all that special about them.

But the thought of Dexter and Susan profiting by it, that burned.

Dexter securing his little academic fiefdom. Fuck. And the idea of Susan building shi-shi boutiques where their house stood—that she couldn't stomach. She wouldn't let that happen if she could possibly help it.

26 · Bodie

Bodie's harvesting cabbages. It's after 8, the sun is sinking toward Marys Peak. Straightening up and stretching his back, Bodie sees, at eye level just a few feet in front of him, a cloud of gnats, backlit, swirling up and down in a leisurely gnat frenzy, all aglow in the low-slanting sunlight. Bodie is briefly mesmerized.

Now his stomach growls. He hasn't eaten anything since lunch. Fleece told him she'd grill some lamb chops whenever he gets home.

Harvesting cabbage is a job he would normally delegate to one of Zebra's crew, but they've had to let go a couple of the seasonals to save money. And besides, he forgot to tell Zebra the cabbages needed to be picked and packed for delivery to the co-op early tomorrow morning, and now all the workers are done for the day.

He's about done in himself. This stoop labor is agony on his bad hip. The surgeon says they can resurface the joint, with Teflon or titanium or something, and make it good as new. But when is a farmer going to find two to four months for rehab? The amount of ibuprofen he takes is bad for his kidneys, especially considering the beer he often washes it down with, but he can't keep going without his vitamin I.

Bodie saws at the neck of another cabbage with the serrated harvesting knife. Zebra insists it's the proper tool for cutting cabbages, but he can't get the hang of it. It just doesn't have enough heft for these big Danish ballheads. Zebra is ridiculously picky about tools. She's always ordering specialty stainless steel weeding hoes and brass spray nozzles and fancy harvest knives from high-end suppliers. He's threatened to take the Visa card away from her, but so far he hasn't had the nerve. He walks back to the pickup and swaps the knife for an old-fashioned machete. He whacks off the lower leaves of a cabbage then lops the head with a single swing. Much better.

He still can't wrap his head around what Ursula told them. About this same time last night, a couple of hours after he'd gotten home from his day-trip to the beach with Joe, she'd knocked on their door. Which was strange. Ursula never visited them unannounced. Stranger yet, when Fleece answered the door, Ursula barged across the living room and gave Bodie a bear hug, whacking him on the back like an old teammate. Her hair was not bound tight in her everlasting braids, but flying frizzy and wild. She looked wild-eyed and Bodie smelled wine on her breath. Ursula stalked back to Fleece and repeated the hug routine. The only thing Bodie could think of was that Joe must be dead. Heart attack probably. He couldn't imagine anything else that would make his sister behave this way.

She stood, trembling, in the center of the room, tugging at her loose hair. "Whew," she said.

Fleece took her by the arm and led her to the sofa. "Sit down, Ursula. You want some water?"

Ursula sat on the edge of the cushions, breathing hard.

Fleece headed for the kitchen and Bodie dragged his chair across the room and sat close to Ursula. "Sis, what's the matter? Is it Dad?"

She shook her head and chewed on her lower lip. Fleece returned with a glass of water, and Ursula took a long drink. "Whew," she said again. "Okay. I've got some very weird news."

As she'd proceeded to detail her conversation with Becca, Bodie noticed that Ursula looked more often at Fleece than at him, as if she thought Fleece would understand it all better and have a better idea of how to respond. And she'd been right. Bodie's mind had lurched in and out of the present as he'd struggled to digest her story. What was she saying? That the university had pulled a big charade with the research farm ploy? That Dexter had been deceiving him all this time? Bodie had replayed his recent conversations with Dexter, trying to spot any lies hidden there. He just couldn't see it.

He'd come back to the present when Ursula said, "So, we have to stop these bastards."

"Yes," Fleece responded. "It all makes sense. We have to hold onto the farm. Somehow, we have to keep this land out of their hands."

Now Bodie hacks at the base of another cabbage and accidently slices off one side of the head, ruining it. "Gahhh," he growls.

He's just not sure he can fight them anymore. Only last week he had finally come to terms with having to give up the farm. After months and months of dogged denial, he'd turned the corner. Last Wednesday, to be exact, after meeting with Gary, their accountant. Gary had explained to him how, given the failure of Lehman Sachs and the turmoil in the real estate and investment markets, the Tunder family's deal with the university was undoubtedly a boon. The terms of the sale had been negotiated back in a stronger market, and the appraisal last year had settled on the highest value ever for the farm. They would get a great return, and then Bodie could go shopping for other farmland in a depressed market, a buyer's market. He should be able to purchase comparable land for a lot less than they would receive for Tunder Farm.

Since that conversation he'd begun thinking ahead. He knows of a farm in North Albany that might be for sale. It isn't on the market yet, but he's heard that the owner has some health issues and might listen to an offer. He'd walked that land a year ago. He can picture the nice southwest exposure, the gentle slope of the fields.

But now, according to Ursula and Fleece, the fight for Tunder Farm is back on.

Bodie tries again to make sense of it. Could Dexter have been playing him all along? It was true that Dexter had handled the sale of the farm in the first place, but no one in the family objected to that at the time. He had still been in Denver, recovering from his shoulder injury. Ursula was in Pullman. And Joe couldn't take care of the place after Alice died. So, no, Bodie didn't hold the original sale against Dexter.

If Dexter is not being honest with him, there should have been signs. How could he have missed them? Dexter has given him a lot of solid advice about managing the farm. It was Dexter who'd dissuaded Bodie from going too far into debt by trying to start a brewery, counseling him instead to grow hops. And further, Dexter lined up the private loan that enabled Bodie to install the trellises for the hops. Why would Dexter have helped him so much if he plans to sell him down the drain?

Maybe something has changed? Maybe this new donor guy, Modini, has told the university, told *Dexter,* to get the Tunders off the farm ASAP? Maybe there is something extra in it for Dexter, enough that he is willing to screw Bodie over?

Nah, he just can't believe Dexter would do that. Maybe in the beginning Dexter really believed that Bodie could make a go of the farm. Maybe Dexter didn't think the university would ever find a big enough donor, so the sale would never proceed, and Bodie would be in a decent position to keep going as a hop farmer. But then maybe, when Modini's big money arrived, Dexter knew Bodie was stuck. The farm would have to be sold. And the money this Modini is bringing will make it a good deal financially for Bodie and the rest of the Tunders.

That is the most generous way Bodie can rationalize Dexter's actions.

But that doesn't account for Dexter's blatant lying. Or for the university's deception about their actual plans for the farm. And Susan Sauer coming away with a chunk of the land to build more of her shit shopping mall! That has to be Dexter's true motive for lying. To hide Susan's involvement. Bodie has never even met the lady. All he knows about Susan is that she owns Bliss Fits. She owns the sodium vapor security light that blasts into his father's backyard.

Oh, right, and she slept with Dexter while Dexter was still married to Ursula. Ursula hates Susan even more than she hates Dexter. So, yeah, Dexter would know that Ursula would go into full battle mode if she thought Susan was going to make a profit from this.

Bodie looks down at the damaged cabbage and takes another whack. He puts his whole arm into the motion, hacking again and again at the miserable head. Shards of cabbage leaf go flying. His jeans are splattered with green flesh.

What did Fleece say last night after Ursula left? "We are meant to look after this place, Bodie. We can't let the university get hold of it. They'll ruin the land."

He stands up straight and stretches again, feeling calmer now, ready for whatever comes next. The sun slides below the horizon, and the air instantly cools. A red-tailed hawk sails low over the sheep pasture in the distance, searching for gophers, no doubt.

"Go get 'em, bird," Bodie urges the hawk, then hoists the plastic tote full of cabbages and shoves it into the truck.

27 · Nu

Nu got to the farm a little late. Ursula had told him the family meeting would start around 7, and he'd left Bend in plenty of time. But he forgot about the paving repairs on Highway 20. He was stuck in thirty-minute delays *twice*. The late-afternoon sun had glared in his eyes all the way, and by the time he made it to the farm he was tense and grumpy. His T-shirt was soaked with sweat.

He wasn't sure why he had come. He was still resentful of the way he'd been stranded at the farm to look after Joe while Ursula went to work in the mountains. When Ursula had called and told him what she'd learned from Becca about the university's true intentions for developing the farm, she'd made it clear that she wasn't asking him to return. And she'd apologized more than once for abandoning him at the farm. "You've done more than your share already," she'd told him. "I just wanted to keep you in the loop, as a family member, about what's going on."

He should be back in Bend, in his studio. He'd just barely begun to get a little traction on the Furman painting. It was not a good time to be distracted from a paying gig. But he shared Ursula's outrage at what Dexter and Susan and the university were trying to pull over on the Tunders, and as he listened to Ursula, he began to imagine ways he could help them fight back.

When Ursula had growled, "We're gonna make those assholes wish they'd never tried to cheat us," the fury in her voice had excited him. He supposed he'd come back to the farm to see what her angry resolve looked like in the flesh.

When he pulled up to the house, Ursula came out to greet him. Road-weary and damp with sweat, he tried to give her just a quick cousinly, one-shoulder hug, but Ursula wrapped both arms around him and squeezed him hard.

"I'm so glad you came," she said. "I can't tell you how much I appreciate you taking care of Daddy while I was gone. I shouldn't have left you alone with him."

He wasn't quite ready to accept her apology. Maybe he was holding out for something more, he couldn't tell. So he just nodded and followed her inside without speaking.

"Everybody's here," Ursula said, cheerily. "There's pizza and beer in the kitchen. Help yourself."

Fortified with food and drink, they sat around the big dining room table, each with a manila folder of paperwork—budget spreadsheets, a couple of official-looking government documents, photocopies of news stories pulled off the Web—that Ursula had provided. Nu pushed his paper plate with his uneaten pizza crusts to the center of the table, where it formed a bad still-life with a package of Oreos, several empty beer cans, a bottle of white wine.

Ursula was sitting at the head of the table, with Joe at the opposite end. Bodie had the far side to himself. Fleece was next to Nu. Nu had angled his chair back from the table a little so he had room for his sketchbook on his knee. He was aware that it might seem like he wasn't fully engaged, not quite "at the table," but that was okay, because that was in fact how he felt. Keeping his sketchbook between himself and the world was a strategy he'd adopted in childhood. If people sometimes thought he seemed aloof, so be it. They were probably right.

It was hot and stuffy in the house. Bodie had wanted to meet on the deck, but Ursula was adamant that they gather here at the dining room table and *concentrate.* Before Nu left for Bend two weeks ago, this table had been piled with seed catalogs, integrated pest management manuals, and books on greenhouse operation, along with samples of potting soil and fertilizer, drip irrigation emitters, plastic pots. Now Ursula had cleared away all her business paraphernalia.

Ursula's braids were coiled on top of her head in a fashion Nu had not seen before. Maybe she'd put her hair up because of the heat, to keep it off her neck. But it made her seem formal and business-like, a style for the office more than the farm.

"So if your figures are right, Bodie, it looks like we can cover our bills through the end of the year." Ursula had just led them through the accountant's latest report, complete with spreadsheets. She was clearly taking the helm of the Tunder Farm ship, and everyone seemed to be grateful to her for doing it.

"Well, that's if we tap into *your* savings," Bodie said, sheepishly.

"That is the plan, and I'm fine with it," Ursula said.

"Okay, then. Thanks," Bodie said. "I may have been a little optimistic about our tomato income, but I really believe the melons will save our ass. Our honeydews will be ready before anyone else's. We'll make a small killing."

"Cool," Ursula said, smiling warmly at Bodie. "So, bottom line is, if we turn down the university's offer, we won't immediately go bankrupt."

"But I still owe Dexter $5,000," Bodie added gloomily.

"Dexter can go fuck himself," Ursula said.

"It doesn't seem like that much money," Fleece said. "Can't we get a bank loan or something?"

"No. We're all tapped out, Fleece," Ursula said. "Since the housing market went bust, the banks are freaking out, and money's super tight. Nobody will give us any more credit unless the sale of the farm goes through."

Nu's attention drifted. He really had nothing to add to the discussion of the family's financial woes. He was down to a few hundred dollars himself. The 5 grand he would make on the first Furman painting, a sum that had seemed princely when he'd been offered it, now looked paltry. It was the most he'd ever earned on a single painting, but it wouldn't last long. He'd pretty much locked himself up in his studio for the past four days, subsisting mostly on instant ramen. He'd roughed out dozens of studies in pencil, but he still hadn't put any acrylic on the canvas. He was stuck. Flummoxed. Full of doubts. But even though he hadn't been making much progress in his studio, he wasn't sure he belonged here either.

After he'd talked to Ursula on the phone yesterday and told her, to his own surprise, that he would come over for the family meeting, he'd called Mina to tell her he might need an extension on the deadline for the Furman painting.

"Nu, I hope you aren't letting that farm distract you," Mina had said. "There's nothing for your art there."

He wasn't so sure about that. He'd never told Mina about the willow sculptures he was dreaming of building here. As far as she knew, he was completely focused on the Furman commission.

Nu could hear Ursula getting riled up again, and he pulled his attention back to the meeting.

"...but we can't just tell CVSU the deal is off," she was saying.

"We're still bound by the contract. We need *them* to back out of the deal."

"How the fuck are we going to do that?" Bodie asked, his jaw grinding.

"That's the next item on the agenda," Ursula said, poking her finger at another sheet in front of her. Nu shuffled his messy pile and found the page titled, officiously enough, "AGENDA."

    I. Overview of current finances
    II. Strategies for blocking CVSU
        a. Dirt on Modini
        b. Camas easement
        c. Daddy's grave
        d. Other options???

Ursula tapped some keys on her laptop. "First thing," she said, "I did some snooping online to see if I could find more about Modini. I sent you some links. Here's a news story about poor treatment of field workers at Earthwide Farms. It's from a farmworkers' union newspaper, though, and I can't see that anyone else ever picked up on it. And here's some stuff about that salmonella outbreak in spinach back in 2003; they had to recall a shitload of greens. But that was nationwide, and I can't see any evidence that Modini's fields were identified as a source for the contamination. Might be more to that, though. I'll keep looking." Ursula typed something, a reminder to herself, Nu figured, then looked up. "Questions?"

"Yeah," Bodie said, pushing his chair away from the table. "Anybody need another beer?"

Ursula scowled. She didn't wait for Bodie to return from the kitchen, but charged ahead. "Fleece, what have you got on the easement?"

Fleece opened her laptop and looked at her screen. "You know the tribe is looking for sites to do camas restoration. They have some casino money. Not enough to *buy* land, but enough to buy *easements,* where they give landowners a yearly payment to take the ground out of production so they can try to reestablish camas. One of my cousins is a tribal biologist, and he brought some folks to the farm back in May.

"Originally they wanted some of our cropland, but we convinced them that the band of wetlands between the farm fields and the lake would be perfect. It's only twelve acres but, can you imagine, twelve acres of camas all in bloom!" Fleece's face lit up. Nu could tell she was *seeing* that field of camas.

"Wonderful," Ursula said. "I know the money won't happen for another year or so, but still, it's something to throw at the university. They won't want to hassle with easements on their property."

"But it won't be very hard for their lawyers to block it, either," Bodie said.

"True. But at this point we're just trying to throw up obstacles, right?"

"Make it too big of a hassle for them to deal with us?" Fleece offered.

"Correct. And speaking of hassles. Daddy?"

"What?" Joe said. "Am I up?"

"Can you do it? Want me to do it?" Ursula asked.

Joe scowled at her. With a grunt, he pulled his chair closer to the table. He picked up a document and waved it at them. Nu plucked his copy from the pile in front of him. It was an official form, he could tell by the intricate, filigree border. It said, in part, "Joseph Tunder shall be hereby permitted to establish a private family cemetery on the property described herein."

"Urse found this the other day," he said, "going through my old papers." He coughed, took out a handkerchief, and blew his nose. "I'd forgotten all about it. Even when Ursula dug this out, I couldn't remember doing it. So bear with me. I'm trying to reconstruct some old history here." He paused again. "I don't know how far back to start."

"Anywhere you want, Pops. We're here for the long haul," Bodie said. "You need another beer?"

Joe inspected his bottle and seemed surprised to find it empty. "Water," he said. Once Bodie had fetched him a glass from the kitchen, Joe began.

"You remember that your mother and I met in grad school in Berkeley. Right after we graduated, we moved here to the farm to look after her father, Warren. That would have been 1965. Warren had been a professor of horticulture at cvsu for a couple of decades. He and Charlotte—that's Alice's mom, I never met her; she died before Alice and I got married—they bought the farm in 1942 from a Japanese family that was interned. Manzanar, I believe. Those folks had been actual farmers, vegetables and fruits. A big truck farm like what Bodie's doing now. Warren had told them that after the war he'd sell it back to them if they wanted. But they never returned. Bitter or broke or maybe just old, I don't know. Warren and Charlotte didn't farm, of course. They leased out the cropland to Norbert. But Warren planted all the rhodies around the house and Charlotte had the big garden.

"Anyway, Warren died just a year after we came, in June or July? Oh, shoot, Alice would remember. He's buried, along with Charlotte, in the Blevenger plot up the hill at Priory Cemetery. So that meant we were now the owners of a thirty-eight-acre farm and a too-big house, without any money to speak of.

"Alice..." Joe sighed, then paused. He shook his head slightly and continued. "Alice got a job as a kindergarten teacher right off. And I clerked at Barnett's Hardware. About that same time Alice saw an announcement for an opening to teach art at cvsu, and she made me apply. I had no teaching experience, hardly any track record as an artist. Oh, I'd had a show of my oil paintings at the local art center, and I'd sold a few of my sculptures. But, you know, enrollment at all the colleges was going gangbusters. Baby boomers. Lots of boys trying to stay out of Vietnam. And the colleges were hiring faculty left and right. I knew some of the people on the art faculty, and Warren's reputation at cvsu didn't hurt. Plus, I knew enough to put on a suit for the interview. So they didn't look too close at my résumé."

Joe took a drink of water and studied the glass. "I don't think I was all that good as a teacher, but I did feel mighty fortunate to get to make art with my students. And they seemed to like me well enough." He set the glass down and looked up. "Am I wandering too much?"

"No!" Bodie said. "You're fine."

"Please tell us the whole story, Father," Fleece added.

The sun had been lowering toward the Coast Range, and just then it sliced in through the living room window, clear through the house, and hit Joe sidelong. Joe squinted and winced, as if the sunrays pained him.

"I'll get the blinds," Ursula said, jumping up and running into the living room.

Nu had seen something different in Joe's face when the sunray struck him, and he wanted to sketch him again. All Joe's scars from welding–burns, deep age wrinkles, and the recent pockmarks from where he'd had patches of skin cancer burned off gave his face a startling porosity. As Joe resumed speaking, Nu sketched quickly, almost without looking.

"So, I'll make this fast," Joe said.

"Take your time, old man!" Bodie shouted.

"Yeah, yeah, yeah," Joe said, patting the air in front of him. "Okay. So I was teaching art. Alice was teaching kindergarten. We were squeaking by. And then Alice got pregnant and she had the first miscarriage. She got rheumatic fever and lost the baby. She was real sick for quite a while, and she missed most of a whole year of teaching. So that was the first time we nearly lost the farm."

"Oh, Daddy," Ursula said.

"Yep. My wages as an art instructor were comparable, I would guess, to the janitor's. And without Alice's paycheck, and then those big doctor bills, we fell behind on the mortgage."

"I thought Warren gave it to you free and clear?" Ursula said.

"Nope. We still owed the bank. Norbert's rent for the cropland helped, but not enough. That was the first time we talked to CVSU about selling. To the Horticulture Department, you know. Old friends of Warren's were in charge. They wanted the land, but they didn't have any money."

"So what happened?" Bodie asked.

"I got a raise! Wouldn't you know it? The Art Department had an opening for a tenure-track position, and I applied and I got it. Assistant Professor Joseph Tunder. I felt like a complete fraud. I was not very confident in my teaching, not even sure I wanted to be an academic. But my salary more than doubled. I liked that."

Nu gave up on the sketch. He'd never capture the permeability of that strange moment. He set his sketchbook on the table and pulled up his chair so he could hear Joe better.

"As it happened, that was the year, 1969, when the students at CVSU started to get riled up about the war in Vietnam. Years after Berkeley started protesting, or even U of O. But that was our ag school. Conservative. Heads in the sand. But then we had a sit-in, then teach-ins. And a lot of my students, they wanted their art to comment on the war, to be *relevant*. Which I understood. I got that. I felt that way, too. So there was going to be a big rally in a month, on the anniversary of the battle of Huế, if I recall. I proposed to the students that we work together to make a couple of bigger-than-life puppets. Caricatures. LBJ. Westmoreland, maybe. Or Uncle Sam decked out in skulls and bombs. Whatever they wanted. It would be art. They'd learn some techniques. And it would make a statement. All good, right?"

"I've seen pictures of them," Nu said. "The puppets. They were really cool."

"Really?" said Ursula. "Where? I've never seen them."

"Andy Patterson has tear sheets from the *Gazette*. They did a big spread on the protest."

"Daddy, why have you never showed those to us?"

"Burned them."

"Oh, god, Daddy..."

"Now don't you scold me, Urse. That was a rough time. Your mother was still sick..." Joe's eyes glazed for a moment, lost in a memory.

They all let a few breaths pass quietly. Finally Ursula said, "I'm sorry, Daddy. Please, go on."

Joe tried to rouse himself. Lifted his water glass, then set it back down without drinking.

Nu felt a need to ask about something. "Andy took photographs of the whole march. I've seen them. He's got a scrapbook full of the original prints. A big crowd along the street. Lots of smiles. Those puppets were really cool. But the thing that made the news, the *national* news, was one of your sculptures. *The Grieving Mother*."

Joe looked at the ceiling, as if considering what to say, then lifted the glass again and took a sip. "You've talked to Andy, huh?" he said. When Nu nodded, he added, "How's he doing?"

"He's good. Still trying to stick it to the man."

Joe chuckled with pleasure. "Love that guy. It was his fault, really. It was his photos that got me fired."

"I never understood why they fired you," Ursula said. "Or if you cared. You always said you were glad you didn't work there."

"Yeah, well, that's true. But at the time, I wasn't looking to be unemployed."

"What happened, Dad?" asked Bodie.

"We had our march. Started at the Student Union and wound through downtown. The puppets were, I have to say, a huge success. There were hundreds of people out along the streets, some out of curiosity, some to jeer at us. But what happened is, when the puppets came along, a lot of kids—and I mean high schoolers all the way down to kindergarten—they wanted to follow the puppets. And they grabbed their moms or their friends and joined in. It got pretty, you know, festive, like a celebration as much as a protest."

"What about your sculpture? Where does that fit in?" asked Fleece.

"*The Mother*? Well, for a month or more, while the students were making puppets, I worked on her, nights, here in the shop. I was thinking of a photo I'd seen, a young woman standing alone on the tarmac as a coffin was off-loaded from a military transport. Her posture. Grief-stricken. That's what I started with."

"What was the sculpture's body made of?" Nu asked.

"Rebar, covered with hardware cloth. Just a rough armature. Alice helped make the final shape, with quilt batting. And she sewed the cape." Joe went silent, remembering.

After a moment, Nu asked, "The head? Was that ceramic?"

Joe nodded. "I wanted to do a bronze but there was no time. So..."

"Her face is so expressive. Andy said you were thinking of Liv Ullman."

Joe shook his head. "No. Maybe. I took a cast of the department secretary. Olga. She was Russian, I think. Slavic, anyway. Big eyes, broad features. She always looked sad, even when she smiled."

"And the hands?" Nu asked.

"The hands. I don't know. They just took me over. It was like I was in a dream for a week or so, carving them." Joe's eyes turned inward. "Never had quite that experience again."

Joe seemed to have slid back into memory. Everyone waited, the ceiling fan in the living room emitting a mousy squeak with each slow revolution.

Bodie was the first one to squirm. He reached for the package of cookies and asked, "Then what happened?"

Joe nodded, the spell broken. "Right. Well, that morning, before the march, we'd set *The Mother* up on the quad. Nobody paid any attention to her at first. I made sure she was stable on the paving there, and then I stepped away from her, and I remember thinking, 'Well, she's nothing special. But making her was.' Alice had brought bunches of flowers from her garden, and we figured we'd pass those out to people as they returned from the march. Alice thought folks might want to lay the flowers at the feet of *The Mother*.

"Well, that didn't happen. When the march got back to campus, there was a handful of militant protesters bunched up beside *The Mother*, and that really pissed me off. They had a bullhorn, shouting some stupid slogans. And there were cops in full riot gear standing behind them."

Joe took a deep breath. "The fight happened right there, all around *The Mother*. I saw one protester turn around and try to hang a North Vietnamese flag on a cop's truncheon, and the cop smacked him and then the fight was on. A couple of students got injured, I remember, and one of the cops, too. Nothing serious, but holy shit. It was big news when a backward ag school like ours had a riot."

"Andy told me about it," Nu said. "The fight was what made the papers. He showed me his photo. There's two or three people on the ground, and one of them, a long-haired guy in army fatigues, is being punched by a cop in a riot helmet. Behind them there's a ring of a half dozen or so cops. And standing there right in middle of the action is Joe's sculpture *The Grieving Mother*."

Nu heard Ursula gasp.

"That's what made it into the papers," Joe said, his voice flat with disdain.

"Andy sold it to the *Camas Valley Gazette*," Nu resumed, "and it got picked up by the wire services. *Oregonian, LA Times, Washington Post*. Andy has all the tear sheets in his scrapbook, too. Impressive coverage. It was your fifteen minutes of fame, Joe."

"Yeah," he scoffed. "And three days later, they fired me. I'd only been in the job for five months, still on probation, so they didn't need any justification. What they did need was a fall guy for the flak they were taking from their alums, and I was handy. No due process required."

"Oh, Daddy," Ursula said.

Nu saw Fleece put her hand to her cheek, as if she might be on the verge of crying. Nu wondered what the family would make of this long-buried story from Joe's past, his career as an artist, an academic, a war protester.

Fleece was the first to respond. "Father," she said. "This is such a hard and beautiful story. I'm just so surprised that Bodie and Ursula have never heard it."

"We have heard it, Fleece," Ursula said. "But only in pieces. It never made much of an impact on me, I'm sorry to say."

Joe thought for a moment, then sighed. "I'm sorry, too, Urse. I don't know how that happened. It was never a secret, but it wasn't a story that I was proud of, or much wanted to share. I don't know."

"Where did the sculpture go, Daddy?"

"Dismantled it. She was out in the hop barn for a few years, and the mice got into the batting. So I took the head and the hands off. They must be up in the attic."

"And the body?" Bodie asked.

"Bone yard. Might have cut her up for the rebar. I'm not sure."

Nu looked down the table and caught Ursula's eyes. She nodded, her face flushed with excitement. She was thinking the same thing: they could possibly resurrect *The Grieving Mother*.

Nu picked up his copy of the burial certificate. There was no easy transition to the question of the cemetery, but Nu figured it would be less awkward for him to bring it up than either of Joe's kids. "Why did you want to do this?" Nu asked, holding up the document.

"Don't rush him, Nu!" Ursula said.

Joe lifted a hand to shush her. "No, that's good," he said. "We've got to stick with the *agenda*," he added, winking at Nu.

"Long story short, after they fired me, I started the welding business, and it wasn't long before I was making better money than the college had paid me. It wasn't easy work, mind you. But all the farmers knew I was good with machinery. During summers, especially during harvest, I had to work pretty much seven days a week, any hour of the night or day, you know, keeping combines in the field and stuff. Alice got healthy, went back to work. And you kids came along. You were born," looking up at Ursula, "in 1973. Easy baby. Alice only took a couple of months off from work. And, Bodie, you came along in '75."

"'76," Bodie corrected him mildly, with a smile.

Joe wrinkled his brow as if doubting Bodie's memory, but then lifted a hand to acquiesce. "You were a difficult birth."

"I was big."

"Huge. And Alice got sick again, and missed another year of work. But we survived. We made out okay." Joe rubbed his eyes. Nu could tell he was getting tired. They'd need a break soon.

Joe's voice got quieter. "Then something happened that led to the burial thing. You were too young to remember it, but you may have heard since. You know about Ben Jurickson, the musician? His son William got killed in an accident. He was a soccer player in college like his dad. The soccer team was going to a match somewhere, Montana maybe, and their van slid off the road and William and another kid died."

"I've read about it," Ursula said. "Is that, like, 1980? '81?"

"Yeah, thereabouts. You two were still just whippersnappers. Anyway, I knew Jurickson a little bit. We knew some of the same people from the Bay Area. I'd been down to his farm in Titusville. In fact, I welded a bumper extension on his camper bus. So I was invited to the funeral, and I went. They'd arranged to bury William there on the land. It was pretty amazing. There was a handmade coffin, beautiful, a work of art. William's soccer team buddies came and dug the grave. There was singing and poetry. People were wailing, laughing. And I came home all fired up. I wanted to be buried like that someday, here on the farm.

"Alice thought it was silly. She hadn't gone to the funeral. She didn't know Jurickson. I don't recall whether I went in to the county courthouse or what, but, somehow I came away with this," he squinted to read the paper in his hand, "'Certificate of Home Burial.' And now I propose to use it, especially if it puts a twist in the guts of those CVSU dicks."

Bodie chuckled. "Where did you plan to have your plot, Dad?"

"Oh, hell, I don't know. Up on the rise, probably. Somewhere out of the way. But now I'm thinking right smack in the middle. Between your house and the hop barn."

"That's our garden," Fleece said. "We'd love to have you in our garden."

Everyone laughed at that. Fleece hadn't intended it as joke, but she smiled.

"I have to tell you," Joe said. "I'm kind of excited to be dead." He took a drink of water and thumped his glass on the table. "But I'm not dead yet, and I need to use the facilities."

Nu saw Ursula gaze at her father with unabashed love. "Okay," she said. "Potty break." Then added, and Nu was put off by how quickly she dropped back into boss mode, "But we still have work to do. So don't wander off."

Joe traipsed toward the downstairs bathroom, and Fleece headed to use the one upstairs. Nu went out the back door with Bodie following him. The evening was finally cooling down. The air was thick with the heavy, pungent fragrance of some flowering shrubs Nu didn't know the name of. They crossed the yard and ducked inside the thicket of Warren's big old rhododendrons.

"Whew. Never knew the old man was such a troublemaker," Bodie said.

"Your dad has done some amazing things," Nu answered. "His artwork deserved more recognition."

"Art doesn't pay the bills," Bodie said. "I remember Dad saying so on more than one occasion. But then I guess farming doesn't pay much either."

Back at the dining room table, Ursula was busy at her laptop. Fleece was in the living room doing some exercises, stretching her back. Joe hadn't returned yet.

Nu took his seat and picked up his sketchbook. He tried again to draw, now from memory, the way Joe had looked earlier in that last stab of sunlight, carved up by shadows and a hard life. A few minutes later, Joe returned, shuffling back with his eyes lowered, looking completely worn out. By the time everyone was settled around the table, Nu had made up his mind.

Ursula snapped down the lid on her laptop and said, "Okay, I just want to make sure everybody knows their assignments."

"I've got something to add," Nu said, "to the obstacle list."

"Great. Let's hear it."

Nu tossed his sketchbook onto the table and scooted his chair up. "Andy Patterson told me about a Canadian artist, Robert Gottlieb, pretty well known. Guy has a farm in Alberta. It's prairie country, and it's also fracking country, and these oil goons keep bugging him to let them drill on his land. Gottlieb says no, absolutely not, but they keep coming around, offering more and more money. So what he does is, he already had some sculptures around his farm. He works in wood mostly. So he's got some cool boatlike sculptures, and some human figures, and some big abstracts. Andy showed me the pics on-line. Really interesting, solid work. And the guy decides to put more sculptures around the land and, get this, to *copyright* his farm."

"Copyright," Bodie said, clearly unimpressed.

"Yeah. He applied to the government copyright office. He said, 'Look, the farm is a work of art. The whole thing is a single work of art.' Which is the only thing you can copyright. Single works of art. He copyrighted his farm."

Bodie looked incredulous. "What, and the fracking guys just said, 'Oh, excuse us. We sure wouldn't want to fuck with your artwork'?"

Ursula said, "That's really interesting, Nu, but what does it have to do with us? We can't just declare the farm is an artwork and expect the university to, what, back out of the deal? I can't really imagine the government would even approve an application like that anyway. Is there any precedent in the U.S.?"

"I know. It's pretty iffy," Nu said. "But it's something to try at least."

"Doesn't make any sense," Bodie said.

Fleece reached out across the table and took Bodie's hand. "Let's hear Nu's idea before we dismiss it, Bodie."

Bodie scowled. But Nu could see that Fleece was interested. She looked excited even.

Nu forged ahead. "You know how I made that brushwood hut in the woods? Rough, I know. Nothing to get excited about. But, I've been dreaming up, sketching this idea for putting willow sculptures—

people, I think, and maybe animals, too—all around the farm. They'd all be related somehow, I haven't figured that out yet. They'd be part of a, you know, a single art installation."

"Sounds dopey. Not to mention a shitload of work," Bodie said.

"Tons," Nu agreed. "But Andy told me he'd help line up a bunch of volunteers. I think we could do it in, I don't know, a month, two months maybe."

"I love it," Fleece said.

Ursula fussed with the braids coiled on her head and the loose end of one of them splayed across her forehead. She wrestled it roughly back into place. "It sounds beautiful, Nu, but I still don't understand how this helps us hang onto the farm. Is there a payoff for these sculptures?"

Nu shook his head. "Not in money. Not much anyway. Andy thinks he could raise some funds to support the art if his people were involved. And maybe we could find a grant or two. It wouldn't amount to much."

"So...?"

"It sounds like our strategy is to just create as many obstacles as we can. So, Andy's idea is to get a lot of people out here making art on the farm. Taking an interest in the farm. Having some ownership in the farm, I guess. Make it so the university and their donor guy will start to wonder if it's worth the hassle. We might be able to make a PR thing out of it, make them look like bad guys."

"They *are* the bad guys," Bodie said. "I could just fucking punch those..."

"But," Ursula made a karate chop in the air to cut Bodie off. "But what's the point of the copyright thing, Nu? I just can't believe it would hold up in court."

"I hear you. Andy told me the fracking people in Canada haven't even tried to go to court. It's probably just a hassle for them. And they might be afraid that a court would actually uphold the copyright. Then there could be an outbreak of protest art. Imagine, a line of frack-blocking, pipeline-blocking art stretching clean across the Canadian prairie."

"An art blockade," Fleece said, her eyes wide.

"So it's really just a bluff," Ursula said.

"Or a gesture of beauty!" Fleece said. "I think it's wonderful. It's worth doing for its own sake, whether it works or not."

"It's theater," Nu said. "Copyright might or might not hold up in court, but the art would be good theater. People would come to see it. We'd make friends."

Bodie clapped his hands to both sides of his head, then leaned down and clunked his forehead on the table. Sitting up straight again, he said, "You guys are amazing. I can't believe you're all trying to knock yourselves out to keep the farm. But I don't want to drag you all down with me." He sat up straighter and took a deep breath. "Say Ursula gets some dirt on Modini. And let's say the tribe wants to do the conservation easement and the money comes through sooner than we think. And, okay, say Nu even gets a little grant to make his willow people. It ain't enough. Not even close. If we turn down the university's offer, knock ourselves out with pointless labor and unrepayable debts, and then we go bankrupt, what's the point?"

Nu noticed that Ursula was turning red in the face. Her coils had finally come undone and she was tugging a braid. "Wait a fucking minute!" she shouted, standing up so fast her chair crashed over behind her. "Let me get this straight. For years you've wanted to keep the farm at any cost, while everyone else was against it. Now everyone wants to keep the farm, but you're ready to give it up? I can't believe this shit! I can't believe my badass brother, one of the best goddamn farmers in the valley, is gonna turn tail." She put her hands on the table and leaned toward Bodie. "Are you suddenly okay with them bulldozing your house and your fields and the hop barn?"

They all sat still, watching the muscles twitch in Bodie's face. After a long minute, he stretched his jaw and took a deep breath. "Okay, people. You're crazy, and I guess I wouldn't have you any other way. I guess we're gonna love this damn farm straight to death."

"*Art Farm*," Fleece said. "Let's call it *Art Farm*."

Joe struggled to his feet, looking wobbly and worn out, but willing, maybe even inspired. He gripped the table edge with one leathery old hand and lifted his glass with the other. "To *Art Farm*," he said, turning to smile at Nu. They all hoisted their drinks. Joe looked across toward Ursula, then Fleece, and then to Bodie, and added, "We might outfox those bastards yet."

Part III
September 2008

28 · Ursula

Bart, the hospice nurse, came in the afternoon, so Ursula seized the opportunity to catch up on housecleaning. She had just tidied up Joe's room and was changing the bedsheets when Nu came in and offered to help. She tossed him two clean pillowcases, and he slithered the pillows into them.

Nu had been back for ten days. Before that he'd spent a week in Bend, where he'd finally completed his commissioned painting. Since his return to the farm, he'd been immersed in work on his *Art Farm* willow sculptures.

They changed the sheets on Nu's bed next, then hers. Nu was wearing baggy white painter's pants and a blue T-shirt with an ambling black bear stenciled across the chest, and Ursula kept sneaking glances at him, wishing she could see the intricate tree tattoo on his back again. When they'd finished, she hugged the bundle of dirty linens and headed downstairs.

Ursula dumped the sheets on top of the washing machine in the mud room, and they went to check on Joe. He and Bart were out on the back deck playing checkers. "I'll be here until 6," Bart said. "You two should go do something fun."

Ursula was about to dutifully refuse, but Joe growled at her. "Do as the man tells you!"

So they grabbed some apples and nut mix from the kitchen, stowed them in a daypack with a bottle of water, and headed out the front door.

"Where do you want to go?" Nu asked her. "We could hike up Skull Hill."

Ursula thought for a moment. "You know, I don't want to go anywhere. I like being here."

"Well, let's climb up to the cupola," Nu suggested.

Ursula had to concentrate hard on the ladder rungs; the one time she looked down, her head spun. They clambered up through the opening in the cupola floor and sat on opposite sides, admiring the views and talking about the family's chances for holding onto the farm.

"Did you hear Fleece found five $100 bills in the bottom of Bodie's underwear drawer?" Ursula asked. "Bodie doesn't even remember where it came from. Makes you wonder what else he's misplaced."

"Hey!" Nu said, popping up suddenly. "I haven't told you yet. The Furmans want me to do three more paintings."

Ursula stood up, too. A congratulatory hug seemed in order, but she suddenly felt dizzy and had to hang onto the railing. "That's so cool," she managed to tell him.

"Twenty thousand dollars," Nu said.

"Excuse me?"

"They are paying me 20K for three more paintings. I told them I couldn't get to them until after the New Year, and they were cool with that. They gave me 5 grand in advance."

"I thought you weren't sure about working with them," Ursula said. "It's kind of creepy, what they're doing." She knew about the Furmans' survivalist mansion, how conflicted Nu had felt about doing the first painting. She was kind of surprised he was so eager to do more work for them, the hefty commission notwithstanding.

"Truly, I do have reservations. Painting ornaments for a doomsday hideout is not my highest aspiration." He turned to look out over the farm fields. "But I tell you. That first painting, the *Airplane Graveyard*, came out, I have to say, great. And I already know what the next three paintings will be. I wish they weren't going to be socked away in the Furmans' house, but," he turned back around to face her, "I'm on fire, Urse. I went into my studio and painted the *Airplane Graveyard* in *four days*. I wanted to get back here and work with willow so bad I just knocked it out. I can do the same with the other three in January, after we save the farm."

He smiled across the hole at her. "Now I can get the AC fixed on my pickup," he said. "And maybe go to the barber, too," he added, rubbing his hand over his fuzzy scalp.

Ursula sidled around the hole until she was standing in front of him. "I can cut it for you," she said, reaching out to run her hand through his half inch of hair. She tried to make it seem like a professional appraisal, but her skin shivered, her ears felt hot. "I used to cut Daddy's all the time. I've got good clippers."

If he'd reached for her at that moment, it might have been dangerous, there in that too-small space, with the open hole in the center and the long fall below. But Nu had only looked at her sidelong. "Okay," he said. "If you'll let me cut yours."

When they got back to the house, Bart was packing up to leave. "Your father is in bed," he told Ursula. "I just gave him his morphine, so he'll probably sleep for three or four hours at least."

While Nu walked Bart out to his car, Ursula went to look in on Joe, who was indeed snoring peacefully. When she came out, Nu was tidying up dishes in the kitchen.

"Where shall we do it?" he asked her.

"Out on the deck. It's still nice outside, and it'll be easy to sweep up," Ursula said. "I'll get the clippers and the scissors. They're up in my room."

Upstairs, she pulled off her jeans, T-shirt, and sports bra and put on a loose blue shift. For comfort, she told herself. She went back downstairs and found Nu already on the deck sitting on a stool with his back to her. He'd taken off his T-shirt, and his elaborate pine-tree tattoo climbed the smooth skin of his back and shoulders as if it were alive. She plugged in the clippers and, starting at the nape of his neck, she worked up and over his skull. Resting her free hand at the side of his neck, she could feel his pulse there, strong and slow. When she moved around to do the front, she felt his breath blowing warm into her chest. It made her happy to imagine how deep he could see inside her dress, but when she glanced down at his face, his eyes were closed. She took a deep breath, focused, and finished up.

"There you go," she said, her heart pounding. She'd done a nice job.

"Feels good," Nu said, running his hand over his head. He stood and brushed himself off. "Scissors? Hairbrush?"

She handed them to him and took her place on the stool. Nu stood in front of her, appraising her hair.

"I really don't want..." she began to say, but he leaned forward and put two fingers on her lips.

"Just a trim," he said. "And I'd like to try braiding it a different way. Okay?"

He undid her braids and brushed her hair out, running the brush through it over and over again. There were tangles, as always, but he prized them apart with his fingers and worked the brush firmly through them. He must have brushed her hair a hundred strokes, two hundred strokes. It felt like warm ocean waves washing over her. He took up the scissors and, combing together little handfuls of hair with his fingers, snipped off the ends, less than an inch. She could see the wisps of hair as they landed on the deck. It took him quite a while. She was quaking inside, but she held herself still. Neither of them spoke. She could smell his body, salty and a little sour.

Then he parted her hair with the comb, not down the center as it had been parted for some thirty years, since she was a child, but off-center an inch or two. And once he'd established the part, he picked up the brush again and stroked some more. He gathered up her mane and divided the tresses into three hanks, then drew them over her left shoulder and braided them loosely in front.

She watched his face, surreptitiously, because she didn't know what she'd do if their eyes met. Or, no. She knew. And she didn't want it to happen a moment too soon.

He pulled a length of ribbon from his pocket. Where in the world had he found that? It was deep blue, scrub jay blue, and he wrapped it around the loose braid once, twice, three times, and tied it off with a bow.

He stepped back and regarded her. "Beautiful," he said.

Now she looked him full in the face, and he met her gaze. His eyes were enormous.

"I'm going upstairs to put the clippers away," she said. "Why don't you come and help me?"

It was three days later, and Ursula had spent the whole day getting her accounts in order, organizing all the manuals, spreadsheets, and client account information that Becca would want to look at. She had hoped to have her papers in better shape, but this would have to suffice.

When she had shut down the greenhouse earlier in the summer, she'd felt no regret about closing the business. But now, with Becca interested in buying the operation, she felt the faintest twinge of nostalgia. It had been a well-run business. Anyone could tell from looking at her books. She'd built up a modest but loyal clientele.

Her customers had valued her products, had recognized what talented growers she and Cat were. But she was done with that phase. She was looking forward to moving to Pullman, to working as a botanist again.

She tried to remember which hospice volunteer was coming this afternoon. Two months ago, when they'd first talked about signing up with hospice, she'd expected her father to resist the idea. She thought he'd hate having strangers in the house, hate being so deeply dependent, hate having his infirmities so intimately witnessed. But in the end, he was the one who'd insisted on it. "Because," he had argued, "you and Bodie and Nu need your hands free to work on the Opening." The Opening was shorthand for the combined Third Annual Tunder Farm Harvest Fest and the *Art Farm* art installation opening, now less than two weeks away. The amount of work they had to do to prepare for it was staggering, so Joe's logic had made sense.

She'd dreaded hospice, herself. The idea of having strangers in the house who might judge her caregiving, her housekeeping, her personal hygiene had given her the creeps. But hospice was working out better than any of them had imagined. Joe liked his primary nurse, Bart Yardley, and most of the nurse aides. And the volunteers who came to offer respite care—the "babysitters," as Joe referred to them—they were fine, too. Ursula had surprised herself by not trying to be especially friendly with any of them. She was cordial, of course, but all business. She knew her mother would have baked cookies and inquired after the volunteers' kids, dogs, or favorite movies. Ursula had no time for any of that. She was incredibly grateful to each of them, and she told them that often. But that was all she had the energy for. Otherwise, she used every moment of the freedom they granted her to work.

She'd expected the hospice people to be a big distraction, but that wasn't really the case. They came and went without fuss. What *was* a huge distraction was Nu, the way he would suddenly impinge on her thoughts throughout the day. She'd be making notes for questions to ask Giles, the attorney, about the potential sale of her business, and all of a sudden she'd be flooded with a fantasy of undressing him. It felt wonderful, but aggravating. She needed to stay focused on the Opening.

Nu had been out working on sculptures since early morning. Joe had been up fairly early, too. She'd made him breakfast, and they'd gone for a short walk to Bodie's house and back. He'd taken a nap, then sat in his chair in the kitchen watching birds for a while. She'd found him there around noon, dozing. She got him to eat half a tuna sandwich for lunch, and reminded him that Becca was coming over later in the afternoon to talk about buying the greenhouse business.

Becca arrived precisely at 4. She looked gorgeous as always, wearing a forest green track suit that molded nicely around her conspicuously pregnant belly, and pretty pale yellow trainers. Ursula watched her reach back into the car and pull out a new-looking leather briefcase, a good sign, Ursula thought. Becca was already accessorizing for her new business career.

"Come in," Ursula said, giving her a brief hug. "Let's go sit in the kitchen. I'll make tea."

"Can I say hi to your dad? How's he doing?"

Ursula made an exaggerated frown. "He's asleep. He's going down pretty fast, actually. He's just trying to hold on until the Opening."

In the kitchen, Ursula set two cups of tea on the table, and Becca drew some papers from her briefcase. "Before we talk about the greenhouse, you should have a look at these." She passed a handful of pages to Ursula.

"Are these...?" Becca had told Ursula the general drift of the correspondence between her husband Randy and Dexter. It appeared that these were printouts of the actual emails.

"Just read them," Becca said, with an edge to her voice.

The emails dated from more than a year ago up to nearly the present. The two men discussed how to preserve the deception about the purpose of the proposed research farm, and the secret deal to sell some of the property to Susan Sauer. The more Ursula read, the angrier she grew. There weren't any big revelations beyond what Becca had already told her, but seeing the scam unfold email by detailed email made her feel faint with loathing.

"Sick, isn't it?" Becca said. Then, sounding concerned, "Hey, don't get stuck there, Ursula. Take some deep breaths."

Ursula did as told, until her breathing returned to near normal. "Do you think Dexter has money in the deal?"

Becca leafed through the papers. "Look at this one. 'Going to Sonoma this weekend to confirm my investment.' That's where Susan's living now. There's another reference to Sonoma somewhere. I can't find it right now, but it seems like he's been down there a couple of times."

"Jesus, he's still screwing Susan," Ursula said.

Becca frowned, then shrugged. "I wouldn't put it past him, would you?"

"His poor wife," Ursula said. "She deserves to know."

Becca shook her head. "No doubt. But we don't know anything for sure about that."

Ursula put her head on the table for a moment, then sat up and sipped her tea. "I don't give a shit about Dexter. The only issue is his role in Susan's real estate deal. It's clearly unethical. But is it *illegal?* Maybe. Maybe not. There's nothing in our contract with the university that says they can't change the plan for the use of the land. That's our bad. We weren't on top of that one, *at all.*"

"Your dad was sick, your mom had just died."

"Yeah, yeah. We forgive ourselves," Ursula said impatiently. "But now we really want to get out of this mess."

"So what is the plan? How can I help?"

"You know most of it. We've had our attorney send them the conservation easement we're doing with the tribes. We're not asking for comment or anything. Just presenting it as a done deal. Likewise with the cemetery plot."

"Are you really going to bury your father in Bodie and Fleece's garden?"

Ursula laughed. "Where'd you hear that?"

"Fleece told me."

"When did you talk to Fleece?"

"We're in baby group together. Didn't you know that?"

Ursula shook her head. "I can't keep track of myself anymore, let alone the rest of my crazy family. But yeah, maybe. I don't know if we'll actually end up burying Daddy there. For now, it's just another way to mess with the university. If he really wants a home burial, we'll probably put his grave more out toward the driveway. Andy wants to make a fake headstone and have it in place for the Opening."

"Seriously? Oh, god, that's good. Doesn't it creep your dad out, though?"

"Becca, he is so excited to be buried here."

"You *are* a crazy family," Becca said, then pointed down at the papers on the table. "So what are you going to do with these emails?"

"We've debated that. As you know, we don't have any way to break our contract. Our only hope is to get Modini to withdraw his backing, or for CVSU to get cold feet. So here's the plan. Bodie has invited Dexter and Modini to come to Nu's art opening. He told them we want to have a ceremony to honor their vision."

"That's balls."

"Right? Bring the crooks into our trap."

"Will they come though?"

"There's a football game that night. Dexter told Bodie that the university invited Modini to come up for the day, do some schmoozing and a business meeting, probably, and attend the game that evening. I don't really expect him to come to the farm, but maybe he'll send a stooge. I don't know. But Dex is coming. He's already confirmed. He might bring the dean. And Dexter is the one we're after, anyway."

Becca looked around the kitchen. "You got anything to eat?"

Ursula found some shortbread cookies and refilled their tea cups. Then she detailed the rest of the family's plan. At the Opening, they would give Dexter an envelope containing copies of these emails and any other dirt they had on him. If Modini or anybody from Earthwide showed up, they'd give them printouts of all the stories about poor sanitation in their handling facilities, the labor complaints. If nobody from Earthwide came, those would be FedEx'd to corporate headquarters in Fresno to arrive on Modini's desk Monday morning. "Just to let them know there will be resistance. That we'll make sure everyone here knows what kind of an outfit might be coming to town."

And the piece she really liked—it had been Fleece's idea—immediately following the Opening, they would spread the word in the local media that the deal was off. That Modini and CVSU had come to see the true value of Tunder Farm to the whole community, and wished them continued success as a family farm.

"Taking the high road," Becca said. "That's brilliant. But will any of the media go for it?"

Ursula waved a cookie at her friend. "You'd be amazed what people will do for a former football star. The editor of the *Tattler* is an old friend of Bodie's. And he likes to stick it to the university whenever he can."

Ursula glanced down at the sheets of email, and a bad thought suddenly dawned on her. "What will Randy do when he finds out you gave these to me?"

"He knows," Becca said. "I told him. I told him what he and Dexter were doing was *wrong*. That he needed to help you get out of the sale."

"And he agreed?" Ursula gasped.

Becca made a stern face. "Let's just say he decided not to cross me. Modini's money would have meant some big opportunities for Randy, so he's disappointed about that. But now, thanks to some compelling arguments from his wife," Becca paused and smiled, "Randy understands what the farm means to you and your family."

"Oh, my god, I can't believe you're doing this for us."

"It's not just for you, Ursula. We can't let the university ruin this place. It's too special. It belongs to the whole community, not some lettuce empire."

Ursula felt tears trickling down her cheeks. She swiped at her face with a napkin. "I..." she said, and had to stop and blow her nose.

"I'm in a good space, Urse," Becca said. "I love Randy, but he screwed up. I think he realizes that now, and he's going to help fix it, to the best of his ability. I think we'll be okay."

"And buying my greenhouse? He's supportive?"

"Oh, well, sure. I don't think he feels like it's a good time to *not* be supportive. It's my money." She shrugged and gobbled down another cookie. "Hey, let's go look at my new business venture."

The afternoon was overcast and cool. For more than a month it had been miserably hot without a stitch of rain. Today there was a slight chance of a shower, with rain forecast for later in the week.

They needed it. But with all the work they had to accomplish before the Opening, Ursula wished the rain would hold off.

They strolled down the driveway and veered off to the overlook. "Holy moly," Becca said. "Who are all those people? I thought this was Sunday."

Ursula surveyed the scene below. It was even busier than usual. "Well, that's Nu there in the middle of the pumpkin patch. He's got a couple of Andy's people helping with one of the willow sculptures there. Andy's around somewhere. There he is, out by the far end of the lake. See the tractor and the wagon? Looks like they're harvesting more willows. There's Bodie. Can't miss him. He and, I think that's Arnold, are moving irrigation pipe. The farm work goes on all the time, even if you're trying to get ready for an event."

"How is Fleece doing?" Becca asked, reaching out to wrap her arm around Ursula's waist. "She's due about twelve weeks before me. So it's coming up pretty soon."

"Well, there she is," Ursula said, pointing far out toward the pasture beyond the cropland. "See that? They've made that little temporary paddock with electric fence so she could shear a couple of the ewes."

"I didn't think this was shearing season," Becca said.

"That's right. But Nu needs some loose wool for his sculptures, and Fleece had a couple of ewes she was willing to do a trim on."

As they watched, two men flipped a sheep to the ground, and Fleece bent over it with what must be electric shears. "Wow, eight months pregnant. What a woman." Becca turned to look back down again toward Nu. "Tell me more about Nu's art project."

Ursula described the *Art Farm* concept, how the twelve life-sized willow sculptures would be spread around the farm, each of them depicting some aspect of farm life. "There'll be a woodcutter in the woods over there, big muscly dude, except she'll be female. The *Pumpkin Man*. And there's a *Chicken Lady*. That'll be in Fleece's backyard. I can't remember all of them. Nu sees it as a single work of art, bringing together the whole farm."

"How is it coming?"

"He's pretty freaked out, to tell you the truth. He's only finished, I think, three. He has them all started, at least."

"But the show, the Opening, is...?"

"I know! Thirteen days! It's going to be chaos. Everybody feels a ton of pressure. And it sounds like there will be gobs of people coming from the arts community, maybe from all over the state. Because of Andy. He is so connected. And then it's the annual Harvest Fest, too." Ursula shivered, thinking of all the work she had still to do. "Music. Food booths. Craft vendors. Porta Pottis. Parking lot attendants. Flowers. Cat and I promised to make bouquets for the volunteers. Oh, Becca, I really don't know if we can do it."

They sighed at the same time.

"I remember when you brought me to this lookout point back in June," Becca said. "I was stunned. I still feel it right now. What a gorgeous farm. Shangri-la!"

"I have to tell you," Ursula said, "shit happens in Shangri-la. But, yeah, thanks. It's a pretty place." Ursula felt Becca tighten her grip around her waist. The two women swayed together, quietly regarding the scene below. "We'd better head over to the greenhouse," Ursula said. As they walked, she asked Becca, "How do you know Cat anyway?"

"We did phone bank together for the Dems last month."

"Cat?" Ursula said. "I can't imagine her doing anything political."

"She's hot for Obama, I can tell you that," Becca said. "When she mentioned that she was out of a job since you closed the greenhouse, that's when I got the idea of buying in."

"Well, here it is," Ursula said. She gave Becca a quick tour, starting with the seeding room, then the potting shed, and on into the main greenhouse.

"Cat should be here any minute."

"I've been meaning to ask you," Becca said. "Did Cat do your hair? I really like it over your shoulder like that."

"Uh, Nu did it," Ursula said.

"Mm-hmm," Becca said. "Nu has talents I wasn't aware of."

Ursula led Becca to the desk and opened a big binder. "Here are the seeding charts. Irrigation and fertilizer schedules. All the basic operational stuff."

Becca paged through the binder. "This looks good, Ursula." Then she took a step back and let her gaze roam all around the greenhouse. "I just love the feel of this place, the way the air tastes. Randy thinks

I'm nuts to take over your business, but I tell you, I've never been so excited about anything."

"Not even yoga?"

"Oh, I'm tired of yoga. Of teaching anyway. This," she gestured toward the benches, "this will be such a great new challenge. But I'd need Cat to coach me. And, really, to run the show."

As if on cue, Cat flung open the sliding door and barged inside. "What's up, ladies?" she called out.

Cat was dressed in a filmy summer frock, sand-colored with a floral pattern, and black pumps. She must be coming from church, Ursula guessed. Cat strolled up to Becca and shook her hand, and she gave Ursula a wink and a nod.

"You look great, Cat," Ursula said. "Love that dress."

"You look pretty spiffy yourself, girl." Cat said. She turned to Becca. "What do you think of her new hairstyle?"

"I like it," Becca said.

"Yeah, it's cute," Cat said, and to Ursula added, "Makes you look like a dairy maid. At least you're finally sleeping with him."

Becca stifled a laugh. Ursula tried to look outraged, but she knew the blush rising in her cheeks gave her away. "Well!" she said. "What of it?"

"Damn right, girl. What of it? Nobody's business but your own. But sweet Jesus, I can't believe how long it took you two to figure it out."

29 · Bodie

As the packaging promises, the IKEA crib is easy to assemble. Until the final step. Bodie can't seem to get the side rail aligned in the channel. It won't raise and lower like it's supposed to. He swears quietly. Fleece is already asleep. He can hear her sawing logs in the bedroom next door. She never snored like that before she was pregnant, loud and growly. But lately she sleeps best flat on her back and snores galore. Bodie figures he'll sleep in the spare bed here in the baby's room if she's still making noise like that. They could both use a decent night's rest.

He can't believe how Fleece continues to work, helping him in the fields, helping Nu with the willows. Last week when they'd harvested the hops, she drove the tractor, and she also made huge lunches for all the extra help. Yesterday she stood in the packing line for two hours, sorting and bunching green onions for the Wednesday market at the fairgrounds, chattering away with Zebra and the crew. And this evening she sat down after dinner—a nice dinner of Irish stew and tossed salad that she made from scratch—and paid all the bills. Their hops were going to fetch the best price ever, and their finances were looking ever so slightly up.

"We're not flush," she'd told him, smiling wearily and blowing a loose strand of hair from her eyes. "But we'll make it to the New Year."

He lifts the crib rail out and tries again to position it. Nope. It still won't lower. He kicks it in frustration and hears something crack. Groaning, he bends down to inspect the leg of the crib, gives the crib a shake. Seems okay. Might have been his bad knee popping.

Maybe tomorrow he can get Nu to help him align the rails. It's been a shock, a goddam revelation, to discover how good Nu is with fix-it stuff like this. For an artist, he's incredibly handy, and not afraid to get down in the dirt. But part of the deal with Nu staying here and helping the family try to hang onto the farm is one, no more plumbing, and two, no more fieldwork. And Bodie has stayed true to his promise, leaving Nu to work on his willow sculptures.

Nu surely wouldn't mind helping him assemble this crib, though. And besides, Bodie spent a couple of hours today cutting willow withes for Nu, carting them over to the pumpkin patch where Nu was weaving a bigger than life-size farmer. Bodie recalls the ribbing he'd been subjected to. He'd been off-loading the sticks when Juano had walked over from the tomatoes, pointed to the sculpture, and exclaimed, "Señor Bodie, it is you!" And then Zebra dashed over and made him stand beside the sculpture while she snapped photos with her phone. The sculpture didn't look anything like Bodie. It had sad brown eyes and a bushy mustache, and its body was round and bulging. It looked like a cross between Sam Elliot and the Michelin Man. But he'd played along.

He's still not sure about the whole *Art Farm* thing. He's only seen a couple of the sculptures. The shepherdess and the ewe out in the pasture, that one he likes. The willow withes that form the lady's long skirt swoop out as if billowing in a breeze. The ewe isn't particularly well proportioned, to his mind. The muzzle is too long. But Nu tucked some tufts of real fleece into the weaving along its back, a nice touch. The only other sculpture he's seen is the girl on the horse. It's the only one Nu isn't constructing in place. It's kind of fragile, Nu told him, so he's making that one in Joe's shop. He'll install it out in the paddock behind the hop barn the day before the *Art Farm* opening. It's pretty special, Bodie has to admit. Nu made the framework out of welded wire, then wove willows around it, finishing with a beautiful smooth hide of fine dried grasses. How Nu could make it seem so alive is beyond him. And the girl on the horse's back exudes the same life-force as the horse. Her painted face looks Asian, with narrow, slanted eyes and a button nose, but her hair is blond, made of sweetgrass in twin braids.

It's cool how they've made the faces on all the sculptures. Andy and his people formed papier-mâché masks from everyone's faces—his, Fleece's, Ursula's, even Joe's, plus some of the helpers—then Andy and Nu painted them with semi-realistic features. With the horse girl, the contrast between the sleek, stylized body and the girl's vivid face is kind of eerie.

He still can't really believe that the art will make any impression on the university, though. Nu and Andy have filed their application for a copyright, and Giles, the family attorney, sent a copy to CVSU, but they haven't even acknowledged receiving it. Nu says it takes months to process copyright applications. Which is good, because they'll almost certainly get rejected, but until then it might give the university something extra to fret about.

Suddenly hungry, he goes into the kitchen. There was one piece of apple pie left after dinner, he remembers. But, nope. Here's the pie pan in the sink with nothing but crumbs remaining. Fleece and her fetus have beaten him to it. There might be some Bodie cakes in the bread drawer, though. Ah, yes. He takes one out and peels away the paper. As he leans on the counter and takes a big bite of the pumpkin-ginger muffin, he notices the little green light flashing on the answering machine. He punches the replay.

"Hello. This is a message for Mr. Bodie Tunder. This is Gladys Allie calling from CVSU. I am administrative assistant to Dean Cockburn and I'm calling about your interest in hosting Edward Modini at your farm this coming Saturday. Mr. Modini is interested in seeing the property. The dean notes that Mr. Modini has a forty-five-minute window available in his schedule, 1:45 to 2:30, on Saturday. Please call me back as soon as you're able and let me know if I can tell the dean that that is a good time for his visit."

Holy shit. He's coming. Mr. Spinach himself, the king of mass-marketed salad mix. Bodie glances at the clock on the stove. After 11. Too late to call Ursula.

The Harvest Fest and Nu's *Art Farm* opening are—Bodie counts with his fingers—"Thursday, Friday, Saturday. Three fucking days away." Well, if Modini is in fact coming, it doesn't really change the amount of work he has to do. His work load remains impossible. But it slightly increases the chances of their success.

Does he really believe that? No. There's no chance of success. No way they can scare off Modini and the university. He remembers how he used to approach football games when his team was going to be seriously outclassed. He raises his muffin as if making a toast or invoking the gods. "We don't have a prayer," he says aloud, reciting again his private locker-room mantra. "But I swear to do my absolute best to bust as many heads as I can."

30 · Nu

Nu tucked the end of the willow withe under another stem in the woman's armpit, but he wasn't confident it would stay put. "Hand me a piece of wire, would you?"

The sculpture they were working on was a woman gathering eggs. Short and stocky, she was modeled loosely on Fleece, though the painted face mask made her out to be African American. She was standing beside Fleece's chicken coop. On Saturday morning, Nu would come by and hang a willow basket from her hand, placing a couple of fresh eggs in it.

As Andy was clipping a length of copper wire from the roll, the willow sprang free and whacked Nu across the cheek. "Arggh. Fucking willow," Nu cried. He pressed his hand to the wound. When he drew it away, there was a thin wisp of blood on his palm.

"Buck up, Nugie," Andy said, handing Nu a Band-Aid from the stash in his shirt pocket. "You're an Artist, are you not?"

Andy had the disposition of a Labrador retriever. Nu had never, not once, seen him dispirited or mean. Angry, sure. Outraged at the wholesale exploitation of humans and nature. But even in his anti-capitalist rants, Andy seemed full of innocent joy. He could be occasionally irritating, the way a Lab, staring up at you with big eyes, wet nose, and slobbery tongue, begging you to throw the ball for the hundredth time, could be irritating. But on this project Nu would have been lost—practically, aesthetically, and emotionally lost—without Andy.

"Seems like you're wound up a little tight there, Van Nuys," Andy said. "Are you getting enough sleep?"

Andy's tone was so genuinely solicitous that Nu didn't realize he was being teased until he glanced up and saw Andy leering at him, smacking his lips.

Nu flung a ball of twine at Andy, but missed by a yard. Andy laughed and fetched the twine from where it fell under a shrub ten feet away. "Seriously," Andy said, tossing the twine back to Nu. "You and Ursula are burning the candle a little close, aren't you?"

Nu fussed with the squiggly twigs that made up the *Chicken Lady*'s hair, manzanita branches he had gathered near Santiam Pass on his last trip back from Bend. A delicious henna color, they snaked out from her head like a hundred mini-dreads. They were her most beguiling feature.

"What are we supposed to do? Take a vacation? The Opening is…"

"Three days away!" Andy said.

Nu groaned and shook his head.

Andy clapped him on the shoulder. "Just don't wear yourself out, Van Nuys, okay? After the Opening, you and Ursula can stay in bed for a week."

Nu recoiled at the suggestion. A week in bed was for sick people. Even if he were with Ursula, he couldn't fathom spending a whole week *indoors*, much less in bed.

Where were he and Ursula headed? He couldn't foresee it. They had found only stray moments in the past few weeks—during meals, on walks, in bed at night—to share their thoughts about a possible future together. Ursula was committed to working as a scientist again. She would almost certainly be offered a job at Washington State University, working with Marlys, studying *Xeropyllum tenax* and all the other wild fiber plants of the Pacific Northwest. Nu wasn't sure how his more nebulous ambitions might dovetail with Ursula's. Their paths might twine, or they might diverge. Everything was in flux.

The only sure pivot was Joe's impending death. After that, the farm would be sold or saved, though "saved" would be a tenuous condition. If Bodie and Fleece continued to live and farm here, this place would be, in some sense, the family home, the center of the Tunders' small realm. Nu admired Bodie's and Fleece's fidelity to this land, and he could sense the energy and inspiration that flowed up from the earth into them. He'd been changed by his summer of working and living at Tunder Farm, he knew that.

But farm work was not what fueled him. And the wet west side of the Cascades would never feel like home. He got his energy from art, and from the air—hot, dry air. He needed to be in the high desert most of the year. If there was some halfway place, some middle ground where he and Ursula could be together, they hadn't figured it out yet.

The *Chicken Lady*'s hairdo still needed something. Nu tweaked another manzanita twig. "Should we maybe twine a scarf through her hair?"

"Look, mate, we're running out of time. You're going to have to lower your standards if you're going to survive this."

"My standards went belly-up a month ago."

"Yeah, well, it's folk art we're making here, right? Embrace mediocrity." Just then Andy's phone buzzed. "Better get this. It's Bolo."

While Andy talked, Nu made a few final adjustments to the *Chicken Lady*'s tresses. His friend Bolo, Andy had told him, was the editor of the *Camas Valley Tattler*, the entertainment weekly that came out every Thursday. A lot more locals would come to the Opening if it were well covered by the *Tattler*.

Andy snapped the phone shut. "He's gonna run the story."

"Sweet," Nu said. "How about your photo of Joe and *The Grieving Mother?*"

"Yep. We got the centerfold. Bolo says the announcement for the Opening will be on the left-hand page, with the story about Joe's art career on the right."

"Fantastic," Nu said. He dropped his pruners into the tool bucket and started gathering up the rest of the supplies. They'd have to call it good enough on the *Chicken Lady*. "It would be nice if the cvsu people knew our ceremony was on record. Think any media people will show up?"

"Nugie, my friend, you *know* this. Publicity is not something left to chance. The fourth estate has to be coddled," Andy said, grinning mischievously, "or else cloned. I've asked some friends to come dressed, shall we say, in journalistic costume. I can promise you there will be a large and conspicuous, if mostly bogus, media presence."

31 · Ursula

"Want to see it?" Zebra stood and tugged up the hem of her tank top to reveal the horse tattooed low on her belly. "Stallion," she told them.

Ursula leaned across the corner of the kitchen table to get a closer look. The horse was in full gallop just above Zebra's navel. She wanted to touch it but the skin all around the new tattoo was red and raw-looking. "Cool," Ursula said, and she couldn't help adding, even though she knew it would make her sound like a nagging mom, "Does it hurt?"

Zebra ignored the question. "Let's see if I can do this," Zebra said, and rolled her abs. "Does he look like he's galloping?"

"Not really," Fleece said. "When you squinch your muscles, his legs just disappear."

"Ah, shit."

"He's very beautiful, though," Fleece hastened to add.

Ursula gathered the sheets of paper on the table in front of her. The three of them had just spent an hour going over the script for tomorrow's ceremony. Everyone—the three of them, Bodie, Nu, even

Joe—had a role to play and everyone needed to be in sync. Once Dexter and Modini arrived, everything had to go fast and snappy. Crucial pieces of information had to be delivered at exactly the right time and place. Thus the script. Not that they'd be able to memorize it, or speak their parts verbatim. But they did need to stick to it super closely. Zebra had proven to be the best writer among them, and she'd composed most of the text over the past few days. They had just now made one last round of revisions, and Ursula volunteered to type up the final draft and print out copies to give to everyone tomorrow.

"Are we done?" Ursula asked.

Joe wobbled into the kitchen doorway and stood leaning against the jamb. "Need some water," he said, his voice hoarse and weak. Hanging onto the counter, he shuffled into the kitchen. Ursula popped out of her chair to fill a glass, but Fleece had gotten to the sink before her. Zebra was up and at Joe's elbow, supporting him, as Fleece handed him his drink.

"We could have brought this to you, Daddy," Ursula said.

"Heard you out here. Figured I'd better make sure you weren't causing any trouble. Let me see that tattoo."

"How long have you been listening to us?" Ursula asked. Joe had been asleep in the living room when Zebra and Fleece had arrived.

"Sit down, old man," Zebra ordered, spinning a chair around for him. Once Fleece had lowered Joe onto the chair, Zebra stood right in front of him and pulled her shirt up again. "What do you think?"

Joe blinked a few times and leaned forward till he was just a few inches from Zebra's stomach. "Damn," he said. "Makes me want to hop on and take a ride."

Zebra slapped him lightly on the side of his head. "Down, cowboy. Your wrangling days are over."

"You want something to eat, Daddy?"

Joe shook his head. "I'd better go lie back down."

"Beatrice will be coming in a little while." Ursula told him. Zebra helped Joe stand up, and she and Fleece shepherded him back into the living room. Ursula closed her eyes and let her chin sink wearily to her chest for a moment. She heard the murmur of their voices from the living room, then Fleece chirping, "Chick-a-dee-dee-dee." They must be watching the birds at the feeder.

Beatrice, Joe's favorite hospice volunteer, had asked if she could move the feeders from the backyard and install them in front of the living room windows, where Joe could bird-watch from his bed. Despite all the people coming and going to the front door, lots of birds—finches, sparrows, chickadees, nuthatches—had quickly adapted to the feeder's new location. Beatrice was a serious birder. She particularly loved the LBJs: little brown jobs. She and Joe would sit there for an hour, each with a pair of binoculars, and try to identify individual birds by telltale distinctions—a ragged tail feather, an oddly shaped beak, a neurotic habit of flicking wings while at the perch. They were like an old married couple, and Ursula was somewhat concerned that Beatrice might be getting attached to Joe. But that was a risk that hospice volunteers were willing to take, she supposed.

She'd been surprised at how readily her father had given himself over to the hospice people. Bart, the main nurse guy, was easy to like. Incredibly competent. But Joe talked with all the volunteers, swapping life stories with near strangers. Had her father been more like this before Alice died? Ursula tried to remember. Amazing how difficult it was to recall how Joe had been just those few years ago. But yes, her father had been more outgoing and friendly. Joe could seem gruff and a little scary to some people, Ursula remembered, with his ragged eyebrows and burn-scarred cheeks, looking like a pirate in his greasy coveralls. But he had been quick to laugh and could draw anyone into conversation. It was only when Alice died that Joe had become so angry and withdrawn.

But now he seemed to be reverting to his younger, easier way of being. His pain meds helped, no doubt, making him comfortable and more gregarious, but Ursula thought there was some deeper transformation happening, too. She'd expected him to fight every stage of his dying, but that hadn't been the case at all. For instance, she'd put off broaching the subject of bringing in a hospital bed because she thought Joe would regard it as waving the white flag of surrender. But Joe said sure. It would make it easier for Bart when he came to administer drugs. The only thing he insisted on was that it be placed so he could look outside. So they'd moved the sofa over to Bodie's house, and put the new hospital bed in the living room facing the picture window.

Ursula heard another, louder voice enter the living room. Bodie. Probably come to fetch Fleece. Ursula put the tea cups in the sink, and headed in to say hi to her brother. There was a knock on the front door, and Beatrice came in, followed, to Ursula's surprise, by Nu.

Beatrice made a beeline for Joe's bed. "Look what I've got," she said, holding up a copy of the *Tattler*. "You have to see this."

She shook open the newspaper and handed it to Joe. Ursula caught Nu's eye and he slid past Bodie and joined her. With his arm around her back and his hand on her hip, Ursula felt some of her tiredness drain away.

Joe thrust the paper back to Beatrice. "Read it out loud, would you?"

Beatrice looked around, flustered. "Nu? Maybe you should..."

"No, no. Please," Nu told her.

"Well, alright."

Fleece and Zebra took seats on Joe's bed, and Bodie leaned back against the wall. Nu squeezed Ursula tighter, brushing his lips along her ear.

Beatrice pushed her glasses up her nose and read aloud.

ART FARM PROJECT WEAVES COMMUNITY TOGETHER

Artist Nu Van Nuys's new art installation is comprised of nine life-sized willow sculptures of people engaged in everyday farming activities tucked among the fields and gardens at the Tunder Family farm.

An opening art reception will be held at the farm on Saturday, September 26 as part of the farm's third annual Harvest Fest. The day-long event includes food and craft booths, a beer garden, and live music by Camas Valley Grass.

Van Nuys says his sculptures are intended to weave the farm into a single work of art. He has even taken the unusual initiative of applying for a copyright. The *Tattler* asked Mr. Van Nuys what the point of a copyright would be.

"A well-managed farm, with both wild and cultivated lands, is a human construction, and some of the best of them, such as the Tunder Farm, rise to art," Van Nuys said. "These sculptural installations are meant to awaken an awareness of the larger artwork that the farm already is. Copyrighting the farm as whole is really just a further gesture toward acknowledging the integrity of the ecosystem as art."

The farm is the longtime home of sculptor Joseph Tunder. Tunder's work received national notice when one of his sculptures, *The Grieving Mother,* was captured in a photograph of a local Vietnam War protest that turned violent (see photo on facing ' page). Though Tunder had no direct role in the riot, he was fired from his position in the CVSU art department.

Local artist Andy Patterson helped Van Nuys restore Tunder's sculpture. "Joe Tunder is a true original. It's been thrilling to revive this important example of his early work," said Patterson. The restored sculpture will be on display on Saturday as well.

"Here's the picture of your sculpture," Beatrice said, handing the paper back to Joe.

Joe sighed and dropped the paper onto the bed. "You know," he began. His voice was just a murmur and Ursula had to move closer to hear what he was saying. "If you all want me alive for the show tomorrow, you'd better let me get some sleep."

Ursula saw Joe pat Beatrice's hand. Fleece and Zebra leaned down to give him hugs, and then everyone headed out the front door. Ursula remained with Beatrice while she gave Joe a pill and a drink of water.

"I'll just stay till he's asleep," Beatrice told her. "Then I need to scoot."

"I've got him," Ursula said. "Thank you so much. For everything."

Ursula went looking for Nu and found him standing at the kitchen sink eating straight from a bowl of leftover potato salad. He finished a glass of apple juice and said, "I've still got a shitload of work to do. Way more than I'll be able to finish. I'll see you in bed." He kissed her, sighed, and went out the back door.

Ursula picked up the script from the kitchen table. She needed to type up the edited version and make copies for everyone. She should iron her clothes for tomorrow, too, and while she was at it pick out a shirt and pants for Joe and iron those as well.

The *Tattler* story would bring out more people tomorrow. That would be good for the cause, she supposed, but make the day even more stressful. She wasn't sure Joe could participate. The cancer was spreading. His skin had gone to paper, blotched everywhere with bruises. His cheeks were sunken, his face skeletal. And his pain was getting more constant, harder to manage. Bart had told her it could be dicey if Joe wanted to be part of the events tomorrow. And he'd told Joe he would have to stay in his wheelchair, and he'd have to have an IV to keep him hydrated.

Ursula heard some muffled sounds from the living room and figured she'd better go check on him. In the kitchen doorway she paused to peek around the doorjamb. Beatrice was whispering to Joe. The bed was still tipped up and facing the windows, so Ursula couldn't see her father, only the purple-veined, emaciated hand that Beatrice held and stroked.

32 · Bodie

The morning of the Harvest Fest, Bodie is up before 4. In a pre-dawn stupor, he starts the coffeemaker. He draws off the first, extra-strong cup of coffee as the pot begins to fill, then blows and sips at the steaming mug, leaning on the kitchen counter in his underwear. He promised Fleece he'd make her an omelet for breakfast, but she won't be up until 6, so, with his second cup of coffee he eats a ham sandwich to tide himself over. Now it's time for the most important part of the day, his pre-game shower.

For years, beginning in high school, before each football game he would try to arrive at the locker room well before his teammates. Offering just the briefest of greetings to the equipment manager, the trainer, and any teammates who'd come in earlier, he'd head for the showers. Within the privacy of the needling hot water, in the shelter of the enveloping steam, he would imagine all the plays the other team might run at him. He would watch, from his helm at middle linebacker, the opposing linemen dropping back into pass protection, or trap-blocking his left guard to open a lane for an inside run. Keying on the quarterback's eyes, he would be able to read whether the QB would be passing or handing off. And Bodie could sense his own footwork as he'd almost take the bait and believe the fullback was coming off tackle, but recover instantly as the quarterback pulled the ball and rolled to his left looking for his tight end. If the pass came out quick and accurate, Bodie would close ground fast and take the tight end down for a short gain with a rib-bruising tackle. Or else he'd be there in time to break up the pass, maybe even pick it off and take it to the end zone. He'd done that more than a few times.

Now, as Bodie stands under the shower, he envisions the Harvest Fest, the coming day. He sees himself making his rounds, starting out by the road, where he will clap his old teammates on the back and thank them for volunteering to manage the car parking. Then he can make a quick detour over to the cut-flower beds, where Cat will be gathering great bunches of asters and sunflowers and black-eyed Susans, maybe give Cat a big kiss on the cheek, make her laugh and blush. Next he'll check in with Juano running their vegetable stand, make sure he has people who can fetch more produce from the cooler if anything starts running low. Then he'll wind past the craft booths, over to the pod of food stands, maybe grab a sun burger at the Nearly Normals' booth. From there he can wander into the beer garden—it was his idea to put it at the edge of the hop yard under a row of hop vines he left unharvested for the occasion. He will keep his beer consumption modest, even though he's eager to sample Camas Valley Tapster's new IPA, and it is his job, after all, as host of the Harvest Fest, to help his vendors feel appreciated.

Bodie closes the cold-water handle a tick. The longer he stands here, the hotter he wants it. The water almost scalds the back of his neck. He probably has another ten minutes before it starts to cool. He wishes they had a bigger hot-water tank. Or a hot tub! That would be nice for the old sciatica. A guy can dream. He just hopes the heater recovers before Fleece gets up. She'll be pissed at him if there isn't enough hot water for her shower.

He feels good. Despite getting just four or five hours of sleep every night this week, he knows he won't get tired today. Crowds give him energy. He'll be calm, practically euphoric as he moves through the crush. He chuckles, recalling something one of his college teammates once told him. "Bodie, your body uses so much energy, you get an endorphin high just from breathing." He can still move quick as a linebacker, he likes to think. Big as he is, he will nevertheless glide between knots of visitors without bumping a shoulder. No one will feel threatened by his size; rather, they'll be put at ease by his demeanor. Some old-timer will no doubt shake his hand and recall Bodie's tackle-for-loss on the final play of the game against Stanford twelve years ago. Zebra's Goth friends, sulky young adults of indeterminate gender, will welcome his hugs.

Last year almost three hundred people came to the Harvest Fest. Today, with the publicity about Nu's art opening, plus all the advertising they've done, Bodie thinks they may get twice that many. He just hopes his dad will be well enough to make it through the day. The plan calls for Bart to wheel Joe outside after lunch, let him sit in the sun for a while, watching the crowd from a safe distance. Andy and Nu will be leading a select group of art people on a walking tour of the *Art Farm* installation. They'll wind up at the booth where Joe's few surviving sculptures are mounted, and then on to *The Grieving Mother* standing nearby in all her restored glory. Then, the hope is, some of these art poo-bahs will swing by to congratulate Joe, say something nice about his work. Bodie will go over and join them for a bit. He'll put his arm around his dad's shoulder, maybe tease him about the patchy white beard he's sporting now that he is, as Joe himself says, "beyond shaving." Then, if he has a chance, he'll catch up with Nu and tell him how much he likes the willow sculptures, maybe not the *Pumpkin Man* so much, but the *Shepherdess* definitely. How much he appreciates the effort Nu has made to help them hold onto the land, regardless of the final outcome.

He might even have time to jump onto the hay wagon and ride down to the fields, playing peek-a-boo with the babies on board, flirting with their cherubic young mothers. He will stay in constant motion until it's time for Dexter and Modini to arrive.

Then things will get tense. Then the team will begin their final series of maneuvers. He's got his playbook in writing, everything he's supposed to say as he and Zebra and Fleece chaperone the enemy toward the stage. And it's a good thing he has it written down, because he's no good at ad-libbing. And he can't actually see how the climax will unfold. Try as he might, with the hot shower water beginning to cool slightly, he can't envision it. Once Dexter arrives, the scene goes dark.

33 · Nu

It was past noon before Nu saw an opportunity to sneak off. He'd planned to go up into the cupola first thing this morning, before anyone else was out and about, in order to survey the Harvest Fest setup. But Andy had arrived at the farm even earlier to do some last-minute tune-ups on a couple of the sculptures, and he'd intercepted Nu by the hop barn. Emergency. The *Chicken Lady*'s ribs were springing loose.

Other emergencies had followed. He and Andy had performed minor surgeries on four of the sculptures. *Art Farm* was intended to be a temporary installation, of course, but Nu had hoped the sculptures would hold together for weeks or months rather than mere hours. It appeared that the springiness of the willow was just too much for the thin copper wire binding it.

Now he extricated himself from the circle of arts administrators he'd been sucking up to and ducked into the old part of the hop barn. It was dim and cool inside, even on this warm and sunny September day, and relatively quiet. Nu sighed with relief. Bodie had hung some of his hop vines from the rafters, and their pungent fragrance sharpened the air. Bodie had told Nu that most of his hops had been dried mechanically, but he wanted to try old-school air-drying with the smaller part of the harvest he planned to reserve for his own home brewing.

Nu had forty minutes or so before he was due to give his artist's talk and he needed this quiet time. He scaled the ladder to the cupola. The view from high above the farm was glorious. No other word for it. Fifty miles to the east a few classic cumulus clouds sailed like gigantic ships toward the high Cascades. He took the binoculars off the nail where he'd left them and looked to the south, where he caught a glimpse of the river, a silver shimmer beyond its fringe of cottonwoods trees. Nearer, in the bottomland, the patchwork quilt of Bodie's farm fields was as intricate as a medieval tapestry, though with a more vibrant palette of colors. He tried to locate the *Shepherdess and Ewe*. There they were, far out in the pasture. It surprised him to see Fleece still out there, making little dolls from felt scraps. There were half a dozen kids sitting on the ground in front of her, and maybe twenty adults, mostly women, standing behind the children, watching Fleece work.

He swung the binocs to the southwest and spotted the *Pumpkin Man*. Surrounding the sculpture, a field full of sprawling vines lay spangled with small ornamental pumpkins like orange soccer balls. Arnold was helping kids pick out free pumpkins, then herding his charges onto the hay wagon for the trip back up the hill. Further to the west Nu could just glimpse the *Woodchopper* in the oak copse, her axe poised over her head. The sculpture's only company was a lone male in blue jeans and white T-shirt snapping a photo. To the northwest, beyond Bodie and Fleece's house, he could see the *Chicken Lady* beside the coop in their garden. She had drawn a nice crowd. A volunteer in a pink gingham pioneer-style dress, one of Fleece's friends, probably, sat next to the sculpture holding a chicken in her lap for the kids to pet.

Closer in, Nu looked down on the makeshift stage, where a one-man band played musical saw and harmonica, the plaintive melody wafting like thin clouds of sound into the clear air. Bodie had borrowed a couple of hundred old metal folding chairs from the Marys River Grange and set them up in front of the stage. There was a good crowd already, though the main event was yet to come. Below Nu, tucked in close to the hop barn, the beer garden was standing room only, the white plastic chairs and round plastic tables pretty much all occupied. The babble of laughter mingled with the strains of the musical saw wafted up to Nu's private perch.

Between the beer garden and the stage, in the shade of one of the old oak trees, *The Grieving Mother* stood, looking forlornly down on Joe's fake tombstone. Nu still felt amazed at how easily they'd been able to restore the sculpture. Bodie had found her rebar body intact in the scrap heap; Joe's welding had held up through the years. The *Mother*'s head and hands were in the attic, as Joe had remembered. The gray, hooded, full-length cape had been re-created by one of

Fleece's seamstress friends. Andy had also tracked down a few more of Joe's sculptures, which were on display now under the canopy, standing beside *The Grieving Mother*.

Nu swung the binoculars around to the north and spotted Cat seated under a sun umbrella beside her cut-flower beds. As a bevy of kids disembarked from a minivan and headed toward the festival, Cat plucked asters from the plastic bucket beside her and gave one to each child. The new arrivals merged with the stream of people moving among the booths and exhibits that lined the entry drive and arced around the shop building and hop barn. Nu wasn't great at estimating crowds, but there had to be five or six hundred people all told.

He'd been on the move all day. Between doing emergency surgeries on his sculptures, trying to photographically document the show, plus engaging in countless conversations with friends, well-wishers, and visiting dignitaries, he hadn't had a moment's peace. He hadn't even eaten since breakfast, he realized. He checked his vest pockets. There was a carrot in one pocket and a molasses cookie in the other. Lunch and dessert. Nu slouched against the cupola wall and took a bite of carrot.

Andy had been true to his promise. The turnout by the art community was fantastic. There were artists, gallery owners, arts administrators, and representatives of foundations and granting agencies. Nu had all their business cards in his pocket. He'd received a number of genuine-seeming invitations to apply for grants, residencies, commissions. And everyone he'd spoken to had had nice things to say about the sculptures. Even Bodie. He'd crossed paths with him near the food booths, talking to Becca. Bodie, with a sandwich in one hand and a beer in the other, had beamed at Nu, handed his beer to Becca, and absolutely crushed Nu in a bear hug.

Bodie turned back to Becca and said, "I love this dude's art."

"It's amazing!" Becca had said. "Your willow sculptures are just fantastic!"

He'd gotten lots of "amazings" and "terrifics" as he'd circulated through the crowd, though, to be honest, he'd also heard some more nuanced appraisals from some of the art crowd. "You've done it, Nu," Carrie Lupine had told him. She was the head of the Oregon

Arts Commission; he'd met her on a number of occasions and liked her. "You've foregrounded the farm without diminishing your own creations. Very impressive."

In other words, he'd heard every imaginable variety of positive bullshit. His *Art Farm* installation, Bodie's Harvest Fest, the whole thing seemed so depressingly cheerful, so Norman Rockwellesque. Hay rides, petting zoos, free flowers and pumpkins. They were the main attractions for most of the visitors. His artworks were just signposts telling them where to get the goods. Sure, he had enjoyed the process of making the sculptures, for the most part, but the results were disappointing.

But then he always felt this way at his art show openings. Hyper self-criticism was his default response. It was just the insecure, underappreciated, self-loathing artist talking, he reminded himself. He probably shouldn't take his own cynicism too seriously. This installation was not just "art," per se. It was meant to focus and reflect the farm and its community. And everyone seemed to enjoy it, so he could give himself permission to do so, too.

But he probably wouldn't. And in any case, he was right. The *Art Farm* installation was amateurish, a mishmash of styles, of slapdash quality and dubious artistic merit. He suddenly felt overcome with weariness. He shuffled around the cupola and peered below him. A little crowd was already gathering just outside the beer garden, many of them holding plastic glasses of wine or beer. He looked at his watch; ten more minutes until he was supposed to give his artist talk. He dreaded it.

He sidled back to the east and looked down toward the house. There was Joe, sitting in his wheelchair, bundled up despite the warmth of the day in his wool pea jacket and a watch cap, a plaid blanket draped over his lap. Bart stood behind Joe, hanging up something like a lantern on a post beside Joe. Nu trained the binoculars on them. Oh, right. An IV bag. Nu could see the plastic tubing that snaked up Joe's coat sleeve. Jesus. This whole effort had just about used Joe up. Even if they succeeded in foiling the university's purchase of the farm, Nu had to wonder if it was worth it.

He was hoping to catch a glimpse of Ursula. He'd slipped out of bed without waking her this morning, and he hadn't seen her since.

He wondered what she thought of his artwork. Just then Ursula emerged from the house. She hadn't changed into her good clothes yet. She still had on jeans and a blue T-shirt. But even from this distance Nu could see she'd put on some makeup, even lip gloss, and her hair was draped in its loose braid across her left shoulder. She looked, not tense exactly, but alert, ready for the big finale. He put down the binoculars and gazed bare-eyed at her face, hoping she'd look up at him. And she did. She looked right up at him and smiled.

34 · Ursula

The odds of Nu being up in the cupola were tiny, but Ursula, as she stepped outside the front door, had known that when she looked up, he would be there. She wasn't the least surprised. That kind of coincidence had been a common experience these past few weeks. She'd never been superstitious about love, hadn't believed two people could be in extrasensory communication, but, as a scientist, she couldn't deny the plain facts.

Bart had parked Joe's wheelchair in the yard in front of the house, and now Ursula brought a lawn chair over. It was far enough away from the festivities that they could watch without much risk of random people coming over to talk to them. Ursula was glad to see the bag of electrolytes hanging from the wheelchair pole. Joe had resisted the IV, but Bart had convinced him that he'd feel a lot better if they kept him juiced up. "Everybody else will be drinking," Bart had reminded him.

Ursula settled into her chair and sighed. As a substitute for obsessing one more time over her to-do list, she concentrated on the early-afternoon sunlight settling warm on her arms, cheeks, and chest. She could sense Joe's alertness as he sat beside her. He'd taken a long nap before lunch, then declared himself ready to go outdoors and observe the chaos from a safe distance. Joe had a small but crucial role to play in the ceremony in a couple of hours, and Ursula hoped he would hold up alright. She hoped *she* would hold up alright, for that matter. *She* had not had a nap. She had not had a full night's sleep in weeks. She had not had many moments free from worry and stress, either, excepting her nightly trysts with Nu, and while the lovemaking no doubt alleviated some of her stress, it hadn't done anything for her sleep deprivation.

The exhilaration of being in love was all jumbled up with her grief over Joe's impending death. Together, it was exhausting. One winter term in grad school, she'd volunteered as a subject for a friend's research project, mapping brain functions using electroencephalography. She remembered the rat's nest of electrical receptors they'd attached to her scalp, how her eyelids had flickered as she watched the images of car wrecks, laughing children, pustulant wounds, and bucolic lakeside scenery flashing briefly before her eyes, while a computer recorded what parts of her brain were stimulated. She'd like to see what her EEG would look like now. Flat, staticky, and indecipherable, she imagined.

In any case, she was completely drained. They all were. Just a few more hours and it would be over, whatever the outcome. She turned her arms over to let the warm sun get at her wrists. She closed her eyes and listened to the weird keening of a musical saw drifting over from beyond the barn. Dreamily, she floated above the farm. She imagined Cat gathering bunches of flowers, Arnold on the tractor pulling a hay wagon full of kids through the pumpkin patch. She saw clusters of people bunched around each of Nu's willow sculptures, how altogether they made a loose necklace of humans strung around the farm. Then she drifted over the center of the festival, saw the one-man band on the makeshift stage with Joe's *Grieving Mother* statue standing in the wings as if listening to the saw-man's lamentation. When she noticed the faux granite cardboard gravestone beside the rectangle of bare earth that signified her father's future grave, she startled from her shallow sleep with a gasp.

She shook her head and tugged at her ear to wake herself. Reaching out to touch Joe, her fingers accidentally landed on the IV port taped into the back of his wrist. She flinched and withdrew her hand.

Joe looked over at her calmly. "It's okay, Urse," he said. "Relax."

She looked sideways at him and tried to smile. Bart had dressed Joe for winter. In his heavy wool pea jacket with the collar turned up and a blue watch cap pulled down over his ears, her father looked like an old salt who'd spent the better part of his life at sea. A seaman's life might have suited him, it occurred to her.

Ursula glanced over toward the front door and saw Zebra come striding out. When Ursula had seen Zebra earlier this morning, she had been dressed in muddy rubber boots, grubby tights, and a black hoodie. Now she was wearing a stunning white dress and white pumps, her mouth outlined with siren-red lipstick. Ursula couldn't take her eyes off her. As Zebra strolled toward them, Ursula studied her. It looked like a wedding dress: gleaming white silk with embroidered edges and lacy perforations. The long sleeves were pinned at the wrists but open at the seam, offering glimpses of the menagerie of tattoos on Zebra's arms. The openings in the lace were dime-sized or larger. Clearly the dress was meant to be worn with a blouse or camisole, but all Zebra had underneath was a black bra and her constellation of tattoos.

Zebra curtsied in front of them. "Whatcha drinking, old-timer?" she asked, nodding toward the IV bag.

"Schnapps."

She gave him a thumb's-up, but added, "Go easy on that shit. It's bad for your teeth."

She leaned down and kissed Joe on the forehead, then stepped back and faced them, her lips moving silently. It seemed to Ursula that Zebra was struggling for words—a first, as far as Ursula could remember. "You two," she finally said, "are my heroes. Thank you so much."

Ursula waited for the punch line, but Zebra just gazed down at them a moment longer, pooched her brilliant red lips into two little kisses, then turned gracefully away and walked back toward the house.

Zebra was a marvel. Ursula could hardly believe how much effort Zebra, along with Becca and Andy and so many others, was putting into this charade. Especially given how slim the odds of success were. She was pretty sure that the university was not going to be deterred by any of the obstacles that the Tunders were trying to create. If the idea of a cemetery in the center of their future campus gave them a slight pause, she knew as well as they did that graves can be moved. If they'd even noticed the Tunders' letter informing the university that an easement was being granted to the Confederated Tribes to perform camas restoration, the university's lawyers would have assured them that the contract would not hold up in court. On the other hand, how would it look for the university to take the local tribes to court? It would be a public relations nightmare. Or at least that was what the Tunders were hoping.

Their best chance to abort the sale was to freak out Modini. If the family could, in front of a big crowd of Tunder Farm partisans and no small number of reporters and media people, publicly assassinate Dexter's character, would Edward Modini reconsider his partnership with the university? Well, she had her doubts. Dexter and the university still coveted their farm, coveted the money that Modini was putting up. They'd find a way to reassure their corporate sugar daddy.

Ursula squeezed her father's hand—his non-IV hand—and went inside to put on her own costume. In her bedroom, she took down the outfit she had ironed yesterday. She hadn't dressed up many times in the past few years, and she no longer had much of a wardrobe to draw from. For this occasion she'd decided to wear her favorite knee-length tan skirt and her lemon-yellow linen jacket. She had surprised herself by going to Macy's and buying a fairly expensive pale-peach sleeveless top.

She tugged open her underwear drawer and was suddenly overcome with a memory. She used to stash money in here. She didn't like to carry more than $40 or $50 in her purse, so sometimes, if she had more cash than she needed, she'd stick some bills under her bras and panties. Now she remembered the time, early in her marriage, when she and Dexter were here for Christmas and some of her money—a wad of 20s she'd just stashed in this drawer—had gone missing.

"You didn't happen to take some cash out of my underwear drawer, did you?" she'd asked Dexter that evening.

He'd made an exaggerated face intended to convey hurt and incredulity. "Are you kidding me?"

She was almost positive she'd put the money there. Almost. It had felt a little crazy-making, but she had decided not to make a big deal of it.

It had taken her a couple of years to finally realize how much of a thief and a cheater Dexter was. He had been from the beginning, and he still was. He had cheated the university on travel expenses. He had fudged his research data on beet seed field productivity. Back when Dexter had offered to handle the sale of the farm after

Alice died, it had seemed like an act of generosity. Certainly Joe had thought so. But Dexter had seen it as a business opportunity. Whether Dexter had planned to make a profit over the sale, whether he'd planned to have an affair with Susan Sauer, or whether those were just convenient options that emerged along the way, Ursula couldn't say. But she did know that Dexter was always looking for an advantage.

Two days ago Bodie had told her that he was worried Dexter might not show, and he'd asked her to email him. She didn't want to, but she understood the power she still held over him. She knew he still craved her forgiveness so that he could go on cheating with a clear conscience.

"I'm glad you're coming to the farm on Sunday," she'd written him. "I'm looking forward to talking to you."

She had never really processed all her feelings about the affair, the divorce, and especially her miscarriage. She should have done some therapy, shitloads of therapy. She just wasn't all that much of a believer in talking. She hadn't spoken to Dexter in nearly four years, not since the divorce. But she would, once and for all, speak to him today.

35 · Bodie

Bodie is down in the parking lot, checking in with the volunteers who've come to help direct the parking. He is good at making people feel appreciated, and he's happy to be backslapping with some of his old buddies. But mostly he's on the lookout for the delegation from cvsu, due to arrive any moment.

That might be them, he thinks, as a shiny limo van with the "Fighting Muskrats" logo on the door enters the gate from the road. Yes, as the van stops at the gate, he sees the volunteer guy point up toward the house where there is a special parking space reserved for them. Fleece and Zebra are supposed to be up at the house keeping an eye out, and sure enough, as he hustles up to the yard, the two women come strolling out. They couldn't be more different in appearance. Fleece, always short and wide, is now, with her enormous pregnant belly, the shape of a tree stump. A graceful tree stump, but still.

She's added pregnancy panels to each side of her deerskin tunic, but it's still taut across her belly, and the leather tassels at the bottom hem dangle way out in front of her shins. Her black hair is glossy in crisp braids, wound through with ribbons and scrub jay feathers. And her cheeks are shiny as chestnuts. Pregnancy, anyone can see, suits her beautifully.

Zebra, by contrast, in her screaming white dress with the lacy holes that let her black undies peek through, looks like the queen of some Hollywood hell, elegant and deadly.

Dexter and another man who must be Modini climb out of the van. Their driver, Bodie's friend Xavier, an old football teammate, steps out from behind the driver's seat and waggles his hand in a *shaka* sign. All good. Bodie just nods, careful not to blow the chauffeur's cover. Instead he hastens to shake hands with Dexter, squeezing hard enough to make Dexter just begin to wince before releasing him. "Glad you could come, Dex," he says.

"Wouldn't miss it," Dexter says, clapping Bodie on the shoulder. "Bodie, this is Edward Modini."

Modini has a handshake as strong as his own, and Bodie hangs on while he studies the man. He was hoping Modini would have a steely gaze or a mean-looking twist to his lips, but Modini's smile seems genuine, and his handsome face is hard to look away from. Bodie finally releases the man's hand and turns to the women. "Mr. Modini, this is my wife, Felicia, and my farm manager, Zebra Gillespie."

The two men nod their greetings. Dexter says, "Bodie, the dean wanted me to invite you and your wife to join us in the box for the football game tonight. How about it?"

"Uh," Bodie mutters, looking around for help.

"How generous of you," Fleece says. "Regrettably, we have another engagement."

Zebra sidles up to Dexter and touches his arm. "Is your wife coming today?"

Dexter smiles at her, and Bodie sees Dexter's gaze crawl up and down Zebra's chest. "No, no. She's in Pullman, staying with her mother. She's pregnant too," he adds, pointing at Fleece's stomach.

Bodie has some lines here, he remembers, some points he's supposed to cover, but he's already so flustered he can hardly speak. Fleece squeezes his bicep and looks up at him expectantly. He clears his throat. "Right. And how about Susan? Is she coming?"

Dexter looks puzzled. "Susan? Susan Sauer? Is she invited? I'm not sure she would have any particular interest…"

"Oh, she's interested, alright," Zebra says. "Deeply involved, you might say."

While Dexter shakes his head in puzzlement or irritation, Zebra turns him by the arm and leads the group along the drive until they arrive, exactly on schedule, at the overlook. Bodie is supposed to say something here, but he's gone blank with anger. He stares down at Fleece with a pleading look, but Zebra once again is quick to the rescue.

"Look at that!" she says, sweeping her arm across the entire vista. "Tunder Farm in all its glory."

"Well, that is beautiful," Modini says. "You've done a great job here, Mr. Tunder."

"Zebra did it," Bodie chokes out. "Juano, too." He points haplessly at the fields below. "The whole crew."

"The university will try to be as good a steward of the land as you've been, Bodie," Dexter says, and Modini nods in agreement. Bodie wants to shout, "Bullshit!" but stifles himself.

"Oh, look," Zebra says, "you can see a couple of Nu's—Mr. Van Nuys's—willow sculptures. See there," she leans against Dexter, practically cheek to cheek, and points in the distance. "That's the *Shepherdess* with a ewe. It's got real wool woven into it."

Bodie turns and starts to walk away. "Next," he calls out.

"Yes, but we should just point out while we're here," Fleece nearly shouts, "the camas restoration we've written to you about. The conservation easement funded by the Confederated Tribes? It's going to be in that swale of low-lying wetlands around the lake. Twelve acres. We hope to begin next summer." She hands them each a three-fold brochure titled *Tunder Farm Camas Restoration Project*.

Modini glances at it, then turns to stare at Dexter. "What's this about, Blount?"

"I, uh, I don't know anything…," Dexter stammers.

"Excuse me," Fleece says. "You are aware that these are all unceded traditional lands of the Kalapuya people, right?"

"No," Modini says, eyes still lasered on Dexter. "I hadn't been told that."

Bodie senses that Fleece is about to school Modini, which he would dearly love to witness. But he has enough presence of mind to know that that is not part of the script. He grabs Fleece by the hand and, nodding toward the others to come along, turns away from the bluff and heads for the next station. Halfway there he glances back to make sure they're following. Zebra has her arm entwined with Dexter's, chattering away at him as if they're on a date.

So far they've been able to keep their two charges bunched together within their tight group, but now they have to enter the crowd. Bodie and Fleece wait for the others to catch up.

"What the heck is that?" Dexter says, pointing at the big granite tombstone and the freshly dug grave twenty yards behind the face-painting table. They had decided they wouldn't take the party directly to Joe's cemetery plot. The volunteers who'd made the gray-painted cardboard gravestone—a few of Andy's developmentally disabled adult clients—weren't very skilled, and the result was pretty amateurish.

"That is the family cemetery plot," Zebra jumps in. "The artistic mock-up of Joseph Tunder's headstone and grave is intended to serve as a reminder of the constant presence of death."

Bodie sees Modini's jaw clench. Sensing that the men might be about to cut their mission short, he strides over and grabs Modini by the arm. "This way," he orders the men. Fleece gives him a slight scowl. His tone must have been wrong. "Please," he adds, "over here."

Under a free-standing canopy, Joe's surviving sculptural works are displayed. There are two bronze castings—a sleek and beautiful tree frog and an agitated raven, each about the size of a football—along with several wire sculptures of human subjects: a man shoveling something, a woman with a scythe. There's also a table with photos and other information about Joe's and Nu's artwork. Bodie knows it's his turn to speak again, but Zebra upstages him. She has entered a zone, Bodie realizes. He is more than happy to yield to her.

"As you know," Zebra says, "we're celebrating the opening of Nu Van Nuys's extensive art installation, *Art Farm*." Her tone, Bodie would say, is a cross between an art museum docent and a high-end hooker. "His sculptural works are placed around the entire property, weaving the farm into a single work of art. Since you, regrettably, won't have time to tour the exhibit, we wanted to make sure you received Mr. Van Nuys's artist statement and his map of the installation." She hands them each a copy of the handout.

"Alright, Miss...," Modini interrupts.

"And here's the best part," she continues. "Mr. Van Nuys has taken the extraordinary measure of copyrighting the entire farm, ensuring that all future development will preserve his unique artistic composition."

Modini's eyes narrow. He tugs up a sleeve to consult his watch.

"We're right on schedule, Mr. Modini," Fleece tells him. "Your people told us to make sure you were free by 2:30. Correct?"

"Alright," he says. "Let's just get this over with."

"I believe we are almost ready for the ceremony to begin," Fleece says in a cool, formal voice. "Right this way."

Bodie lets Fleece lead them through the crowd, past a couple of booths where vendors are selling leather goods and pottery, past a face-painting station where a bevy of noisy children are having vegetable shapes painted on their cheeks, until they arrive at the edge of the stage area. The bluegrass band is still playing. Bodie walks toward the stage until he catches the fiddle player's eye.

He returns and tells the others, "They're just gonna finish this tune."

Fleece gestures forward. "Let me show you to your seats."

The two men follow Fleece to their reserved seats, front row center. Bodie sees Arnold, in his dusty farm garb and backward-pointed ball cap, come out from behind the stage, give Modini a slightly crazed eyeballing, then take the seat beside Dexter. And now Xavier, the chauffeur, comes over and gives Bodie a shoulder bump, then heads down front to take the chair next to Modini.

Zebra stretches up on her tiptoes and gives Bodie a kiss on the cheek. "Nice job, big guy," she whispers. Then she sashays down the aisle and takes a seat directly behind Dexter and Modini.

36 · Nu

Nu stood beyond the last row of seats as Andy took the stage. Andy didn't have a great stage presence. He fancied himself as a rock concert emcee and hit all the hokiest clichés. But he had the script they'd written for him, and he'd promised he would stick to it.

"Hey! Hey, thank you, Camas Valley!" Andy called out, tilting the mic stand over like a dance partner. "What a great turnout! Let's hear it for the band, Camas Valley Grass. As you know, we're here to celebrate a terrific art exhibit by Nu Van Nuys. But first," Andy held up a three-by-five-inch note card, "I've got a few people and organizations to thank," and he let his taped-together *stack* of note cards accordion all the way down to floor. Nu chuckled along with the crowd, though he began to worry about how long Andy might hold the stage.

Once he got rolling, though, Andy ran through his performance briskly. He thanked the art community, including a couple of prominent regional funders in the audience, whom he pointed out and recognized by name. He thanked the local newspaper and other media people in attendance. "Hey, hold up your hands if you're media," and a dozen or more people, many with cameras or camcorders, raised their hands. Most of them were probably Andy's friends—imposters, Nu figured, but it was an impressive showing in any case.

Nu saw Modini and Dexter look over their shoulders to see who was covering the program, then Modini gave Dexter a stern glance.

"Big shout-out to the Confederated Tribes," Andy resumed, "for the conservation easement to preserve twelve acres of wet prairie for camas restoration here at Tunder Farm." He pointed out a couple of representatives of the tribes, who smiled at the round of spirited applause. Finally Andy thanked the directors and funders of his own program, Keystone Support, and when he asked everyone who'd volunteered to help create the *Art Farm* sculptures to stand up, forty or more people, including maybe twenty developmentally disabled adults, stood. The applause was loud and genuine. Nu checked the time on his phone—he was concerned that Modini might bolt at any moment—but they were only four minutes behind schedule.

"And now," Andy said, holding up his hand for silence, "Before we hear from Nu Van Nuys, we have a very special treat for you. Joseph Tunder, the owner of Tunder Farm, Bodie and Ursula Tunder's father, is a skilled metal worker and a talented artist whose work I've admired for a long time, but who has never received much recognition. Today, for your amazement and edification, we have restored one of his signature sculptures, *The Grieving Mother*, and I hope you will all spend a few moments in her company. Joe Tunder was on the faculty at CVSU in 1975 when he constructed *The Grieving Mother* as part of a student-led protest against the Vietnam War. Photos of Mr. Tunder's sculpture appeared in the *Washington Post*, the *Seattle Post-Intelligencer*, the *Los Angeles Times*, and other national outlets. Sadly, some vocal CVSU alumni objected to this national coverage of a protest on campus, and Joe, shortly after the incident, was fired."

A rumble of comment buzzed though the audience, along with a few boos, and Nu noticed Dexter shrink a little. Modini, on the other hand, stiffened up even straighter in his chair.

"Ladies and gentlemen," Andy said, "let's give it up for Mr. Joseph Tunder."

As Bart rolled Joe out, Bodie and Fleece came down the aisle to meet them, and the three of them hoisted Joe and his wheelchair up onto the stage. Joe looked exhausted, Nu thought, but determined to see this through.

Andy walked over and handed Joe the mic. The crowd quieted. Joe let his eyes roam over the audience and then, in a low, rusty-throated voice he said, "You've made a used-up old man very happy. Thank you." The crowd started to clap, but Joe held up his trembling hand. He wasn't done. He just needed a moment to gather his strength, Nu could tell. "You might have noticed I have a grave waiting for me over there," he continued, pointing off to his left. "I'll be using it soon, and that way I'll remain here among you. Long live Tunder Farm."

The crowd roared. A bunch of people chanted back, "Long live Tunder Farm!"

Andy let the chanting continue for a minute, then retrieved the microphone. "Awesome!" he said. "Just awesome. Thank you for your beautiful art, Joe Tunder." Bart parked Joe at the back of the stage, and Fleece and Bodie took seats behind the podium. "People,"

Andy resumed, leaning forward and looking the audience in the eye like a preacher, "to introduce Nu Van Nuys, I want to invite up to the stage my good friend Ursula Tunder."

Nu didn't know where Ursula had been hiding, but the moment Andy said her name, she appeared from somewhere behind him, swept past Nu, and strode down the aisle. She wore calf-length boots, a tan skirt, and a crisp yellow jacket styled, Nu observed, like a dressy lab coat. She climbed the three steps onto the stage, then crouched down and took her father by the shoulders and said something that made his sunken old cheeks lift into a smile. Ursula stood and gathered herself, walked to the podium, and took the mic from Andy.

She looked graceful and beautiful, and she already had the audience in the palm of her hand. But she wasn't here to entertain. Her poise and focus were that of a scientist, and her main audience was the two specimens in the chairs below her.

"Nu Van Nuys is a very sweet man," she began, "and a terrific artist." She ran quickly through his vita, his group shows and one-man shows, fellowships and grants. In writing her script, the team had agreed that listing Nu's accomplishments might risk boring the audience, but the bona fides were for the benefit of the two men—one fidgeting, Nu noticed, one staring unflinchingly up at her—in the front row.

From where he stood in the back, Nu gazed over the heads of the audience at Ursula. He knew she wouldn't look out at him and risk meeting his eyes. He knew how nervous she was, though no one else in the crowd would have guessed it. Lost in gazing at her, he didn't hear the last few sentences of her introduction. But now everyone was applauding and some people were craning around to look his way, and he realized she'd just said his name. He took a deep breath, jogged down the aisle, and leaped onto the stage, then stopped a few feet away from her. He was excited about what came next.

Ursula was still standing at the mic, waiting for him. Now they approached one another, opened their arms and embraced. Then, as they'd so carefully practiced it, they leaned back, regarded each other for a moment, then kissed. The crowd *ooh'd* and clapped. They kissed some more, and the crowd went berserk.

It maybe wasn't the most appropriate behavior for an art opening, and Nu did worry a tiny bit that some of his potential funders in the audience would be put off. But it was good theater, he was pretty sure of that, and he gave it everything he had.

37 Ursula

As Nu went to the microphone, Ursula settled in her seat beside Andy at the back of the stage. Andy reached out and squeezed her hand. "Perfect," he whispered, and made a little kissy face.

Her pulse was thumping and she knew her cheeks were aflame from stage anxiety and, even more so, from that drawn-out kiss. Now she wriggled in her chair and tugged her skirt down to her knees. Wasn't there supposed to be water here? She looked at the floor on both sides of her. Andy leaned over again, reached under her chair, and grabbed her water bottle. He unscrewed the cap and handed it to her. She took a deep, steadying breath, then a stiff drink of water. Whew. Okay, she thought. I'm okay.

She glanced to her right and saw Fleece sitting with her eyes lowered as if she were meditating, radiating a peaceful energy. Ursula imagined Fleece was communing with her Creator, or maybe with her baby.

Now she let her eyes roam out over the audience. There was Cat, smiling from the third row, sitting with Becca and a couple of women from the yoga class. And there was Juano with some of the farm temps. Near them, Andy's team of twenty or so developmentally disabled adults, who'd put in so many hours helping to create *Art Farm*, were seated in a block.

Now everyone, even the little face-painted kids scattered throughout the crowd, quieted down, focused on Nu.

"I hope you've walked around the farm and seen our willow sculptures," Nu was saying. "So many of you helped make *Art Farm*. It's really your creation. But I have to thank a few people in particular. Andy Patterson, he made this happen," Nu said turning to point back to Andy, "and Andy's team. Stand up!"

Andy stood and lifted his hands in a "stand up" gesture toward his team, and a few of the bolder adults tugged the others to their feet. A short round serene-looking man—Rodney was his name, Ursula remembered, and he had Down syndrome—suddenly punched the air and shouted, "Yeah!" and then the whole group went wild, waving their arms and shuffle-dancing. Nu began clapping and the whole crowd joined in with loud applause. "You rocked it!" Nu shouted.

After a raucous moment, he held his hands up for quiet. "You know, many of you were already aware of how a farm can be a work of art," Nu said. "I call myself an artist, but I really *didn't* know that. I hadn't really looked at farms the right way before. You all knew it, because you've seen it, *here*. You've seen what Bodie and Fleece and Ursula—and Zebra, Juano, Arnold, and all the gang—what they've made here: not just great produce and healthy food but also beauty. Capital B Beauty. The beauty of a productive and abundant ecosystem."

Ursula stifled a cry. Between love, pride, and exhaustion, she was on the verge of tears. She sucked down another deep breath and tried to steady herself by staring at the back of Nu's head. She loved the modeling of his head, the perfect knob of his occiput. His ears did stick out pretty far. It was more obvious from behind. Cat thought Nu should grow his hair longer, but Ursula loved to be able to see the shape of his skull. Stick-out ears were part of his charm.

"Making all these sculptures," he was saying, "with the help of so many of you fine people has been a privilege, and an education. Hard work, sure, but also a lot of fun. All the sculptures, all the weird Willow People, they've grown out of this soil, Tunder Farm soil, and they'll eventually go back to the soil. But Tunder Farm will still be here. Tunder Farm will continue as long as this community wants it to."

Ursula could tell by his cadence he was winding up. She felt a moment of panic; she couldn't recall how she was supposed to begin her final speech. But then she remembered: it was all typed up. All she had to do was read it. She drew the paper out of the pocket of her jacket and smoothed it across her knees. A deep calm came over her—she thought that it might be Fleece's doing—and when Nu once again said her name aloud, she was ready.

38 · Bodie

Bodie drains his bottle of water and wishes he had more. He hadn't wanted to be onstage, but now he's glad that Nu had insisted. With no further responsibilities, he can sit back and gawk at the audience. Pretty much all the chairs are full, and folks are standing five and six deep around the edges. Must be two, maybe three hundred people all told.

Fleece is sitting close beside him, hands folded in her lap, eyes lowered. He finds her blissed-out Buddha mode slightly irritating, but, hey, whatever it takes. Glancing across the stage, he catches his father's eye and Joe winks.

Nu is finishing up. "Thanks, everyone," he is saying. "Finally, for a special note of appreciation to conclude our ceremony, I want to bring back Ursula Tunder."

Ursula bolts upright and strides to the mic. No kiss this time; she barely acknowledges Nu. She's all business, reading directly from prepared notes. "Among the many people who have helped make this day possible," she reads—woodenly, Bodie notices—"we need to give special appreciation to the people at Camas Valley State University who have *in the past* taken an interest in purchasing Tunder Farm. We will understand if they are no longer interested. Also, we have a special guest today, Mr. Edward Modini, who went so far as to propose that his company, Earthwide Farms, fund the purchase of our farm in order to create a marketing program aimed at extending his company's monopoly over plastic-wrapped vegetables."

On cue, Bodie sees Zebra lean in between Dexter and Modini and give each man a big manila envelope. Bodie knows that Modini's packet contains the news clippings about his company's labor and environmental issues, and a copy of the letter signed by more than a hundred Camas Valley citizens petitioning the university to pull out of the deal to purchase the farm. Dexter's packet includes more personal, possibly libelous, items, including the evidence of his continuing affair with Susan Sauer, which, the Tunders assure him, will not become public if the purchase of the farm is aborted. Remembering the contents of the two envelopes, Bodie smiles.

The crowd can tell that someone is being dissed, and several people are pointing at the suits down in the front row. Dexter half rises and says something to Modini. He looks like he's getting ready to bolt. But Zebra puts a hand on Dexter's shoulder and pushes him down. She bends forward and speaks to both men. Bodie knows she's telling them that their limo driver—and now she nods toward Xavier—is an old friend of the Tunders. They won't be leaving until she tells them it's time.

"The community has come out today to witness how important Tunder Farm is to everybody," Ursula continues. Bodie notices that a little warmth, a little cadence has returned to her voice. "The art community has come out today to see that our farm is itself a work of art, a singular and integrated and living work of art.

"I want to conclude on a very personal note." Bodie sees that she's dropped her script onto the lectern. "My brother and sister-in-law are pregnant, as you can see," she says, smiling and glancing behind her at Fleece, "and their child is going to be born very soon, right here on the farm. A few years ago, I became pregnant. My child might have been born here at Tunder Farm, too, but I had a miscarriage. Recently, we, the whole Tunder family, nearly allowed another miscarriage to occur here. A social and ecological miscarriage. Tunder Farm is not just what you call a 'family farm.' It's a community farm. Legally it belongs to us, but we belong to the community."

She hesitates for a moment, and Bodie is afraid she's going to lose it, start bawling or something. But, no, after a pause that he realizes is deliberate, and just the right touch, she picks up her script again and reads, not warmly now, but forcefully. "We want to thank CVSU and Mr. Modini for providing the opportunity for us to clarify our values, and to begin to seek out broader, noncorporate partnerships among the wider community in order to help Tunder Farm remain a public asset in perpetuity.

"Thank you for coming, everyone. Please stay, get some food, beverages. Absolutely go look at Nu's willow sculptures and my father's *Grieving Mother*. Thanks. Thanks, everyone."

Warm applause as people get up to disperse. Bodie sees that Dexter and Modini remain seated. Zebra is standing behind them with a hand clenched on each of their shoulders, while Arnold and Xavier stand alertly at either side.

As Ursula comes out from behind the lectern and steps toward the front of the stage, Bodie jumps up to accompany her. He can't believe how much he admires her, his beautiful, smart, and very brave sister.

Nu and Fleece and Andy step forward as well, and now Bart pushes Joe over to join them.

Ursula stares down over the front of the stage to address her small subdued audience. "We're done with you two," she tells the men. "You can leave now."

Epilogue · October 2014 · Ursula

Ursula looked up from her computer and gazed dreamily out the window. The sight of rain was so soothing. All summer the weather had been brutally hot, the air fouled with smoke from all the forest fires. Even the rhododendrons in the backyard had gone droopy in the drought. But now, with the return of the rain this week, their leaves were once again turgid and glistening.

She spotted a robin splashing in her mother's old birdbath tucked among the shrubs in the back border. She never remembered to fill it, but the rain had done the job. The robin was ducking its head and flapping giddily, flinging water every which way, probably drunk on fermented holly berries.

She felt pretty good herself. She'd accomplished most everything she'd hoped to today. After she'd bundled Alicia into her rain gear and walked her over to kindergarten this morning, she'd finished painting the bedroom. It was a surprise for Nu. He was always grumbling about their boring off-white bedroom walls, so in his absence she'd repainted the room in desert colors: three walls a pale sage green and the fourth a sandy ochre. Then after lunch she'd baked a tin of pumpkin muffins, and still managed to put in a couple of hours typing up her field notes. She'd asked Fleece and Becca to come over before school let out and help her put the bedroom furniture back in order, promising them tea and muffins as a reward. They were due anytime now.

She couldn't ask for a better rain: steady and gentle, every drop percolating down into the parched soil. She clicked over to the NOAA weather site. Partial clearing this afternoon. Rain returning late. With luck, they'd get another beautiful overnight soaker. She imagined the rain seeping in, wending its way down through Bodie's beloved Chehalis silt loam.

Nu might not like it, but they needed a wet winter, wet and also cold enough to replenish the snowpack in the Cascades. Nu had told her on the phone last week that he'd been caught in a torrential downpour on a farm in the Mekong Delta. He'd taken shelter in the mausoleum he was studying, but the farmers in the rice field had just carried on. He'd also told her that his time in Vietnam had given him some ideas for a project he wanted to start on as soon as he got home. "*Art Farm Two,* maybe," he'd told her. "And I want to be able to work on it in all seasons, so I might need to make my peace with the rain."

Peace with the rain was easy for her. The record-high summer temps and especially the smoky air had made her field season miserable. Bushwhacking across steep slopes, tripping on trailing blackberry vines, clambering over slash in the heat and the bad air, her body had taken a beating. And the team's findings were depressing, too. There were already so many changes appearing in plant and animal communities, particularly at higher elevations. She and the other scientists on her team would have to be cautious in making any claims about the role of global warming, but the data was sobering nonetheless.

When Ursula heard Fleece and Becca come onto the back deck, she saved her files and shut down the computer. In the kitchen, she waited while the two women shed their rain parkas and boots and then, after quick hugs, she led them upstairs.

"I love the colors," Becca said the moment they entered the bedroom. "Nice and warm."

They made short work of the furniture moving, then returned to the kitchen. "Have a seat," Ursula said, "We've got half an hour before school's out." She poured the tea and handed around the cups, followed by the plate of pumpkin muffins.

"Bodie cakes," Becca said, taking a bite. "Mmm, I love the crystallized ginger."

"I had to use canned pumpkins," Ursula admitted. "I just ran out of time."

"Nu's coming home tonight, isn't he?" Fleece asked.

Ursula nodded. "He lands in Portland in a couple of hours."

"I'll bet you've missed him," Becca said.

Ursula smiled and took a sip of her tea. "I *have* missed him. But it's good, too, being apart. You appreciate the things you love them for."

"Yeah, and you get a break from the things that drive you crazy," Becca said. "I wish Randy was gone more. I could really enjoy missing him."

Ursula glanced at Fleece. It occurred to Ursula that their talk about missing people was pretty insensitive, but Fleece didn't seem to mind. She was intent on tucking the end of a flat reed into the loosely woven basket she held in her lap. Ursula gazed fondly at her sister-in-law. There were new strands of gray in Fleece's hair, and the dark patches under her eyes seemed like they were there to stay. Being a widow and a single mom while still keeping up the farm had been rough on Fleece. Ursula wasn't sure she could have done it herself.

She glanced out the living room window. It looked like the rain had stopped. There were even a few ragged patches of blue sky in the west.

"Remind me what Nu was doing in Vietnam," Becca said.

"He got a grant to study their funerary arts," Ursula said. "Did you know there's a Buddhist sect that buries their dead in temporary graves, digs them up after two years, scrapes the remaining flesh off the skeletons, and reburies the clean bones? It's supposed to make it more likely they'll be reborn into the same family."

"Ugh," Becca said. "That's gross."

"Different strokes, I guess," Ursula said. "In any case, Nu's work seems to be catching a wave. He's been invited to Japan this winter to be part of a design team. A memorial for victims of the Tohoku tsunami."

"I hope he's not going anywhere near Fukushima," Fleece said.

"Me, too," Ursula sighed. She sipped her tea for a moment, then said, "I already told Fleece this, but Nu found some of his birth family in Vietnam, an aunt and uncle and some cousins."

"Oh, my god!" Becca said. "His mom's side or his dad's?"

"His mother's sister. He didn't go over there with the idea of searching for family. He had his grant, so he was focused on visiting as many cemeteries as possible. And besides, there are thousands and thousands of Nguyens. It's the main surname among the Vietnamese, like Smith and Jones rolled together. But his mother's name was more unusual, Khab or something like that. She was Hmong. That's one of the reasons that Nu's parents got out of Vietnam just before Saigon fell. His mother's family was involved in the Hmong resistance in the highlands. Nu came across the family name in a cemetery in a village in the mountains north of Dalat. And that was where she was from, that village."

"And how did it go?" Becca asked.

"Oh, Nu told me on the phone it was odd. They didn't exactly embrace him with open arms. You know, they have a term, *Viet Kieu,* for Vietnamese who leave the country. They seemed a little suspicious of him. Nu is still not sure what his father was doing during the war. Maybe something his wife's family wasn't happy about. Anyway, they warmed up to him when he started talking about cemeteries and ancestor worship. They took him to where his grandmother was buried. It was a crypt right in the middle of a barley field. His mother's people were hill farmers."

"So burying people on the farm runs in his family," Fleece said.

"It makes perfect sense," Becca said. "But I still think it's crazy that Nu's parents wound up in America. That you two ever met."

"It could have been crazier," Ursula said, then stopped and looked out the window. She wasn't sure she wanted to share this other bit of news. She was just getting used to it herself.

"Yes?" Becca said. "Let's have it."

Ursula sighed. Oh, well, she thought. No holding back now. "You know that Nu was adopted by my aunt Constance."

"Your dad's sister?" Becca said.

"Yes. And she was a lousy mother. Truly bad. She had no business adopting. She was not interested in kids whatsoever. But here's how it happened. My parents had been trying to get pregnant for a couple of years, but it wasn't working. I know Mom miscarried at least once. She wanted a baby something fierce, so she convinced Daddy they should adopt. And they jumped through all the hoops, which, if I understand correctly, were a lot less complicated in the '70s. So, they were in line to get an orphaned Vietnamese baby. And then they got pregnant."

"With you," Fleece said quietly.

Ursula nodded. "Mom wanted to have me *and* do the adoption, too. You know Mom."

"I didn't," Fleece said. "I so regret I never met her."

"Well, Becca knew her," Ursula said. "She was a strong woman."

"Strong as a horse, and wicked smart," Becca said. "I remember asking her once when she planned to retire. And she said, 'Oh, Becca, honey, I love my work so much, I can't imagine retiring. But at sixty-five, I plan to cut back to just full-time.'"

They all laughed, though sadly. Alice hadn't made it to sixty-five.

"But they didn't adopt a baby, obviously," Ursula went on. "The agency wouldn't let them, what with Mom being pregnant already. And then Joe called his sister to tell her the good news, that Alice was pregnant, and the bad news, that they wouldn't be able to adopt. And Connie said, 'We'll take it.'"

"'We'll take it!?'" Becca said. "'We'll take *it*?'"

"Enough said, right? That about tells you Connie's approach to parenting."

"Wait a minute, wait a minute," Becca said. "How do you even know this?"

"Daddy told Nu the whole story a week before he died."

"But how did your aunt get them to let her adopt? I mean, there's gotta be some kind of screening."

"Yeah, Daddy didn't say. Nu wondered about that, too, but it didn't occur to him to ask until it was too late. Money, probably," Ursula said. "But here's the clincher. Daddy always felt guilty about it."

"About what?"

"That his sister got the baby and she was such a rotten mother. He told Nu that he wished he and Alice could have found a way to adopt him. That he always felt like Nu was supposed to have been his son."

The women all fell silent.

"I think Bodie always sensed that," Fleece finally said. "That Joe treated Nu like a son. That Joe maybe even liked Nu better."

"But Ursula," Becca said, looking solemn. "If they *had* adopted Nu...?"

Ursula sighed and nodded. "Yeah. He would have been my brother. Adopted, but still..."

"Wow," Becca said. "Just wow." She took a deep breath. "But hey, I hate to break the spell, but we're going to be late picking up the kids."

"I want to gather a few flowers," Fleece said, holding up her little basket, and she and Becca went into the backyard.

Ursula hurriedly cleared away the dishes, then met up with Fleece and Becca in the front yard. They walked around the hop barn and over to the little cemetery. *The Grieving Mother* was still there, looking sad and decrepit. Her left arm had come loose at the shoulder and hung limp at her side. Her gray cape was coming apart at the seams. Ursula wished they'd either fix her up or take her down, but Andy and Nu wanted to document her decomposition with drawings and photographs.

Ursula stood gazing down at Joe's headstone. It wasn't anything like the cardboard monstrosity they'd mocked up for the *Art Farm* opening, just an upright slab of granite the size of a bag of fertilizer. Along with Joe's name and dates, they'd had his goofy epitaph carved on it: UNDER NEW MANAGEMENT.

Fleece set her basket of flowers on Bodie's grave. Ursula put her arm around her sister-in-law, and they both sighed. It was coming up on two years since Bodie's death, Ursula realized. She flashed again to the moment she'd found him. Fleece had called her after dark that evening to ask if she knew where Bodie was. He was two hours late for dinner. Ursula had taken a flashlight and looked for him in the hop barn and the shop, then gone down to the fields, where she found him facedown in his pumpkin patch. He'd been harvesting pumpkins—the old "No Further" pickup was loaded near to full—and he was already cold. He'd had a massive aneurysm, the doctor told them.

The women wandered around the hop yard and past Fleece's chicken coop till they came to the woven-willow gate at the edge of the school yard. Selling the front parcel of land to the Camas Valley Cooperative School had gotten the family out of debt, and it also brought a hundred of the community's children to the farm each day. Ursula reached out and, taking Fleece and Becca by the hand, paused at the gate. She loved this moment of anticipation.

A bell rang and then a chorus of young voices burst from the school building. Most of the children were exiting by the front door on the street side of the building, she knew, but the preschoolers and kindergarteners had their Exploritorium class last period. Ursula could see them out in the play yard already. As the women stepped through the gate, the teacher, Blue, pointed their way and said something to their three children, who spotted their mothers and came running.

Fleece's boy, Joey, the biggest of the kids by half, proudly held up a block of wood with a couple of bent nails protruding.

"Did you do carpentry today?" Fleece asked him, and his smile, Ursula thought, was wider than a pumpkin.

Becca crouched and her daughter Katy ran into her arms. Ursula was so glad that Becca would be teaching yoga again, and the class for mothers and children was going to be at the fitness club right next door. It was called Every Body Up now, a corny name, but a huge improvement over Bliss Fits. And the new owners had consented to Ursula's request to turn off the security lamp at the back of the building.

Becca swooped Katy into her arms and waved goodbye. Fleece and Joey, holding hands, headed back toward their house.

Alicia was the last one to come running. Her T-shirt, shorts, knees, and cheeks were all smeared with dirt. Even her straight dark hair was muddy. "Blue let me make mud pies!" she cried out. Ursula remembered how Bodie used to take up a little pinch of soil and taste it, smacking his lips. He'd approve of Alicia's mud pies.

Ursula picked her daughter up and rubbed noses with her, feeling the mud slide onto her own cheeks. "We'll have to give you a bath," Ursula said. Alicia loved baths. She would take it as just more play time.

Ursula gazed into her daughter's brown eyes. They were so big and bright that Ursula felt her own eyes brighten.

"Your daddy's coming home tonight," she said. And Alicia's eyes opened even wider.

Acknowledgments

I can't imagine completing a novel without the help and encouragement of a writers' group. I've been so fortunate to regularly share work in progress with accomplished novelists Rick Borsten and Gregg Kleiner, who read every word and made this book better on every page.

Writing residencies at PLAYA and the Sitka Center for Art and Ecology gave me time and space to work on key chapters. Thanks to the devoted staffs of these two fine organizations.

Working with the dedicated people at the University of Nevada Press has been a great pleasure and privilege. My deepest thanks.

Boundless gratitude to my wife, Kapa Korobeinikov, a gifted garden designer and a restless reviser of our backyard gardens. Garden labor never fails to feed my imagination.

I've written poetry and essays for decades, but when our son, Elliot, left home for college, I saw an opportunity to take on a bigger project—perhaps a novel—to occupy all the time I'd previously shared with him. *Weave Me a Crooked Basket* is how I filled the empty nest.

About the Author

CHARLES GOODRICH is the former director of Oregon State University's Spring Creek Project for Ideas, Nature, and the Written Word. He is the author of a collection of personal essays, *The Practice of Home,* and four books of poetry: *Watering the Rhubarb, A Scripture of Crows, Going to Seed: Dispatches from the Garden,* and *Insects of South Corvallis.* Goodrich is also the coeditor of two anthologies: *Forest Under Story* and *In the Blast Zone.* He lives in Corvallis, Oregon.